D1362336

WALKING AFTER MIDNIGHT

RICHARD NUSSER

VILLARD BOOKS NEW YORK 1989

 Published in the United States by Villard Books, a division of Random House, Inc., New York, and simultaneously in Canada by Random House of Canada Limited, Toronto.

Library of Congress Cataloging-in-Publication Data
Nusser, Richard.
Walking after midnight.
I. Title.
PS3564.U79W35 1989 813′.54 88-40609
ISBN 0-394-56314-X

Manufactured in the United States of America
9 8 7 6 5 4 3 2
First Edition

For Sherlock Holmes,
Philip Marlowe,
Jules Maigret
and all their children.

All things ephemeral
Are but a reflection;
The unattainable
Here finds perfection;
The indescribable
Here it is done;
The Eternal Feminine
Still draws us on.

Goethe, *Faust*

ACKNOWLEDGMENTS

The author wishes to thank all the people whose help and cooperation allowed this book to be written, particularly members of the New York City Police Department and the outlaws they pursue; without each other we would be lost; also to Dr. Donald Hoffman of the New York City Medical Examiner's office, Dr. Thomas Manning, chief toxicologist of the Nassau County Medical Examiner's office, and Dr. Robert J. Berk. The book could not have been written without the support and encouragement of friends like Fran Meneker, J. B. Moore, the late Roman Kozak, Doris Toumarkine, and the many fine reporters and editors who taught me the basics of the journalism trade, particularly the gentlemen at Newhouse High. I am deeply indebted to American Express; had I left home without my card I would have starved. (Can I have it back now?)

I wish also to pay special tribute to the memories of Brandy Alexander and Candy Darling and to all the other drag queens, transvestites, cross-dressers, transsexuals, and transgendered persons I ran across in my research for this book. Thanks, girls.

I am particularly grateful to my agent, Barbara Lowenstein, and my editors, Peter Gethers and Alison Acker, for seeing what I saw, and seeing it with clearer eyes than mine. Alison deserves special thanks.

And, last but certainly not least, to my wife, whose presence saw me through it all.

ACKNOWLEDGMENTS

[illegible]

WALKING AFTER MIDNIGHT

1

I'm not one of those people who think life is beautiful. I imagine it could be, if you had loads of money and a clear conscience. Experience tells me that's rare. Life is a coincidental journey from womb to tomb, riddled with meaningless work and unfulfilled desire, ending in death. There have been times when I've lapsed into a less jaundiced frame of mind, but something always happens to restore my basic belief in man's inhumanity to man. Greed, stupidity, ignorance, and lust rule the planet while mankind dreams of heaven, its mind in the gutter, its eyes on the stars.

Luck plays its part. We swing through life on a rope we weave for ourselves. If we're lucky it's a pendulum ride; if the knot slips it's a noose. I was lucky. I stuck my neck out but I managed to grab the rope before the knot slipped. A woman I loved wasn't so lucky. She was exploring the wild side of life when it happened. She was an artist. She was an innocent victim of a society so corrupt that blame can only be apportioned, never fixed. I miss her terribly. Thereby hangs this tale.

It all started on a crisp, clear Monday morning in December. I was holed up in a secluded, sixty-year-old stone cottage on the sandy cliffs of Montauk, Long Island, 125 miles east of Sodom and Gomorrah, AKA Manhattan. The owner of the property, a friend, had reluctantly put the place up for sale because the sea had clawed huge chunks from the base of the cliffs, imperiling the foundation of the house, which had been a rich man's hunting lodge when game was still plentiful on the East End. Gatsby. It was pure comfort—knotty pine built-ins, windowseats, and quiet corners with an occasional flourish of twenties' ostentation, such as the stained glass, Tiffany-designed stag hunting scene over the front door. The stag was holding a noble pose while the hounds bayed at his heels. I came to identify with that scene, but I still can't decide if I'm the hunted or the hunter.

I was recuperating there, earning my keep by showing the place to potential buyers who, hopefully, wouldn't notice the erosion of the cliff. I had taken a leave of absence from my job as the star reporter on a tabloid called the *New York Graphic* because I needed a rest. I had gotten lost on the High C's—cocaine, Camels, cognac, and coffee—and wound up in a hospital with bronchial pneumonia. I had sunk into the misery I was chronicling daily, using pot to feel happy, booze to relax, and cocaine to stay awake while I wrote about eighty-year-old rape victims and people who scalded their children to death for discipline's sake. A critic described my columns as "embittered, lurid slices of urban life."

On top of that, I had fallen desperately in love with a lady photographer who sported a butch haircut that did nothing to diminish her beauty, had stopped wearing skirts, and was working on a portfolio of portraits of Latin transvestites. At twenty-nine, Denise Overton was already a critical success in Europe and a rising star in the United States. Being a gorgeous strawberry blonde didn't exactly hurt. She was also sharp, witty, a tad arrogant, and smarter than me—until luck, and I, deserted her.

There you have it: I was on a loop between drugs and love in the fast lane. Pneumonia was a relief; it gave me time to think. And after a month in the hospital I went to Montauk to try to set my life in order.

I had been there for six weeks. The salt air cleared my lungs and did wonders for my head. I got lost in the ocean's pulse the first week, staring out over the Atlantic from an easy chair. Storms came and went, yielding to blue skies, fresh breezes, and abundant sunshine, and I was starting to feel good about myself for the first time in months. I wanted Denise back.

My days were rich and full, my nights spent in solitary contemplation. Up at eight A.M., the dog scratching to get out. Big breakfasts that took all morning to cook and eat, boogieing to the kitchen radio and laughing at the follies they called the news. Afterward, I hit the local spa for a few hours of supervised Nautilus, just enough to restore the spring to my muscles and sweat out the toxins and antibiotics. I was now up to two-mile runs and seventy-five roll-ups a day followed by a sauna, a plunge in the surf, and a nap before dinner. When the weather didn't allow running on the beach with Honcho panting and splashing along behind me, I read Melville and listened to the rain beside the fire. The nights were long and sweet. I spent them thinking about ways to avoid returning to Manhattan. I even fooled myself into thinking there might be a literary market for cosmic thoughts about the tides and the moon, and a career for me as a freelance writer. I went so far as to plan a budget to see how cheaply I could live without going back to work as a reporter. I had begun to think I could have it all—live in Montauk year-round and have Denise visit me on weekends. I would remain in Montauk and build our nest while she conquered the world. I'd survive on my literary jottings, spinning tales of time, tides, and the changing seasons until she was ready to make babies. I was starting really to believe it could happen when I caught the one-two punch that changed my life.

It was Monday, shortly before noon. The sun was playing hide-and-seek among scattered clouds and the sea was an undulating carpet of dappled blue and gold. I was on the deck sweeping away pine needles and considering saving the cones to make a Christmas wreath when the phone rang. It hadn't in days. The caller was Dixie Cupps, a semifamous female impersonator, who was a mutual friend of mine and Denise's. Dixie was calling to tell me that Denise was dead.

The words "Denise is dead" roared in a vacuum that filled the room and pulled the breath from my lungs. Denise can't die! No way. I had plans. Dixie kept talking. It looked like an overdose. The story was in the papers—with Denise's address, a description of what she was wearing, a description of her. I implored God to change the news to a terrible mistake. No mistake, Dixie said. Denise was dead. I began trying to conjure a vision of the last time I saw Denise alive when a wave hit the beach like a thunderclap, swallowing a few tons of sand before departing. I was going under with it.

Dixie offered more details as my mind fought the undertow. I had been full of hope when the phone first rang. I remember thinking for a fleeting instant, This might be Denise calling. The details were bad.

Her body was found in a vacant lot on Staten Island. She very likely had died elsewhere. "An apparent overdose," the papers said. Dumped like garbage. Honcho stirred and came over, gently wagging his tail. I slid off the couch and let him rest his head in my lap while I wept and struggled to make sense of something that fit all the journalistic adjectives: senseless, brutal, *wrong*.

According to newspaper accounts and Dixie's own grapevine, Denise had been dead some twelve hours before her body was found. That was two days ago. The story got worse. The vacant lot where the body had been found was in a neighborhood Dixie said was Mafia turf.

"There's a drug war going on," Dixie said laconically. "The Latins are killing each other for a piece of the crack market. Denise could have gotten close to that scene. She was working with nothing but Latin drag queens."

As Dixie saw it, the drug war involved rival Latin gangs, one of which was hell-bent on eliminating the competition and dumping the bodies in Italian neighborhoods so the cops would think it was a traditional mob war. Denise's latest project had brought her into contact with that twilight world of sex and drugs that flourished in certain quarters of Manhattan after dark. These days the Latins ran the action because everyone else was on Wall Street or in real estate. And labor was cheap in the sex and drugs rackets; lots of people found it easier getting high and getting laid than paying attention in class. Dixie figured Denise had wandered into a drug deal or taken a picture of someone who was pathologically camera shy. In any case, she had been in the wrong place at the wrong time. That was Dixie's opinion, and Dixie had strong opinions about everything.

Dixie Cupps was in her mid-thirties, headed her own drag queen revue, and knew her way around, from gutter to penthouse. Unlike some female impersonators, Dixie actually lived as a woman. It was even hard to relate to her as a man, hence the feminine pronoun. She was wise and insightful like a woman. As a man, she was dull and stubborn. She liked a good time and thrived on gossip, mostly intimacies collected along Manhattan's sexual freeways. Denise had met Dixie at the very start of her project.

I sat in silence as Dixie described other recent events in Gotham.

"There's lots you don't know about, Max. I know you've been sick, but life goes on. You never called Denise once in the past six months, so how could you know?"

My mind was far off, bobbing on a darkening sea. Denise and I could have been lovers again as soon as I wrote the letter that would win her back.

"I've been trying to get myself together, Dixie. I wanted to get her back."

"She's dead, Max. You weren't fast enough. Now listen to me."

There was an edge in Dixie's voice. She had become tight with Denise, one of the girls, and she wasn't fond of me. In Dixie's view, I had squandered a golden opportunity.

"There's something else you should know," she added. "Denise was the second person who hung around the drag scene to die from an overdose. They found a kid from Park Avenue dead on the street the morning before they found Denise. I know he was gay because I've seen him at my shows. He might have known her. I think they even died around the same time. It's something to think about."

It was something to think about. How could she die from an overdose? Denise *hated* drugs.

Denise had taken a puff or two—no more—of a joint if it was offered to her. A puff or two maybe four or five times in her life. And she had taken a sedative once or twice because she'd gotten so wound up working in the darkroom, and she couldn't sleep unless I was there to rub her back. That was the extent of Denise's drug-taking. Heroin? Forget it. She hated cocaine—she left me when she discovered I was dependent on it.

We were going to be the perfect couple.

And now Denise was dead, of an overdose.

But what if she started taking cocaine in an attempt to understand the attraction it held for me?

"Forget it," Dixie huffed. "Denise wasn't taking drugs. I can spot a junkie or a faggot a mile away."

Dixie was right when she said Denise had no business prowling the after-hours scene. It wasn't the place for a man, if he thought himself a man, much less a place for a woman. These were the bars where transvestite prostitutes met their clients and drugs were plentiful. When Denise launched the project, I insisted on accompanying her on her rounds.

It all came back like a bad dream. Someone had recommended that Denise start her talent search with Dixie's drag revue, which was playing one-night stands in local gay bars. Denise thought Dixie was wonderful and bought her a drink after the show. Denise had just cut her hair short. I told her she and Dixie looked like two dykes, with *Dixie* as the fem. Denise thought that was great and they became fast friends.

Dixie became Denise's guide to Manhattan's sexual diaspora and I trailed along, staying awake by snorting coke while Denise charmed a bunch of queens into posing for her. She wanted to document their lives and she wanted me to write captions. I thought the project was a waste of her time and I told her so. I wanted to marry her, move to the country, and have children.

We parted six months ago and then drifted apart from there. I got lost in my work and slipped deeper into drugs.

My tears stopped for a while when Dixie told me she had learned that Denise's body was still in the morgue, unclaimed. Denise's parents had both died when she was in her teens; she had no relatives that I knew of.

I told Dixie I would return to Manhattan as soon as possible.

"I think you should, Max," Dixie said. "She loved you. You owe her that much."

I promised Dixie I'd call when I got into town, hung up the phone, and then I cried until the dog wagged his tail and beckoned me to follow him outside.

I stood at the edge of the cliff and watched a fishing trawler bobbing in the waves about a mile offshore. The wind had shifted. The sea was choppy. I listened to the waves nibbling away at the base of the cliff and went back inside. All my foundations were eroding.

I walked aimlessly through the house. Why did Denise have to die? Who dumped her body in the lot? Where did she get the drugs? I would get the answers.

I went into my bedroom and found a picture of Denise, a self-portrait with the same mischievous smile she wore whenever she was setting up a shot. I took the picture and sat down on the bed and stared into her eyes. Honcho drifted in and then went away.

I remembered the first time I saw Denise smile. I was covering a demonstration in Harlem that had turned violent. The police were attempting to clear squatters from an abandoned tenement when a man threw a bucket of feces at a city official who had been arguing the landlord's case in front of a mob who hated landlords. All hell broke loose when two cops got splashed and charged into the crowd to nab the thrower. The crowd swallowed them up and someone grabbed one of the cop's service revolvers and shot him in the chest. The perpetrator shrank away into the crowd.

Denise was covering the story for an Eastern European press service. She knew the pictures were going to feed anti-American propaganda, but the job let her do what she loved and the pay was good.

Her golden-red hair was long then and her face was hidden behind a motor-driven Leica that whirred like a video game gone mad. She was a stalking lion with a third eye and a raging mane. People got out of her way; they had never seen anything like her.

I watched in stunned admiration as a cop tried to lead her away. He grabbed her arm as they both moved stealthily through the now-frightened, angry mob, heading for the spot where the other cop lay dying. Denise flashed that gorgeous smile. "Follow me," she yelled. The cop nodded and fell in behind her with his gun drawn.

Simple as that. "*Follow me.*" I stepped in behind the cop and never took my eyes off Denise for the rest of the night. The next morning half the world looked into the pleading eyes of the dying officer and saw the terror on the faces in the crowd. I had convinced Denise to bring the picture to the Associated Press instead of selling it to the commies. I took her to the Rainbow Grill for champagne afterward. That was our first date.

The romance lasted until I got tired of dangling in the wake of her success. Denise's reputation was growing.

The dark magic of cities intrigued her. That's why she loved Brassai. "The Secret Paris," Brassai's world, was the dance halls and brothels of Paris after dark. It was Brassai who led Denise to the transvestite portfolio.

She had wild ideas about androgyny. Some feminist tract convinced her it was wrong for women to dress provocatively unless they meant what their clothes were saying. But she never failed to entice me. I loved her for her, not the clothes she wore.

How could Denise die of an overdose?

I put the photograph back in the drawer and got my coat. The ocean was calling. I dropped the dog at a neighbor's house for the duration and plodded along the beach until I got into town. I wanted to buy a paper and see for myself what Dixie had read over the phone. I had to go past the post office so I decided to check for mail. That's when I got the second half of the one-two punch: There was a letter from Denise.

I didn't open the letter until I got home. First I went and bought myself a bottle of scotch. Maybe that wasn't a great idea. When I got home, I poured the first drink I'd had in eight weeks and sat down and read the letter. It had been postmarked two days earlier.

Dear Max,
Why didn't you tell me you were sick? I called your office and found out yesterday. Are you feeling better? I hope so. I need your help on this book, Max. I've been in the darkroom for hours, printing the most wonderful

pictures, but they need words to put them in perspective. That's your job.

You must get well soon. I miss you. It's been a long time. Maybe I can come out there to see you.

I have met the most glamorous "she-male," really a transsexual (she actually had the operation!). I want her to sit for a portrait. Her name is Esmeralda and she fancies herself a jet-setter but she's really just a kid. She says she has a rich boyfriend and she shuttles back and forth between here and Florida. What a life! We're supposed to get together tonight. Then I'm free for a while.

I want to see you. I hope you're OK. I do miss your back rubs. Call if you feel likewise. Who knows . . .

Love,
Denise

I already knew it was too late.

2

There's a cemetery alongside the Long Island Expressway near the spot where the Manhattan skyline first looms into view. You see the granite tombstones and right behind them the brooding mass of gray stone and glass known as the Big Apple.

The pewter sky was streaked with red. The sun was shining brightly somewhere over the horizon but not where I was sitting. The temperature had dropped as I drew closer to the city and the car heater wasn't working. I was shivering. I blamed it on the heater but I couldn't help recalling that Denise used to sit next to me in this same car when we'd arrive back in the city on Monday afternoon after a weekend in the Hamptons. That was then. Now was another Monday, I was alone, and the dashboard clock registered four-thirty as I entered the Midtown Tunnel into Manhattan. It took me another half hour to get across town and twenty minutes to realize there were no parking spaces. I put the car in a lot and trudged six blocks to my apartment. Traffic was heavy as the commuters crawled home. The city was the same, but I had changed.

I got to my apartment, threw my one bag into a corner, and sat down in front of the phone. I played back my messages. There were three hang-ups in a row, a call from Denise's neighbor Mary Collins, and a raspy message from Dixie Cupps indicating she'd try and reach me through other means. Mary's voice told me she was calling to tell me Denise was dead. Dixie's voice was a mixture of grief and annoyance.

My message said I had gone fishing. I thought about changing it but decided not to; I was going fishing after all.

I called Mary Collins first and spoke to her roommate. The roommate said she was shocked. She must have sensed I wasn't ready for too much talk, so she told me right away that Mary was planning to claim Denise's body and handle the funeral arrangements. I said that would be fine. There wasn't much else to say. Denise was dead.

I pulled the Rolodex over and wrote down the numbers of the city morgue, the police Major Crimes Unit, and Miss Cupps. I looked around for a cigarette before realizing I had given them up. I finally picked up the phone and dialed. My erstwhile employer might as well know I was back in town. For Denise's sake, it was more important to reestablish my credentials as hotshot reporter by paying homage to the city desk. It was a few minutes past six P.M. Walt Hurley, the *Graphic*'s crusty but lovable night editor, my boss, would just be sharpening his pencils and getting ready to ride herd on the night shift.

I was right. An assistant editor put me on hold; I could imagine Walt toddling back from the wire room, wondering what Darenow was up to now.

"The famous Mr. Darenow returns to life. When are you coming back to work?" There was no mistaking Hurley's voice when it crackled on the line.

I told him about Denise, at least everything I knew so far.

Hurley listened quietly, clicking his tongue occasionally. "Here's what *I* need," he said. "*I* need somebody, preferably you, to follow this whole drug business. I want daily stories on what the cops are doing, what the mayor is doing, or what he's going to do. I need hard news and I need it now. But don't get involved if you're going to make it a personal crusade. Are you up to it?"

"I'm still a little weak," I answered.

"Then you're wasting my time. What did you call for? To annoy me? Think it over."

Hurley didn't want to hear my excuses. He had carried me through some bad times and now he was calling in my debt.

"When do I start?" I asked.

"Right now. This is a big story. Get a list of the people who are turning up dead. Overdoses, shootings, there's been a shitload of them in the past month or so. Find out who they are and profile them. The cops say they're all related to drugs."

"Who's handling the case?"

"Call our man at police headquarters and ask him. He has lots of friends. There's another angle. Congress bankrolled a federal–state task force six months ago to look into the drug trade. Some big shots from Washington blew into town a month ago—Justice Department, State Department, who knows. We need a follow-up. They're probably hiding out in some office building on Foley Square playing gin rummy. Check it out."

"Where do I start?"

"I don't suppose you want to profile your friend, so try this: kick off a series by showing that drugs are an international problem that affects rich and poor alike. They found another overdose victim on Park Avenue the other morning, a rich kid. Beef the story up with statistics on how many people use drugs, why they take them, and where the drugs are coming from. I'll have someone dig into the files for you."

If you were nice to Hurley, he was nice to you.

"I'll get on the Park Avenue angle after I go to the morgue," I said. I spoke too soon. Hurley's crust was disturbed.

"Look, Max, I realize this girl was your friend, but don't waste time at the morgue. I want quotes. Go after the politicians. Go after this rich kid's parents."

"I have to say good-bye," I said.

"Make it brief, Darenow, you're supposed to be a professional."

I went straight to the morgue. I took a cab and reminded myself to charge it to expenses. One of the assistant medical examiners reluctantly agreed to discuss Denise's autopsy after I assured him the meeting was off the record. I also reminded him that the *Graphic* had endowed the pathologists' lounge with a color television set last Christmas as a show of thanks for news tips that had turned into front page stories, and hinted that Santa might be generous again this year.

The doctor had style. He was wearing white clogs, brown tweed slacks with fancy suspenders, and a Grateful Dead T-shirt. His black curly hair was gathered at the back of his neck with a rubber band. He was young, newly married, and anxious to get home for dinner, so our meeting was brief.

"You don't have to be Sherlock Holmes to suspect foul play," he began, thumbing through a manila folder and pulling out a couple of forms for inspection. "Both victims—" he meant Denise and the Park

Avenue youth— "ingested a rather large quantity of heroin and another drug we strongly suspect is scopolamine. It was probably administered in capsule form, judging from the stomach contents."

I was full of questions and the doctor was ready with answers.

"Scopolamine hydrobromide is sometimes used by prostitutes as knockout drops. They usually pour it into a drink and if they're not careful, the dose can kill. It's hard to detect unless you have a trained eye and sophisticated test equipment. I've seen a couple of cases, so I recognized the symptoms when I examined your friend. It dries out the skin and affects the bodily secretions in an unusual way."

"So she *was* murdered."

"Not for you or me to say," he cautioned. "The district attorney makes the charge. I can tell you, off the record, that visual evidence alone suggests doses that would have killed a linebacker. Both victims had eaten recent meals, so the drugs were readily absorbed. There's usually a period of severe mental disorientation before the onset of death."

I wished he hadn't told me that. I thought of Denise, lying on a slab in the next room. Six months ago, who would ever have thought she'd be there, and I'd be out here?

"Denise would never fool with heroin," I said. "If it's scopolamine too, it has to be murder."

The doctor shrugged noncommittally, put his folder aside, and glanced at the clock.

"We'll know more after the toxicologists complete their report," he said with finality. "They have instructions to be real careful on the chemistry."

He pulled on an overcoat and we walked in silence to the exit. I had thought about asking him if I could say good-bye to Denise on the way out but I changed my mind. He was going home to his wife.

But I couldn't help looking back when we reached the sidewalk. The doctor caught my mood and reminded me of the Latin inscription carved over the portals of the medical examiner's office: "Let laughter cease, let conversation flee: this is where death delights in helping the living."

I thought about that all the way home.

3

Clarence Henry was a detective lieutenant assigned to the Manhattan Major Crimes Unit who owed his rapid rise through the ranks to a series of stories I had written about him. Henry was thirty-five, black, and the possessor of a master's degree in psychology. He started out as a cop on Broadway, pounding a beat in the West Nineties. He began cleaning up the neighborhood, and the sharper hoods and drug dealers retaliated by filing complaints with the police department's Civilian Review Board. The rules of the department called for immediate transfer if the complaints exceeded a certain number.

The hoods knew this and Henry was transferred. Leaving the job half done angered him, so he came to me with his story. I did a series on the neighborhood, interviewing residents and shopkeepers who had nothing but praise for him. They made it clear they wanted him back. So he came back and the junkies moved uptown.

Henry owed me a favor. I called him and told him I had been assigned to cover the so-called drug wars, from top to bottom. I knew how the New York cops hated it when the feds moved in to steal their thunder, so I dropped a disparaging remark about the boys from D.C. to let him know whose side I was on. I let him chew on that a while and then I let him know that Denise had been more than a friend.

I asked him if he had heard the rumor that Latin mobsters were deliberately confusing things by dumping bodies on Mafia turf. He snorted loudly and opined that the story was probably more than a rumor. I described Denise's photo project and told him what I knew of the preliminary autopsy report. I also told him how Denise had been on her way to meet Esmeralda, the jet-set drag queen, and offered the description from Denise's letter. He became very interested.

"The case sounds like it's up for grabs," he mused. "The girl's body was found in the 120th Precinct on Staten Island. I could pick it up if we can establish that the crime took place in Manhattan. Can we get a picture of the queen?"

I thought of the postmark on Denise's letter and counted back. Denise may have completed a photo session with Esmeralda sometime Friday night, the night she probably died. We'd have to look through her files.

"I'm gonna make an effort to get this case," Henry assured me. "Call me tomorrow. I like the idea of returning a favor."

I thought I handled the call nicely, balancing my own interests with Hurley's need for hard news. If the lieutenant got the case, I had a direct line to the police department. And if I got tight with the feds too, who love trading information for publicity, Henry too would have a line to their camp. And I'd use Dixie for everything else.

My next call was to police headquarters. Hurley had been in touch with our man there, and he was ready with facts from the police reports and copies of them for me. He reminded me that Hurley thought the Park Avenue angle was top priority. Then he read me the report.

The Park Avenue resident was identified as Jaime Santiago, twenty-two, male Hispanic. He lived at a rather fancy address in the Eighties. The next of kin was listed as Mrs. Ethel Watèly of New York, same address. A detective from the Central Park precinct had the case.

I wondered momentarily what a kid named Santiago was doing living on Park Avenue, but I let it drift. Mrs. Watèly might have been married to a Spanish duke. This town was full of foreigners who preferred the risks of getting mugged to paying taxes back home.

I called the Central Park precinct, but the detective there wasn't much help. The investigation was hardly underway and he had already drawn a list of dead-end conclusions. The Santiago kid was "destined to meet a bad end," he said, and "the girl"—he meant Denise—"was in the wrong place at the wrong time." I already knew that much. He already suspected drag queens or prostitutes were involved but didn't seem anxious to pursue that angle.

"You can't ever find these people," he complained. "Maybe a year from now some snitch will give you a line, but that's the best you can hope for."

He did give me a few more facts. The Santiago boy's body was found on the street, wedged between two parked cars. A neighbor who was walking his dog discovered the body Saturday morning at 6:30 A.M. The detective had interviewed Mrs. Wately, whom he described as "a typical rich dame," and her housekeeper, a Mrs. Rosa Torquenos. Neither one had much to offer.

"The kid was adopted," the detective said gruffly. "He had a problem with drugs. He was also a little queer, from the looks of it. The Wately dame and him weren't very close. It's a shame, but what are you gonna do?"

I decided not to tell him about my chat with Lieutenant Henry or my visit to the morgue. The less he knew, the better the chance Henry would take over.

"If there's an arrest, you'll be the first to know," the detective said. He didn't mean it.

I called the Wately residence. The phone rang eight times before a woman with a Spanish accent and a tiny, hollow voice said, "Allo?"

I took a guess and asked, "Mrs. Torquenos?"

"Who is this?"

"My name is Max Darenow. I'm investigating young Mr. Santiago's death. I'd like to ask you a few more questions." No sense mentioning the *Graphic*, I thought. Let's see how far this goes.

"Are you police?" Not very far.

"A very close friend of mine was also found dead of a drug overdose, Mrs. Torquenos. She may have known Mr. Santiago. She was a photographer. Her name was Denise. Denise Overton. Does that ring a bell?"

"I'm soo-rry. We have nothing to say. It is very sad what happen. Please leave us alone." Click.

I called again. The phone rang three times. Mrs. Torquenos picked up.

"Allo?"

"Mrs. Torquenos, this is very important—"

She put down the receiver but didn't hang up. There was a resonating echo that had the clarity of marble and I thought I heard voices far away.

There was another click on the line.

"May I help you?" It was a younger woman's voice, crisp and cool, businesslike. I shifted gears.

"Is Mrs. Wately in?"

"Who is calling, pleez?" The voice got crisper. A Latin touch was evident. Another servant? She sounded bitchy, but not old and bitchy.

"My name is Darenow. Max Darenow. I have some information I'd like to share with Mrs. Wately. It's about the young man, Mr. Santiago. Who are *you?*" I demanded, to put her on the defensive.

"Uh . . . I work for Mrs. Wately. Are you with the police?"

"A friend of mine was found dead under similar circumstances," I answered. "My friend may have known Mr. Santiago. They could have been given drugs by the same person."

"Mrs. Wately is very upset," she said flatly. "She can't come to the phone." I could tell she wanted to get rid of me. Whoever she was, she was more than a housemaid.

"I think she'll want to talk to me," I said, stalling. "We might be able to put these drug dealers out of business."

"Oh?" she said, her voice rising. "Let me have your name, pleez."

"D-A-R-E-N-O-W."

"And you say your friend knew Jaime?" There was a hint of coyness in her voice now, as if she were really interested.

"Right. She was a photographer. She was given an overdose of drugs, like Jaime. She might have known Jaime or the people who killed him."

There was a long pause, as if she were writing everything down or someone were listening over her shoulder.

"OK. I give Mrs. Wately the message." The crispness in her voice had returned. I was being dismissed.

"Wait a minute. Do you want my phone number?" I gave her my number at home and told her I was a reporter for the *Graphic*.

"But I'm not doing a story *per se* on Jaime," I said. "I'm concerned because my friend was involved. Do you understand?"

"I understand. Thank you." She was being polite but slightly condescending. If your name's not in the society columns, don't bother calling.

"What's *your* name?" I asked testily.

"Aurora Carrera." She trilled all the rrr's.

"It's very important—" I started to say.

She had already hung up.

I was certain Ms. Carrera was Mrs. Wately's personal gatekeeper, and good at her job. Hurley wasn't going to like it one bit if I failed to develop a sob story on the Santiago kid. Finding out where he went to school, then trying to get his friends to talk about what a sterling lad he really was would take a lot of legwork.

What a way to make a living. I unpacked my bag and drew the curtains to shut out the night. I was itchy and hungry and I didn't know what I wanted. There was nothing in the refrigerator but a jar of mustard and a single can of beer. I would have to go out for food, but I wasn't ready for the street.

I made myself a gin martini, heavy on the vermouth, and dug into a drawer full of memories. I came out with two manila envelopes crammed with more of Denise's work.

The photographs were of friends, couples mostly—writers, photographers, actors, artists, playwrights, an occasional poet. They were candid shots, taken in bars and cafés, studios and street corners: artists at work and artists relaxing with their mates. Only they didn't look relaxed. Their smiles were either tired or forced—manic. Everyone looked driven and uncomfortable. Denise couldn't decide whether to call the series "Under the Influence of Art" or simply "Modern Lovers."

I was the subject of a few photos myself, always trying to look hardboiled. And there were some of Denise and me, looking lovey-dovey, happy.

I left the photos spread out on the desk, finished the martini, and caught myself wishing for a joint to float me downstream. I had some pot hidden away, but I resisted the urge. I was back in the land of the quick fix, instant profit, and too much ain't never enough. I took a couple of deep breaths and walked to the Chinese restaurant on the corner, where I wolfed down a platter of sliced fish and vegetables and drank two bottles of Chinese beer.

I went back home, put away the memories, and took a shower. A sour taste rose in my throat. I had started drinking before I left Montauk, and the gin and the beer hadn't done my digestion any good. I was out of practice. I had forgotten how drugs work their devious magic: the more you take, the less you notice. You pull the wool over your own eyes until you're so out of step with everyone else that you can't see why they can't understand you. I stepped onto the cold tiles, swallowed some bicarbonate of soda, and vowed to take better care of myself if I expected to accomplish anything.

"I was a fool, Denise," I said out loud. I went into my room, turned off the light and quietly cried myself to sleep.

4

The phone rang at 7:15 A.M. It was Aurora Carrera, phoning to say that Mrs. Ethel Wately was returning my call before catching a plane to Florida. She was going home to bury Jaime. I snatched the phone from the night table and grabbed a pencil and a piece of paper. There was no need for haste. Mrs. Wately took her time getting on the line.

"Mr. Darenow?" Her voice was full of character, silky smooth and heavy with innuendo. She was wide awake and in command. "What can I do for you?"

"I'm a reporter, but my interest in this affair is personal, Mrs. Wately. Denise Overton was a very close friend of mine. She didn't take drugs. If my information is correct, she and your son may have been murdered. They . . . ah . . . shared some common interests and . . . ah . . . there may be a connection."

I let out a sigh. This was getting to be some balancing act. I wondered how long I could serve two masters, Hurley and myself.

"You've brought this to the attention of the police, I would expect?"

"I have."

"I see. Well, that's very good. What do you think the connection is? Did your girlfriend know Jaime? He wasn't my son, incidentally. I'm his legal guardian. Were they friends?" Mrs. Wately apparently did more than shop for clothes and lunch with the girls. She knew how to handle herself with nosy reporters.

"Can I come by and see you before you leave?" I begged. "I can be there in twenty minutes."

"I really don't see any reason. . . . Well, all right. But I don't want our family name dragged through the media. We tried to help the boy. Can you assure me there'll be no publicity?"

I promised, though Hurley wouldn't be happy.

"Can you get here by eight o'clock? Our car leaves for the airport at eight forty-five." She gave me an address on Park near Eighty-sixth. We made a date for around eight.

I made some tea, never drank it, shaved, and put on a brown wool suit, green knit tie, and sensible shoes. I called the city desk and asked them to send a photographer to Seventy-second and Park. It was the wrong address, but Hurley would think I had tried.

I grabbed a cab at the corner and made it up Eighth, through Central Park, and to Eighty-sixth and Park Avenue by 8:10.

The Watelys lived in one of those elegant, well-kept prewar buildings that bespeak old money. The doorman rang upstairs and turned me over to the elevator operator, who took me to the twelfth floor. He waited until a short, squat, brown-skinned woman who looked about sixty opened the door. I could see a man's leather suitcase and a woman's overnight bag in the foyer. A long marble hall and a marble staircase leading to an upper floor were in the background.

The maid wore a black uniform dress, black cotton stockings, and cheap white sneakers. She asked me to come inside and led me down the marble hall to a living room the size of a tennis court. I felt like Puss in Boots coming to con the mean old ogre on behalf of his master.

I asked the maid if she was Mrs. Torquenos.

"I'm the maid," she said. "I work for Mrs. Wately."

"Is Mrs. Torquenos here?" I asked.

"I am," she snapped. "Mrs. Wately will be right here. Sit down." She padded off down the hall.

I strolled across a floor parqueted in octagons of polished light oak bordered in a slightly darker wood and took a seat on a beige silk couch. The first thing I noticed when I sat down was a portrait of a contented man in a business suit which hung over a light brown marble fireplace that belonged in a castle. The walls were covered in a nubby, moss-colored fabric, also probably silk, and hung with more paintings. Some of them were oddly out of place. There were a Rivers, two Lindners, and a Hockney. I had been to enough galleries with Denise to know that much. Otherwise it was all beige and moss green. The room looked like the inside of a very old hundred-dollar bill.

Despite their provenance none of the pictures was any competition for the full-length portrait that dominated the wall opposite the marble fireplace. The subject was a woman about thirty, with brown hair tucked into a stylish roll at the nape of her very long neck. She was wearing a full-length blue silk evening dress that could have been from the fifties. It had lots of elegant folds and pleats. The woman was posed against the very mantelpiece she now faced. She looked serenely happy and self-assured. Norman Parkinson's portraits in *Vogue* came to mind. I could almost smell the Chanel No. 5.

"Mr. Darenow? We haven't much time. This is Edgar Wately. He'll join us for a moment."

The voice was Mrs. Wately's; so was the Chanel. She was a stunning blonde with a smile you could get lost in forever. I was checking her out when behind her I heard a gruff, distinctly unfriendly male voice growl hello. Yogi Bear with a prep school accent. I stood up, expecting to shake hands with Mr. Wately, but he put his palm up and told me to sit down. He was a big man, brawny but flabby, who looked to be about fifty. He was deeply tanned, with a firm jaw and a pair of dark blue eyes under a sparse crop of blond hair going gray. He checked a large gold wristwatch and sat down in a wing chair facing me.

Mrs. Wately was the perfect size eight, no doubt about it; slender, medium height, late thirties, maybe older. It's hard to tell with women who take meticulously good care of themselves. I found out later she was forty-seven and he was forty-five. Her ash-blond hair looked natural, but women her age sometimes select that shade to hide the gray. It was pulled straight back, not in that eyebrow-stretching style that looks painful, but tucked lightly, neatly, at the nape of her neck, held in place with a tortoise-shell clip. It was a young touch for her age bracket. She had green-brown eyes, and like Denise's, they caught you in their gaze and held you there. Her smile was all-knowing, a Mona Lisa smile, beckoning, but it also carried a warning: be good or begone. Yet for all her impeccable grooming, something suggested Ethel Wately wouldn't mind being tossed on a blanket at a lifeguard's clambake.

She was still standing in the doorway and despite her schedule she looked cool as a cucumber. She wore an elegantly simple short-sleeved black linen dress, a single strand of pearls, and gold-hooped earrings.

Several gold bracelets hung idly on her wrist. Her feet were clad in black alligator pumps. I was drinking this all in, standing between a couch and a coffee table, unable to move because I couldn't take my eyes from hers. I was a callow thirty-five myself, and until then had thought younger women were best suited to me. I suspected that Mrs. Wately had a few years on me, but she looked very good.

She came forward, offered her hand, and withdrew it the instant I touched it. It fluttered away like a little jeweled bird, soft and sharp, coming to rest in her other hand in a state of elegant composure.

I stood transfixed until she told me to sit. I sat, right in the middle of smart money.

She sat down herself, taking the matching wing chair on my right.

"Would you like a cup of coffee?" she asked.

She turned in the direction of the hall and addressed Mrs. Torquenos in Spanish, the kind of Spanish they teach at Sweetbriar, but she used too many words to be just asking for coffee.

"Milk and sugar?" Mrs. Wately inquired.

"Yes, please." I heard Mrs. Torquenos shuffle down the hall as I turned my attention to Mr. Wately, expecting him to talk, or growl, or whatever he did. But it was Mrs. Wately who did the talking.

"So . . ." she said. "Let me get this straight. You think your friend's death is connected to Jaime's? Why?" The smile was gone. She was all business now. The green-brown eyes positively burned with intelligence. Mr. Wately probably got his jollies just watching her. I couldn't blame him for that. My eyes had wandered back to the two portraits. Mrs. Wately noticed. "My parents," she said. There was a hint of pride in her voice.

Edgar cleared his throat and checked his watch again. His impatience was showing. He stared at Mrs. Wately.

"The car will be here in twenty-five minutes, Ethel," he said.

"Did you have much contact with the young man?" I asked him, just to get the conversation going.

"He's Ethel's problem, I'm afraid." His eyes were fixed on her. Ethel smiled enigmatically by way of reply. They were as distant as two people could be and still live under the same roof.

"Everything is my problem, Mr. Darenow," she sighed. "We have extensive family holdings in Florida and this is a very busy time for us. Unfortunately, Jaime insisted on going to school in New York at a time when we've had to remain in Tampa."

"Where did he go to school?"

Mrs. Wately looked at Edgar as if she expected him to answer. He was busy sizing me up.

"New York Design," she said. "He was interested in fashion. The Latins have a flair for that."

"Jaime's parents were Spanish?"

"I raised him from the time he was six years old," she said. There was pride and sadness in her tone.

Edgar stood up, jammed his hands in the pockets of his pants, and addressed me like a spoiled brat talking to a servant.

"Mr. Darenow," he said, "we've told the police everything we know. We were under the impression you were coming here to enlighten us. You are a newspaper reporter. Your newspaper has a reputation for . . . overkill, shall we say? I'm beginning to think we're being led down the garden path. This was not to be an interview. Am I correct?"

"Yes, sir, you are," I answered politely. "I came here to find out if my friend, Denise Overton—she's the other victim—knew your young man. There's reason to believe they moved in the same circles."

"Get to the point," he said. "We don't have much time." He moved back to the mantel and leaned against it, under the father's portrait. He looked a lot like Mrs. Wately's father. Maybe that had been the attraction.

I glanced at Mrs. Wately, who glanced back with the Mona Lisa smile. If Edgar was a pain in the ass, Mrs. W. was capable of giving as good as she got. Their spats must be monumental.

I described the project Denise had been working on, nimbly avoiding the fact that Jaime Santiago had been described as a conoisseur of transgendered flesh himself. I didn't want to rock the boat just yet.

"I thought Jaime might have bumped into Denise somewhere. They might have gone to the same clubs," I said. "It's mostly a Latin crowd and Denise had a professional interest in those people. She was an excellent photographer. She wasn't a drug addict. Far from it. There's no way in hell she would have swallowed a capsule of heroin unless she thought she was taking something else. There's evidence she was murdered. Your ward," I turned to Ethel Wately, "may have known the people who murdered both of them."

Edgar stared at Mrs. Wately. I couldn't read either one of them. If what I implied shocked them, they weren't letting on.

Mrs. Wately looked at me kindly, like an understanding aunt. She leaned forward and spoke with emphasis.

"My ward is dead, sir. I have no idea who his friends were. He had very few friends, I think. A few old school chums in Tampa, perhaps. Although I imagine he made some acquaintances here."

She sat back in her chair and looked me in the eye briefly, then she shivered and looked away. She was crying—or trying not to. Her eyes reddened and returned to the portraits of Mummy and Daddy, who continued to stare impassively.

Mrs. Torquenos arrived with my coffee. She placed it quietly on the table alongside a linen napkin and shuffled off. Edgar Wately moved from the mantelpiece to a position behind Mrs. Wately's chair and placed his paws on its sides as if he were going to shake it. Without looking, Mrs. Wately put her arms up and lightly stroked those paws before she addressed me.

"The lower classes will always be a problem, Mr. Darenow. No matter what *ethnic group*—" she fairly snarled the words— "is involved. Now I really must finish packing some things. I'm very sorry."

I didn't know whether she was putting on a brave front, or controlling some deep-rooted wrath over her ward's death. She rose from the chair. So did I. I was a bit annoyed. Things were just getting interesting and I hadn't touched my coffee.

"Edgar? Will you see Mr. Darenow to the door?"

She held out her hand again and waited until I crossed the room to her. I shook it very gently. It was hard staying annoyed when she was that close.

"Thank you for coming," she said. "Help us forget this terrible tragedy. And don't hurt our family. We tried our best." She drew back her hand and moved away. Her first steps were almost stiff-legged and I thought she was faltering, but she recovered with an elegant stride.

At the doorway she was joined by a Spanish woman in her late twenties whom I hadn't seen earlier.

This had to be Aurora Carrera. She wore a blue poplin suit, the Brooks Brothers look for the young professional woman, a white blouse with a trim little black bow tie, sensible black pumps, and sheer stockings. The outfit didn't hide any of her curves. Her jet-black hair was cut short on the sides, swept up in front, and disproportionately long in the back. She also wore too much eye makeup.

She was carrying a black linen bolero jacket, which she draped carefully over Mrs. Wately's shoulders. Mrs. Wately whispered something and both of them drifted down the hall, but not before Aurora stole a glance over her shoulder.

Edgar Wately waited until they were gone and then lumbered around the wing chair, looking mildly embarrassed. He took my hand and shook it, too.

"This has been a very rough time for all of us," he said. "You hear about this sort of thing, but you never think it will strike so close to home."

I uttered something forgettable in reply and began moving toward the front door. I didn't have much time left and I knew the Watelys weren't eager to invite me back. They were going to Florida. Who knew when I'd see them again? If I were Detective Henry, what would I ask Edgar Wately at this moment? I could only think of the drag queen, Esmeralda, and something Dixie had said about the kid turning up at the gay bars where she did her shows.

"Has anybody gone through Mr. Santiago's things?" I asked. "There could be a photo or an address book with names in it. Maybe a matchbook or something. You never know where these things will lead you."

He frowned and glanced at me sideways, as if the prospect was appalling. The man just wanted the whole thing to go away. I didn't blame him, but I was suddenly curious about how his wife wound up adopting a kid with a Latin surname. I tried another tack. The man-to-man approach.

"Look," I began with cautious deliberation, "let's say he was hanging around with the wrong crowd. There are people in this town who would cut your throat for a quarter. Maybe he . . ." I was searching for a word when he smiled, took my elbow, and began escorting me down the hall. His voice took on a conspiratorial tone.

"I think a couple of hookers knocked them off," he confided lightly. "You're never gonna find them. Jaime was spoiled. The, uh, girls probably smelled money. He was naive. I'm sorry about your friend."

I searched his eyes for more information but there wasn't anything there. He had an enviable talent for concealing whatever emotions lay beyond his words. He must have been a tough businessman. I guessed then what Mrs. Wately saw in him. He was hard when he had to be.

"Is that what the police think?" I said.

"I would assume that's what took place. Unless you come up with a better explanation. Give me a call in Tampa if anything turns up." He drew a wallet from inside his blazer and handed me a business card. I put it away without looking at it.

He shook his head in anguish or disgust, I couldn't tell which. The meeting was over, and the hall didn't seem quite so long this time. We were standing at the front door.

"I really wish we could help you but, frankly, the boy was left pretty much on his own. It wasn't right. She's not a mother and I'm not a father and we lead pretty busy lives."

"What business are you in, Mr. Wately?" I asked, realizing that men like Edgar Wately had to be prodded to talk about money or business among strangers.

Wately grinned and reddened.

"Making money so we can pay our taxes," he said. "I'm a banker." He was serious now. He sounded like a banker. "I manage some rather complicated family holdings. They've been occupying most of our time." He opened the door. "Please call if you find out anything, won't you?"

We stepped into the hall and Wately rang for the elevator. We said good-bye and he went inside, closing the door behind him.

But I had forgotten to ask for a picture of Jaime. I turned back and buzzed the doorbell. Edgar answered the door, looking annoyed. I asked him if we could print a picture of the Santiago boy, without mentioning the Wately name. He disregarded the question momentarily and began moving luggage into the hall. I held the door open for him.

"I don't know," he frowned. "That may be asking for trouble. But let me ask Ethel if she has one. Is the elevator coming?"

It was just arriving, and we said good-bye again.

"Tragic family," the elevator man said when the doors had closed. He was addressing my reflection in a mirrored panel. He was a wizened little Irishman who looked as if he had been working in that elevator most of his life.

"Did you know the young man who died?" I ventured.

"Sure," he said. He glanced over his shoulder. "He was mixed up. He brought some real showgirls in here once, but I don't think he was that way. A real pity."

"Do you think they were really showgirls?" I was pushing my luck but time was short.

He shot me another glance and smiled.

"Now you're talking. He had some friends, all right. Weird."

"Weird?"

"Not the type you see around here," he said. "Village types. Punks. Spanish from Harlem. Not the sort of crowd you'd want your kid to hang out with."

"The Watelys weren't home much, I guess."

"Sure they were," he said. "Well, *he* was, but I don't think he bothered much with the kid. They never spoke to each other when they were together. Like the mister was embarrassed. Frankly, the kid hadn't been hanging out here much lately."

"What about Mrs. Wately?"

"What about her? She stays mostly in Florida."

"Did she *ever* live here?"

"Years ago, right after the parents died. She had lots of parties, lots of guests. The governor was here once, Rockefeller, and so was that guy who was secretary of state, the big guy from Wall Street. She went out with him after his wife died."

"She's still a beautiful woman," I said.

"Yeh," he said, without much enthusiasm. He didn't agree, for some reason. I guess he saw her in a different light.

"Things changed when the Spanish came on board," he said.

"What do you mean?"

"Aw, the parents had a swell couple, a maid and butler. Lovely people, lovely. High-class, educated blacks. She got rid of them when the kid came here to live. I guess she wanted him to be with his own kind."

We had reached the lobby.

"Well, have a nice day," he said.

I walked a few blocks in the winter sun before hailing a cab to Denise's apartment.

I took Wately's business card out and examined it. It said Edgar J. Wately, Chairman of the Board, The Suburban Bank of Tampa.

I wondered how long he'd been married to Ethel. And how the Santiago kid and the rest of the Latinos fit into their tight little family.

5

Denise had been living on the top floor of a five-floor walkup on Grove Street in the Village, and I had arranged to meet Lieutenant Henry there. The apartment was great by New York standards. She had four small rooms, a fireplace, and a skylight. She had built a darkroom in the kitchen and installed a small stove and refrigerator combination in the back room under the skylight. We had prepared some memorable meals on that stove. Two french windows overlooked a couple of spindly trees and a courtyard in the back. You could hear the birds in the morning and watch the moon move across the sky on a summer's night. In that room there was also a green convertible sofa, an ornate, six-foot-long Louis XIV writing and dining table, a couple of gilded bamboo chairs from a prop house, and an easy chair covered with a wool paisley shawl. A metal file cabinet sprayed in ersatz gold leaf and waxed to resemble the real thing stood in the corner, and there were photo lights on stands.

Everything was where it ought to be, except Denise.

The door was ajar. I pushed it and walked in. Detective Lieutenant Henry was standing behind the Louis XIV table. A man in a gray tweed suit and turtleneck sweater stood next to him. He was the detective from the Central Park precinct. He was about forty and he looked like one mean cop. He had dark wavy hair and thick eyebrows that hung like dark clouds over a permanent scowl.

There was a third cop, a faceless rookie who jumped up quickly from the easy chair and just as quickly sat down again.

"Max, you have to forgive us for getting started already," Henry said. "We don't like having to go through personal effects without a next of kin if possible. You and I can take a look around the other rooms later. Meanwhile, here's what we have."

He referred to the two dozen stacks of contact sheets, envelopes, and loose prints piled before him.

"Miss Overton was organized," Henry said admiringly. "Most of these negatives are keyed to file folders in the cabinet that identify the material."

"There's a lot of stuff without names," the mean cop huffed. He picked up a bundle of proofs in varying sizes and dropped them back on the table. "She did not identify the drag queens."

Henry joined in. "We found some release forms that might belong to those pictures but you'd have to know their names to match them up."

The other man's scowl was deepening. "You know any of these people?" He was talking to me.

"I doubt it," I replied. "I often went out with Denise when she was taking the pictures, but I was just along for the ride."

His mouth curled as if he'd bitten into a piece of bad fruit. "She hung out with these people?"

"She was going to make a book." I said, and then I drew a breath and pressed my lips together. I wasn't ready for this horseshit. I calmed myself by trying to imagine how Denise might have reacted to the insult, but then Henry threw his palms up and defused the situation.

"Look," he said wearily, motioning to the faceless rookie. "We have a plainsclothesman here who knows a few of these people, at least by sight. We're gonna make copies and circulate them around to various precincts where they congregate. We'll try to bring a few in for questioning. Can you identify the one Miss Overton was supposed to be meeting Friday night?"

"I don't think so," I replied. "She's been described as a sex-change. Blonde. Spanish. A hot number, well-heeled. Denise called her a jet-setter."

"She's a high-class prostie for rich freaks," the mean cop scoffed. "She'll go back to Puerto Rico and disappear. Change her name, her looks. Forget it."

Henry shook his head.

"Yeh, Max, it's gonna be a problem. It's hard finding these people, even harder getting them to talk. They're drifters with no identities, made-up names, and phony birth certificates. It's not the real world."

"It ain't no fairyland, either," the meanie interjected. "A human garbage heap is what it is. They don't talk because that's the code of the street and that's where they live. If they talk they got nowhere to go home to. They're worse than dead."

"I get them to talk," the faceless rookie bragged over my shoulder. "I put 'em in a holding pen with two sex-crazed bloods with twelve-inch schlongs." I tried concentrating on the bare trees outside the window.

"That's enough of that." Henry bristled. "You seem to forget there's a member of the press here."

"Only kiddin'," the rookie whined.

"You have a job to do," Henry said.

Henry was not only a good cop, he was also a smart, decent human being. He played by the book when he had to, but he knew how to manage hard-boiled dicks and the rookies without losing their respect. He had made his point, now he beckoned to the younger man. "Please tell us which of these ladies you're familiar with."

The rookie blushed slightly and sidled up to the table.

"Sorry, Loo," he muttered under his breath.

We spent the next hour going through the proofs, slides, and contact sheets they'd found in the darkroom. We put most of them back, except the ones that made up the transvestite series. Some were candid shots, in color and black and white, taken in drag clubs, on sidewalks, in hallways, hotel rooms, and apartments. Transvestites at work, at play, and at home. All of Denise's subjects were Latin. Baby-faced boys with baby-fat bodies. Slim little boys with sultry eyes and girlish pouts. A few posed with their "husbands," surly-looking lizards with "loser" written all over them. There were a few middle-aged "matrons" with naughty, defiant stares, but there was always a wistful quality in their eyes, too.

There was a series of posed studio shots, black and white on a neutral background, of six different models wearing the same floor-length gown. It was a period costume from a prop house, which looked like velvet and had a jeweled neckline, cut low but sculpted so you couldn't tell the models were flat-chested.

Not all of them were. I kept flipping to new photos. Several displayed remarkable cleavage. It could have been silicone, or, as Denise once explained, it could be done with wide surgical tape that pushed and squeezed a man's flat chest into credible lumps.

Denise had undoubtedly rearranged their hair and redone their makeup, as she did for all portraits. The models wore no jewelry, but each conveyed a kind of regal grace. They didn't look like men or boys; with a couple of striking exceptions, they looked like ordinary, sad, not especially attractive women modeling an antique gown.

The hard-boiled dick snorted in disgust when we uncovered a few proofs of the boys in their undies, stepping into the gowns. Denise had probably been joking with them, putting them at their ease. The drag queens reflected the mood by grinning mischievously or smiling demurely. I thought of how Denise used to move nonchalantly around the studio, setting lights, tilting the reflectors, all the while keeping up a running conversation with her subject. The camera, with shutter cord, would be aimed and ready on the tripod. Denise, with an air of disarming distraction, would then ask pointed questions as she drifted over to snap the shutter at precisely the right moment.

"Fuckin' AIDS carriers is all this freak show is about," the mean cop said.

The rookie recognized a couple of the "girls."

"This one I know. We picked her up about six months ago for prostitution. She did three days." He pointed to another one. "Charro. She's done time for shoplifting. She needed a new dress."

"The question," Henry said, looking at me, "is whether any of them had a reason, real or manufactured, for killing your friend. It's true that most of these people are street queens and prosties, but we've run across some from good families. We've picked up drag queens who fit a certain description, brought 'em in for a line-up, and found out their parents were diplomats at the UN.

"What I'm saying is that this type of person might have second thoughts about having posed for your friend," Henry continued. "It's something to think about."

"They're like cockroaches," the other detective sneered. "They come out at night and go back into the woodwork. We'll take a shot at it, but I'm not optimistic."

He and the plainclothesman gathered up a dozen photos. The rookie would pass copies to sector cars in various precincts and barrios, and the other man was going to try to match the faces to known felons. They were to work together under Henry's supervision. The rookie seemed to like the idea. The hard-boiled dick looked as if nothing ever pleased him. I imagined he'd seen too much, thought about it too much, couldn't understand it at all, drank to forget it, and couldn't. The job was his life and he hated every minute of it.

None of the photos featured anyone you could describe as a stunning blond transsexual. Esmeralda may never have made it to the sitting, or her photographs might have been in Denise's camera when she died.

I looked around the apartment. There were several cameras and a bag of lenses in the darkroom, but Denise's favorite Nikon FTN was missing. The room didn't look like it had been set up for a photo session, either.

When the two men left, Henry and I looked through Denise's personal things. It didn't take long. Denise didn't believe in having a lot of stuff, except books.

"Her address book and her appointment book aren't here," I pointed out. "She carried them with her in the camera bag."

"All she had when she was found were the clothes on her back," Henry said. "No bags, no ID. Whoever dumped her has all that."

"Who identified her?"

"A neighbor from upstairs saw the story in the paper and called 911. Mary Collins."

We hadn't found anything worth noting. We were in the bedroom now, and I was torn between wanting to get out fast, right on Henry's heels, and tossing myself down in the rocking chair where Denise's nightgown was still draped. I went over to the rocker and ran my hand over the fabric. It was pink flannel, soft and worn, with a white lace collar.

"Let's go in the other room," Henry said. We crossed through the darkroom and a room full of books on shelves, books everywhere, and went back under the skylight. I wondered again where Denise had met Esmeralda.

"See if you can get a better description of this Esmeralda," Henry said. "We'll pick her up if we can find her. Otherwise, it ain't gonna be easy. The other detective is right. They only come out at night and the ones who talk don't live very long. The others tell you what they think you want to hear."

I didn't mention Dixie's name, but I said I'd talk to some people and look around. Then I wrote up a list for him of places where Denise hung out. He said he'd let me have a peek at the autopsy report after the toxicologists finished their tests.

"Need a lift somewhere, Darenow?" he asked. I told him I wanted to walk for a while. He stuck my list in his pocket and taped the police order on the apartment door again.

We went back outside, onto the street. I saw faces of people I'd seen while walking with Denise—shopkeepers, neighbors, the cat in the Italian bakery window. I missed coming here.

"Wait a few weeks, we'll release the seal," he said. "Who's gonna clean out her things?"

"Maybe I will," I said as we walked through the scent of baking bread. I wanted to take that nightgown Denise loved so much and tuck it in a drawer, out of harm's way.

Henry promised to keep in touch and left me on the sidewalk. I walked a couple of blocks east, stopped for an espresso, then called Dixie before I left the coffee shop. Maybe she had gotten a line on Esmeralda.

"Esmeralda had a sex-change eighteen months ago," she crowed. "Complete makeover, silicone from stem to stern, state-of-the-art. Loves to go dancing and show off her tits. Lives in Florida, has a sugar daddy. Hits town regularly."

"Where does she hang out?" Dixie had obviously done some snooping.

"Besides Bloomingdales? Well, she's been seen in some of the drag clubs, flaunting her prosthetics and her wardrobe. The Santiago boy was her frequent escort."

"Is she a prostitute?"

"No-ooo. Not from what I've been told. She's a kept woman, kept in style. Her surgery bill must have been enormous."

"Is she Spanish?"

"Yes, but very fair. A blonde. Supposed to have gorgeous hair."

"Short or tall? What about her eyes?"

"No one mentioned her size. Medium height, I guess. Dunno about her eyes."

"Where's she staying?"

"I'm not on intimate terms with her. Several people said she stayed at the Plaza. The girl travels first class. She hung out in the Toucan Too. You might want to start there."

"I know the Toucan. Latin high rollers," I interrupted.

"That's her scene, and tonight's a good night to go there. It won't be too crowded and there're always a few uptown queens hanging around."

"Want to come along?"

"Is this a date, darling?"

Dixie was going to be a problem.

"Call me when you're ready to leave and I'll be downstairs waiting for you," she said. "I'm doing you a favor."

I spent the next eight hours at the *Graphic*, matching clips pulled from the morgue marked "drugs/homicides" with the raw data which had been routinely copied and sent over from police headquarters. I started writing the story around 5:30 P.M., after the day shift cleared out and I could concentrate.

The bare bones of the story were simple. A dozen Latins, male and female, had been shot, blown up, or thrown from a roof by a person or persons unknown to the police, all within the last two months. The victims were found throughout Manhattan, Brooklyn, and Staten Island, almost always in locations that had been traditional Mafia burial grounds. That alone had convinced the simple-minded people who ran the federal task force—code-named LEGAL, for Law Enforcement Government Assistance Liaison—that New York's Italian mob was behind the slaughter. But the New York cops knew that was too simple. It wasn't what they were hearing from the street, and the street, for anyone with half a brain, was a barometer far superior to the political appointees in the Justice Department.

The victims ranged in age from twenty-four to forty-eight. Ten were Cuban-born. Two were Marielitas, "boat people." Another two were identified as former troopers in the Nicaraguan National Guard. Four of the Cubans had been arrested one time or another for possession of narcotics with intent to sell. *All* were Florida residents.

A Cuban husband and wife died separately; he was blown up with a car bomb in a parking lot at Kennedy Airport, she was raped and shot to death in their apartment in Kew Gardens an hour later. Most of the others were executed, Mafia style, shot in their cars. The Nicaraguans, thought to be killers themselves, were among the last to die. A .22 caliber pistol and a 9 mm automatic were used in most of the shootings.

According to their written reports, the detectives handling the murders believed the Nicaraguans were responsible for most, if not all, of the murders that preceded their own demise. They were described as professional killers, former members of one of Somoza's death squads, who fled to Florida when the Sandinistas took over. According to which source you believed, they were either hired guns or undercover guys from the DEA. All of the victims had been part of a gang that for a year or so had been running drugs into New York, and new information suggested that *they* were set up by the very syndicate which had supplied them, burning its bridges with bloody efficiency. You could see from the files that the cops were eager to find out who was behind it, but it was tough sledding. Every time they thought they had a lead, the feds stepped in, took charge, and the lead got lost in a bureaucratic thicket called LEGAL.

It was a juicy story, easy to write until Denise's name came up. I described her in the lead story as a brilliant photographer and wrote a brief biography as a sidebar, tracing her career. I identified Jaime Santiago as a fashion student but didn't mention his connection to the Watelys. I said the police thought they had stumbled across a drug deal and were executed.

The execution theory was Lieutenant Henry's. Henry had called me at the *Graphic* late in the day to say a toxicologist from the ME's office told him the lethal doses of heroin and scopolamine had almost certainly been concealed in a Tuinal capsule. The official cause was respiratory failure. Denise had suffocated on her own vomit as her stomach tried in vain to reject the junk. And she thought she had taken a sleeping pill.

I had to move to a far corner of the city room after hearing Henry's news. Denise was dying in front of me, over and over. I couldn't stop imagining what it must have been like for her as the heroin pulled her under despite her desperate struggle to cling to life. I wept quietly and fought like hell to concentrate, ignoring the stares I was getting from copy boys and editors, who were pointedly leaving me alone. I finished the story about 8:30 and handed it in.

I stood at Hurley's side and watched with red eyes until he scanned it, approved it, and sent it down the copy line.

"Now," he said gently, "why don't you burn off some of your vitriol with a nice scathing editorial aimed at getting that federal task force off its ass? Don't waste time thinking about it, just hammer it out. About two hundred and fifty words."

It would be a nice exercise in controlled rage, so I sat back down and worked like a good soldier. I wrote that Emma Lazarus's invitation to wretched refuse from foreign shores didn't mean that America "had to roll out the red carpet for drug dealers, spies, arms merchants, assassins, born liars, and common criminals."

Hurley loved it. Before meeting Dixie at her Bowery loft I killed an hour by stopping for a beer and a sandwich at a seaport café. I found a quiet table, read over copies of my editorial and Denise's sidebar, and then slowly, deliberately tore them into strips and dropped them in an ashtray.

Would Denise have needed a sleeping pill if I had been there to take her home? Forget it, Darenow, I told myself, she's dead.

Dixie was the height of fashion. She wore black ski pants, black leather low-heeled boots, a fox parka, and her auburn tresses cut in a short flip. I hadn't seen her in several months.

"Do I pass inspection?" she asked.

She looked a little like Ann-Margret, but I still hoped I wouldn't run into anyone I knew.

During the ride uptown, Dixie was as somber and serious as any drag queen could be. We talked about Denise. Dixie appreciated Denise's work on transvestites, but she had some reservations about the way she had approached the assignment.

"She didn't make judgments, Max. I liked that. But why she had to concentrate on Spanish types and street queens is beyond me. She was asking for trouble."

"I don't know, Dixie. I just don't know."

But I did know. Denise had identified with these people. They were orphans, like her. They had no identity except the one they created for themselves.

Dixie read my eyes as my thoughts strayed.

"Max, the Latins are blowing people away. You just came from writing a story about it. There's a war going on. Denise might have taken a picture of someone who didn't appreciate it. Or maybe some jealous queen killed her because Denise *wouldn't* take her picture."

We were in a partitioned cab, but I still wondered if the driver was picking up any of the conversation. His command of the King's English consisted of Manhattan street names and directions to three airports, but I was getting antsy about everything.

"What are you going to do if we run into Miss Esmeralda?" Dixie asked.

"Call the cops," I said out of the side of my mouth. "She's a suspect as far as I'm concerned." I was beginning to sound like Sam Spade. Dixie pursed her lips and frowned.

"Instead of coming on like gangbusters, why don't you let me make some discreet inquiries first? If she is the guilty party, chances are she's not out nightclubbing. The police are looking for her too." She nodded thoughtfully. "So let me handle it."

We were in the Fifties, way west near Eleventh Avenue, in a neighborhood filled with warehouses and truck depots. The cab pulled up in front of a broken police barricade. Behind it, half a dozen people stamped their feet in the cold under an unmarked, unlighted canopy which marked the entrance to the Toucan Too. We crossed the street and I recoiled when Dixie looped her arm through mine. She squeezed it and told me to relax.

We climbed a flight of stairs and stepped into someone's vision of what a tropical village would look like after it was carpeted in acrylic, lined in chrome, lit with neon, and covered with a dome of plastic palm fronds and stuffed birds.

"Just remember one thing," Dixie said as we went inside. "These queens usually stick together so I certainly wouldn't go and tell them Esmeralda's wanted for murder."

There was a ten-dollar cover charge, per person. My receipt was an ink stamp on my right hand visible only under ultraviolet light. If I spent more than twenty-five bucks I was going to have to Xerox my hand in order to claim it as a business expense.

The Toucan boasted three bars. One in the lounge as you came in, another overlooking the dance floor from across the room, and a third tucked way in the back of the club, near the fire exits. The dance floor and stage were visible from all, but the smart money hung by the fire exits. Dixie opted for a booth in the middle of the room.

"Orchestra seats," she pronounced.

I followed her through the crowd of Latins and their dates who were arriving for the merengue party that started at ten. Prizes would be awarded to the best couple.

I ordered a glass of white wine and Dixie did the same.

The drinks had barely arrived when Dixie said, "Wait here, I'll be right back." For ten minutes I drank alone and thought about the last time I had been here.

For what it was, the Toucan Too was a fairly legit nightclub. It attracted a mixed crowd. There were always a few yuppies who had a yen for Puerto Rican girls, a few lesbians with similar tastes, a smattering of gay Latin males, a bevy of drag queens who were dressed to the hilt and looking for sugar daddies, and smart-talking Latins with their girlfriends. If you knew somebody, it was also a place to score coke and smoke.

Denise had been thrown out of there one night for taking pictures of drag queens in the ladies' room while coke was being snorted. One of the real ladies sent two bouncers in. Denise coolly informed the bouncers she had permission from the drag queens, but the real dames were still very uptight. I convinced Denise to call it a night and leave.

That incident marked one of the first arguments we were to have about Denise's preoccupation with these people and the world they inhabited. What was it that so fascinated her? She couldn't answer the question to my satisfaction. Denise felt sorry for them. They were little boys, she said, dressing like Mommy to attract the daddy they never had.

I once wore dark glasses so I could observe them, these painted birds and their swains, without meeting their eyes. I saw things Denise could not see, or did not want to see.

Denise saw hunger and sadness. I saw anger. I think I was more on the mark.

I finished my wine, ordered another, and watched about twenty people jumping around on the dance floor. I recognized two of the songs, "Dogs of War" and "Future Sex." The DJ knew this crowd.

Dixie returned with a buxom brunette on her arm. The brunette was wearing a bright green North Beach leather cocktail dress with shoes and a slouch bag to match. She looked about nineteen, and there was no way in hell you could tell her tits weren't real.

Her name was Linda. She had long, stringy hair and she primped and pulled stray hairs from her face as we talked. She ordered a vodka and Kahlúa.

"Your frien' tell me you looking for Esmeralda. Why you want her?" Linda had a slight lisp. Her voice was soft, but it came from a man's throat.

"She may be in trouble. I could help her if she'd get in touch with me."

"You a frien' of that girl, the photographer, who get killed?" Linda asked warily.

"That's right," I said.

"Esmeralda wouldn't hurt nobody," she said.

"Maybe not, but the police have other ideas." Dixie nudged me.

"The police looking for all those girls she took their pictures. Lucky she don't take mine." She moved her shoulders around and smiled shrewdly. "Why they look for those girls, the police?"

"That's what cops do," I said noncommittally.

"Make trouble for people." She pulled the stirrer from her glass and pointed it at me. "Wha' you want to say to Esmeralda?"

"That's between me and her." I said. She wouldn't look directly at me, but I kept my eyes on her.

"Maybe I talk to her but I doubt it. She maybe gone to Europe." She flicked her hair and turned away to look at nothing in particular.

"When did she say that?"

"Tha's wha' I hear." She shrugged. She was lying.

I gave her one of my business cards. "If she wants to reach me, tell her to call this number."

"Ooh," Linda trilled. "You're a reporter. Tha' must be nice."

Better than being a dead photographer, I thought.

"I'm not writing a story and I'm not going to the cops," I said. "I might be able to help her out. Tell her that."

Linda dropped my card into her purse and finished her drink.

"I better get back to my frien'." Linda nodded, stood up, rearranged shoulders, hips and hair, and traipsed off into the crowd.

"Tell Esmeralda to call me," I shouted after her.

"We had a little chat before we came over here," Dixie said. "She knows Esmeralda and I wouldn't be surprised if she isn't going to call her right now."

Dixie launched into a flawless impression of Linda. " 'Ooh, that girl in trouble. The cops want her and her boyfrien' don't. She gonna have to sell her pussy at las'.' "

"Sounds good," I said. "Let's hope Esmeralda gets the message."

"Max, if the girl is running scared, something is up."

Dixie was right. My hunch was that Denise hooked up with Esmeralda around the same time she was given the poisoned Tuinal. Could Esmeralda have had a motive for killing Denise? Or would she know who might have given Denise the drug?

Dixie had an idea. There was another transvestite hangout, about ten blocks away, where, she said, "a few bucks could loosen tongues." I remembered it. We had gone there once with Denise. It was a trashy little Times Square hole-in-the-wall that attracted a steady stream of hookers, pool sharks, and assorted low-lifes who seldom strayed more than a few blocks from the bus station, as if someday they'd wake up, see the light, and go home. It was called The Gateway.

I settled the tab with the waiter, who carried himself with an arrogance far above his station in life, and Dixie and I headed for the exit. A gaggle of drag queens waited at the entrance to the ladies room and eyed us as we swept past. They oohed and aahed and giggled. I caught Dixie's arm. Shouldn't we ask if one of them knew Esmeralda? Dixie drew back and spoke into my ear.

"Vampires, Max. They'll take your money, drink your blood, drain your vital fluids, and laugh at your corpse. They're looking for husbands. Are you good with your mouth?"

I shuddered at the thought.

"But . . ." I started to say.

"You need to find envious queens," Dixie said chidingly. "Jealous bitches who may bear a grudge against Esmeralda."

"Bear a grudge?"

"Have you ever wanted to be a woman, Max?" she said tersely.

"Certainly not," I huffed. What was it about this world that so intrigued Denise? Dixie pulled me along through the throng.

We took a cab to The Gateway. It was filled with smoke, and had a pool table in the back and a jukebox whose blare cloaked Dixie's voice and mine. There were a dozen middle-aged men at the bar, some in business suits, all of them staring into their drinks, and a couple of Spanish kids in the back shooting balls around on the tattered green felt. We slid up to the bar between a man in gray tweed and another who appeared to have passed out standing up. We ordered white wine, which Dixie recommended we sip through straws to avoid touching our lips to the glass.

"You don't know where their lips have been, honey," she observed.

Dixie toasted to better days.

It was fifteen minutes before fate dealt us a pair of jealous queens. Both were Spanish. One of them was wearing a fake fur coat that she doffed to reveal a red Spandex halter and a black leather miniskirt. The other wore white boots and a white minidress under a red plastic raincoat. It was only twenty-three degrees outside. They sized up the place and took seats at the bar next to Dixie and me.

I told the bartender I'd pay for their drinks. They ordered rum and cokes, gushed their thanks, and turned to appraise Dixie, then me.

The one in the Spandex halter was tall and flat-chested. She turned and asked for a match. Dixie passed her lighter down the bar while I tried to think of a conversation starter. The tall one found it.

"Aren't you Dixie Cupps?"

Dixie smiled. The tall one introduced herself as Carmen. Her friend's name was Tallulah.

Dixie introduced me offhandedly as "a friend."

"Ooh, you're not together?" Carmen cooed.

"Not really." Dixie smiled. She took four quarters from the bar and went to play the jukebox. Carmen was delighted. She moved her drink closer and asked me if I liked drag queens. Normally, Spandex turned me on, but Carmen had muscles and a faint mustache.

"There's one I'd like to meet," I answered casually. "Her name is Esmeralda." Carmen looked momentarily insulted, then impressed. Tallulah, who hadn't been paying much attention, perked up.

"You have good taste." Carmen sniffed. "But Esmeralda has a boyfriend. She don't have to work." She said it as if referring to the Princess of Wales. "You know her?"

"A friend of mine knew her. Esmeralda was supposed to have posed for her."

"Ooh, the photographer!" Carmen cooed again. "*She* was a friend of yours?"

I nodded.

"Tha's too bad, what happen. Esmeralda's friend died, too. He was so cute. The police are looking for Esmeralda, yes?"

"Probably," I answered. "Have you seen her?"

"Yeh," Tallulah cracked. "On her broom."

Tallulah could have made it at the Toucan if she let someone else pick her clothes. She had a sense of humor.

"Honey." Carmen looked at me seriously. "Esmeralda ran with a different crowd. She was lucky. But maybe her luck run out."

"I'd like to get in touch with her," I said.

Carmen started to laugh and had a coughing fit.

"I gotta make a living, baby," Carmen said. "I can't be worrying about no high-class queens. You want a date? Then we relax and talk, do whatever turns you on."

I slipped a twenty-dollar bill from my wallet, folded it in quarters, and pressed it into her palm. She took it without comment but examined it before tucking it into her halter.

"A twenty-dollar question gets a twenty-dollar answer," she said, crossing her legs and getting down to business. "Go ahead."

"Where can I find Esmeralda?"

"She's high and mighty," Carmen huffed. "I don't wish her harm. But she travel with the big boys and they don't like their women getting too big for their boots."

"Oh," I said. "Who are those boys?"

"Tha's a sixty-dollar question," Carmen said. Tallulah's eyes lit up but she said nothing. Dixie had returned from the jukebox and was trying both to eavesdrop and to avoid contact with the drunk who was stirring on her left.

I peeled off two more twenties and dropped them into Carmen's waiting palm.

She removed the first twenty from her bodice and put it together with the ones I had just handed her. She wrapped them all in a napkin from the bar and tucked them back into the halter. She turned, looking grave, and placed both hands on my knees.

"I ain't gonna tell you nothing secret, OK? But I gotta make money, and you want to know these things, OK?" She moved her hands midway up my thigh, squeezed gently, and smiled. "All I know is you paid me to touch you. Now I'm gonna tell you what you want to know. Esmeralda hang out at the Toucan."

She looked to make sure I was following her.

"Tha's where the big shots hang out. Esmeralda's friends run it."

"What are their names?"

She flicked her eyes. "I don't know. They just run it. Her boyfrien' owns it."

"Who's her boyfriend?"

Carmen shook her head and pulled her hands away.

"I don't know about her private life," she said. She was clamming up. Maybe it was time to let Dixie take over.

"Let me get this straight," I said. I put my hand on her thigh and looked her in the eye. Big bold Darenow. "Esmeralda's boyfriend runs the tough boys. He owns the Toucan?"

"Maybe. He got money." She frowned and looked at me as if I was born yesterday. She took my hand away and took a long swallow from her drink. Tallulah was breathing down her neck and Dixie was breathing down mine.

"You wanna meet my girlfrien'?" Carmen grinned.

"Does she know who Esmeralda's boyfriend is?" I grinned back.

"Ai-yi. You got a one-track mind!" Carmen squealed. She looked serious again. "No, baby. Tha's the truth. Tha's all anybody know."

"Where does Esmeralda live?" I asked.

"Florida, I think."

"Florida?" I don't know why I was surprised. Everyone was from Florida these days.

Carmen shrugged her shoulders, then chattered in Spanish to her friend. Tallulah replied with an admonishing look.

"Where does Esmeralda stay when she's in New York?" I asked Carmen.

"The big hotels," she minced. "Once she stay with her friend, the cute one who die."

"Jaime?" Esmeralda and Jaime were friends?

"Listen, baby," Carmen whined, "I gotta make money. I can't be answering your questions all night."

I was running out of money. I gave her another ten dollars. I had sixty left. Hurley would never buy *this*.

"The cute one, Jaime, had his own apartment. Is that what you're saying?" She fingered the ten spot and pouted.

"I guess so," she said. She put the ten on the bar and ordered another drink.

"I think he had his own place on the West Side. I'm not sure." She questioned Tallulah in Spanish again.

"Someplace on the West Side," she repeated. "We really don't know. Honest, baby."

Dixie leaned closer, looking slightly bored.

I didn't think I was going to learn much more from Carmen, and Tallulah was eyeing me suspiciously. I wasn't sure where we were going, but I had a sense it was time to leave.

We said good-bye and Carmen pulled me toward her and kissed my cheek.

"I hope you enjoyed yourself," she said, loud enough so the bartender heard it.

Dixie and I walked over to Ninth Avenue to get a cab.

"The Torres gang runs the Toucan," Dixie said as she adjusted the hood of her parka.

"Who are they?"

"Very macho, very hip. Very big in the Cuban community."

I spotted a taxi but didn't hail it.

"Are they drug dealers?" I asked.

"That's what I'm thinking," Dixie replied, walking on. "Maybe Denise heard something about them and repeated it to Esmeralda. Max, Denise was naive. She didn't know the code so she could have blurted something out and maybe Esmeralda ratted on her and her boyfriend ordered the hit on Denise."

We walked another block in silence. The avenues were a moving blur of cars and people. We paused at the corner for a moment.

"You really loved her, didn't you, Max?"

"I did." That was all I could say.

"Maybe you should let her rest in peace, Max. She told me she didn't want to marry you. Call it quits and get her pictures published. That's all she'd want from you."

Dixie spotted a cab and waved her glove. "Are you coming downtown?"

The cab squealed to a halt at Dixie's side. We got in and told the driver to head downtown. "I want to know where Denise was meeting Esmeralda the night she died," I said.

Dixie sighed. "If they were meeting for dinner or someplace to talk, wouldn't Denise have taken Esmeralda to Eddie's?"

Eddie's Coney Island was the hippest bar in SoHo and the food wasn't bad, either. It was on the list of places I had given the detectives. Denise was a regular customer and often entertained clients there over a hamburger.

"Eddie's," I said. "That's a good idea."

"I have an early call. I'm going home." Dixie smiled and patted my leg. "Don't get too wrapped up in this, Max. Let the police handle it." Then she added, "Stop chasing her."

I dropped Dixie off and headed for Eddie's. It was nearly midnight and the regulars would be arriving soon.

I slumped down in the seat of the cab and thought of what Dixie had said. Is that how it looked to other people? Max Darenow, fading star reporter, trailing a brilliant photographer whose star was on the rise?

What happened, Denise? What went wrong, besides me?

7

The liquor license said "Eddie's Coney Island of the Mind." The middlebrows called it Eddie's Coney Island and we just called it Eddie's.

It was a two-story former deli on Houston Street that had been taken over and transformed by a sharp young lawyer and art collector named Eddie Kozen, whose roots were Sheepshead Bay and Allen Ginsberg.

Eddie's was a clearinghouse and bulletin board for downtown café society, a launch pad for the party circuit, a beehive for punks, tastemakers, swells, and artists of all stripe, where the fifties, sixties, and seventies met in the eighties, where uptown and downtown debated relative property values over chicken pot pie and fine wines by the glass. Denise and I were celebrities there. Her photos, blown up and hung in frames, were the decor.

Eddie's had been a special place for us. After we had both logged twelve- to sixteen-hour days pursuing our crafts, we'd make loose arrangements to meet. "If you're at Eddie's around twelve I might be there," Denise would say. "Or the Short Stop, or the Bistro, or the Lion's Head." She'd laugh and apologize. Where she'd be depended on where her mood took her. Denise liked to be with certain people at different times, and I never had to chase her to more than four or five places before I ran her down.

But once I arrived, it was always different. Denise would make room next to her, kiss me on the cheek, and bring me up to date on the conversation. I'd be full of piss and vinegar, not to mention a few Jack Daniels manhattans, a couple of hits of grass, and a snort or three of coke. I'd wow the table with stories taken from that day's police blotter and join in the irreverent gossip about people across the room, the sort of gossip that makes New York a small town.

I used to think it was important, knowing all that horseshit. That's what I'd tell Denise when I needed an excuse to stay until closing time. At first we always left together, but as drugs claimed more of my life I'd find an excuse to hang around and meet her later. You go ahead home, I'd say. I just heard the mayor is going to appoint a Puerto Rican commissioner of cultural affairs and I want to see if anyone knows anything about it. I could easily have left with Denise and gotten the information in the morning by dropping into City Hall and whispering in the ear of the little blonde in the press office. If she didn't know, she'd find out because she was curious, too. Virgin gossip was a passport to all the right places.

It was nearly twelve-thirty when I walked inside. Joe Bop, an ex-Golden Gloves champ who liked the nightlife more than the ring, was on the door. Joe had fast hands. One night he cold-cocked a wise-ass so neatly, no one even saw the punch—not even the guy's partner, who thought he'd had a heart attack.

Joe Bop wrapped both his hands around mine. "Everybody's in a state of shock, babe. We all loved Denise but there's nothing we could tell the cops. It's bad for business, the drugs and all. You saw what happened to that preppie hang-out uptown after that girl was murdered. People stopped going there. It died."

It turned out the hard-boiled dick from Central Park had stopped by earlier with four eight-by-ten glossies, including a picture of Denise.

"I loved the girl, Joe. I just want to know what the hell happened to her."

He bobbed around awkwardly for a few seconds and frowned before he settled down and told me Denise had been there Friday night, less than twelve hours before her body was found. She came in alone around midnight and left after a short while. Joe didn't remember who she sat with or if she met anyone.

"C'mon Joe." I smiled. "You know more than that." He rocked on the balls of his feet and looked at me sideways.

"Talk to Sacha and Britt. They're in the back. Don't say I told you anything."

Sacha and Britt were the local Frick and Frack, two Madonna clones who ran a used clothing store in the East Village. They were in Eddie's every night. They dressed like rag dolls and had matching geometric haircuts.

They were alone so I joined them and bought them a drink. We talked about Denise for a while and then I popped my questions. Had they seen Denise Friday night?

"She was trying to score Tuinals," Sacha said gravely. "And we didn't have any. She was chasing some drag queen, but she wanted to go home to sleep." They exchanged glances and sipped their drinks in unison.

According to Sacha and Britt, Denise had hung around for an hour and then left, saying she was going to look elsewhere for her drag queen and a sleeping pill. She told Sacha and Britt she was going to try The Crib. I knew the place well.

"Was the drag queen named Esmeralda?" I asked.

"She's a sex-change, a blonde, right?" replied Britt.

"Right."

"That's the one."

I went over to the bar. The bartender shook my hand and offered his condolences. I ordered another white wine. That made five so far tonight. I told myself to take it easy on the booze, but I obviously wasn't listening.

The Crib was a funky, gay, Mafia-run bar in the West Village on the waterfront, near the meat-packing district. And if that was where she bought the Tuinal, no one would want to talk about it. In a bar like that, you could do anything with your lips except flap them.

Unless it was in the owner's best interests to cooperate.

The Crib was owned by Rocco Cardinale, a garrulous, gentrified, New Age mafioso who knew and liked Denise and me. She had taken his portrait, and I once devoted a whole column to him, noting his activities on behalf of the community planning board and his contributions to the Gay Men's Health Crisis. Rocco admitted his contributions to the latter were self-serving. He had an instinct for public relations and AIDS was wiping out his customers.

But would Rocco talk if he knew Denise had been given the fatal dose in his bar?

I put the thought aside, caught the bartender's eye, and ordered another drink. He had heard Denise was at Eddie's Friday night, but the place was packed and he hadn't seen her.

I sipped my wine and my thoughts went back to The Crib and Rocco Cardinale. Rocco was well-connected. He might be interested in helping me find Denise's murderer, considering the fact that the feds were blaming the Mafia for the wave of drug-related murders.

I left Eddie's and walked up through the Village to The Crib. It was cold and brisk and I felt wide awake, despite the fact I'd been up since 7:15 A.M. I was chasing a story, and the deadline was all mine. I got to The Crib around 1:30. Rocco was standing at the end of the bar, eating a sandwich. He exchanged pleasantries before Denise's name came up.

Rocco was amiable and good-looking. He sponsored a mixed gay softball team, Guys and Gals, and marched in the Gay Pride parade every year. He was married and had a couple of kids. He liked the column I did on him. His uncle liked it, too. His uncle was Anthony "Tony Beef" Coraggio, who ran a fleet of meat trucks that serviced some of the best restaurants in town. Tony Beef was way up there in the Mafia scheme of things.

The Crib was one of Denise's favorite haunts whenever she wanted to go slumming. It had been a longshoreman's hangout in the early sixties, then a go-go bar, a comedy showcase, a piano bar, a disco, until finally, The Crib emerged as a raunchy cabaret that drew a mixed crowd of locals and tourists on weekends, when Dixie's Drag Revue was the main attraction.

Rocco had a couple of years of college and he certainly didn't act like a thug. He had well-informed opinions on lots of things, especially the legalization of marijuana, one of his favorite causes.

Rocco came up in the sixties, when I did. Rocco believed that if the government looked the other way and let "good smoke" into the country, people wouldn't be going after heroin, coke, speed, and crack. Rocco still smoked occasionally, and starting in the sixties there was always a regular at the bar who knew where to get good pot.

Marijuana wasn't the only thing Rocco was interested in. His wife, rumored to be the daughter of a Mafia don, was a college-educated mother and activist who worked for reform within and without "The Family." I never met her, but she sure had made an impression on Rocco. She made him read *The Second Sex*, and the fact that he liked it elevated him into Denise's male pantheon. The three of us—Denise, Rocco, and myself—spent more than a couple of nights sitting at the bar discussing the battle of the sexes and the eternal feminine, while Dixie and her troupe mimed songs and cracked bitter jokes.

I ordered a white wine spritzer. I had to be on my toes for Rocco. He told me to put my money away.

"Denise was a nice girl," he said, shaking his head. "A real artist. But she wasn't too smart. She ran with a bad crowd."

"What do you mean?" I asked.

"Spics," he said. He spat out the word and picked a piece of food off his tongue.

"What's wrong with spics?" I knew I had touched a nerve. Rocco handed me my drink and started to talk. He seemed agitated.

"You know me, right? I'm a guinea. I'm supposed to be a Cosa Nostra, right? I run a gay bar. I don't sell drugs. I don't police my customers. They take drugs. What am I gonna do? Search everybody? Your girlfriend comes in looking for drag queens. Most of them are black or Spanish, right? She starts taking pictures in here. What am I, crazy? I got guys in here don't wanna be in pictures. You see what I'm saying?"

"I think you're trying to tell me something."

"Look. The guineas aren't in the drug business no more. *Capice?* No way. It's all Spanish now, except maybe for a few jigs who gotta earn a living. The Spanish are killing each other. You read the papers? It's all about drugs. And now the feds are trying to blame the guineas. Now you understand?"

"I heard something about it," I answered, looking into my spritzer. "How does it relate to Denise?"

"She hung out with the wrong people. I don't want the drag queens in here anymore. They're into coke, crack. They attract a bad crowd. Let them all stay uptown with the Torres brothers."

"I think I've heard that name before," I said. Dixie had mentioned them. I was trying to keep Rocco talking.

"Spics," Rocco huffed. "Big-time operators from Florida. They been running a bunch of clubs for a year. They got connections. Their joints are wide open still. They got that one place on the West Side that's legit. The Toucan Too."

I told him I had been to the Toucan Too earlier. I felt an adrenaline surge. Florida and the Torres brothers kept coming up.

"Do you think Denise had some contacts with these guys, Rocco? Do you think she was murdered?"

He put down his beer and looked at me like I was stupid. I was then, very.

"You helped me out once," he said. "That story you wrote made me look good. I run a gin mill. I got a family. My uncle trucks meat. Your girlfriend hangs out with a bad crowd and winds up dead, and where do they find her? In a vacant lot in an Italian neighborhood on Staten

Island. Somebody's putting the squeeze on the guineas, and we don't like it. Maybe your girlfriend overdosed and some of her spic friends packed her up nice and dumped her there so it looks like the guineas did it. See what I'm getting at?"

"What time did she leave here?"

"Look. You're my friend, right? You were in love with this girl, right? What are you gonna do, write a sob story? That ain't gonna help her, it ain't gonna help me, and it ain't gonna help you."

"I'm not writing a story," I lied. "Denise died of an overdose of scopolamine mixed with heroin, hidden in a Tuinal. She didn't take drugs."

"I know scopa-what's-its name," Rocco said. "It's knockout drops. The hookers use it sometimes. It can kill you if you take enough of it."

"All right," I said. "If Denise was in your club Friday night, it was one of the last places she was seen alive. I have no intention of sharing that information with anybody. OK? But I want to know how she died, and why."

Rocco sighed deeply and took out a pack of cigarettes. He offered me one and I took it. When in Rome. We lit up and he ordered another round before the talk turned back to Denise.

"Denise was here Friday with a bunch of spics, like I said. They were high rollers. Denise was with them and a gorgeous drag queen—too flashy to be a real girl. She left here with them."

"Did you know any of the people she was with?"

"Look," Rocco said. He paused for a beat. "You're not printing any of this?"

I shook my head. "No." I meant it.

Rocco went over to the door and tapped one of the bouncers on the shoulder. The bouncer was a gay man in his twenties, a cookie-cutter version of a lumberjack. He was into body building and God knew what else. Rocco beckoned him and me into the back. He opened the door of his office.

There was room for a desk, two chairs, whiskey bottles lined up on floor-to-ceiling shelves, and the three of us. Rocco and I took the chairs. The bouncer closed the door and stood facing us.

"This is Alfred," Rocco told me. "Alfred, this is Max. He's gonna forget everything you tell him, so tell him the truth. He's an OK guy, *capice?*"

Alfred nodded. Rocco continued.

"Alfred, you remember the blond drag queen in here Sunday night?

The dish? She was with the girl who got dead. Do you remember her friends?"

Alfred remembered. A drag queen arrived in a limo and came in with two men, one a cute, well-dressed Latin and the other an older man, also Latin. Denise joined them, as did three other Latins known as Los Tres Cucarachas, or the Three Kooks. He ticked off their names. I knew the one named Manolo best. They were low-level drug dealers who doubled as musicians. They had aspirations of becoming a Latin punk rock band. They were considered harmless buffoons. I had bought drugs from Manolo many times, grass and coke. He didn't handle weight, just sold enough to support his own habit. He had quality dope, which meant he had quality connections.

"Was the drag queen a blonde named Esmeralda?" I asked.

Alfred concentrated hard. "I believe so," he said.

"She was really a sex-change," I corrected him.

"The cute one, I think he was the trick, he was in charge," Alfred continued. "I don't go for drag queens—or sex-changes—but this one was really a piece of work. The trick was cute, too."

"Did Denise leave with them?"

"Naw. I was standing outside. The sex-change and the two guys got into the limo. Your girl went with the Three Kooks. It was late. Maybe about three-thirty."

"Did you know the trick?" I asked.

"Never saw him or the other one before. But, uh, she acted like she knew the older guy—and your friend, the girl, seemed real friendly with the sex-change."

"Were they high?"

"Hey, I'm no mind reader," Alfred sniffed. Something in Rocco's eyes made him think twice. "Maybe," he muttered.

"But you're sure Denise left with the Kooks?"

"The last I saw, she was walking up to Hudson Street with them. *She* looked a little wobbly. I know she wanted a cab because she waited here first but there was nothing. That's why they hiked."

Rocco jerked his head toward the door. Alfred took the hint and left.

Rocco had an I-told-you-so look. "Any more questions?"

I didn't have any. Rocco got up and walked me to the door. I had a lot to think about. I thanked him and started walking toward Hudson Street myself.

It had started to snow. Big flakes, wet and cold on my face. I pulled the hood of my parka up and kept walking. When I got to Hudson Street the crosstown bus was idling at the corner. I knew the Kooks lived at the end of the line. I'd been there before.

The inside of the bus looked nice and warm. I came up with a buck in change and took a seat. I didn't know what I was getting into. I probably should have called Lieutenant Henry and let him handle it from that point, but I didn't. Maybe it was better the way it turned out.

8

The bus driver took his sweet time getting there. The snow was coming down harder as we lumbered lazily across Fourteenth Street to the east side of town. I had no business going there except a hunch that the Kooks might know who at The Crib would be capable of passing out Tuinal capsules laced with scopolamine and heavy-duty skag. According to the autopsy report, Denise died about twelve hours before her body was found. The medical examiner said the junk hit her hard and fast, which meant she took the fatal dose and died between the hours of three and four A.M. That made good odds that someone at The Crib had slipped her the drugs.

I never once believed the Kooks gave it to her. That was the farthest thing from my mind. You have to understand the Kooks; they were guileless social climbers, middle-class runaways from the Cuban exile community, products of Catholic schools who craved acceptance in the downtown, hip Anglo world of art and commerce. They logged a semester or two at City College, just enough schooling to encourage the foolish notion that art could be profitable, before dropping out to seek their fortunes as musicians.

I wanted to know where they had parted company with Denise. Or did they part company? It wasn't like Denise to go traipsing off to the East Village at three-thirty in the morning, but who knows what was going through her mind when the junk started dancing in her veins. Where was she then? If she was with the Kooks they surely would have brought her to an emergency room. They loved celebrity and they respected Denise. She was only eight blocks from her house when she left The Crib. How the hell did her body get to Staten Island?

I got off the bus at Fourteenth and Avenue A and walked the three blocks to their apartment through an inch of cold, wet snow. The streets were empty with the exception of an occasional passing car or a lone straggler on foot. There wasn't a cop in sight.

The Kooks' building was the only inhabited building on a block lined with vacant, abandoned tenements still waiting to be spruced up. They lived on the first floor in a railroad flat that ran from the street to a garbage-strewn courtyard. Their front door was at the end of a dark hall. Someone had snatched the bulb ages ago. Rock music and the sound of a cheering audience seeped out from under the door. Someone was playing an old Stones' concert tape. I rapped a "shave and a haircut" signal and waited. No response. I took off my gloves, stuffed them in my pants pocket, and knocked again, louder.

Strange. One of the Kooks was always home. They had to be home, guarding their speakers and amps. They lived on a block where if people thought you had something valuable inside and weren't home, they would simply kick in the door and take it. No one called the police unless someone was having a baby. I knocked again and glanced out into the street. Nothing was moving there except snowflakes and rats in the garbage. I heard voices inside, so I knocked until I got a reply.

"Bennie?" It was a man's voice, harsh and guttural. It wasn't Manolo.

"It's Jimmy Olson," I said. The Kooks had a sense of humor. They knew I was a reporter and had given me the name of Clark Kent's assistant. "I have to talk to Manolo."

"He's not here. Everybody's asleep," the voice shouted.

"I'll talk to one of the others," I shouted back. "It's important, man. Tell them it's Jimmy Olson."

The guttural voice told someone to shut up, but it was ignored.

"Jimmy! Stay there! I'll be right out." It was Manolo. He sounded awake to me. I heard more movement and I heard Manolo tell someone to "knock it off." Was it just the two of them or were the other Kooks there? I knew that Manolo slept on a couch in the living room, which overlooked the courtyard. His buddies bunked in the front room, overlooking the street. That room was dark when I came up the stoop.

"Wait there, Jimmy!" Manolo cried again. He sounded wide awake and there was a note of urgency in his voice. What were they doing? Hiding the stash? I wasn't a cop, what did I care?

I waited for about three minutes, a long time in a dark tenement hallway. I no longer heard the other man. The Stones were caterwauling through an old Robert Johnson tune and somewhere down in the basement a boiler heaved to life. Manolo's voice rose above the music several times. He was arguing with his visitor. I looked out and watched the snow falling through the arc of the street lamp and wondered when I was finally going to get to bed. The thought raised a bitter taste of guilt and déjà vu. I used to sneak over to Manolo's to score before rushing off to Denise's bed. The peephole opened and I heard Manolo's voice. I heard my name mentioned, too.

"Hang on, Max, we got heavy-duty phone calls." Another minute went by before I heard the sound of bolts sliding in locks. One, two, three locks. The place was a fortress, triple-locked and soundproofed with egg cartons that had been stapled and glued to the walls and ceilings so the Kooks could rehearse without blowing the neighbors away. Manolo stepped aside and let me in.

He looked like hell. His eyes gleamed from deep ravines. He needed a bath, a shave, a shampoo, and six months in a rehab center.

The room was poorly lit, the only light coming from a small Tensor lamp illuminating a couple of very expensive ounces of flaky white powder piled on a broken mirror on top of a trunk that was also serving as a cocktail table. About three thousand dollars' worth of white powder was on the mirror.

There was just enough light to see that the rest of the place was still a dump. Newspaper and magazines littered the floor. One wall was occupied with steel shelving that housed some expensive recording equipment and a collection of tapes. Cases of electric guitars and a portable electric organ took up most of the floor space.

The visitor was sitting on the edge of a desk in an alcove in the rear. He glanced away quickly when I came into the room; he was more concerned with whoever he was talking to on the telephone. There was enough spill from the lamp to let me size him up. He was a little man, dapper in a beige suit, loudly striped shirt, brown tie, and brown boots with a Cuban heel. His face was in shadow, but I could see he was clean-shaven, dark-haired, and pushing forty. Someone on the phone was giving him a hard time. He spoke in short, rapid clips of Spanish and clenched his jaw in anger whenever the other party did the talking. My

Spanish was rusty but a couple of phrases told me he was having trouble getting the right person to come to the phone. I knew exactly how he felt. I heard him say, "Get that bitch on the phone," but there must have been some confusion at the other end about which bitch he was talking about. "No!" he shouted, "not *la vieja*," the old woman; he wanted someone else, but I couldn't make out the rest. The urgency in his voice told me it wasn't a romantic quarrel.

He saw me eavesdropping, tucked his head, crossed to the tape player, and turned the volume up. That was fine with me. I didn't want him eavesdropping on my conversation with Manolo either.

Manolo shivered and pulled a flannel hospital robe tighter around his chest. It was all he had on, except for a wide-eyed look that told me he hadn't been roused from sleep. He shot the other man a nervous glance and forced a smile at me but he wasn't happy. The other man had moved back into the shadows.

"Get yourself high, Max," Manolo said, using my real name again. Then he added, "He thinks you just came to score." He poured warm Coca-Cola into a dirty glass, topped it with lots of Spanish brandy, and pushed it in front me. I drank it. It tasted like cough medicine. He took a razor blade, carved a man-sized hunk from the coke pile, and shaped it into four hefty lines. His robe fell open, exposing a well-muscled chest and a roll of fat around his midriff. The coke hadn't entirely wasted him, yet. He smiled wanly and motioned for me to dig in.

For once it looked repulsive to me. "What's going on, Manolo? What happened to Denise?"

Manolo rolled his eyes and leaned closer. "I dunno what's going on. Get high and go," he whispered. I had the impression Manolo had arranged to buy this rather substantial amount of cocaine from the man on the phone and didn't have the money to pay for it. The brandy and cola made me gag. Was the other man a cop?

"Who's your friend?" I asked, nodding toward the man on the phone.

"He's a go-fer," he replied glumly. "An errand boy for Bennie Torres. Thinks he's tough." The name Torres was everywhere tonight, it seemed. Judging from Manolo's tone, the errand boy wasn't a cop or a friend. I turned around to see if he was still on the phone. He saw me, cupped the mouthpiece, and addressed Manolo impatiently in Spanish. Manolo answered too quickly for me to understand.

"I told him you had money and you needed the coke real bad," Manolo whispered.

I hated the idea of doing coke after all these months just to placate

Manolo's paranoia or get him off the hook of a drug deal gone sour. My reluctance showed. Manolo grabbed my arm and squeezed it hard. He was trying to tell me something but I was too suspiciously dumb to grasp the truth. Coke was absolutely the last thing I needed. I tried once more to shake his tongue loose without having to dip into the powder. I picked up the razor blade and toyed with one of the lines.

"What happened to Denise?" I articulated each word.

"Trust me, Jimmy," Manolo muttered under his breath. He spoke up again so the other man would hear. "It's primo coke, man. I give you a good price." I decided to go along, at least for the moment. It was Manolo's game and I had to see his cards.

I sucked up one of the lines he had offered me and immediately sat up to catch my breath. The coke hit my frontal lobes like four-way traffic screeching to a halt. It was primo coke, all right. First cut and fine.

I recovered and looked Manolo firmly in the eye. "Talk," I said.

"I think it was a mistake," he whispered. "They weren't after Denise. The sex-change must have given Denise some of what Bennie gave her."

"Why?" I looked at Manolo, but I wasn't addressing him in particular. "What does that mean, *a mistake?*"

Manolo squirmed in his robe and looked hurt.

"Somebody wanted to kill them," he replied offhandedly. He turned away and shivered, but it wasn't because he was cold.

Somebody wanted to kill them! I stared at the pile of coke and wished it weren't there.

"*Who*, Manolo?" I was suddenly very aware of the other man's presence, but I held Manolo in my eye until he answered.

"Maybe Bennie," he whispered. "Maybe the sex-change's boyfriend. I don't know."

"Who's the sex-change?"

"I dunno," he muttered. "C'mon, Jimmy! Snort and go."

"Who's her boyfriend?"

Manolo shrugged and ran a finger around the edge of the mirror. He didn't know.

I caught Manolo's eye and silently mouthed Bennie Torres's name. It was a question. Manolo frowned and shook his head.

"Where's the sex-change?" I demanded.

Manolo leveled a cold, gray look from under his eyebrows.

"Bennie would love to know," he said sullenly.

"Do *you* know?" I asked.

Manolo tried to look exasperated, but he was too wasted to care. "Jimmy," he said wearily, "go."

The Torres boys were center stage. I let my eyes drift over to the other man.

"What's he up to?" I asked.

"I don't know!" Manolo hissed. From Manolo's reaction, the prospects weren't good. "Jimmy, finish your lines and get out of here, OK?"

I nodded and snorted some coke off the end of the straw to settle Manolo down while I gathered my wits. I was supposed to be playacting for the man on the phone because the man on the phone was a tough guy. How tough? I was in the best shape I'd been in since boot camp. But maybe Manolo was playacting himself, trying to get rid of me.

"Snort some coke, Jimmy, please!"

"I don't like it, Manolo. How did Denise get to Staten Island?"

His eyes flickered apologetically.

"Bennie," was all he said.

"What's wrong, amigo? You no like the coke?" the visitor drawled. His voice startled me—there was a cruel challenge in it. I spun around to face him. He was still on the phone, holding the receiver away from his mouth.

I told myself I'd handled more coke than this in one sitting before, sighed, bent over the mirror, and sucked up two of the shortest lines. My eyes watered and my pituitary did cat flips trying to sort out the conflicting images in my brain.

Manolo squirmed and pulled the robe tighter around him. He wet his lips and sucked some coke off his fingertips. The other man mumbled something into the phone and shook his head.

"Go, Jimmy, before Bennie gets here. Otherwise it's gonna be too late."

I heard the phone being cradled and turned my head. The little man in beige was eyeing me like a fly looking at dead meat.

Manolo began furiously chopping up more coke and funneling it into a gram vial.

"I thought you came to buy," the visitor intoned lazily. I turned again and squinted, but I couldn't see his face. I didn't like him and the coke wasn't doing anything to make me change my mind. He was just a light brown man glowing with bad vibes.

"It's good shit, man," I said earnestly. "I appreciate it."

He wasn't rushing me. He smiled, baring all his teeth, and told me to finish the other line. I knew his type; he didn't take drugs, he just worked for people who sold them. He relished the idea of selling smart-ass Anglos the rope so they could hang themselves while he watched.

"That's OK," I said. *"No es necesario."* I stood up, took my wallet out, pulled out one of my last twenties, folded it, and passed it to Manolo, who was having a problem screwing the top on the vial. I hoped the other gentleman wouldn't notice I was about eighty dollars short on my purchase. I was saving the other twenty for traveling money.

"Finish it," the visitor said. He wasn't going to take no for an answer.

I sighed, bent over the trunk, sucked up the fourth fat line, and straightened up. The coke was making me cocky. Cocky and stupid.

"I'll see you tomorrow, Manolo." I winked and didn't care if the other man saw me.

"Sit down," the other man sneered. "Nobody's going anywhere until we hear from Bennie."

I turned and faced him. He was about four feet away. I hadn't noticed he was wearing one glove on his left hand and bouncing a thick roll of quarters in it. It made a nice sap and it was legal. When you hit someone with it, it hurt. Things were going downhill.

"Pepe, listen." It was Manolo, pleading.

He was trying to reason with the little beige man called Pepe, but it wasn't working. Manolo addressed him in Spanish, slowly enough for me to get the gist of what he was trying to say. Manolo was in trouble after all. And so was I.

Manolo patiently explained to him that I was a good man and a friend of Denise's but Bennie was not a good man. He told Pepe I was a big journalist and Bennie was just using him, Pepe, to do his dirty work.

Pepe wasn't buying it. "Shut up and sit down!" he said. Pepe was agitated now, confused and agitated.

"I gotta go, Manolo," I said, inching closer to the door. "I got somebody waiting for me in the car."

Manolo cried out, "Wait, Jimmy, let me try again. I'll go with you." Manolo's voice was cracking. *He* was in a panic now and I was beginning to understand why. This wasn't cocaine paranoia. This was big trouble. Something happened on the phone while I was there and it wasn't good news.

Manolo switched to impassioned English.

"Pepe, you know Bennie better than that. You do his dirty work and then he turns you over to the cops, blames *you!* This guy's a reporter, man. You can't hurt him without bringing all kinds of shit down on everybody's head. There's other people saw Bennie with Jaime and the dead girl. It ain't gonna work, believe me. Let us go. We're not gonna say a fucking word to the cops. Take the coke. Take the guitars. I'll make it up to you, man, I swear I will."

I reached the door, turned, and slipped the first bolt back. I saw the brown man slide off the desk and move briskly toward me. I saw the gloved fist hook into the air and I saw his jacket fly open and his right hand jab into his waistband. He was moving too fast to be effective. The laws of physics were going to give me leverage. I was almost lulled into thinking he was all bluster when his right hand came out with an automatic pistol in it.

He wasn't going to be satisfied just breaking my jaw. He brandished the sap in his gloved hand but slowed his pace when he saw my reaction to the gun. I was in shape, but not bionic. Guns make a difference.

Pepe didn't appear too eager to shoot. Maybe Manolo's pleading had had some effect. Shooting a journalist was probably routine stuff where he came from, but the idea of sweating out fifteen years in Attica had little appeal for him. Besides, Bennie was on his way, let Bennie figure it out, it was his problem. I was thinking what a nice guy Pepe was turning out to be when Manolo scrambled off the couch yelling, "Get his gun!"

That startled Pepe. He wasn't sure what to do. He waved the gun in Manolo's direction and then aimed it at my chest. That settled it for me. I had already crossed my arms at the wrist so Pepe couldn't tell which hand was going to block his punch and which one was going for the gun, a martial arts manuever I learned in boot camp. Pepe saw what I had planned and hesitated.

Manolo scooted across the floor, grabbed Pepe's gun with both hands, and tried twisting it down and away from my chest, but he wasn't strong enough to shake it loose. It gave me time to grab Pepe's other wrist and twist it till he dropped the sap. By that time he had jerked his gun hand free but lost his balance in the process. I grabbed the gun this time and pulled it straight up. I had the advantage of height, but Pepe had more experience. He butted my jaw with his head and drove his knee into my groin. My head was so full of coke my jaw didn't notice, but my legs buckled as the pain flew down my legs. It didn't affect my grip, though. I pulled his arm down with me and kept twisting the gun up and away from my chest until his trigger finger snapped. He was screaming bloody murder when the gun hit the floor. Being in shape was paying off.

Manolo dived for the gun while Pepe hopped around screaming in pain, clutching his broken finger. I had to fight the fire in my groin to stand erect, but Pepe's pain exhilarated me. He had tried to kill me. I wanted to get him in a headlock and squeeze his neck until he was blue, but I never got the chance.

Manolo's reaction was slightly different. His eyes seethed with fear and hatred as he pointed the gun at Pepe's chest and pulled the trigger. I went limp and let the sound carry me down to the floor. I rolled against the front door, the shot roaring in my ears.

Pepe threw his hands out in front of him. He lurched forward and Manolo shot him a second time, then a third. It was all one big roar. I braced my back against the wall and watched in mute horror as Pepe dropped to his knees and made a gurgling sound before his body collapsed like an accordian. He fell into a heap on the floor, the gloved hand crumpling under his chest. His right leg quivered and then his body relaxed. A little pool of blood started forming in the crook of his arm.

Manolo enjoyed watching Benny die. He kept backing up for a better view until he nearly tripped over the trunk. It jarred him from the stupor he had fallen into, thanks to the coke. Manolo stared at his weapon and then pointed it again at Benny's prostrate form, like a kid playing guns.

I struggled to my feet and casually put my hand out. "He's finished, Manolo, give me the gun."

Manolo shook his head and continued to stare at Pepe's lifeless body. Killing your dealer brings a mixed reaction.

I bent down and lifted Pepe's head. His eyes stared sorrowfully off into a corner of the room. There was no pulse in his neck. I stood up and put my hand out again. I wanted the gun.

Manolo held on to it and backed away. His jaw was down around his ankles. Killing was new to him but he liked it.

"Give me the gun, Manolo. He's dead."

Manolo shook his head.

"I had to, man. He would have killed us both. Bennie is on his way over here right now. I gotta get dressed. We gotta go, man, before Bennie gets here."

"Wait a minute, Manolo. We're gonna call the cops. I saw everything. It was self-defense. It seems obvious Denise got the Tuinal from Bennie. The cops will want him for questioning."

"No way!" Manolo raged. "You gonna deal with Bennie Torres when he sees this? He's runnin' around town claiming he's working for Hector Melendez. You know who he is? He's the guy the CIA calls when *they're* in trouble. He's God. You think a man like that needs this shit?" He stared at the body on the floor and laughed a dry laugh. "No fucking way, man. The police ain't gonna get here before Bennie comes and if they did it wouldn't matter. We wouldn't live to testify. We're goin'. Now!"

I was losing it. I screamed and lunged at him. "I want to know what happened to Denise, man!"

Manolo dodged away, went through the kitchen, and turned on the light in the front bedroom. He muttered an oath and flicked it off again. I stood in the doorway as he placed the gun on a bed and started pulling clothes from the drawers.

"Manolo, tell me what happened to my girl," I said softly. He shook his head in exasperation and started telling me what little he knew while he jerked on a pair of jeans and pulled a sweater over his head.

He confirmed that Bennie Torres was with Jaime Santiago and the sex-change, Esmeralda, when Denise met them at The Crib. Bennie was in a good mood until Denise arrived, Manolo said, then claimed he had to leave and insisted that Jaime and Esmeralda accompany him. There was an argument, but Bennie prevailed. According to Manolo, Bennie always prevailed.

"Who gave Denise the Tuinal?" I asked.

"Denise said the sex-change. She was feeling wobbly when we left the club, so it figures. She passed out in the cab and we brought her back here."

"And then what?"

"We put her to bed," he whined. He pulled on socks and started to simper while he laced up his Nike high tops. "We didn't know what she had taken. There was nothing we could do, Jimmy."

I slammed my fist into my palm. "Why didn't you take her to a hospital? You could have saved her." Manolo shook his head. His eyes swung like lost planets.

"She was already dead. I swear. We called Bennie because we figured he might know what she took. Bennie went wild." Manolo picked up the gun and started into the living room. He drew a cloth coat from a pile of clothes and put it on. I fought an urge to hurt him.

"And you let Bennie dump her like garbage?"

Manolo shook his head wearily. "She was dead, Jimmy. Bennie warned us not to say a word about what happened. He said he'd take care of us good if we ever talked. He took the other Kooks with him and left me here with this guy." His voice cracked. "I ain't heard from them since, Jimmy. For all I know they're dead and I'm gonna be next."

He buttoned his coat, jammed the gun into an outside pocket, pulled a ski cap down over his ears, and started for the door.

"Let's go," he said.

I didn't have time to ask him for the gun again. The phone started ringing. Manolo was right. The cops weren't going to break their necks getting here in the snow and I wasn't looking forward to meeting Bennie Torres under the present circumstances. Manolo unbolted the door and peeked out to check the hall. It was empty. He stepped out and I followed him, closing the door behind me without locking it.

We were halfway to the front door when I heard a car door slam, followed by the whistle of tires on snow. We froze for a moment until Manolo turned and whispered: "Upstairs."

Manolo was rounding the bend to the stairs when the front door flew open. I knew from the looks exchanged between Manolo and the man entering the hall that we were in for trouble. The first words out of the man's mouth were "Where's Pepe?" So this was Bennie Torres.

Manolo said nothing at first. He started backing up and so did I. Bennie knew something was wrong. He had pulled a gun from his coat by the time I reached the apartment door. Manolo blurted out something about Pepe being inside, but Bennie wasn't interested. I turned the knob, backed inside, and resisted the urge to push Manolo into the hall and bolt the door. I stepped quickly behind the door, hoping to let Manolo in and keep Bennie out, but it was no use. Manolo was moving too fast and Bennie was helping him. I ducked down the narrow hall that led to the room overlooking the street. I was planning to climb on top of the dresser that was flush against the inside wall and pounce on Bennie if it came to that. I would have jumped through the window but there were steel gates in front of it. I was trapped.

I could still see into the main room. Bennie shoved Manolo inside and closed the door. The sight of Pepe, lying in a pool of blood, must have surprised him and then he realized he had lost track of me. He whirled and tried using Manolo as a temporary shield. He didn't know Manolo had Pepe's gun.

"No! No!" Those were Manolo's last words.

I was clambering to the top of the dresser when I heard a roar, twice as loud as the ones I heard before. I don't know how many shots were exchanged; I thought I had gone deaf until I heard the steady thump of Charlie Watts's drum again and the persistent ring of the telephone. I stayed on top of the dresser until I felt sure nothing was moving except me and the roaches, the kind with six legs and hard shells. Nevertheless,

I first kicked a bottle of cologne off the dresser and into the hallway, half expecting it to draw Bennie's fire. I don't know what I would have done if a round flew down the hall. I had already pissed my pants. I waited for what seemed like an eternity before I hopped down, lay on my stomach, and peered cautiously, at floor level, around the corner of the dresser.

Manolo was in plain view, also lying on the floor, near the metal shelves, very still in the glow of the Tensor lamp. The blood had drained from his face like water from a sink. His mouth was open and he was staring at a paper lantern that hung from the ceiling. Bennie Torres's head lay against Manolo's knee. Bennie wasn't moving either. A .38 caliber revolver with a standard barrel was lying by his right hand. I crawled down the hall for a closer look.

The phone stopped ringing so I could hear my heart pounding in time with Charlie Watts's bass drum. Call the cops, I thought. Call the cops now, before someone else arrives with a gun. I stood up, tiptoed to the door, and triple-locked it. I whispered Manolo's name but got no reply. Manolo wasn't breathing. *Call the cops. Call the cops.* I had a gram of cocaine running through my brain. I was in no shape to be talking to the police and I had to be sure the man in front of me was indeed Bennie Torres. I checked his pulse but then remembered the gloves in my pocket and put them on before going through his pockets. I found a thick wallet but no pulse. I carried the wallet into the light.

There was a driver's license in the name of Benjamin Torres, age forty-five, resident of Tampa, Florida. The wallet also contained five hundred dollars in traveler's checks, drawn on a Union City bank, and a bunch of business cards, neatly wrapped in a rubber band. There were nine cards in all, including two from agents in the Miami office of the FBI. So Bennie was an informer. He also had a red address book wrapped with a rubber band. I slipped the address book into my pocket and returned the cards and the license to the wallet. I was putting the wallet back when I saw the envelope.

The envelope contained two Panamanian passports and a pair of airline tickets for a morning flight to Bogatá, Colombia, with a stopover in San Juan, Puerto Rico. Bennie's picture was on one of the passports, but his name wasn't listed as Torres. It was Corrado, Eduardo, and his place of birth was listed as Panama City. The other passport carried the name of Corrado, Fulgencio. Fulgencio looked enough like Bennie to be his brother. I dropped the passports and the tickets into the envelope and returned it to Bennie's pocket. No trip to Bogatá for Bennie.

I made a quick search of the apartment to see if Denise's camera was there but I couldn't find it. Then I took a damp cloth from the kitchen and wiped my fingerprints off anything I might have touched, including Pepe's gun, which I replaced in Manolo's right hand after first pressing it into Pepe's. I rolled the glass, the brandy bottle, and the metal straw I had used to snort the coke over Manolo's palm and fingers and put them back on the table, next to the coke. I was trying to make it easy for the police. They wouldn't spend much time on a drug-related triple homicide in this neighborhood.

I walked quietly into the front room and looked out the window. The snow was falling more heavily now. I heard a car coming down the block. I moved into the center of the room and waited until it came into view. It was a yellow Chevrolet. The driver slowed to a crawl when he drew abreast of the front door, and then kept going.

I went back to the living room, careful not to step in the blood that was glistening in the pale light. I went to the rear window and unlocked the gates. The keys were on a hook alongside. I opened the window and looked outside. The buildings in back were abandoned. A narrow alley ran between two of them and led to the next block.

Forget the front door. Bennie had been dropped off by someone who was coming back to pick him up. I stood at the window, half expecting the rush of cold air would help me think straight, but the cocaine kept flashing *GO! GO!* I heard a noise in the room behind me. A steam pipe? I wondered again if I should call the cops, but that no longer seemed like such a good idea. Had I checked Manolo's pulse? Could he still be alive? *GO!* He wasn't breathing. *GO!* Maybe I should have one more snort of cocaine for the pain in my groin. *GO!* I climbed up on the sill and peered down. I couldn't judge the distance to the ground. *GO!*

I listened to the cocaine and jumped.

Flip, flap, and fly was my motto. I hit the ground, rolled, staggered to my feet, and hobbled gaily off into the teeth of the storm. And a snowstorm at that! How apropos! Keep marching, Darenow. You're far from home and the snow doth fall. Maybe, I prayed, it will cover my tracks.

March, Darenow! Isn't that what they call snow in the Andes?

Peruvian marching powder. Hah-hah, aren't we witty. Cocaine must have been a big help to the Incas who built Machu Picchu. Thousands of campesinos toiling in the thin air, chewing on little green leaves while they pushed two-ton boulders around before dropping them neatly into place. Cocaine might be great for building cities in the sky, but it's no way to run a railroad. I knew why. Cocaine lets you think you can do things you can't. Aside from jumping out of windows, pushing boulders around, and killing people, it's not much good for anything except expensive daydreaming, but you don't catch wise until it's got you in its nasty grip. Either your brain's going 16 rpms while the cocaine alkaloids jam your synapses, letting you boogie when you should be dead on your feet, or your feet can't move because your brain is spinning at 78, busy with too many options. You're wrapped in an aptly named cloud of *dope*.

My legs and ankles hurt from the jump and my crown jewels had been rocked loose from their settings. I dragged my ass across the courtyard, shuffling to obscure my footprints in the snow. It was no effort to shuffle. I reached the little alley across the way that led to the next block and sank into more muck. I was knee deep in garbage and decaying mattresses.

A car alarm was wailing somewhere off in the distance when I stepped from the alley to the sidewalk. The street was lined with the ghostly, snow-covered shapes of cars and trucks. The amazing thing about neighborhoods like this is that no matter how poor the inhabitants are, everyone seems to have a car. It doesn't matter if they run, it just gives the men something to talk about when they're not getting drunk or beating their wives and children.

The subway was two blocks away. It was my best bet for anonymity. It was too easy for the cops to check the destination sheets of cabs to see which one had picked up a suspicious looking male around the corner from a triple homicide the night before. By now I must look suspicious.

But the snow on my face felt good; my brain felt like walking. The rest of me hurt.

The coke kept my brain marching along. Did I wipe my prints off everything?

What about Manolo? I forgot to take his pulse. He might still be alive. Wanna go back? Ha-ha, just joking. Wait, I owe him that much. He might have saved my life.

I fished a token from my pocket and dropped it in the turnstile. The platform was empty but it did have a pay phone. Call an ambulance. Manolo was young, maybe his body could take a lot of punishment still.

I fished around some more and found a quarter. I dialed 911 and put on a Spanish accent. I gave the operator the address and told her to send an ambulance, first floor, rear. I said I heard shots and people screaming. I said it sounded like they were killing each other and hung up before she could ask me any questions.

It was four by the time I got back to my apartment. The dope was still twirling in my skull but the circles were getting smaller, neater, tighter. *What I have done isn't as important as what I am going to have to do.* That thought settled like a lava pool in my cerebral cortex. My heart was a distant drum, pounding a rhythm I thought I had left on Avenue A. I was in bad shape. I flopped on the couch, lay back, and stared at the ceiling while I tried to compose myself. It wasn't going to be easy.

I'd snorted a gram, *or more*, of very good cocaine at Manolo's. I was still percolating, begging to come down from the mountain but wishing I could go higher. I was in the foyer of addiction again, but at least this time I had my hand on the door. I looked at the clock. It had been exactly seventy-seven minutes since I ducked into the subway and dialed

911. I recalled seeing no more than half a dozen people on my journey. The snow was still coming down. Only real gluttons for punishment were out roaming and half of them probably hadn't seen me. The other half looked as if they couldn't remember their own names. I hoped I was right. The police were probably there by now, stepping gingerly over the corpses. I had given the operator the address and the location of the apartment. Maybe that was a mistake. The longer I waited to tell the real story, the worse it was going to be for me. What if they found something to link me to the crime? Footprints? My sensible brogues could have left an impression, at least in the soft muck under the window. No, I remembered messing the dirt with a stick.

What if Manolo lived? Forget the pulse; he wasn't breathing. I'd seen men die. Manolo was dead. I wasted a quarter on the phone call. Yeh, but what if . . . what if Rocco realized I was going to call on the Kooks after I left his place? So what? I tell the police I went there, discovered three bodies, got scared, and beat it. Darenow, ace reporter, runs from big story. And what if that little fable makes a smart detective dig a little deeper? What if I left a thumb print on the crystal of Bennie's Rolex when I took his pulse? On Pepe's gun? The *what-ifs* were rolling in now like mortar rounds in the rain. I was Teddy at Chappaquiddick, Nixon at Watergate, Regan protecting Reagan. Then one of the rounds landed with a thud and didn't explode.

What if I had an alibi?

I got up from the couch and went into the kitchen. I didn't turn on the light. I put the kettle on the stove and made myself a cup of chamomile tea to calm down while I thought about this. *If I wasn't there, how could anyone think I could have done it?* I got up, went into the bedroom, and dug around in the night table drawer. I found the little envelope with three joints of home-grown marijuana. I fired one up, took three hits, and put it out. Good, Darenow, throw another log on your paranoia. Stay up all night and get really fretful. By dawn you'll be confessing to murders you didn't commit.

I went back into the kitchen, sat down, and sipped my tea in the dark, letting the steam drift into my tortured sinuses. My heart suddenly skipped a beat. It must have been the last of the coke giving my conscience a twist. Denise was my excuse! I'm a hero, for God's sake. The Torres brothers were scum. Who'd blame me for blowing one of them away?

The tea and the grass defused that one. It was no good. A headline from the *Times* kept getting in the way:

VENGEANCE SEEN AS MOTIVE FOR REPORTER IN SLAYINGS

The thought of a righteous prosecutor and twelve skeptics headed by a foreman who didn't like reporters capped that pipedream. No matter how you sliced it, I had a lot of explaining to do—*unless I had an alibi.* I sat in the dark for a long time. I thought about something Bob Dylan once said: "If you live outside the law you must be honest." And I decided to call Dixie Cupps.

I got the answering machine, left a brief message, and dialed again. Dixie was at home, sleeping. She'd probably pick up now on the second ring. I was right. Dixie's sleepy voice got stronger while mine got weaker. She had connections, and she'd know how to handle something like this. I pulled down a bottle of Remy, sat in the dark, and spun several yarns. Dixie didn't buy any of them. She said I sounded terrible, as if I'd seen a ghost. I told her I had seen three. She asked some more questions and then she said she was coming over. Don't worry about anything, she said, and don't drink too much. Too late. I gave her my address and hung up the phone. I felt all alone. I was thirty-five years old and I'd just watched three people die. Now I was going to confess to a drag queen. There had to be some meaning in that. It didn't matter. I poured another shot of cognac and sat down to wait for the buzzer to ring.

10

A distant bell rang in my head and bile rose in my throat. I opened an eye and the clock radio winked at me. It was 12:15, Wednesday, the afternoon of the morning after the night before. The phone was ringing. It wasn't going to stop so I answered it. It was Danny Tung, one of the day editors at the *Graphic*. He wanted to tell me about a triple homicide on Avenue A.

I heard Danny say, "Drugs, blood, bodies, Max, right up your alley." I remember those words and something about the day shift being shorthanded, and a memo from Hurley saying I was to be alerted to all drug-related crimes. Then the sluice gates opened and the cold sweats came: *It's a trick to get me to the scene of the crime so they can grill me.*

No. I expected this. I had given it some thought over the bottle of Remy. It was simple: the city desk merely wanted me to cover the story; I report only what I learn from this point on.

Danny innocently, incessantly, fed me details while I struggled to a sitting position in bed. Three dead in a shoot-out in Alphabet City. No IDs pending notification but we know one of the guys was a heavy hitter. Name of Torres. Ring a bell? *Rings general fucking alarm!* Quarter of a million dollars in uncut cocaine, blah-blah-blah. Police are still on the scene. How soon can I get over there? Nervous laughter suppressed. Choke, gag. Need time to think.

I tell Danny Tung I have the flu. A bad taste in mouth. Sore teeth.

Swamp gas in throat, bad images flooding fevered brain. Cold sweat.

Danny dropped into sardonic low-low gear.

"Maa-aa-x! Guaranteed page one. The story writes itself. Take a couple of aspirins. It's a beautiful day. You oughta be outside. The drug war's your beat. I can't spare anybody." He gave me the name of a detective in the Ninth Precinct, a Detective Gonzalez, and told me to call him back in half an hour or less.

Drugs, blood, bodies . . . the possibility of returning to Manolo's apartment had never been considered over the bottle of Remy. Story, yes. Eyewitness report, no. I was going to avoid that by getting the information on the telephone. I was sorry I had left Montauk. I was sorry for everything, but I knew that wasn't going to be enough.

I needed coke; I settled for aspirins. I shuffled into the living room, cracking my knee on an end table. The empty bottle of Remy rocked lightly but didn't fall over. I made a grab for it anyway and knocked over a snifter half full of it, spilling the contents. I caught a whiff, shuddered, gagged, and saw Dixie.

Dixie was curled on the couch, a robed chorister stirring awake. She wore a red flannel nightgown with a puritan lace collar and cuffs and was wrapped in my old army blanket. She yawned, opened her eyes, and smiled. What was she doing here? The telegraph key started tapping in my brain and I dashed straight for the bathroom.

I clung to the towel bar and let the shower beat on my back. I must have been there for fifteen minutes because Dixie began beating on the door, asking if I was OK. I turned the water off, did a lot of coughing over the sink, and almost succeeded in avoiding my own gaze in the mirror. When I saw myself, the night before tumbled over the dam.

I toweled quickly and made a run for the bedroom. I slammed the bedroom door behind me, realized I hadn't shaved, and ran back to the bathroom again, wrapped in a towel. I felt stupid avoiding Dixie, but the feeling subsided when I smelled food. *Dixie was cooking breakfast.* I wiped the last bit of shaving cream off my earlobe and slapped my face awake. It wasn't a good idea. There was a bowling ball in my skull that wobbled around when my head moved.

I trembled my way into a fresh white shirt, pulled my pants on very slowly, and decided on a blue tie. I invoked several holy names and stepped out to face the music.

Dixie was standing over a hot stove in a red Mother Hubbard, her hair pulled back in a loose knot, *a guy*, doling out eggs and advice with the impunity and calm innocence of a suburban housewife. Everything was natural; everything was satis-factual. Zippity-doo-dah, things could only get worse.

Dixie poured me a cup of coffee. I gulped it, scorching my tongue and throat. It had the strange effect of helping me focus on the events of the night before. I blew on the coffee and concentrated. I was hazy on details, but I remembered Pepe waving a gun and looking confused. Whoops! Pepe goes down. Manolo shouts and shoots Pepe. Bang! Bang! Bang! Manolo down now, sitting on the floor. Lots of blood on the floor. Throw your shoes out, Darenow, they might have blood on them. I got up with some effort, found the shoes, put them in a wastebasket, and put the basket by the door. Dixie said nothing. I came back to the kitchen table and sat down. The silence between us was beginning to roar.

But I didn't remember telling the police all this. That set off the telegraph bell again, which rocked the bowling ball, which opened my pores and made the hair stand up on my neck. I was sweating again. How the hell had Dixie gotten here?

Dixie read my mind and refreshed my memory without being asked. I was in trouble; I called her; she came. She was my alibi, remember?

The bowling ball went on a big roll and the muscles in my neck froze to support the weight of my head on my shoulders.

Dixie cracked an egg into a hot pan and it sizzled while she talked.

Did I remember talking to Rocco about Bennie Torres? No. Yes!

Dixie raised her eyebrows, cooked an egg, and jogged my memory.

Bennie Torres was the man blaming the Mafia for all the murders. Bennie Torres was the man in The Crib with Denise, Jaime Santiago, and the sex-change called Esmeralda.

"The chauffeur?"

"Yes," Dixie nodded pleasantly. "And there's more good news!"

The Mafia, Dixie told me, knew all about last night. They think I'm a hero for taking care of Bennie Torres so they're going to take care of me. Rocco had generously answered my request for an airtight alibi and had two witnesses to back it up. He'd been working on it all morning. Now Dixie and I had to get our stories together.

"What's the alibi?" I coughed. Dixie told me. It was simple. A Mafia-owned car service picked Dixie and me up at her house at about 4:30 this morning. I'd been there all night, grieving over Denise's death and getting very drunk. I refused to sleep there, so Dixie took me home. The driver and Dixie will swear to it.

In addition, Dixie informed me, Rocco will swear I told him I was going to Dixie's when I left The Crib because Dixie had pictures of drag queens that might be useful to the investigation.

The bowling ball rocked dizzily in my skull.

"I can't use an alibi fabricated by the Mafia, Dixie."

"Look, Max," Dixie sighed. "It's only if someone *asks*. If no one asks, there's no problem."

"Why is Rocco doing this?"

"You said Bennie Torres was killed last night, right? Well, Rocco's friends are almost positive Bennie Torres was the guy dumping bodies on Mafia turf. You're a hero, Max."

"You didn't have to tell Rocco anything, Dixie," I said without conviction. "I confided in you because you were a friend of Denise's."

"Darling, you said you needed an alibi—so I called Rocco. He's a very dear friend. He liked Denise and he likes you. Rocco is connected, Max. His uncle is—"

"I know who his uncle is." The alarm bell trilled. "Does his uncle know what happened?"

"You walked in on a rub-out, Max. *A hit*. You defended yourself and you're lucky you're alive. You're a hero in the eyes of some people who've been very good to me. Call them the Mafia. Call them anything. They owe you, Max. The Torres brothers were blaming the guineas for all those murders. You did the world a favor."

Dixie shook her head in disbelief and slid the egg smoothly onto a plate.

"That was my office calling before. They want me to go back over there."

"Not *back* over there, Max. You were never there, remember?" Dixie shook her head again and sat down. "Do you have time to eat something?" she asked.

I picked at the food and discovered I had an appetite; not much of one, but I managed to eat half an egg and half a slice of toast. The coffee had cooled and it tasted good. I was starting to feel human but I wasn't going back to Avenue A. Excuse me, *going* to Avenue A. Watch them stuff the body bags? No thanks. Besides, what if some old biddy saw me coming or going last night and recognized me again today? *That's him, officer. That's the man I saw!* We're talking grand jury, triple homicide, a fortune in lawyer's fees, and no guarantee anyone will believe my story. *I left the scene of a murder and didn't report it!*

Dixie and I exchanged looks while I sipped lukewarm coffee in silence.

When I finished and pushed the plate away she began clearing the table and putting the dishes in the sink.

"I'll do that," I said none too eagerly.

"It's OK," she said. "I like to do it."

"Please . . . you've done enough."

There were only three plates. By the time we finished arguing they were cleaned and racked.

"Are you going over there?" Dixie asked.

"Oh, the crime boys are there," I said airily. "Taking pictures and looking for clues. I'd just be in the way. What are *you* going to do?" I shouldn't have asked.

"I'm going to take a bath if it's all right with you."

"A bath?"

"I want to relax."

For the third time that morning I was speechless.

"Look, Max, I'm part of your alibi. And this thing is far from over. Rocco wants me to stay here until he calls again."

She sat back down and looked at me over the rim of a coffee cup. I remained speechless. She put the cup down and smiled.

"Rocco says there may be some details that need looking after. I can help. What time does the mailman come?"

"The mailman?"

"The mailman. You insisted on going downstairs last night to put an address book in the mailbox. I had to find an envelope and stamps. But you didn't really want to mail it. You were playing safe, you said. You better get it before the mailman comes."

"I put it in my mailbox?"

"Right."

I remembered. It was the address book I had lifted from Bennie Torres's pocket.

"I better get it now," I said. "The mailman comes soon."

"So you won't need the bathroom for a while?"

"Dixie, look . . ." I wasn't sure what I wanted to say.

"It's OK, Max. I don't have AIDS. I've never been very sexually active. Once I started living as a woman my sex drive became, well, manageable. And I never really fucked around."

"That's not what I mean . . ." I blushed. "Go take a bath."

I got her a fresh towel and face cloth and went downstairs to retrieve the address book.

It was there, stuffed in a envelope addressed to my friend in Montauk.

I must have been very drunk because the address was block-printed as if a child had done it. I put it inside my shirt and went back upstairs.

The bathroom door was closed. Dixie was running water in the tub and humming to herself. I disconnected the phone in the living room, brought it into the bedroom, and called the number the day editor, Danny Tung, had given me. It was the squad room in the Ninth Precinct. I asked for Detective Gonzalez. He wasn't in. I identified myself and asked if Gonzalez was working a homicide on Avenue A. He was.

"Is there a phone where I can reach him?" As if I didn't know. The cop on the line gave me a number.

"If anybody asks," he said, "you tell them you looked it up in the book. I hope it's in the book."

I told him not to worry and thanked him. I thought about being in Manolo's apartment and the telegraph bell trilled in my mind. Something to do with telephones and Pepe, the man in the brown suit. There was a lot of static in my brain. I couldn't get the connection. I made a note: "Torres, brown suit on phone." It made no sense, but it had the earmarks of something I ought to be concerned about.

I called Danny at the *Graphic* and told him I was going to try to dig something up over the phone. He was disappointed I wasn't going in person but I told him I'd be in the way and the cops wouldn't like that.

"We might only run two more editions," Danny reminded me. "So you have an hour to catch the first one and then we're due for a final at three forty-five. That's press time. Deadline for you is three fifteen. Can you do it?"

No sweat, I said. That was a lie. Little rivers of it were rolling down my back. I hung up and called Manolo's apartment. I identified myself and asked for Detective Gonzalez.

"This is Gonzalez. What can I do for you?"

I asked for details on the homicide. I told him it was a page-one story.

"I want a good write-up, now," he returned cheerily. I promised him his name would be used, spelled correctly, and featured prominently so every junkie in town who could read would know who to call with a tip.

"OK, we got a slight problem with names. Two of these guys had two sets of ID and we don't know yet which are the right names. Plus we haven't gotten confirmation on next of kin so I can't actually give you any names. OK?" I indicated my assent.

"All right," he said without a pause. "Three dead, all male Hispanics. All shot. We found three guns. Two have been used, most likely for this job. Couple of pounds of cocaine on the premises. That's pounds. Street value around quarter of a mil. That's $250,000. It happened around three A.M., give or take an hour. No one heard a thing, of course. What else can I tell you?"

No one heard a thing. "Who owns the apartment?" I asked.

"The owner can't be found, but the super says one of the victims lived here."

"And the guy . . . the guy who lived there. Which one is he?" I almost said "Manolo."

"The youngest. He got it through the lung and bled to death. But he took one of the other guys with him."

"A shoot-out?"

"Looks that way, but it's hard to say. There might have been a fourth individual."

My pen froze. This wasn't over by a long shot.

"Another hit job, like the rest of them?" My voice quavered. I hoped he hadn't noticed.

"Possible. We think the two older guys are connected. If their IDs match some information we got already, they're part of the same outfit. We're waiting for records from Florida."

Florida again. "Where were the bodies found?" I asked.

"In the living room. You could say it's 'awash in blood,' but don't quote me. All three bodies on the floor. The place is a dump."

"What kind of apartment is it?"

"The occupants were apparently musicians. There's all kinds of expensive sound equipment here. The coke was packed in two guitar cases. It looks as if two of the men came for the drugs and the young one pulled a gun rather than hand it over. The victims only had a few hundred dollars between them so it could be someone tried to take the coke without paying. Or someone else could have beat it with the dough and left the coke. We're still trying to figure it out."

My brain was going a mile a minute. I tried to think of what I would ask if I didn't know anything. I asked him to describe what the victims were wearing, the physical layout of the pad, and the exact nature of the wounds. I asked him what kind of guns were used. He gave me enough detail to make a decent story for the next edition. I thanked him and hung up the phone. I was trembling.

I sat and stared at my notes. There weren't very many. I must have been temporarily paralyzed while Detective Gonzalez was talking. I quickly scribbled down as much of his description as I could remember, trying not to let the information pounding in my skull get in the way. My hand shook, so the notes came out looking like a seismograph.

I took the notes and the address book and went into the kitchen. Dixie was still in the bath. There was some coffee left so I poured a cup.

A .38 caliber Smith & Wesson, a 9 mm automatic, and a .22 caliber automatic were on their way to the police lab. My prints weren't on them. They shouldn't be. I was careful.

I heard the bathroom door and saw Dixie dart around the corner, wrapped in a towel. She had another towel wrapped around her head.

"Give me three seconds," she said. "I left my robe in the living room."

Dixie bounced barefooted into the kitchen wearing her red Mother Hubbard, a towel twisted into a turban on her head. Her toenails were painted rose pink. "I'd love to kiss ya'," she said, Bette Davis style, "but I just washed my hair." She meant to be funny. I didn't laugh. She poured herself a cup of coffee, pulled up a chair, and sat down. She sipped the coffee before she spoke.

"You found your little black book, I see," she said offhandedly.

"I did."

"Anything interesting?"

"I haven't looked. I'll get to it after I file a story."

"Max, be careful. This is a whole other world you're getting into. Believe me."

"I'm a big boy, Dixie."

"You don't know who you're dealing with, Max. You're lucky you're not dead."

"Then why don't *you* tell *me* what *you* know?"

"I'll know more after I speak to Rocco." She shrugged. "He's still checking into the Torres brothers. So far he thinks they're the ones blaming the guineas for all the murders, so naturally the mob would like to . . ." She turned her head and shrugged. Her turban came loose and she paused to adjust it.

"To what . . . ?"

"To know more, I guess. Oh, Max. Don't worry about it."

"It's a moot point, Dixie. Bennie Torres is dead. The person to find is Esmeralda. It's fairly clear to me that one of the Torres brothers was her lover and they had a falling out. One of the drag queens I talked to last night said as much. Manolo, before he died, *said* Bennie tried to kill Esmeralda." My palm hit the table. "And he killed Denise instead! I'm going to make damn sure—"

"Max! Let the guineas handle this! You write your story! Let other people do the dirty work. They enjoy it. Denise wouldn't want you jeopardizing yourself. It proves nothing. Quit while you're ahead."

I got up and walked to the window. The courtyard was covered with snow and the clotheslines were cat's cradles of icy gossamer.

When I first moved into the building I had heard a crash in that courtyard, and when I approached the window to look, the first thing I saw was a man's legs, spread-eagled, silhouetted in snow. As I moved closer to the window I saw the body, wrapped in clotheslines that had snapped around him on the way down. The dead man was a burglar who slipped in the void of crime.

My tongue could slip like that man's foot slipped and the result would be the same: a fatal fall. But I wasn't a criminal.

Ah-ha! Darenow, that's the point. You're not a criminal. You're just a babe in the woods, a puppy in a tiger's cage.

"Okay, hang around until you talk to Rocco," I said. "We'll take it from there."

And let's just hope the need for an alibi never arises. The Mafia is not noted for doing favors unless the favor can be redeemed upon demand.

I turned, picked up my notes and the address book, and retreated to the bedroom.

11

My best bet was to play dumb and keep moving, one hand on the rosary beads, the other on the telephone.

Dixie got dressed after her hair dried and went to the supermarket. She wanted to get ready for "hitting the mattress." I assumed she meant the Mafia term for hiding out and laying low. I called the number for the federal task force—LEGAL. The man in charge, a Mr. Owen Reed, assistant attorney general for international affairs, was not available, of course. I huffed and puffed and told his secretary the public had the right to know what the task force was doing in response to a killing wave that showed no sign of abating. But my speech had all the force of an old maid haranguing the dogcatcher to get those mutts out of her daylilies. The secretary thanked me for calling and hung up.

I knew what was wrong; my body craved more coke. I shivered off the urge and dropped my notes on the floor, Bennie Torres's well-worn address book among them. Some pages came loose and I sat down at the desk to put everything back in order. I found myself caressing the address book and wishing I had left it at the scene.

It was a funny little book. I had a hunch it represented a market plan for the distribution of lots of cocaine. Lots. Fourteen pages of numbers, mostly Florida, New Jersey, and New York area codes. There were some names and addresses next to the numbers, but the majority of listings were just initials or a single name. "Carmen 673-4043." "Alvarez 704-2867." "HJ RH-2-9000." Torres had drawn a box around four phone numbers on the inside front cover. There were no names, no initials, and no area codes next to those numbers. I was going to need a lot more information before I struck gold.

I had a friend in the local bureau of one of the wire services who had covered the Florida state house before winning a slot on the New York desk. We met at a press conference, hit it off, and I'd been coaching him in the vagaries of New York politics ever since. I called and told him a little of what was happening in my life and asked him to recommend a reliable source in the Sunshine State. That's where most of the victims had come from and where Bennie Torres had resided.

My friend gave me the name of a reporter in Tampa named Terry Compton, who, he said, was young, aggressive, and reliable.

I thanked him, hung up, and called Terry Compton in Florida. I was told he worked nights and left a message for him to call me, mentioning, of course, my friend's name as a reference. I was starting to feel like a journalist again.

My next call was to our man at police headquarters. I needed an official statement on the NYPD's role in the drug wars, as soon as possible. Let someone else rattle the police commissioner's cage. The less I had to do with cops the better. Hurley said go after the politicians, so I would. Better them than me.

I sat down at the typewriter and went numb. Blank page, blank mind. I got up, paced the floor, then peeked into Dixie's dance bag. I found pantyhose, a bra, a romance novel, a bag full of makeup, a pair of blue pumps, and two large Tampax. I was looking for cigarettes but there was none. What the hell was she doing with Tampax? I went into the night table drawer and lit up what was left of the joint I had smoked last night. I took two hits, snuffed it, and put it back. Old habits die hard, what else can I say?

I hate to think the grass helped. Here's what I rapped out:

> An apparent dispute over a quarter of a million dollars' worth of cocaine sparked a shoot-out early this morning in an East Village apartment, leaving three men dead and boosting the number of drug-related homicides in New York City to 24 in the last two months.
>
> A combined federal and city task force assigned to root out the evil seems powerless against the drug lords, who have turned New York into a latter-day Dodge City. The body count boosts New York into

the nation's no. 1 slot for homicides and raises again the questions most decent people are asking—When will the drug madness stop? Who will stop it? How can it be done?

The latest victims of the drug war were found, etc. etc. etc.

I added the gory details and left room for the identifications of the victims. The desk would punch in comments from the police commissioner and whoever else we could collar in the next couple of hours for additional quotes. When I phoned the story in to the rewrite man, he told me Hurley had called from his home in Kew Gardens and said to keep after Owen Reed, the head of the task force. "Stir the waters" was his message. He meant rake muck.

But Reed remained unavailable to the press. I told his secretary to remind him it was an election year, and he ought to at least pop out of his bunker once in a while to rally the troops. I used all the right buzzwords but the fire still wasn't there. I was tired and sore from my little romp the night before.

I decided I needed a break. My stomach was having second thoughts about food so I made a cup of mint tea, ate some yogurt, and lay down on the bed to digest it. I heard Dixie come back from the store, rustle around in the kitchen, and then hit the couch herself. I spent the next ten minutes watching a cobweb tremble in a corner of the ceiling near the radiator. I was falling asleep when the phone rang.

It was Rocco.

"How ya' doin'?" he inquired with what seemed like genuine concern.

"I'm alive," I said. "My teeth hurt."

"You had a workout," he said. "But you did good. We're gonna help you out, don't worry. Dixie said you got some phone numbers from the dead guy, from Torres. We got a PI in Tampa who's gonna check it out for us. An ex-cop. A friend."

A shudder rose in my throat. I wasn't expecting this. Dixie had no business telling Rocco I had those numbers. I sidestepped his request with a question. Why was he so sure Bennie Torres was the guy blaming the Mafia for all the murders; and if he was, why bother pursuing him? Bennie was dead.

"Max, trust me. Bennie was small potatoes, all right? We're looking for the big man, the guy who bankrolled his operations. The more we know about Bennie, the more pressure we can put on his boss."

"Pressure who to do what? Turn himself in?"

"My people want to sit down with this guy. He's done us a very bad turn and he's gonna have to make amends. Otherwise we really go to war."

"Let's hear some names, Rocco. Who's the guy behind Bennie?"

"We don't know who's behind Bennie," Rocco replied sourly. "That's why we need those phone numbers."

"I thought I told you that Manolo, the other guy who died, said Bennie was working for a man named Hector Melendez. Manolo thought Melendez was God."

"Chrissake!" Rocco scoffed. "Hector Melendez *is* God, if you're a spic."

"Who is he, Rocco?"

"Forget it," Rocco said dismissively. "We're talking big time."

"Who is he, Rocco?"

"A boss of the Spanish in Florida," Rocco said grudgingly. "A big boss. We call them a *capo di tutti capi*, a boss of bosses. If anything, Torres was a wild card in his deck. That's why we need your information, and a news story to rattle his cage. I'll let you know."

Great, I thought. Max Darenow, the Mafia's own scribe.

I reminded Rocco I wasn't a vigilante. There was a long pause before his voice turned cold. This wasn't the Rocco that Denise and I knew and loved, the Rocco who read Simone (de Beauvoir) and smoked a little weed. This was Rocco whose uncle was Tony Beef.

"Max, come down to the club, now," he said icily. "We gotta have a talk. See you in fifteen minutes."

Rocco hung up on me.

The walk to and from The Crib was sobering. I dropped a perfectly good but possibly incriminating pair of shoes into the garbage on the way down and seriously pondered my fate on the return. Fresh air was a relief, both ways.

Rocco and I sat in his claustrophobic office for about an hour and "talked turkey about the facts of life"—his phrase. I was going dancing with the Big Boys, whether I liked it not.

Charles Baldasano, Brooklyn's boss of bosses and heir to the Mafia's crumbling New York empire, had taken a personal interest in my problems. Mr. Baldasano, AKA the Big Guy, AKA Charlie B, would "stand behind" my alibi, providing I returned the favor by supplying Rocco with information relevant to the Torres brothers, including, of course, Bennie's address book.

It was, Rocco emphasized, an offer I couldn't refuse.

Rocco said Charlie needed me. The Big Guy was the mob's last chance to consolidate what little power the Mafia had left in New York. Rocco began earnestly, leaning across his scarred pulpit, punctuating his sermon with shrugs and assorted body language, all indicating he was as new to this as I was.

Rocco pointed out that the feds' prior assault on the Mafia (he called it "the families") had resulted in prison sentences for 75 percent of the established Mafia leaders. That much I knew.

"They deserved it," Rocco huffed. "They got lazy pushing heroin and they let everything else slide. Charlie wants to set things right. These spics and niggers pushing crack are no good punks—sociopaths, Max—there's no place for them in this country. We gotta have law and order and the cops can't handle it. These punks get busted, hire a lawyer, and they're back on the street."

"What's your solution, Rocco?" As if I didn't know.

"Charlie will give 'em a warning. Once. Then they get whacked, permanently. End of story."

"The, uh, families, then, they become a vigilante force?"

Rocco dismissed the remark with a sour look. He bobbed his head in thought before replying.

"Listen, Max, the spics've got connections in Washington. All they have to do is finger a couple of commies once in a while. If they can't finger a commie, a priest or a nun with liberal ideas will do. That's all it takes, baby. It makes them legit, and the CIA and the State Department and whoever else look the other way. It's all about drugs and guns, Maxie. Drugs come in and guns go out, all to fight commies, except they aren't always commies. They're just people who won't roll over when the Great White Corporation tries to make a sweetheart deal for their crops and their lands. Catch my drift?"

"Look, Rocco," I said patiently, "I'm not saying you're wrong. I'm just saying that my beef with these people begins and ends with whoever murdered Denise. Charlie will have to fight his own wars."

Rocco smiled grimly, leaned back, and sized me up.

"The Torres boys are just a piece of the mosaic," he slowly replied. "Charlie's gonna make it tough on the people who let punks like them operate."

"I don't know, Rocco, it sounds like pie in the sky to me."

"Bennie Torres was an embarrassment to his own people, Max. There are decent spics—Latins, I should call them—who are glad he's gone and they're gonna cooperate now with Charlie to set things right."

"So I give you the names in Bennie's address book and Charlie starts bumping them off, one by one. Is that what you mean by setting things right, Rocco?"

"Ain't necessarily so, chum," Rocco answered blithely. "Charlie's gonna meet with the Latino Mr. Big, Mr. Hector Melendez himself. They'll make a list. There's other ways of leaning on people than whacking them. Charlie wants to avoid bloodshed, believe me. Listen, they got guns, too."

"So Charlie's going to shake these people down?"

"Max, when you have the goods on a guy, when he's cornered, he gotta sit down and negotiate, unless he's a dumb punk, all right? Then he gets whacked, but only then."

Headlines were dancing in front of my eyes again:

MOB USES REPORTER AS SOURCE IN TURF DISPUTE

Rocco tried another approach.

"A lot of politicians are getting tired of playing games with guys like Bennie Torres and whoever was behind him, Max, but it ain't easy freeing yourself from the sort of deals the government has made over the years. But if Charlie gets the goods on these guys he'll feed that information to the right people. That's a fact, Max. He's counting on *you* to fork over Bennie's address book. That's where it all begins."

My head was aching and my back sagged under the strain. I stood up, hunched my shoulders, and tried working the kinks out by craning my neck this way and that.

"And what does Charlie get from all this?" I asked between spasms. "He nails these guys and then what? He takes over the rackets from the Spanish?"

Rocco shook his head.

"You're a cynical guy," he replied without rancor. "But I can understand why you think that way. When Charlie gets back in the driver's seat you ain't gonna have thirteen-year-old kids smokin' crack. Follow me? First off, he won't tolerate the sale of crack *or* heroin. OK? That's out. Maybe he'll tolerate a little grass, for consenting adults only. You're always gonna have some vice, so it's better if the right people enforce it and regulate it."

I stopped jerking my neck around because I had to laugh.

"And the right people would be Italians, I presume." It came out more derisively than I had intended.

"America is never gonna collect the money it's owed from places like Mexico, Colombia, and Brazil unless we make use of their cash crops,

Max, and one of the biggest cash crops is marijuana, let's face it. You just make sure the peasants get their fair share and you won't have to worry about communism, OK? Money talks, Max."

"You're dreaming, Rocco! What have you been smoking?"

Rocco grinned wickedly, but something told me he was serious.

"It ain't just my theory, Maxie. Lots of people think likewise. It's bite-the-bullet time at the White House. The politicians are looking for somebody to keep things manageable, that's all."

It was so bizarre, so way out, and so deliciously silly that I stopped arguing. I told Rocco he could make a copy of Bennie's book, but I had to keep the original.

"No problem," Rocco agreed, patting a hand-held personal copier. "That's what this is for."

"And I want guarantees, Rocco. Number one, I want to share in whatever information you guys uncover from Bennie's book. I want first crack at a story, if one materializes, but mostly, I want this information to help me find who in hell murdered Denise, and why. That's really what I want, and I want Charlie's solemn word on it."

Rocco stood up and offered me his hand.

"I'm shaking your hand, Rocco. That means we have a deal." I hoped I wouldn't live to regret it.

"You help The Big Guy out and we'll make sure you have your alibi and your story," Rocco said emphatically. "So help me God. That 'man of honor' thing ain't bullshit. Charlie keeps his word."

"Honor can be a cloak among thieves," I said, "worn when convenient."

"You don't know Charlie," Rocco answered tersely, "or you wouldn't say that."

I made no reply. I'd said enough already. Enough to implicate me in a Mafia conspiracy, perhaps. My dance card was full. Rocco set to work copying the book, running the scanner over the pages with the zeal of a kid running a set of electric trains.

The Crib was empty now. I went out to the bar, got a bottle of beer for Rocco, and made myself a weak brandy and water. I delivered the beer and then I went and shot a game of pool.

I beat myself, effortlessly.

It was nearly five o'clock when I got back to my apartment. I had missed filing an update for the last edition. Dixie was asleep when I returned, so I let her sleep. It would have been nice if she was waiting for me with a hot meal and fresh coffee, but I didn't want to encourage her housewife fantasy. If I wasn't in such deep, serious trouble it would have been funny.

I had barely doffed my coat when the phone in the bedroom rang. It was Lieutenant Henry, calling from the Major Crimes Unit. He had just returned from the apartment at Avenue A.

"We found your girlfriend's handbag with some notebooks in it and a camera that fits the description of the one you gave us," he began. "How it got there we don't know."

I held my breath. The one thing I should have done at Manolo's—call the cops—I hadn't, so now Henry had Denise's bag, and all I had was deep trouble. Act natural, Darenow, I reminded myself.

"Do you think those guys killed her?" I asked.

"We don't know if it's those guys or what," Henry replied, "but I wouldn't be surprised. We're looking for the other people who were supposed to be living there."

I'd forgotten about the *others*. Such as the other two Kooks, if they were still alive. Such as whoever Pepe was talking to on the telephone. Such as anyone who could place me at the scene.

Act natural, Darenow.

"Well," I said, clearing my throat, "do we have any identifications yet?"

"Oh yeh," Henry said.

He read the names of the victims. Alberto Cruz, known as Pepe, Benjamin Torres, known as Bennie, and Manolo Pearson, no nickname. I should have known Manolo had Anglo blood in his veins.

"Manolo Pearson lived there, according to neighbors. He was going to night school. He has family in Florida. So do the others."

Bennie and Pepe had police records. Armed robbery, assault, attempted murder, possession and sale of narcotics, the usual. Most of the charges were dismissed on various grounds, such as failure of witnesses to appear. Bennie had once served fifteen months in prison for illegal possession of firearms, namely a pair of BARs, an antitank gun, and a .50 caliber machine gun allegedly stolen from a Florida National Guard armory.

"Bennie has a brother named Ralph," Henry added. "They're both known to police in Florida and New Jersey. Cuban wise guys, I guess."

I cleared my throat. "So what do you think happened?" Tread carefully, Darenow, minefield ahead.

"Maybe the boys in the band owed Torres money and couldn't pay.

When Bennie and Pepe came to enforce the debt the kid pulled a gun, they shot it out, and he got killed himself."

"Anything's possible," I said innocently.

"The kid who lived there had no arrest record, nor did he seem the type to be buying quantity from a guy like Bennie Torres. The neighbors said he was a college student. One never knows, does one?"

"No," I said feebly.

"I'd like to be identified as being in charge of the investigation, OK? And please try to get the other cops' names, especially Gonzalez from the local precinct, in the paper. We want to pursue that drag queen angle."

"That's good, too," I said. "Good copy."

"I'm reporting directly to the commissioner's office," Henry added. "You can't print that, but I just want to let you know the department is taking your friend's death very seriously. And the fact that Bennie Torres was involved seems to have stirred the feds out of their stupor. The Torres name rang bells in certain quarters."

I cupped the phone and let out a deep sigh. Maybe Rocco's grandiose theories weren't so grandiose.

"I couldn't ask for more," I said.

"We all want to get to the bottom of this, Mr. Darenow. You mentioned having some sources among Denise's friends. I'd appreciate it if you kept your ears open."

I told Henry I'd gladly turn over any leads I found.

We left it like that.

I hung up and went to adjust the window shade to coax what was left of the daylight into the cold and dark room. I kept thinking of Denise, and how things might have turned out if I hadn't been such a jerk. I ran the shade to the top but it didn't make much difference. The night was closing in fast. I'd missed a deadline. I promised myself to get to bed early and to call Mr. Owen Reed, assistant attorney general, first thing in the morning.

I heard a faint knock. Dixie was awake, gently tapping on my door. She read the annoyance in my eyes and looked hurt.

"I need something else from the stores," she apologized. "But I have to come back because Rocco wants me to stay here."

Lovely, I thought. I'm under house arrest, with a drag queen as my keeper.

She was trying to help, but Dixie made me nervous. I think it had something to do with what she was wearing. I hadn't noticed it before, but she wasn't wearing her slacks and storm boots. She was dressed demurely, like college girls used to dress years ago—plaid pleated skirt, white sweater, sheer nylons, and navy blue low-heeled pumps. And she had tits, for God's sake. Not much, just two discreet little hillocks that jiggled when she did. It was all so bizarre.

I was staring at her.

"I must look terrible," she said. "I have no makeup on."

"You look fine," I stammered. "I'm just not used to this . . ." I made a vague gesture.

"The way you were staring at me," she said, "I thought something was wrong."

"No . . . I might take a nap. Why don't you take the key in case I'm sleeping when you come back."

I gave her an extra house key and listened as she went out and closed the door. The sun had given up. I lay down on the bed and closed my eyes. I wished I could talk to Denise one more time. I turned my face into the pillow and surrendered to the darkness.

12

I was in dreamland, somewhere in Manhattan, on a side street lined with empty buildings. It was raining and I couldn't find a cab. I was late for something, or some*body*, and I had to get there right away. Heading for the subway, I heard Dixie's voice rolling through the raindrops.

"Max! Telephone . . ."

I ran toward the voice in the dream and saw Dixie peering through the window of the back seat of a limousine; she held a portable phone in her hand and offered it to me, but the car drove off before I could reach it. I heard her voice again and woke up. It was Dixie, in the flesh.

"Max, wake up. There's a call for you."

It was Terry Compton, reporter for the *Tampa Times*. My friend at the wire service had told him my story. I wasn't surprised; drugs, money, and murder made good copy.

Terry Compton smelled a good story and immediately asked how, and when, we would share it.

I was waking up quickly. In my bedroom the shades were emitting silver slivers of light from a street lamp, and traffic noises and voices drifted up, too. It could have been eight o'clock or midnight. In New York you never know.

The clock said 9:15. I began by giving the names of all the victims of the recent New York rubouts, and whether they had Florida addresses or not. He'd run them through his files. Had he ever heard of the Torres brothers? Negative, but he'd run them through his newspaper's morgue and check with the local cops.

"What about a young man named Jaime Santiago, the ward of a Mrs. Ethel Wately?"

"The Watelys' ward—what a story."

"You know them?" I should have known.

"Sure," he said easily. "We picked up the story of the kid's overdose from New York, but none of the local papers would touch it. The Watelys have *lots* of friends. Tampa society is ultra discreet and Ethel was very popular—in her prime. Her family came from Philadelphia when the money boys ran the railroad through here."

I told him to hang on while I got a pen and paper.

The Watelys were everything a tabloid writer could ask for, money in excess and enough domestic tragedy to reassure the common man that it couldn't buy happiness. It was a pity my readers wouldn't see the dirt Terry Compton was shoveling my way, but I had promised Mrs. Wately I wouldn't drag the family name through the mud and she was the sort of woman for whom men love to do favors.

Without stopping to take a breath, Terry Compton explained he'd been raised in Tampa, knew everyone, and thought it was just great working with a real "Noo Yark" reporter. In a minute and a half, I found out that Mr. Wately senior, the patriarch, was Avery Wately. He had been a major stockholder and general counsel of the Sunshine Line, founded in the 1920s, the railroad that brought fresh oranges north and wealthy Yankees south. Avery built a mansion overlooking Tampa Bay, added a cattle ranch and a phosphate mine to his portfolio, played polo with the Duke of Windsor in 1929, lived long enough to fish with Hemingway in 1954, and died still holding the patent on refrigerated boxcars in 1963.

"We're talking big bucks," young Mr. Compton said reverentially.

Ethel had certainly married well. But there was more. Compton's voice dropped.

"Avery committed suicide," he said. "After that the Watelys took a real low profile."

"The Santiago boy, Mrs. Wately's ward," I said. "He's supposed to be gay. Apparently had a drug problem. I'd like to know all about him: who he hung around with, where he went to school. Things like that."

"I'll do my best," Compton said, "but that's a tall order. You'd need a private detective. That kind of stuff is good for the tabloids, not for the wire services or a hometown paper. I can't use it."

He was right, but I was offering better information in return. Any story that developed from our collaboration would undoubtedly break first in New York, where the killings took place. It would be hard news, maybe an account of the breaking up of a drug cartel. Wouldn't he like to have that story at the same time it was breaking in New York?

"Tell you what," Compton said. "The society editor is a gold mine of information. She loves to talk and she knew the Watelys. Likes martini lunches, too. Can you spring for expenses?"

I liked young Mr. Compton already.

"One more thing," I said. "Did you ever hear of a Spanish gangster named Melendez? He's supposed to be a big wheel in southern Florida."

"There's plenty of people named Melendez in southern Florida," he laughed. "I'm sure some of them are gangsters, but I'd need a first name and more information before I can answer that one."

My mouth started to form Hector Melendez's first name, until I remembered what Rocco had said. Charlie's meeting with Hector Melendez was supposed to be a secret. I told Compton I didn't have a first name.

"I'm working the lobster shift, so I can run some of these names through the morgue tonight," Compton said. "Will you be up?"

"I'll take the call," I said, then put the phone back in its cradle.

It wasn't my intention to air Jaime Santiago's dirty linen in public. But dirt is dirt, and in a sordid world, the world where Denise had died, dirt was currency. I sat up and started organizing an outline, something to keep Hurley at bay, when Dixie, my very own raven, came tapping at my bedroom door.

"Hi, Max, sorry to disturb you. I thought you might be hungry."

Dixie couldn't have sounded nicer. I *was* hungry, and although I didn't like the idea of Dixie camping out here, I was tired, I didn't feel like hitting the streets yet and I didn't want to be alone. The truth was Dixie made me nervous. Her ease and familiarity with women, and the fact she seemed to know more about men than I did, bothered me. Was I jealous because Dixie got along so well with Denise and I, in the end, hadn't?

I suggested we send out for Chinese food but Dixie had dinner planned.

"You have an excellent fish market on the corner," she said. "I bought calamari. It was on sale. I can sauté it and toss it with some spaghetti. It'll only take a minute."

I had to laugh. She remembered we had eaten it one night when we went out with Denise, down at a place on Mulberry Street. It seemed like yesterday.

"You'll feel better when you get something in your stomach," Dixie added softly.

Relax, I told myself. You're gonna get fed, it's a free meal, and you have a pretty thing serving it up, just forget for a minute it's a guy who carries Tampax in his gym bag and wears makeup. It sounded too much like jail, but I was too tired and hungry to care.

I took a beer from the icebox and went into the living room while Dixie clattered around in the kitchen. I spun the dial on the television, flipping back and forth through the financial news, *Shopping on Cable, Fitness with Finesse, Tarzan's Legacy*, a financial update, *Cartoon Express, The Vanishing Prairie*, reruns of *Bonanza*, another financial update, and a *National Geographic* special on bats.

I discovered that Argentina and Bolivia were defaulting on their loans, again, and Mexico was soon to join them. The mob was certainly up to date on international finance. I switched back to bats.

I found that bats eat lots of insects, drop valuable seeds, propagate the dwindling rain forests, and keep to themselves, packed tight and clinging to the walls of caves that are carpeted in bat shit, called guano. The guano is home to maggots, who feed on it. The bats eat the maggots if they're hungry and the weather's no good for flying. The maggots reciprocate by devouring bat babies that fall off their perch before they can fly or get fouled in the guano while foraging for food. You have to be a clever old bat to poke through guano without getting stuck in it.

There was definitely a lesson there for me.

It took Dixie thirty minutes to put a meal together that I couldn't have done in less than an hour. It was delicious, but my appetite wasn't robust. I picked at the food and worked on a bottle of beer while Dixie ate with gusto and told me more about herself.

Dixie was an Air Force brat, California-born, the youngest of three children. She was the only boy, "a mistake," she said, "something to keep my mother from going crazy when my father got transferred to the Philippines." Her father had been a master sergeant and the service was his life. Women were his hobby.

"My father did come back from the Philippines—once, in order to get a divorce." Dixie shrugged. Her sisters married right out of high school, leaving Dixie alone with her mother, who worked for a dress-maker in La Jolla who catered to rich old ladies. Lots of designer knockoff gowns for charity balls. Dixie went there every day after school and did her homework while the ladies came in for fittings.

"By the time I was eight years old I knew what I wanted to be," Dixie said. "I wanted to be just like them."

"A rich old lady?"

Dixie hemmed and hawed for a minute. "Well, not quite," she said rapturously. "They just seemed to know so much about men, how to get around them, how to manipulate them. They were so vivacious—and smart. *Nothing* fazed them. They led charmed lives and they knew it. They made the most of their femininity; they appealed to a man's fancy."

"That sounds like an expression Queen Victoria might have used. Two queens!" I laughed. I couldn't help it.

"*Cute*," Dixie replied sarcastically. "I mean, *appealed to their fantasy*. OK?"

The food had restored my vigor, making me feel feisty. I pursued the topic of a man's fantasy.

"Oh, Max!" Dixie blushed. "Men project their fantasies on women. The better a woman plays her role, the more power she commands. It's her meal ticket, tit for tat."

Well, I thought, that explains it all. Dixie shrugged and demurely lifted a spoonful of calamari to her mouth.

"When did you start . . ." I wasn't sure how to say it, but Dixie knew what I meant.

"Being a woman? Easy. I was so damn feminine my mother was relieved the first time she saw me dressed up in her clothes."

"God, how old were you?"

"Twelve. I had stopped going to her shop after school so I could go home and dress up. One day, I got all dressed up and just stayed like that until she came home. We had a long talk about it and agreed it would be our little secret. Afterward she started teaching me how to make my own clothes, boy's and girl's. By the time I was fourteen I was working in the shop every day after school. I thought I was Coco Chanel. I had my own designs, but they were a little far out for La Jolla, so I just basted and stitched, and stitched and basted until I was seventeen, then I hitchhiked up the coast one weekend to San Francisco. I had heard about the drag clubs up there and . . . well . . . the rest, as they say, darling, is history. I made my own costumes and worked up an act."

"When did you find out you were gay?"

Dixie looked insulted.

"I don't think I ever was," she replied evenly. "I don't like the word. I've always gotten along with gay men, but they were just a means to an end. It was easier being around them, that was all."

I told her I had heard about men who are heterosexual but have a fetish about wearing women's clothes. Was she in that category?

"If anything, I'm a lesbian." She grinned. "I love women. I see myself as a woman who happens to have a little something extra between her legs."

We both laughed, but the joke, I thought, might be at my expense. Had Dixie been having an affair with Denise?

"But you do go out with *men*," I said, clearing my throat and hoping for an affirmative answer. "Denise told me about your experiences in Paris and Berlin."

"Don't forget Amsterdam," Dixie said.

"But if those men weren't gay, how did you . . .?"

"They caught on." She shrugged.

"C'mon," I said. "How could they be straight?"

"Everybody's bisexual, Max. Most men are suckers for a pretty face. Glamour is its own reward."

"Hm-mm," I said, coming down hard on a piece of calamari. Never talk with food in your mouth, Darenow.

Dixie flashed a cover-girl smile and resumed eating.

I exercised a molar on a hunk of calamari and splashed beer in after it. The more I knew about Dixie, the less I understood. I had the same problems with women. I should have been more help to Denise on her project. I might have learned something.

Dixie insisted on washing the dishes again and said she then planned on going home. Rocco hadn't called so she felt free to leave.

"What's your relationship with Rocco?" I asked. "You two seem pretty tight."

"I'm his diva, Max. When I have good writers there's a line around the block waiting to get into The Crib. Rocco wants to put me on Broadway some day."

I looked askance and Dixie caught me.

"It's strictly professional, honey, if that's what you're thinking. Rocco is my security blanket."

We had coffee and talked some more. Dixie told me about some of the men she dated when she worked nightclubs in Paris and Berlin. German princes, captains of industry, politicians. It was interesting stuff, but predictable, and I found it embarrassing to have to listen to it anymore. There was an underlying sadness in Dixie's voice. These adventures were all one-night stands, usually at the expense of some poor sap too drunk or too dumb to know what he was getting into. Dixie was neither fish nor fowl. She might look like Ann-Margret, but she wasn't someone you brought home to mother or took to the office Christmas party.

I insisted on helping her clean up, which we did in relative silence. When we finished I went into the bathroom. When I came out Dixie was in the bedroom, in front of the mirror, engrossed in makeup chores. She finished her mascara, dipped her finger in a pot of gloss, put a shine on her lips, smacked them together, and winked at me.

"Why do women spend so much time before mirrors?" I asked.

She looked in the mirror again and thought about it while she fluffed her hair.

"Because a man only sees part of him when he looks in the mirror," she smiled. "A woman sees things whole. I mean, she sees her hair as part of her face."

"Are we talking cosmetology or cosmotology?" I laughed.

"Whatever you think best, darling," and she winked again.

We walked into the living room and she put her things away in her bag. I wanted to ask about the Tampax, but I couldn't bring myself to it.

"I need a break, Dixie," I said. "I have to figure some things out. Dinner was great. I mean it."

"Fine, Max," she replied. "Just don't forget what I told you. Take whatever help you can get, but don't try and go it alone. I'll be home all night, working on costumes. But I'm there to help. Just call."

I said I would.

Dixie smiled. A big, starry-eyed smile just brimming with self-satisfaction. Dixie was pleased with herself. What a wonderful feeling that must be.

She took her time gathering up her things, finally put on her coat, threw me a kiss, and left.

It had been a long day. I flopped down in my favorite easy chair and tried sorting it out.

I thought about the guns found at Manolo's house. Facsimile fingerprints from an FBI computer were probably spinning over a telephone wire right now. I wondered whether mine were among them. And what about the fabulously wealthy Watelys? What news would Lieutenant

Henry bring in the morning? What had *I* developed all day that could be used as the lead for a second-day story?

The phone rang at 2:30 A.M., jerking my heart into orbit. I had fallen asleep in the chair. I bolted awake, half expecting someone to be there. It was Terry Compton.

He had pulled the files of half a dozen of the New York victims. He didn't tell me anything I didn't already know, but I went through the motions of writing it down. It was police blotter stuff, arraignments, bail postings, and sentencings. Nothing to suggest who these people were working for.

He also had a file on Edgar Wately. There wasn't much in it. Edgar had been quite a sailor at one time. Compton scanned several headlines from the sports pages showing that Edgar had won a couple of sailboat races. There were also small items from the business pages, including several noting promotions for Edgar.

"I thought he owned the bank," I said.

"His family owns the bank," Compton corrected me. "The clips show that in the past year he was elected president, chief executive officer, *and* chairman of the board of directors. I seem to recall the financial editor here saying something about Edgar and his sister struggling to control the board. The bank is a holding company for a lot of other businesses."

"What's the sister's story?" I asked, trying to visualize a female Edgar.

"His sister, Ethel. The debutante I told you about," Compton replied lightly. "I guess you're still waking up, Darenow."

In more ways than one.

"But his *wife's* name is Ethel," I said uncertainly.

"Wife? Edgar's a bachelor. And Ethel never married . . . Oh, I get it." Compton chuckled. "Of course, she calls herself *Mrs.* Wately. It's just a southern affectation. Edgar Wately and Mrs. Ethel Wately—that's how the society columns refer to them."

I collapsed on the bed in amazement. Ethel was single-O! The Watelys were brother and sister! Edgar's attitude toward Ethel wasn't the begrudging tolerance of a husband for a domineering wife, it was a kid brother's envy of the sister who had it all.

Dixie was right. Glamour is its own reward.

13

Manhattan mornings are not made for late sleepers. The town is brick and steel, anchored in a slab of glacial granite that stretches from the Bronx to the Battery. A big tuning fork, muffled in asphalt. The racket starts with hundreds of tons of steel sliding against steel, screeching through tiled subway tunnels. It provokes a subterranean groan that reverberates upward through miles of cable, conduit, cast iron pipe, and the steel skeletons of skyscrapers. Scramble that with the whine of a few million cars, trucks, and diesel buses rumbling over a roadbed of Belgian granite paving stones, add the ear-piercing wail of ambulance, police, and fire sirens, the jarring rat-a-tat-tat-tat-tat of pneumatic air hammers, the grinding clatter of mechanized garbage trucks, the grating roar of jet engines, and the frantic tread of seven or eight million pairs of shoes on sidewalks, stairs, and hallways and you have some idea of Gotham's noise level.

The din starts around five-thirty A.M. when the trucks labor in from the suburbs and the buses and subways start running every fifteen minutes, then ten, then five. After a while you don't notice it unless you've just come from a place where the only sound is the wind in the pines and waves on the beach.

The clock said it was 6:15 when I opened my eyes to look. I knew I wasn't going to be able to get back to sleep so I got up and boiled water for coffee. I sat in the kitchen, drank it black, and browsed through a copy of *Vanity Fair* Dixie had left behind. The rich and famous seemed to have lots of fun, even when they were out on bail. It was forty-five minutes before I felt bold enough to face the shaving mirror.

I was dragging a dull blade over an aching jaw when the phone rang. It was Ethel Wately, early riser, former debutante, and still eligible beauty.

"I called your paper, Mr. Darenow. They said you were working at home. Am I disturbing you?" She asked with confidence, as if it were noon.

"Not at all," I said warily.

"I won't be a minute," she said, her tone growing warmer. "We buried Jaime yesterday. I've had some time to sit down and think. I want you to know how much I sympathize with your loss."

I stammered my thanks but couldn't think of anything else to say.

"I'm hosting a small gathering in New York, Mr. Darenow," she said cosily. "Saturday night. Will you come? Just some old, very dear friends. I think you'll find it interesting."

I was nonplussed. Beguiled might have been a better word. The old brain alarm was trilling, somewhere deep in my cranium, but I ignored it. Don't be a fool, Darenow, a voice in my head answered. You may never have another chance like this.

"I'd be glad to come," I sputtered.

"Good," she replied evenly. "Come around seven o'clock. I'm looking forward to seeing you there."

"Yes . . ." I said, still trying to form a gracious reply.

"Oh," she added brightly, "you may want to bring your notepad."

"My notepad?"

"You can never tell," she said amusingly. "Well, good-bye. See you then."

She placed the receiver very gently on its hook.

All right. Cocktails with Ethel Wately? Who in his right mind could refuse? But why the notebook? I was sorry the invitation carried a professional caveat.

So what? Ethel had to keep up appearances, didn't she? It made the razor feel good on an aching jaw. I imagined Ethel's soft, bejeweled hand stroking my cheek and approached the rest of the morning with a spring in my step and a promise to myself to get a haircut soon.

I dressed hurriedly—brown corduroy slacks, tweed jacket, and green parka—perfect for a day in the *Graphic*'s library. Find out what's been written about drugs in the last six months before launching my own series. A little reprise to remind the *Graphic*'s readers that Darenow was dishing new stuff. Breakfast? I'd grab a bite on the way. Ah, and don't forget to call the politicians! I paused to write that down. Must call Owen Reed and a couple of congressmen. That would be worth a couple of inches of type.

Was that the phone?

It was Detective Lieutenant Henry. Could I come down to headquarters? Look over Denise's things? Why not, it's on my way. That's the attitude, Darenow, keep going and forget the tolling bells.

But the bell tolled all the same, and I knew it tolled for me. I didn't want to go to headquarters and have to identify the things that were in Denise's possession when she died. That was painful enough, but it wasn't the only reason I was having second thoughts. I was a material witness; I had left the scene of a crime; I was withholding evidence.

Give it up, Darenow. Denise is dead. She was brilliant and beautiful; you loved her, you screwed up, she died. *C'est la vie*. One thing has nothing to do with the other.

Or does it? Did Denise die because I wasn't there to save her?

Forget it. Go to headquarters. Face the music. Think of Ethel Wately.

The camera was Denise's, so were the bag, the notebooks, the watch, and the ring.

My formal identification took five minutes. That was it. Henry slipped the items back into an evidence bag and put it in his locker.

It's amazing how quickly the important moments in life pass, so fast you could almost miss them. Here were the last things Denise had touched before she died, shut in a metal police locker before I had time to feel anything about why I was here looking at them.

"How about coffee, Mr. Darenow?" Henry asked.

In a Greek luncheonette on Fulton Street, I ordered breakfast while he worked on a danish and coffee, filling me in on the last twenty-four hours.

A plainclothes unit had picked up a drag queen on a prostitution charge who admitted knowing both Esmeralda and Jaime Santiago. Upon further questioning and a promise that the arresting officer wouldn't show up in court if the answers were the right ones, she, or he, led police to a brownstone in the West Nineties where said suspect had once spent the night in the company of Jaime Santiago. The apartment was a two-bedroom job on the ground floor. The police found his personal belongings there, as well as a wardrobe full of women's clothes in the second bedroom. Neighbors on the block identified him from police photographs taken of his body. A flashy blond answering Esmeralda's description was said to be a frequent visitor, or, perhaps, a roommate.

"We may just have missed her," Henry said. "And if we're correct, Esmeralda ain't a blonde anymore. We found two empty boxes of Clairol. Dark brown. There were fresh stains in the sink where she did the dye job. It was slopped around, like she was in a big hurry."

I asked him what hope we had of finding her.

He assured me Esmeralda's description was in the FBI computer.

"There's more," he continued. "A sector car from the Sixth Precinct was working Avenue A the night of the murders, they noted a suspicious auto in the area, cruising the block near the crime scene. They ran a stolen vehicle check on it and found it was registered to Mr. Ralph Torres of Union City, Bennie's brother. Only thing is, the Union City cops can't find it. They have, however, supplied us with some other intelligence on the Torres brothers that's very intriguing."

That was putting it mildly, so far as I was concerned. I shut up and put some jam on my toast.

According to someone Henry described as a reliable source in the Union City police department, Bennie and Ralph Torres had been accumulating real estate since they arrived in town a year ago.

"It's funny," he said. "The Tampa cops say the Torres brothers are small-time operators, but they aren't very popular with the local criminals.

"On the other hand," Henry said, "the Union City cops seem to think the Torres brothers are big deals. They own property there and a couple of businesses—an auto body shop, a trucking company and a bar."

"It just seems strange that two punks from Tampa suddenly turn into Jersey entrepreneurs," he mused.

What was the name Manolo mentioned? Melendez? Bennie's address book was burning a hole in my mind. I should have left it for the cops to find.

"I heard last night that the Torres brothers own the Toucan Too, that big disco in the West Fifties," I said, not making eye contact. I smoothed more jam on my last piece of toast.

"Is that so?" Henry said. "Who told you that?"

Now what, slick? "I went uptown the other night," I said, laying down the knife. "To check out a drag bar where Dix—I mean . . . Denise

. . . took me." I took a deep breath. "One of the local drag queens told me she thought the Torres brothers were fronting for someone else. She suggested that the 'someone else' may be Esmeralda's boyfriend."

I felt moisture collecting in the small of my back. I jammed my mouth with bread and jam and thought again of the Melendez guy and Rocco and Manolo and all the other things I was concealing.

"Who's your source?" Henry inquired dryly.

"I forgot," I said, breaking into an involuntary grin. Who could forget Carmen and Tallulah?

"You're slipping," he said evenly.

"Well," I began, "sources are sources." Let him make the next move, I thought.

Henry smiled. "I can dig it," he said. "We all have to protect our sources. But maybe, considering your girlfriend and all, journalistic ethics might be waived, strictly in the interests of pursuing what might be a investigative lead. Off the record."

"Right," I said a little too quickly. "Let me think on that. This is new to me, lieutenant."

Henry said nothing, but his eyebrows twitched in admonition.

Then Henry had a request. He wanted me to print a description of Ralph Torres's car. The description roughly matched the car I'd seen outside Manolo's window—1987 Chevrolet Impala, canary yellow, Jersey plates U-9687.

I said I'd take care of it. Henry said he might have more information later in the day. He was expecting some lab reports from Manolo's apartment, and all I could hope was that the lab boys had been real careless.

14

I was a very nervous man. The overheated newsroom provided no comfort. The damp, grey chill of winter clung to my shoulders and gnawed at my bones. Maybe I was catching the flu. I kept a scarf wrapped tightly around my neck as I went through the motions of being a reporter. Someone had provided copies of past issues of newspapers and magazines with stories about the drug menace. I stuffed them in a large envelope and promised I'd read them all at home.

I called Owen Reed, and much to my surprise, he took the call, apologized for not calling me back, and offered his condolences.

But from there on it was straight party line. He touched on the complex international problems raised by the drug trade blah-blah, the difficulty of coordinating the various law enforcement agencies blah-blah, the government's concern over lost tax revenues blah-blah, and the role of banks in laundering drug money blah-blah-blah.

These topics were being "juggled" by the task force, he said in response to one question, adding sonorously that "matters of such scope" took time to develop. I let him ramble. It wasn't much, but it would be enough to keep Hurley off my back for a couple more days.

I went back to work on the story. I was actually enjoying being back in harness—so long as I didn't have to tell anyone more than 2 percent of what I knew—when the desk shunted a call to my line.

Rocco. He had "a friend" who had to talk to me. Could I meet them for lunch? Right away?

"I can vouch for the guy," Rocco said in response to my silence. "He's at the top." He turned the phone over to another voice.

This was glasnost, Italian-style.

"How ya' doin'? Everything copasetic?" the voice asked.

I figured it was Uncle Tony Beef. He had a baritone voice like grated cheese, softened in olive oil and lightly, very lightly, warmed over a low flame.

I told him I had just gotten off the phone with the assistant attorney general in charge of the government task force on drug trafficking. I wanted to let him know I had friends too.

"So wadde say?" He was referring to Owen Reed.

"A lot of horseshit," I said.

"All right," he said. "You're learnin' somethin', right? All these guys are interested in makin' names for themselves, that's all. I know this guy Reed. He'd love to indict a bunch of paisanos."

"Yeh," I said, feeling those icy fingers on my spine. "Let me talk to Rocco."

Then Rocco was back, assuring me everything was copasetic and I had everything to gain by joining him and his friend for lunch at a very Waspy new seafood restaurant three blocks from the Graphic.

"It's a little fancy so wear a jacket," Rocco added nonchalantly.

I left the name of the restaurant with the day editor, just in case. After all, I had nothing to hide, right?

Rocco and his friend were seated when I arrived. The maître d' scraped and bowed, called me Mr. Darenow, loud enough to draw curious looks from a table of bond traders, and led me proudly to the best table in the house.

I knew immediately who the man with the big smile sitting next to Rocco was. Everybody else in the room knew him, too. It was Charles Baldasano, *capo di tutti capi*, known as The Big Guy, or simply, Charlie B, the man trying to unite the remaining Mafia families. He was a good-looking man, about fifty-five, with a Roman nose and a Florentine forehead, set off by a head of luxurious gray, wavy hair. His eyes were old and searching, like a man always waiting for the unexpected to happen. He dressed like a conservative, well-to-do suburban business-man—blue suit, matching tie and pocket square, white shirt. He was wearing light cologne.

Charlie B rose, bowed, and extended his hand. I grinned stupidly and shook it despite a few stares from Wall Street's establishment.

Rocco beamed proudly and asked me what I wanted to drink. I ordered a Campari and soda, no ice. Viva l'Italia.

Charlie didn't rush his words and he had manners, too.

He started out by thanking me for "taking care of" Bennie Torres, although he never mentioned him by name. He was implying that I had killed him myself. I mumbled that I had done nothing except stay out of the line of fire, but he acted as if I was just being modest.

"You survived." He winked. "That's what we're all trying to do."

He ordered duck à l'orange, sautéed asparagus, and fries. Rocco ordered steak and I don't know why, but I opted for the frog's legs, maybe because I hardly ever ate them at home.

The issue of why I was there was not discussed until the coffee arrived and most of the other diners had returned to their counting houses.

At first, I wasn't all that impressed with The Big Guy's arguments. They sounded as if Rocco had sold him a bill of goods. But I liked the way he used his eyes and his hands to communicate. His eyes shifted like semaphore flags and he fingered his spoon, traced the outline of a cup handle or smoothed the tablecloth as he formed careful sentences in his warm baritone.

"The government can't cope," he said. "Too many people wanna get high. But politicians have to get reelected, so if they can't solve the real problem, they make one up. The feds are after Italian-Americans because, frankly, a lot of Italian-Americans have fucked up, pardon my English, by selling heroin. But the real reason is that the government is trying to save Latin America from the communists and they're doin' it the wrong way."

I shrugged noncommittally and ordered an espresso with Sambucca.

Charlie said the time had come to "settle this among the right people." Charlie would broker the peace talks.

"The Spanish don't want war," he said. "I'm talking to the right guy. Man who can make decisions. You can't print this, but you have my word on it. No more killing, no more drugs—at least from this guy's operation."

"Who is he?" Out of deference to Rocco, I didn't mention Melendez's name.

He chuckled to himself.

"He's the right guy. He's legit. He doesn't want his people involved in this any more than I do."

"So you've arranged a truce, but I can't print this. Why am I here?"

Charlie cleared his throat, carefully folded his hands in front of him, and looked at me, broodingly.

"This guy, or one of his guys, wants to meet you."

"*Me?* What for?" I sputtered.

"He wants to make sure you're who you are. He wants to tell you a few things about how your girlfriend died. Besides, you'll notarize the deal." He paused and scanned the room. We were the last diners. Charlie was looking for the right words.

"He wants you to be like a referee, see, a diplomatic overseer."

"He doesn't trust *you?*" I squeaked.

"Something like that," Charlie said, his eyes betraying affirmation. It hurt and amused him to think he couldn't be trusted.

"Where would I meet him?" I asked.

"Rocco will let you know," he answered, catching the maître d's attention. His voice dropped. "The thing is, it could be soon and you gotta be ready to go when Rocco calls. Can you do it?"

I waited until the maître d' went to fetch the check before asking The Big Guy why I should be sticking my neck out for him. "I thought you wanted to settle a score," he said, wagging his head in disbelief. "The people who murdered your girlfriend are the same ones slandering the Italians, the same ones bringing bad drugs to this country, the same ones lying to the government every day." He seemed baffled. "You know anything about Italian politics?" he asked in exasperation.

"No sir," I replied.

"They got communist parties all over the place, OK, but guess what—they're still America's greatest friend, right? NATO all the way. They're not Russian commies, they're *Roman* commies."

"I don't get the connection," I admitted.

"We're all Latins," he said impatiently. "Treat the Spanish right and they won't need Russian communism. SPQR, you know what that stands for?"

"The Roman senate," I said. " '*Senatus populus quorum romanus*,' I believe. The senate and people of Rome."

"And *vox populi*, you know what that means? It means the people and the senate are one voice," he said. "It means you gotta listen to what the people are saying."

"You have to establish democracy first," I replied.

He glanced at Rocco and then gave me a very cool look.

"You think the guys who eat lunch here want a democracy?" He said it with carefully measured contempt. "They want what *they* want. They don't think ordinary guys have the brains to decide the big issues, see?

"Look," he continued, more benevolently. "You got some problems. I can solve them. Trust me."

He handed the check to the maître d' without looking at it, along with a Diners Club card.

Charlie grinned broadly and patted his waistline. "You want a ride back to the office or you want to walk?"

I wanted to walk.

I returned to the office, switched to autopilot, and went back to putting a story together. It was a rich broth. The mayor, who blamed the drug problem on the feds, suggested the military get involved. "Interdict the borders," was the phrase he used.

The police commissioner's office, upon the request of our police reporter, issued a statement exclusive to the *Graphic*. He needed more men, more money, and stricter laws, he declared. The commissioner's public relations staff understood the need for a more forceful declaration, and hinted something would be forthcoming.

I wove it all into a compact three pages and made notes outlining a reprise for the weekend edition.

It was going on five when I finished cleaning up my desk. I was halfway out the door when a copy girl grabbed me to tell me I had a phone call. Charlie B.

"Chances are we're gonna meet tonight. Be home at seven. I'll call you one way or the other."

"Listen," I was about to say.

Charlie B hung up lightly. He had said what he had to say.

At seven o'clock I was at home watching a rented movie, a spy thriller with Michael Caine and a competent company of English actors who were precisely cast, a welcome relief from the plastic assholes who normally cluttered the TV screen. I hadn't been watching the clock but I wasn't surprised when the phone rang at precisely seven.

Charlie began by telling me he liked my story. He said he thought I was a very good writer and ought to be thinking about Hollywood.

Why do these guys always think Hollywood is the living end? That's when I heard the knock on the door.

"Excuse me," I said. "Somebody's at the door."

"Answer it."

"Do you want me to call you back?"

"Answer it," he repeated. It was a command. I put down the phone and started for the door.

My heart beat a crazy rhythm that stopped me in my tracks. Men with guns. Mob guys.

"Who's there?" I shouted, the phone still in my hand.

"It's Dixie."

I opened the door.

It was Dixie, all right. Dixie and two gentlemen. Dixie smiled and put her finger to her lips.

"It's OK. Friends." She was whispering. "We have to come in." She made a face like "don't blame me."

I stepped aside and let them in.

"I'm on the phone . . ."

The two gents nodded and stepped inside. I closed the door. Dixie's eyes lit up when she saw the phone off the hook.

"The Big Guy?" She was whispering again, all smiles.

I nodded.

She waved her arm toward the phone. "Go ahead," she said.

I stared at her like a lamb about to be slaughtered.

"Be nice to him," she whispered. "He's terrific."

I picked up the phone.

"Everything OK?" Charlie inquired.

"I hope so, I . . ."

"They're friends. They're going to stay with you for a while. For your own protection. And ours. The meeting is on but we're not sure when the guy's plane arrives."

"Wait a second," I said. Charlie must not have heard.

"Tell the guy in the red jacket I want to talk to him," he said.

I turned and offered the phone to a man who was wearing a red down jacket. Why not?

The man in the red jacket took the phone and said hello. He nodded. He said "yeh" and "OK" a couple of times. Then he hung up and took off his coat.

"I'm Number One," he said, offering his hand. "And this," he said, referring to his partner, "is Number Two. That's easy to remember, right?"

I shook his hand. I shook his partner's hand. I was still speechless.

Dixie stepped right in, the perfect hostess.

"These guys haven't eaten, so I'm going shopping. They are perfect darlings, so don't worry about a thing."

"You expecting any company?" asked Number One.

"No," I said. "Not that I know of."

"Good. So relax. Mind if we sit down?"

"No. Go ahead."

Number One asked what I had been watching. In fact, he asked if he could rewind the tape and watch it from the beginning.

Dixie clasped her hands together and looked pleased. She was wearing jeans, her fur parka, and a pair of red high-heeled cowgirl boots with fringe. Her hair was long again, worn down so it fell around her shoulders. She was amazing. The short hair the other night must have been a wig. Or was this the wig? No, it was real.

"You're in good hands," she said. She patted me on the back and went off to do her shopping.

Number One took off his jacket and looked around for someplace to put it. I offered to hang it in the closet. He was of average height and build, mid-thirties, with dark wavy hair and an intelligent face. He wore a navy blue cotton turtleneck, a pair of tan gabardine slacks with a sharp crease, and polished brown shoes.

Number Two was older, forty, maybe forty-five, shorter, and stubbier. His dark hair was flecked with gray and his hairline was receding. He wore a gray suit that needed pressing, and a gray buttoned cardigan under that. His black shoes needed polish. He carried a black raincoat rolled up and tucked under his arm, and when he sat down on the couch he stashed the raincoat next to him, jamming it half under a cushion. I wondered what caliber it was.

We were all being very careful. I asked them if they wanted a cup of coffee before I went back to work. The shorter one, Number Two, said they'd just had some, and then looked at Number One to make sure he'd said the right thing.

I started into the kitchen. Number One nodded to Number Two, who got up to accompany me.

I put some instant in a cup.

"You date her?" he asked. I knew he meant Dixie.

I was about to say no when Number One's voice came in from the living room. "Tell him to mind his own business," he said, and then he was standing in the kitchen doorway.

"You got a nice place here," said Number One. "You read all those books?"

"Most of them," I answered.

"I like Elmore Leonard," he said. "You got some of his I never saw."

"Help yourself," I offered.

"Naw," he said, and drifted back inside.

"Ya' know," said Number Two, "I wasn't making fun. That Dixie is better looking than a lot of dames. Hey, there's nothing wrong with it. You turn the lights out, who knows what it is."

"Dixie was a friend of my *girlfriend*. My girlfriend is dead."

"The photographer, right. I'm sorry to hear that. I get confused over who's who."

The water boiled and I took the coffee inside. Number One was browsing the bookshelves. Number Two wedged himself back into the corner of the couch.

I said I was working on a story and went into my bedroom to stare at the cobweb. The spider saw me looking and froze. He was a small spider, not much bigger than a matchhead. We remained still for a long time, until he got bored and went back to his weaving. I wondered what he did for meals. Flies were out of season and he wasn't big enough for roaches.

Dixie came back from the store with two packages of groceries. Supper was a choice of ham, cheese, or cappicola sandwiches, rye or Italian bread, mustard or mayonnaise, lettuce or tomato or both. Beverages were Amstel Light or San Pellegrino.

Number One had ham and cheese on rye with mustard. He drank mineral water. Number Two had a beer and a cappicola hero with the works. I had the same as Number One. Dixie served us and went back to the kitchen to make herself a cheese omelet.

Hurley called about eight-thirty with a question on my story. I took the call in the living room. Hurley wanted to know why I hadn't asked Owen Reed for a comment on the mayor's idea for "interdicting the borders." I said the mayor's quote came too late in the day for me to follow it up with the feds. Actually, I had no idea when the mayor's quote had come in. It was in my mailbox when I came back from lunch with Charlie and Rocco.

"They phoned that quote in at three," he said. "You had plenty of time."

I told him I hadn't been feeling well and had to leave early. I told him the doctor thought I might be having a relapse. "It happens with pneumonia," I said.

Hurley wasn't pleased.

I put the phone down and shrugged my shoulders. Six eyes quickly avoided mine. Everybody was being very cool. Shifty-eyed but cool.

Bzzz! I stiffened. Doorbell! My first thought was that maybe the peace talks were going to be held in my living room.

"It's Rocco," Dixie calmly announced, getting up to open the door. She looked at me and smiled apologetically. I caught Numbers One and Two exchanging wary glances, but Number One cut the exchange short with a frown and a confident shake of his head, as if to put the other man at ease.

Rocco came in, looking serious and in a hurry. He nodded curtly to Dixie, waved in my direction, and proceeded to shake hands with the two men, who had gotten up to greet him. Rocco poked a finger at Number One.

"I gotta talk to you," he said, jerking his head toward the kitchen.

Number One nodded and stepped aside as Rocco came over to shake my hand.

"I have to talk to these guys first, then I'll fill you in," he said.

I didn't seem to have a choice. I was the prisoner, the house scribe.

Rocco took Dixie and Number One into the kitchen for about ten minutes. I remained in the living room, watching television but not having a clue to what was going on in either place. Number Two and I exchanged glances from time to time to time but the old magic was gone. He was content to sit, hands folded in his lap.

Dixie returned to the living room and sent Number Two into the kitchen, where he remained with Rocco and Number One for another ten minutes.

Dixie stood in the bedroom doorway and apologized for the "secrecy" but implied that everything would become clear after I talked to Rocco. She had put tiny pearls in her ears and had freshened up her makeup.

"Stop looking at me like that," she said. "Everything's going to be fine."

"I'm trying to be nice, Dixie. But it looks like I'm a prisoner in my own house."

She frowned.

"I'm expecting a call from Esmeralda. Last night I made contact through one of the queens at the Toucan Too. Esmeralda wants to talk to you. I gave your number to my answering service. They'll forward the call here. We might have to go and pick her up, so you have to be ready to go if she calls."

"Aw, Dixie," I groaned. "Don't say that."

"I already have," she replied flippantly.

The whole thing was preposterous. I didn't want to *meet* Esmeralda.

She was a material witness. She belonged to the cops. I would be interfering with an investigation. I felt dizzy. I sat down.

"Listen, Max," Dixie said sternly. "We're on to something big. Esmeralda's *boyfriend* is who The Big Guy wants. We think he might have tried to kill her. He has a lot of clout—*a lot of clout*. They'll pin Denise's murder on Esmeralda and make her disappear before she ever gets near a jury. She trusts me, and she thinks you can help her out. She's the key to this whole operation, Max, and she wants to talk to you."

I frowned and shook my head.

"Dixie, this is a job for the police. I'm not interested. What's The Big Guy trying to do, take justice into his own hands?"

"The Big Guy trusts you, Max," she said. "He likes you."

"What's his game, Dixie? That's what I want to know."

Dixie avoided the question. "There's more to it than Denise, Max. She got close to somebody and her death opened a lot of doors. Rocco says the feds are running scared. There's a scandal brewing, Max, and you're going to be right on top of it."

"You're right on top of it, Dixie, aren't you?" I sneered. "Why not tell me what *you* know. You want to be my friend? Start being honest with me."

Rocco came in from the kitchen. Dixie stepped lightly aside and addressed him.

"Rocco will tell you," she said coyly. "Max is worried, Rocco. I think you owe him an explanation. He deserves one." Nice speech, I thought.

Rocco glared at her, frowned, and jerked his head toward the kitchen. "When I need your advice, I'll ask for it," he said. "Take a powder."

Rocco beckoned me into the bedroom. He took a seat on the edge of the bed, lit a cigarette, and offered me one. I took it and found an ashtray.

"Look, we can catch some big fish here," Rocco began. He wanted to say more but he was watching his words.

"I'm not cooperating unless I get the big picture," I said impatiently. "You're holding out on me, Rocco."

Rocco puffed on his cigarette and considered his reply.

"Look, Max, Charlie, the Big Guy, is more than just a boss. He's family to me, and I owe him. As soon as he heard Bennie Torres was running around bragging about working for Hector Melendez he got real interested. Bennie Torres was a liar; he never worked for Melendez. Shit, Melendez wouldn't let Bennie wipe his shoes."

"So why is it necessary for me to meet Melendez?" I asked uncertainly. "I'd rather not get involved."

"The Big Guy has something up his sleeve," Rocco said, shaking his head in exasperation. "Be patient. When it happens, Charlie will get the credit. It'll square him with the cops, see? He's like a diplomat, a peacemaker."

"I don't like it," I replied uneasily. "What if Bennie wasn't lying? What if he did work for Melendez? If he did, Melendez would love to see me dead. It looks like I killed Bennie, for God's sake. Can you now understand my reluctance?"

Rocco frowned and shook his head.

"You're safe with me and The Big Guy," he said reassuringly. "I wish I could tell you more right now, but we can't have any leaks, see, otherwise, the big fish will swim away."

Dixie sidled into the bedroom doorway again. I was tired of her vamping.

"What do you have to say for yourself?" I snapped.

"Let's make believe we're Nick and Nora Charles," she said airily.

"Rocco," I turned and said angrily. "You owe me a better explanation than what I'm getting."

"You have a phone call," Dixie told Rocco, ignoring me completely.

Rocco breezed straight past me.

Dixie shrugged, eyed the cobweb on my ceiling, mimed one of Myrna Loy's most insouciant looks, and drifted casually back into the living room, where she resumed buffing her nails.

I was spider food.

15

I slammed the door. I didn't need these people, I thought, pacing. I needed reliable information. I needed someone who could give me a line on Hector Melendez. The Sunshine State was heavy on my mind. I sulked for a few minutes, then mustered the courage to enter the living room and announce that I needed to use my phone.

No one objected so I took it into the bedroom, leaving the door ajar, and dialed my Tampa source, Terry Compton. His line was busy. Why not call Edgar Wately?

I couldn't find Wately's business card so I called Tampa information. I was given a listing for an E. J. Wately. I dialed and got an answering service. I left a message asking him to call me. I was clutching at straws. Edgar Wately, prominent banker and socialite, wasn't interested in helping me, or seeing his name in the tabloids.

I lay down on the bed and stared at the ceiling. Rocco came in and asked to use the phone again. I said sure, why not. He took it back into the living room, carefully closing my door.

The Big Guy's interest continued to nag me. All I had to go on was mutual trust. His motives seemed pure, so far as his wish to bring Denise's killers to justice and help me find Esmeralda and her boyfriend. But there was a lot more than that going on.

It was all part of The Big Guy's master plan. He was helping me nab Denise's killer in order to curry favor with the cops, while he negotiated a separate peace with Hector Melendez to settle their turf war. Charlie as Henry Kissinger.

Don't dwell on it, I told myself. The Big Guy keeps his word.

I was fretting away in my cell when I heard the phone ring. It was Terry Compton. I took the phone into the bedroom and left the door slightly ajar, to dissuade eavesdroppers but keep an ear peeled at the same time. Number One glanced peevishly at Rocco as the door closed. Screw him, I thought, it's my phone.

Compton had boffo stuff, most of it not suited for the story I wanted to write, but boffo stuff all the same. His meeting with the society editor yielded yards of fresh dirt on Jaime Santiago and the Wately family, as well as more details on the Torres brothers. What bothered me was the dish on Hector Melendez. Compton had established a possible link between him and the Watelys.

Compton was not at all eager to peddle scandal. But the society editor, a "Miss" Vicky Forrestal, had presented it to him, unwashed but neatly folded. Miss Vicky was in her sixties and was particularly well informed on the history of the Wately family.

The father, Avery, the suicide, had squandered his fortune on Kentucky Derby entries and died tangled in debt and estranged from his wife, Sissy, mother of Ethel and Edgar. The debts involved money Avery had borrowed from Italian gangsters to cover gambling losses. There were further entanglements. Avery Wately's bank had been the conduit for monies used by the CIA to finance the Bay of Pigs invasion of Cuba.

Sissy (née Simpson) was the only child of the president of Simpson Steel, a major defense contractor during and after World War Two. She died of a broken heart two years after her husband's suicide, leaving Ethel and Edgar a big but complicated fortune.

Edgar, their youngest, graduated from the Wharton School with a degree in finance the year before the old man kicked off, and settled in as heir to the throne with the rank of assistant teller. Edgar was a hard charger. He made a couple of bold moves right after his mother's death and took the reins at the Suburban Bank, the holding company for the combined fortunes of the Watelys and the Simpsons. It took Edgar ten years, and a lot of corporate in-fighting, before he settled his father's debts and put the bank, and the rest of the family holdings, on an even keel.

"Edgar got control of the holdings of both families by casting his lot with the Latin community in Tampa, rather than working out a deal with the local aristocrats, who sided with his sister," Compton explained.

"Edgar outfoxed his sister and, apparently, outfoxed the Italian gangsters who had claims on his father's estate."

I was scribbling a mile a minute and not keeping up.

"Did you ever hear of Santo Trafficante?" Compton asked.

I had. I was glad Number One couldn't hear the conversation. Santo Trafficante and Meyer Lansky ran Miami Beach and Havana for the Mafia during the 1940s, '50s, and '60s. Santo, now deceased, was the mob's Tampa connection and was rumored to have been instrumental in the CIA's plot to assassinate Castro.

Now came the parts that were to launch Darenow into orbits of conjecture.

"According to Miss Vicky," Compton began, "a lot of the Trafficante mob's money was tied up in the Wately bank when Edgar took it over."

I whistled a long, low whistle and cast my eye toward the door.

"That's not all," Compton added, lowering his voice in response. "You asked about a man named Melendez. A guy named Hector Melendez worked for Santo Trafficante years ago. He supposedly ran the brothels in Havana and came to Tampa when Castro took over. He was a leader of the Bay of Pigs and is now a respectable businessman, probably one of the most powerful Cubans in South Florida. He owns a cement plant, a fleet of trucks, a Buick dealership, a few citrus groves, real estate, franchises on a dozen fried chicken outlets along the Alligator Highway . . . Let's see . . . chairman of the Trans-Caribe Shipping Lines . . . director of the Cuban Freedom Foundation . . . Here's a picture of him and two senators cutting the ribbon on a hundred-million-dollar retirement village."

Compton was a gold mine.

"Copy that stuff and send it air express, OK?"

"Sure," he replied amiably. "I'm also sending copies of stuff from the files on those Torres brothers. Highlights of their criminal career, such as it was."

"Do you think the Torres brothers could have worked for this Melendez character?" I asked.

"I highly doubt it," he said. "Melendez wouldn't associate with people like them. Miss Vicky took *great* pains to point out that Melendez is now a solid citizen, super patriot," he continued carefully. "She mentioned his name only because Avery Wately owed the Trafficante mob a lot of favors, and Melendez was once connected with Trafficante. But Darenow, Miss Vicky says Melendez is untouchable." There was a sigh.

"You have to understand Tampa," he continued. "Years ago, when the mob ran the rackets here, some members of the social register were their best customers. But when Castro took over in Cuba, it was like the Bank of Cuba had suddenly moved to the mainland. It was a new ball game. Some of that Cuban money undoubtedly helped Wately gain control of his father's bank."

"I need to know if they're still connected," I said, whispering now. I was on a fast track, heading for a tunnel with no lights. Reason and logic were flashing by in a blur.

"According to Miss Vicky, Melendez is on the bank's board," Compton replied. "She finds the connection intriguing, in light of the death of Wately's stepbrother."

My ears tintinnabulated.

"Wately's stepbrother?"

"Jaime Santiago," Compton drawled, as if I should know. "Miss Vicky's full of stuff like that. She says it was the scandal of the year. Miss Vicky says Avery had been shacking up with one of the maids and everyone knew it but Sissy. That's why Ethel Wately adopted Mr. Santiago. He's kin."

Kin! He's Ethel's half-brother! My heart was pumping overtime. The *mob* was in my living room, on the other side of a thin door. And Jaime Santiago was a rich kid *by birth*. I wondered how much my guests knew about this. My mouth couldn't keep up with the things going through my mind.

"Darenow, you still there?"

"I was thinking of something else," I stammered. I was thinking of Ethel Wately.

"There's more," Compton continued. "Miss Vicky says she's heard that Wately's bank may be involved in a federal probe."

Why the hell was he saving the lead until last?

"I'm going to talk to the federal attorney down here tomorrow," Compton said hesitatingly, "but I wouldn't be surprised if it's more than rumor. There's been lots of talk about Tampa banks laundering drug money since the heat's been on in Miami."

I scribbled a reminder to myself: *Call Reed re Tampa probe.*

"You're doing great," I said.

"Think twice before slandering the Watelys or Hector Melendez," Compton said finally. "Most of what I told you is hearsay about things that happened twenty years ago, soaked in Miss Vicky's gin martinis."

* * *

I took a blue pencil from a drawer and idly traced circles around the names I'd already circled. The Melendez name predominated.

Lots of theories clicked into position. My brain was a pinball game with a shifting layout, and the name of the game was paranoia.

Melendez consents to a meeting with The Big Guy because he's a link to the Italian mob that kept Havana and Tampa safe for sex and good times in its heyday. Fine, but what if Melendez isn't loyal? What if he's a double-dealing sharpie luring the mob into a trap? What if he's seeking revenge on the Watelys and all the other gringos who've been blowing smoke up the ass of the counterrevolution for two decades?

What if the act of revenge was the murder of Jaime Santiago? And what if Melendez hired two greedy bozos like Bennie and Ralph Torres to do the job so he'd have scapegoats to turn over to the police?

I sucked wind and tucked my notes carefully under the mattress, right next to Bennie Torres's address book.

On the other hand, I thought, The Big Guy trusts Melendez, who from all accounts isn't the type to employ certified deadbeats like the Torres brothers. If not Melendez, then who was bankrolling the Torres boys?

I closed my eyes and squeezed them hard, trying to distill answers from the questions that roiled inside.

Fifteen minutes went by. It was 9:15. Another five hung in silence before I coughed loudly and went into the living room. I asked Rocco for a cigarette. I took it into the kitchen and made myself a cup of coffee. No one stirred. I sat in the kitchen, drank coffee, and smoked until the phone rang again. I was up and there in a flash, but Rocco had already grabbed it. The caller was Lieutenant Henry.

Rocco heard the name and handed the phone to me with a questioning look.

I told Henry I was busy with some friends of Denise's. I told him we were making funeral arrangements. I didn't say whose funeral.

Henry said Ralph Torres's body had been found in the trunk of his own car, which had been left in the parking lot across from LEGAL headquarters, the federal building where the task force had offices. Ralphie had been tortured and beaten to death. Cigarette burns, every finger broken. Somebody had apparently tried to make him sing before he died, and left his body where the feds couldn't miss it. It had all the earmarks of a Mafia hit, and I doubted Ralph Torres had killed himself and blamed it on the Mafia.

Another long, low whistle cleared my larynx. It was going to be a night for long, low whistles.

"So *somebody else* is involved," I said, meaning, certainly not me.

"Sure looks that way," Henry purred. "And they're sending a message to the feds, too. Wish I knew what the message was."

So did I. I wondered what Charlie B had in mind.

"I hope we can find that blond sex-change," Henry said.

"Yeh," I replied distractedly.

"Keep looking, Max, but don't take chances. After what happened to Ralph Torres, I think her life span is gonna be considerably reduced."

"What makes you say that?"

"We found out she knew Bennie and Ralph Torres quite well," he said. "And so did the Santiago youth. What it means I'm not quite sure, but we've also picked up some street gossip that could be useful, if it's not a fairy tale."

I glanced over my shoulder. Dixie was buried in a magazine but Number One and Rocco were all ears.

"Something I should know?"

"Why not? We're on the same team, aren't we? Some snitch told the Union City cops that Bennie and Ralph Torres fucked up a major deal and were marked men. Whether that was the deal over the coke on Avenue A or something else, we don't know."

I nodded my head and sighed. Same team?

"You contact anyone on the task force yet?" Henry asked. Jesus, I thought. If he ever knew who was parked in my living room.

I filled him in on my conversation with Owen Reed. Henry snorted in derision a couple of times as I repeated the party line.

"Man," Henry sighed, "I'd sure like to know what those guys are up to. They're not telling us a goddamn thing but they want us to tell them everything. Any little crumb you pick up, babe, I'd be grateful."

"The funeral arrangements ought to be over soon," I croaked. "I'll have more time then."

Henry parted with another tidbit, a random fact and a man's name I never bothered to write down, until it surfaced again, and I had no problem recalling it. The Toucan Too's liquor license was registered to a holding company headed by a lawyer named Oscar Herrera. Herrera gave a Tampa address. The Florida police were checking him out. Oscar Herrera of Tampa, Florida.

"Well, take care of yourself," Henry said. I wondered what he meant by that.

"Who was that?" Number One barked before I had replaced the receiver.

I told him. I also told him that Ralph Torres's body had been found in the federal parking lot.

Dixie glanced up quickly and went back to reading just as fast. Rocco sniffled. Maybe he was catching cold. Number One gave me a deadpan look.

"What else did he say?" Number One asked.

I told him that Ralph Torres had been tortured and there was obviously some meaning to the fact he'd been dumped in the task force's front yard. I felt out of place in my own living room.

Rocco drifted over to the bookcase and fingered a volume. Dixie cleared her throat.

"*The meaning*," Number One said pointedly, "is that Ralphie Torres was garbage. He worked for those clowns. Let them bury him."

"How do *you* know that?" I replied, just as pointedly.

"He don't know," Rocco said heatedly, turning abruptly from the shelves. "Not to give you a short answer," he added apologetically. He frowned at Number One and went back searching for a book.

"Fucking reporters," Number One sulked. "You guys don't know shit. The fucking world's a cesspool, but you wouldn't smell it if the shit was up to your ears."

Ignore him, I told myself. He just needs a nice raw steak to chew on. I moved the phone back into the bedroom and was starting to close the door when I heard Number One growl in Rocco's direction. Rocco said something in reply and then came over and pushed my bedroom door open. He looked at me uncertainly.

"Relax, kid," he said awkwardly. "Everybody's tense." He came in, closed the door and took a seat on the bed. I remained standing.

"Why do we need Melendez?" I demanded.

"Big man, big man. Pulls a lot of strings, Max. He's Mr. Right for this deal. Trust me."

"He's from Florida, right? A Bay of Pigs hero? A Latin power broker with connections to the CIA—and whatever's left of the Havana mob. He might also know the drag queen who was with Denise the night she died, Rocco. Don't tell me he's Mr. Right."

Rocco raised his eyebrows and looked favorably impressed, but only for a second. His reply came when he shrugged his shoulders.

"You mention a *deal*, Rocco? What kind of a deal? A deal where The

Big Guy cleans up Melendez's garbage for him, disciplines his errand boys—terminally disciplines them—and then what?"

I sounded shrill, but I didn't care. Rocco sighed and stood up.

"You're right about a lot of things, Max, but you're wrong where it counts. The Torres crew did *not* work for Melendez. *No way*." Rocco wasn't enjoying our *tête-à-tête*.

"Then who did they work for? And who's Esmeralda's boyfriend? And why did they want to get rid of the Santiago kid? Let's have some answers, Rocco. Otherwise my part of this deal is off."

"You'll get answers when we sit down with Melendez," Rocco said patiently. "He's on his way to New York as we speak. I'm waiting for The Big Guy's call.

"Here," he added, "have a cigarette, piece of gum."

I took the gum and Rocco walked out.

Another ten minutes crawled by. Neither I nor my pet spider moved during that time. We just eyed each other. I was starting to feel like the guy in *Dracula*—Renfield—who went crazy and wanted to eat bugs. That's how they'd find me when they came to let me out of my room. Drooling and delirious.

What was the inscription over the entrance to the morgue? "Death delights in helping the living"? The morgue where Denise was lying on a slab. The girl I loved. She wanted to talk to me before she died. Talk to me now, I thought, I need advice.

I went into the kitchen, poured a slug of cognac in a glass of water, and threw it down. It was an act of desperation but it made me feel better.

I washed out the glass and went into the living room. It was like walking into a dentist's office. I needed a good book. I was sorry I left Melville behind when I left Montauk. I scanned my stacks and saw an old, dog-eared copy of *The Little Sister* by Raymond Chandler. What would Philip Marlowe do if he was here right now?

I took the book down and opened it. I hadn't read it in years. A paragraph caught my eye. I stared at the page and read the passage slowly, to myself.

A man named Ballou, a Hollywood agent with "crisp dark hair and shiny shoes," was talking to Marlowe.

" 'One of these days,' Ballou said, 'I'm going to make the mistake which a man in my business dreads above all other mistakes. I'm going to find myself

doing business with a man I can trust and I'm going to be just too goddamn smart to trust him.' "

My jaw dropped into a crooked smile. I turned a corner of the page down and put the book gently back into its space. I turned, the crooked smile hanging there like a sign twisted in the wind.

At that same moment, Number One drifted over and asked if I had ever met Edgar Wately. It was as if he'd said: "Had a nice day, champ?"

I said I had.

"Rich guy, huh?"

"I think so. He's a banker."

"You think he's queer?"

"What makes you think he's queer?"

"Just asking," he replied.

Dixie looked up from her book momentarily and then went back to it.

The atmosphere was too loaded with anticipation to allow for proper thought. I needed solitude. I sent myself to the showers.

16

I brought a fresh change of clothes into the bath with me, turned the water on, and did twenty-five push-ups before stepping under the spray. Rocco thought the shower was a good idea. He said it would relax me. The cognac had relaxed me. I just needed hosing down.

It was nearly ten o'clock and the phone was ringing off the hook. If the calls were for me no one was letting on. Fine, I figured. More time to think. I had to find out, and quickly, as much about Hector Melendez as I could. I let the water trickle over my skull while I posed questions for Edgar Wately, should he take the bait and return my call. At the time, nothing seemed too farfetched.

Maybe, I speculated, Jaime Santiago, who was *maybe* an heir to the Wately estate, held shares in the Wately bank. Now that he was dead, those shares were up for grabs. Maybe Hector Melendez, who was on the bank's board of directors, wanted to buy those shares. Maybe Hector Melendez helped arrange Jaime Santiago's death. And Denise just happened to be there when the deadly poison was being handed out.

That was one theory. How to prove it was something else. Could Edgar Wately help? How much did he know? Better yet, how much did Ethel know? Would the Mafia, simply out of spite, help prove a case against Melendez if I proved it to The Big Guy's satisfaction?

There was another scenario that really angered me.

Maybe Denise *had* taken a picture of Esmeralda's boyfriend at the

Toucan Too or some other joint, and maybe he—whoever he was—didn't like that. Maybe Denise was the real target, and Jaime Santiago just happened to be along for the ride.

I knew one thing for sure: I was going to have to share these theories with someone else in order to find the truth. I was debating whether to level with Rocco and The Big Guy, or take Lieutenant Henry into my confidence. And how would I handle Edgar Wately? He didn't seem too sorry about the death of his stepbrother. He never even acknowledged the relationship. If Jaime *was* an heir to the father's estate, his death would just leave more pie for the others. But who? Wately himself?

The creek was rising fast and the current was swift. I turned the water off before I drowned in my thoughts, dressed, and stepped into the living room.

Everyone was waiting for my arrival.

"The Big Guy wants to see us right now," Rocco announced gravely.

"I'm expecting a call," I said. "Tell him no can do."

Everyone, including Dixie, shook their heads.

Number One started to say something but Rocco cut him off.

"From who?" Rocco asked.

"Edgar Wately," I protested. "I just found out he's related to the kid who was with Denise the night she died. I have to talk to him."

"No way," Number One snapped. "We know that already."

"Why not tell me?" I bellowed. Dixie cut me off.

"Max," she said, "can we talk?"

"No, Dixie. Your friends know a lot more than they're letting on."

Rocco let out a long sigh.

"In the bedroom," he said.

I went into the bedroom and Rocco followed. He closed the door behind him.

"Mr. Max, you don't fuck with The Big Guy. Wately ain't going nowhere, believe me. You gotta hear what The Big Guy has to say. He's got Wately sewed up. Listen to me. I'm trying to be nice. Don't get these mugs pissed off. They got orders to bring you and they're gonna bring you."

"Is this the meeting with Melendez?"

"Maybe," Rocco said. "Yeh," he added. "Brooklyn. The Big Guy's turf, so you don't have to worry. Everything is gonna be OK."

"You're not sure."

"Get your coat, babe. You got my word of honor nothing's gonna happen to you."

I was sweating profusely. "Rocco, this kid Jaime may have been an heir to a fortune in shares at the Wately bank that Melendez wants to grab. That's for starters." I was scared. "What's Charlie's game?"

Rocco shook his head.

"It could be a fucking setup, Rocco!" I snarled. "Does The Big Guy understand that?"

"Don't yell," Rocco said.

"I'm not yelling," I yelled. "And I'm not going anywhere until I speak to The Big Guy myself."

Rocco sighed another big sigh and opened the bedroom door. Number One was standing there when it opened. He'd heard everything.

"He wants to call the boss," Rocco said. "He's worried about the Spanish guy. Maybe he's right."

"He wants to call The Big Guy?"

"Right!" I said. "The Big Guy. Right now."

I was grandstanding it.

"So call him," Number One said. "It's your dime. Rocco will dial. Get dressed."

Rocco dialed while I stood my ground.

The Big Guy was rather persuasive. He told me, point blank, that "the Spanish," as he called them, seemed to know my whereabouts during the time the Torres brothers were being blown away—independent of anything I had told Dixie or Rocco.

Talk about your blood running cold? Mine was crystallizing in my veins.

"Is this a threat to get me to the meeting, Charlie?"

"He says he can place you there," is all The Big Guy said.

"And you want me to meet him? The Torres brothers might have worked for him. Charlie, come on. It's a setup. Don't fuck with me!"

I was going to have to take another shower. Cold sweat dripped down my spine.

But no, no, no, said Charlie. No, no, no. Melendez just wants to clear his name. The Torres brothers didn't work for him.

"Then who did they work for?" I asked.

"They worked for Edgar Wately," Charlie said with some impatience. "See what I'm tellin' you?"

17

A stretch Lincoln limousine picked me, Dixie, Rocco, and Numbers One and Two up at 10:30 P.M. We dropped Dixie off at her loft on the Bowery and took the Manhattan Bridge across the East River to Brooklyn. I never saw the driver of the car. Except for the windshield, the windows were smoked glass all around and he never got out.

We got off the bridge and took the first exit in Brooklyn, swinging right onto local streets rather than taking the Brooklyn-Queens Expressway. The Lincoln was following the road that curved under the highway and parallel to the docks. We purred along for several blocks before turning right at a Cadillac showroom that sat on the corner of a dead-end street ending at a fourteen-foot steel fence overlooking the water. A Liberian tanker was tied to the pier that stretched behind it.

A disembodied voice broke the silence. It was the driver, speaking through an intercom, announcing our arrival. The Lincoln turned left, put its front paws on the sidewalk in front of a garage door, and announced itself with a neutral purr and a toot of its horn. The door rolled up and we drove into the bowels of a three-story garage. It was the back end of the showroom.

The setup, as Rocco later explained, was very clever. A dark blue Ford station wagon, also with smoked windows, was parked on the left. Its doors were open. Four men who looked like they were waiting for someone to throw a Frisbee at them stood next to the doors. Each man wore a jacket or raincoat. One man had a two-way radio cupped to his ear. They had their eyes on us. They all carried guns. They were the Spanish.

On the right was another Lincoln stretch limo, doors also open, with six men posed around it. Four of them held down the front fenders, two on each side. The other two sat on either side of the front seat, half in and half out of the car. They watched our arrival with some interest, but their gaze was directed across the aisle, where the station wagon was parked. They didn't carry guns. They were the Italians.

Our Lincoln ground to a halt directly between the two factions. Rocco and Numbers One and Two were on the left side. They exchanged glances when we stopped, focusing on the group gathered around the station wagon. I followed their eyes. The man with the walkie-talkie came forward and waved us back. His lips were moving but I couldn't hear him.

"He says move back ten feet."

It was our driver, talking through the intercom.

"Move back," Number One said. "I know what they're doing. It's OK."

I had a sudden urge to go to the bathroom. I wondered whether I should let someone know.

The Lincoln slid back ten feet, no more, no less, and came to rest.

"He says get out—one by one. Their side."

Rocco looked at me. I looked at Rocco. Rocco looked at Number One.

"Don't worry," Number One said. "I'm gettin' out first."

The electronic door lock snapped open and Number One stepped out into the garage. He put his hands out in a papal blessing, bowed from the neck, and turned around, as if to announce the next act. He said something to the man with the walkie-talkie and then he opened the front door of the Lincoln. I saw Number Two step out, wearing his black raincoat, his arms also chest high in supplication. Rocco was next, coming forward on a nod from Number One.

Rocco cleared his throat, slid across the velvet seat, and planted his feet on the concrete. He held his hands in front of his chest, stood up, and looked to Number One for further directions.

"Tell him to look nice coming out," I heard Number One say.

Rocco turned around, hands still chest high, and peered into the back seat, where I met his eyes. His eyes were scared.

"Show them you ain't got no gun," Rocco said. "Just keep your hands high."

I did as I was told.

Number One approached the man with the walkie-talkie.

"Where is he?" he said.

"Upstairs. Only two go."

Number One scowled and shook his head.

Number Two stepped forward and walked slowly toward a set of iron stairs to the left of the station wagon.

"Follow him," Number One said to me.

I followed him.

He got to the foot of the stairs, hesitated, turned, and indicated he wanted me to go first.

No way, I thought. I jerked my head to let him know I was in charge—at least from here to the next blind corner.

He understood, with some reluctance, and proceeded upstairs backward, so he faced the killing floor as he went up, a step at a time. It took me a minute to realize he was covering me, and to sense that he really was interested in whether I lived or died.

The iron stairs went up a half flight and swung left. A man with an Uzi greeted us at the next landing. He said something in Italian to Number Two and escorted us down a narrow catwalk enclosed in wire mesh. He paused in front of a wooden door that featured a brass sign that said CONFERENCE ROOM, knocked twice, pushed the door open, stepped aside, and motioned specifically to me.

"In," was all he said.

I got to the edge of the doorframe and stuck my head around the corner. Four men sat at a glass conference table twelve feet long. The glass, in one piece, was supported on three inverted chrome triangles. It was shiny and clear and you could see everyone's lap. No matter; everyone had his hands on the table.

The two men on my right looked uncomfortable. They sat halfway down the table from the other two gentlemen, who sat side by side at the far end, facing me. The two men at the head of the table were The Big Guy and his muscle. The Big Guy wore a gray worsted suit, a gray shirt, and a matching tie, probably both silk. The muscle wore a tweed sports jacket, brown slacks, gray sweater, and blue sports shirt. The muscle cradled an Uzi in his arms as if it was a baby. His finger was on the trigger.

The Big Guy, who we'll call Charlie from now on, extended his right arm and said: "Sit."

I sat across the table from the other two.

Number Two took up a position in front of the door, but no one seemed to care.

Charlie nodded in the direction of a distinguished looking man sitting at the middle of the table, opposite me.

The man was tall, dark, tanned, and very trim, about thirty-five, with salt-and-pepper black curly hair. He wore a neat mustache. He had on a lightweight glen plaid suit with a bright paisley tie, a matching pocket square, and a blue button-down oxford shirt with a monogram over the breast pocket. I knew about the monogram because he leaned back in his chair and flashed it at me like a badge; or maybe to show me he didn't carry a gun.

"I'm Arthur Melendez," he said. "I'm here for my father, Hector Melendez. This man," he indicated the sour-faced man on his left, "is my lawyer." The lawyer wore a wrinkled brown suit, striped tie, and white shirt. The man needed a good tailor and a few days napping in the sun. His complexion had the texture of boiled mutton. He'd been too long living under fluorescent lights. His face was familiar. It took me a minute to identify him. He was a former federal prosecutor, now in private practice, who had helped draft the indictments against The Big Guy's predecessors, the old heroin-dealing dons. His briefcase was opened in front of him. Among other things, it held a slim black box that twinkled with little red lights. It was an electronic monitor that detected the presence of bugs—as in eavesdropping devices. There was a walkie-talkie on the table alongside the attaché case. Smart move for the Latins, having a mouthpiece who knew his way around the Italian mob, as well as the ins and outs of the latest electronic surveillance techniques.

"Nice to meet you," I said.

Melendez nodded and leaned forward but we didn't shake hands. "I want to offer my deepest sympathies on the death of your friend," he said.

"Yeh," I said.

A flush came to his face. "I've been informed that some . . . *maricon* . . . told you Bennie and Ralph Torres worked for us. *They never did*. They never worked for the Melendez family. They're scum. And the people they worked for are scum," he said.

Something told me he was telling the truth, but a chip invariably blossomed on my shoulder when I confronted men like Arthur Melendez. His manners were better and his nails were clean, but he drank from the same cup as the people who had killed Denise. They shared the same credo: Every man for himself.

"I'm listening," I replied evenly, catching his lawyer's eye at the same time, "but I hope you have the facts to back it up."

The lawyer responded with a bored look.

"You'll get the facts, if you know where to look," Melendez said, cocking an eye sharply in Charlie's direction.

"Then who did they work for?" I asked.

"Ask Edgar Wately," he said.

It was a long, high ball into right field. The sun was in my eyes.

"What does he have to do with this?"

"Maybe a little. Maybe a lot."

"What's your father's connection?" I asked righteously.

"He has nothing to do with this."

"And you do?"

"I don't; my father don't; we don't—get that straight right now. We don't deal with scum and faggots. Don't play games with me, Mr. Reporter."

"I'm not playing games, Mr. Melendez. I'm here to listen."

The guy was tough, but he was in some kind of trouble or he wouldn't be here, forced to be tough without a gun. The pasty-faced ex-prosecutor twitched in his seat and rubbed his nose.

"Edgar Wately has servant problems and they're getting everybody in a lot of trouble," Melendez said agitatedly. "Do you know that Bennie and Ralph Torres were related to Wately's housekeeper?"

That long, high ball was still in the air, drifting down from the sky like a ball of cotton. The pasty-faced man coughed and looked pleased with his client.

"Wately's housekeeper," I repeated.

"Rosa," Melendez sneered.

"So?" I said.

"Bennie and Ralph worked for Edgar Wately, Mr. Reporter. They did not work for me. They wanted to. They came to my father with dumb schemes. Bennie and Ralph had big ideas and no brains. All they could do was kill people—and they weren't very good at that."

"Did they kill . . ." I wanted to say Denise's name, but it got tangled up on its way out.

"They killed, by my count, eight people, including two undercover agents for the DEA," he said without emotion. "They also killed your girlfriend and the Santiago kid."

"Can you prove that?"

He thought a minute and looked at his lawyer, who remained impassive.

"I'm telling you the truth. You're supposed to be a reporter. So far your information is lousy. Bennie and Ralph weren't picky about who they worked for. They might have worked for Fidel Castro. They might have worked for the United States government. They did not—repeat, did not—work for my father. What do you want? That we should write the story for you, too?"

"Why are you telling me this?" I asked. The ball was still in the air.

"To clear my name," Melendez said. "We do business with Edgar Wately. He owes my father a lot of money. He'd like to see my father get blamed for something he didn't do." He looked at Charlie. "*Would never* do," he said carefully.

"Let me get this straight," I said. "Bennie and Ralph Torres were related to Mrs. Torquenos, who works for the Watelys. They might have been Cuban agents, or government agents, or double agents. And they had a grudge against the Watelys for some reason. Is that why they killed the kid . . . and my friend?"

He looked up from under his eyebrows.

"It's possible." He shrugged. "Bennie and Ralph were on the outs with Wately." I had the impression he was only telling me half the story. Maybe that's all he knew.

"Who told you this?" I pressed him.

He grinned and looked at the lawyer.

"The same person who says you killed Bennie."

My blood pressure rose, fell, and rose again in my chest, trying to force its way through a tight neck into a tired, apprehensive brain; I blushed red, breathed deep, shook my head, and grinned like a dumb fool. Tag. I was it. I looked at The Big Guy. The Big Guy had expected this. He grinned, too, and addressed Melendez.

"Tell him what you told me."

"A cousin of Bennie and Ralph's called me the day after Bennie was shot," Melendez said. "She called to deny that Bennie and Ralph ever blamed"—he jerked his head in Big Charlie's direction—"this gentleman for the people who had gotten in Bennie and Ralph's way."

"Who was she and why would she call you?"

"She was scared for herself and Rosa. She wanted to let me know they weren't part of her cousins' business. She wanted me to pass the word."

"You're talking about Aurora Carrera?" I asked. It was a long shot.

He answered with a curt nod in the affirmative. He didn't like the question.

"And you believe her story?"

"Absolutely," he said.

I thought immediately of Pepe Cruz, the little beige man in Manolo's apartment, arguing with a woman on the telephone before he was shot. What was the phrase he used? "Get that bitch on the phone!" The woman was Aurora Carrera.

She can put me there, at the scene! Has she said anything to the cops? I'm a soccer ball in an Italian-Spanish face-off!

I looked to The Big Guy and tried not to show my fear.

"Are *you* happy with the explanation?"

"Let him talk," Charlie said.

Melendez exchanged glances with his lawyer before continuing.

"You know Wately's girlfriend, right?" Melendez asked me.

I did not.

"The freak who was with *your* girlfriend," Melendez snapped.

Bells went off. A silly grin tugged at one corner of my mouth while the other side sagged like a warm puppy. I had to touch my chin so it wouldn't fall into my lap. I knew I looked stupid because I drew a wan smile from Melendez's lawyer.

"What freak?" I managed to say.

"The fucking faggot with its dick cut off—the sex-change miracle." He grinned and looked at Charlie. "Ain't bad looking, either. She's Edgar's girlfriend."

I let my jaw drop. I didn't care. I looked at Charlie. He was beaming. I looked at Melendez. He looked disgusted. His lawyer had turned sour again. I made a vague gesture, like I was brushing cobwebs away.

"Esmeralda . . . Edgar's lover?"

"Look, I'm telling you what's what," Melendez said. He sighed and shook his head. "All I know is that the Torres brothers didn't care who they killed, and they had plenty of reasons to shake Wately down."

"Are you suggesting blackmail?" I asked him.

His lawyer cleared his throat. He didn't like where the conversation was going for reasons only he knew. Melendez caught the drift, and changed his mood. These sons of bitches knew more than they were letting on.

"I just want to make it clear that Bennie and Ralph never worked for me or my father," he repeated. "They worked for Edgar Wately and that's easily proved. You need proof on that, you'll get it." He looked at Charlie. Charlie nodded sagely.

I sat back and took a deep breath. My temples were pounding. Jesus.

"And Aurora *claims—*" I emphasized the word and glanced at The Big Guy— "I was at the place on Avenue A?"

Melendez looked at his lawyer and at Charlie before answering. He spoke into his tie, avoiding my eyes and flicking off a piece of dust.

"The aunt, Rosa, she thinks you were there," he said flatly.

The cocaine cobwebs were blowing like crazy in my brain. I flashed back to Avenue A and the little man in the beige suit on the telephone again. I could almost hear him speak. One word fluttered through my mind this time, a Spanish word. The word was wrapped in a cocaine cloud.

"*La vieja*," I said. "The old lady."

"You met Rosa?" Melendez asked.

"Once," I said. "She's a tough old bird."

Vieja.

"Rosa was the only person who could handle Bennie and Ralph," Melendez said.

"You talked about servant problems. Did the kid, Jaime, do something to Rosa? Is that why Bennie and Ralph killed Jaime?"

"I don't know why they did it," Melendez said with an air of finality. "That's all I have to say. I don't even know why I bothered to come here."

Charlie bristled at the remark. His displeasure was felt by all.

The pasty-faced lawyer looked like he was going to speak but had a change of mind. Arthur Melendez frowned and shifted in his chair.

"What kind of servant problems?" I persisted.

"Edgar Wately owes my father a lot of money and he's gonna pay off one way or another," Melendez replied peevishly. "And we don't need anybody's help collecting, either. My father has friends of his own." He looked at Charlie when he said it. Charlie shrugged it off with a sour grin.

"What's your business with Wately?" I asked.

"Totally legitimate," the lawyer interjected, coming down hard on each syllable. "My client bailed him out. Wately came begging and they gave him money. He promised a big return on their investment but he can't pay off. He got cheap; he got involved with a lot of things he shouldn't."

"Drugs?"

"You're the reporter," he said. "You find out."

"Your father is on the board of directors of the bank?" I asked Melendez.

"Of course he's on the board," he said angrily. "Just leave him out of this. Pay attention to what I'm saying, reporter: Edgar Wately ran the Torres brothers. They worked for him. He made a lot of money and it disappeared. He owes my father."

Melendez was getting tired of this. He looked at Charlie and he looked at his lawyer. He wanted to go and he was making it clear. His lawyer spoke in a flat, bored voice.

"What else can we tell you, Mr. Darenow? Surely you don't expect the Melendez family to solve your beef with the Watelys."

"Tell him about the feds before you go," Charlie said, looking pleased with himself. Melendez's lawyer took note of it and fidgeted in his seat.

"The feds," Melendez said, "are looking into Wately's deals. The ones where he lost money. Wately's trying to stick my father with his bad loans." Melendez turned and addressed Charlie. "There's nothing more I want to say."

Charlie looked at me.

"Does that satisfy you?" he said.

"I don't know. I'd like to ask some more questions."

"No more questions," Melendez said. "You have questions, ask your friend."

He meant Charlie.

"Or ask Edgar Wately." He smirked and stood up to leave. "Just keep my father out of this or you're dead."

His lawyer didn't like that. His face faded into a mottled gray mask.

"My client didn't say that," he said.

The lawyer snapped his briefcase closed. He pressed a button on his walkie-talkie and announced that he and Melendez were coming down.

The meeting was over. Arthur Melendez never gave me a second glance. Nor did the lawyer. Number Two opened the door on a signal from Charlie and the two of them filed out.

"Wait until they go, then tell Rocco I want him," Charlie said to Number Two.

"You surprised?" Charlie asked me. I sure looked it.

"I'm impressed," I said. "Is the guy legitimate?"

"He's Hector Melendez's son, for chrissake," Charlie said. "What more you gotta know? Of course he's legitimate. His old man don't want trouble."

"What kind of trouble?"

"Any kind."

"You believe his story?" I asked.

"A guy like him don't lie to a guy like me," Charlie said with a patient, knowing smile.

"How does he know the Torres brothers killed the Spanish kid, Jaime?"

"He knows the whole family," Charlie said.

He couldn't understand why I didn't get it.

"The spics know each other. Like the Italians know each other. Like the Wasps know each other. You don't know that?"

A car's motor turned over and car doors slammed. The motor settled down, revved a bit, and slid into gear. The garage doors made noise going up and coming down again. The car went away with Arthur Melendez and his entourage.

"What was your question?" Charlie asked when the noise died down.

"I'm trying to figure it out," I said. "Melendez, or his son, believes the Torres brothers killed Jaime and Denise, and maybe tried to kill Esmeralda. Why did they do it? That's question number one.

"Question number two: Did Edgar Wately have anything to do with it?"

"That's what *you're* going to find out," Charlie said.

I didn't like being told what to do by Charlie. A lot of things breezed through my mind.

"I'll talk to Ethel Wately," I said. I made no mention of my cocktail party invitation.

"You're gonna talk to Wately's girlfriend first," Charlie said easily. "Then you talk to whoever you like."

"What's your angle, Charlie? I don't get it," I asked then.

"We're gonna make the brother sweat," Charlie said idly.

Charlie paid no heed to my plight. He glanced at a piece of paper on the table. "She's in the Waldorf. Room nine-forty," he said.

"Who, Ethel Wately?"

"Wately's girlfriend," Charlie snorted. "Whatever . . . the sex-change. She called the other queen, Rocco's friend, *your* friend, Dixie Cupps. She wants to talk to you. The boys are gonna take you there now. Dixie Cupps will go with you. The Spanish queen doesn't trust anybody. She's scared."

"She should be. She's facing a murder rap," I said. "And so far as I'm concerned, nothing Melendez said takes her off the hook—yet. She may have passed out the poison."

"Melendez don't seem to think that's the case," Charlie said, easing back into his chair and giving me a long, searching look. "He thinks Wately's sister's, uh, friends were helping Edgar clean up his act. That makes a lot of sense to me. It needs cleaning up."

"Who are her friends?"

"She's got friends in the right places," was all Charlie said. "They would have done a job on the Torres brothers, too," he winked, "if you didn't beat them to the punch." He still thought I was one of the shooters on Avenue A.

A big, dark cloud was settling over my little ballpark. All the fly balls were gone. There was nothing but line drives heading my way.

"I don't know about this." I laughed nervously. A door opened and I nearly flew from the chair.

Rocco had come upstairs.

"What's the story?" Charlie asked.

"We can pick her up anytime," Rocco replied.

"But I can't be running around snatching witnesses, not with the weight I'm carrying," I said. "I have to think about what I'm getting into."

"You're getting your wish," Charlie said. He bit down hard on the words. "You'll nail whoever did your girlfriend in, maybe you'll get a story, a little glory, the Italians will look good, and that'll be it. What more you want?"

"I don't like this," I said.

"Life ain't always sweet," Charlie said. "Sometimes you just have to eat what you're served."

18

We paraded into the lobby of the Waldorf-Astoria at exactly midnight and headed for Harry's Bar. The limo had dropped Rocco off at Dixie's place and picked Dixie up. Every parade needs a majorette. It hit just the right chord for this reporter. I needed some amusement. Dixie alighted from the limo like royalty, with Numbers One and Two acting like deferential bodyguards. I wished I had dark glasses and a hat. We attracted a few curious stares as Dixie tripped lightly through the lobby in her cowgirl boots, a tight skirt that barely covered her thighs, a fox parka, and a cloud of Giorgio, flanked by two poker-faced palookas and a slightly chagrined member of the press. Number One wanted a drink and I didn't blame him. So did I. Dixie headed for the house phones to call Esmeralda and tell her she was on her way up. From what I was told by Charlie, I was to be Esmeralda's assurance that everything was on the up-and-up. A wonderful role for someone completely in the dark.

The cocktail crowd from an orthodontists' convention was holding forth in Harry's, showing off their wives. It was a well-behaved mob—the men neat and trim in dark suits, the wives in cocktail dresses and mink coats, laughing through capped teeth. Our presence titillated them.

We ordered drinks. Dixie came back and said Esmeralda wanted to see her alone first. Numbers One and Two discussed the pros and cons of that and decided it was OK after Dixie explained that Esmeralda was simply a little nervous. Dixie winked.

I knew what she meant. Esmeralda needed cocaine.

Dixie smiled and went upstairs.

I sipped a Jack Daniels perfect manhattan and watched the world turn while Numbers One and Two exchanged notes on the women in the room. Sure, I was drinking hard liquor. I wanted a cigarette, too. I was a bundle of nerves. Numbers One and Two made light talk. I entered the conversation as Number One was listing the options on the new Caddy Seville. He seemed to have driven every make and model American car in the past five years, at least.

He said he used to be in the "car business." I let it go at that.

Twenty minutes passed. Dixie hadn't come back. Number One told his buddy to call upstairs and see what was going on. I was nursing my second manhattan. The crowd at the bar was thinning out. Number Two came back from the house phone shaking his head.

"We better call the boss," he said. "There's some punk up there with them. He won't let either one of them go. Dixie says he got rough with her. He smells a rat."

"Call the sex-change," Number One said to me. "I want her out of here. Tell her anything, just don't scare her. Tell her we're coming up and we'll handle the tough guy. Tell her you're gonna call the cops if she's not out of there in five minutes. Tell her you'll be in the hall, on her floor, waiting for her."

I shook my head no. He leaned across the table and put his hand on my arm.

"You're going in the garbage pail," he said. "The Big Guy's gonna throw you and all the rest of them to the wolves. Mark my words. What are you, stupid? *Call her!*" He hissed it.

I called. The phone was answered in a bubbly, high-pitched parody of a woman's voice, as if she'd just been goosed.

"Esmeralda?"

"It is she," she trilled.

I told her who I was.

"Yes, of course," she said pleasantly. "The reporter. Please come up. I will talk to you now. You know the room?"

"Nine-forty?"

"Come up now."

She hung up before I could reply.

I went over to the newsstand and studied the headlines on the newspapers. OZONE DAMAGE IRREVERSIBLE; END IN SIGHT. It sure was a crazy world. I bought a pack of Camels, lit one up, and decided I wanted out, soon.

I knew from the tone of her voice Esmeralda was more than a little psycho. She probably thought talking to a reporter was going to make her famous, and legitimatize her in the eyes of the world.

I went back and reported to my keepers. I told them I was going upstairs.

"Is the punk still there?" Number One demanded.

"I never asked," I said.

"Dixie says he's just a punk," Number Two crowed. "Chances are you won't have trouble." He was teasing me.

"Don't worry," said Number One. "I'm goin' in with you."

"No good," I said. "I talk to her first. Then I go. You give me time to leave and then you do what you have to do."

"Fine," said Number One, ignoring me. "Let's go."

He stood up, told his partner to "go down to the car and wait," laid a fifty-dollar bill on the table, and jerked his thumb toward the exit. "And wait for the change," he snapped.

"I'm not doing this," I said. "It's kidnapping a witness." I was having second thoughts for the eightieth time.

"I'm going with you if the punk gets wise," he said. "You talk to her, then you go. You said you had work to do. So go."

Number One and I took the elevator. The bellhops never looked twice at us. Number One carried himself with an air of confidence that reminded me, strangely enough, of some cops who accepted the role of tough guy without losing all due respect for lesser mortals. It was a job.

Esmeralda's room was two down from the elevator. Number One unzipped his jacket, flexed his arms, and let me go first. He stepped to the side, out of view, when I knocked. The door opened about three inches, as far as the security chain permitted. I was looking into a pair of dark eyes set in a sea of studied innocence. It was Esmeralda. She had an abundance of dark curly hair, flawless skin, and lush, full lips. She looked like a chorus girl. She was young and had a mischievous smile.

Esmeralda said 'hello' in her little-girl's voice and sized me up. She liked me. She smiled coyly and scrutinized my photo on the press pass I held under her nose.

"Is that him?" she said, stepping aside so Dixie could see me. Dixie vouched for me, and stepped back. I saw a man's head, neck, and shoulders close behind Dixie—too close.

"Open it," the man said.

Esmeralda slid the chain off, stepped back, and stopped. The man behind Dixie said "Slow," and that's how she did it, slow. I came in slowly, too, the three of them moving back like a wave as I stepped further into the room.

When I had both feet inside, the punk behind Dixie said: "Shut it. Now!"

I kept my eyes on him. His eyes flared when he saw Number One coming in behind me. Dixie winced and said "Oww!"

"I knew it!" the punk said.

He snapped an arm around Dixie's neck and waved four inches of double-edged steel blade in front of her face, reddening with anger.

Number One put his arms on both my shoulders and moved me about three feet to the right and into the room. The guy holding Dixie was a curly-headed greaser with bad skin and a jailhouse tattoo on his left hand. He was wild-eyed and crack-brained, a loose, high-voltage wire.

Number One moved past me as if he was showing a car to a prospective customer. I almost expected him to say excuse me.

"This freak gets it. He gets it!" the greaser yelled. He was referring to Dixie.

I'm not sure what happened next. Dixie said she brought the heel of her boot down on his instep. I didn't see it. I heard the guy scream and I saw Dixie spinning away, her hand throwing blood. Number One kept going for the greaser, kicking at him and throwing hand blocks out at the same time. The kid fell on the bed and rolled off it, snapping back like a rubber band, coming up and under Number One, who was moving too fast to stop. He was going to get his guts ripped out.

I rushed toward Number One, pushing him away and ducking behind him at the same time. He staggered and tripped and the greaser kept coming at him as if I didn't exist.

But the greaser knew *exactly* where I was. He only had to make a half-turn to get there, catching me in an advanced state of stupidity, frozen in the perplexity of those about to die. He had faked me out.

I met him halfway. He snarled something as he came at me but it got stuck in his throat and turned into a scream.

Dixie was on his back, her skirt around her waist, her well-shaped legs wrapped like a snake around his midriff. Her nails were driven deep into his face and eyes and her heels dug into his groin. Dixie's hands were covered with blood.

"Grab his wrists!" she cried.

My eyes found his wrists and I tried grabbing them without getting cut when I heard an ugly sound. The greaser's jaw was breaking. I saw a flash of metal, a gun, and Number One's right hand and arm coming behind it. He was rearranging the scars on the greaser's chin.

He was surprised. Number One hooked him again with a left, but it wasn't necessary. The punk dropped his knife and followed it to the floor, but wasn't watching where he was going. He hit his head on the night table on the way down and managed a weak moan before leaving the party.

I hadn't been touched. Dixie's right hand was sliced above the knuckle. There was blood smeared on her fur coat.

She had saved my life.

Number One muttered some oaths in Italian and then spit on the fallen greaser. He turned his gun on Esmeralda, who was standing in awe, her back pressed firmly to the wall adjacent to the front door.

"Get in here," Number One barked.

Esmeralda danced toward him, holding her hands in prayer.

"My heroes!" she squealed. She curled her lip at the fallen greaser. "He was trash. I didn't want him here. My boyfriend sent him for protection."

Esmeralda was an expensive, custom-designed toy. A five-foot-seven *Playboy* cartoon, state-of-the-surgeon's-art. She had silicone tits, silicone hips, and silicone cheeks and she swung it like a charm bracelet. She had light, creamy skin, with just a hint of mocha. Her eyes and eyebrows were bigger than life, sable showcases for all kinds of hidden pleasures, but with a limited book: "Look at me. Aren't I sexy? Don't you want me?" If she was Edgar Wately's idea of a lover, he had to be a very complex man.

Dixie was hurt. I went to help her, but she was already tearing a pillowcase into a bandage, tearing off strips with her teeth and her free hand. Number One was holding her other arm tight against her chest, which stemmed the flow of blood. Two pros.

"Dixie . . . I'm sorry. I owe you my life. I don't know what to say." I was blubbering like an idiot.

"This little shit is going to pay, personally, if there's a scar," she said, referring to the fallen greaseball.

Number One had a trace of a grin on his face.

"Go home and call Wately. Tell him we're taking care of his little honey. Get a number from him. A twenty-four-hour number. Tell him he better be sitting by the phone."

I nodded yes. I kept nodding.

"This shit is crazy," he said. "You go. We'll go down in a minute."

I looked at the fallen greaser.

"He ain't going nowhere," he said. "Go!"

Dixie smiled.

Esmeralda smiled and gave me the eye. Everybody was having fun except me.

"Max," Dixie said, "we'll be at my place. I'm OK. Come there when you're finished. Give us half an hour."

"And no monkey business, either," said Number One. "Understand? No cops yet. And watch what you say to Wately. Don't let on we're talking to Melendez."

I checked the hall, then used the stairs. I ran and thought about what Number One said. No cops, yet. Was Charlie serious about turning Wately in to the feds?

I beat it down to the fifth floor, and stopped in the stairwell to catch my breath. I had just helped the Mafia kidnap a witness.

I couldn't call Edgar Wately. What would I say?

"Hi, Mr. Wately, we're holding your sex-changed boy toy until you apologize to Charlie Baldasano for sullying the Mafia's reputation, and then you have to tell us what you know about the deaths of Jaime Santiago and Denise Overton, among other victims. After you confess and apologize, please turn yourself in to the NYPD for bankrolling the Torres brothers and other crimes against the People."

Shit!

Ignoring a NO SMOKING IN HALLWAY sign, I sat down on the stairs and lit a cigarette. I was turning into a chronic lawbreaker. It was time to have a little talk with myself.

What did the man say to Philip Marlowe about trust?

I trusted Charlie Big Guy and I trusted Arthur Melendez, although their motives weren't the purest, especially Charlie's. Charlie wanted to shake Edgar down, threaten him with exposure over his love affair with Esmeralda, and punish him for making it look like the Mafia had had a hand in all those drug-related murders. Call it blackmail. When Wately was squeezed dry Charlie would turn him over to the New York City cops, who would then owe the Mafia a heavy favor.

What about Melendez? Melendez wanted to clear his father's name and collect on their investment, probably by taking over Wately's bank. It wouldn't hurt to have Wately arrested on drug charges, in that case. I believed Arthur Melendez, his story rang true. But I still had to eliminate any possible connection between the elder Melendez, Hector, and the Torres brothers.

The one man I knew I couldn't trust was Edgar Wately. After what I'd heard, I could believe Edgar capable of anything. In today's climate, it seemed perfectly reasonable for a buttoned-down banker with ties to the CIA to have a sex-change lover, peddle drugs to fight communism, skim the profits to pay off his own bad loans, and walk through it all with a clear conscience.

It made sense, but it didn't provide enough answers.

Why did the Torres brothers kill Jaime and Denise?

And what about Arthur Melendez's crack about Ethel Wately and her "friends in high places"? Were they already at work cleaning up her brother's act?

I took a deep drag, coughed, cursed Sir Walter Raleigh, and thought maybe it was time to tell the cops everything.

I hightailed it down another two flights, stepped into the hall, and grabbed an elevator to the lower lobby, now quiet, where I found an empty men's room and ducked into one of the stalls. My knees were knocking and my bowels were in an uproar.

When I finally walked out of the hotel's side entrance the streets were quiet. I spotted a cab and headed downtown. The driver thought he was Richard Petty. He turned over to Park, turned left, and hit the Grand Central ramp at forty miles an hour, braked so he wouldn't hit the wall at the first turn, fishtailed, and threw me flying across the back seat. He stepped on the gas again, reversed the maneuver at the next turn, and threw me back in place.

I told him to slow down. The message didn't register until eight blocks later, when he had to stop for a light.

"What were you sayin'?" he crooned.

19

The Waldorf is a great hotel, but I felt a lot better after I stepped into my quiet, empty apartment. Maybe too empty. I wouldn't have minded having Denise's rocking chair, with her favorite nightie draped over the back, sitting in a vacant corner. The red light on the answering machine blinked spastically despite the fact it was well past the hour when decent people conducted business. A lot of folks wanted to talk to Max Darenow.

I lit a Camel and rolled the messages back. I had a call from police headquarters, an Inspector Rossetti. The name was new to me, but I assumed the commissioner was about to issue a new statement on the drug scourge. I made a note to call Rossetti first thing in the morning and moved on. Denise's friend, Mary Collins, left a straightforward message. Denise's body had been transferred to a funeral home on Fourteenth Street. When would I come by? I couldn't answer that question.

Lieutenant Henry called. Twice. He wanted to see me, tonight.

Edgar Wately was back in town. He'd received my message and returned my call. He left a New York number, but it wasn't his apartment.

Let them wait, I thought. I was taking off my coat when the phone rang. Henry was coming off a shift and wanted to drop by. His voice sounded strained.

"What's wrong?" I asked.

"It's a little complicated," he said.

"It's late," I replied. It was almost two. "Can it wait?" Maybe whatever was wrong would go away if I ignored it.

"I'm off the case," he said glumly. "For all practical purposes the NYPD is off the case. Me and Gonzalez, the detective who worked the Avenue A murders, we're going to 'liaison' with the feds, but that's just a formality. Otherwise, we're on hold. Our files were picked up early today by two marshals and brought downtown to the federal task force."

"What files?"

Henry wouldn't say more until he saw me in person. He said he'd pick me up in fifteen minutes.

I met him in front of the house. Henry looked grim. He drove slowly, sticking to side streets, circling blocks, doling out information with deliberative calm.

Henceforth, for reasons of "national security," the feds had taken over the investigations of any and all deaths connected to the Torres brothers—that meant Denise, Jaime, Manolo, Pepe Cruz, Bennie and Ralph Torres themselves, and a variety of other Latins hurled from roofs, blown up or otherwise murdered. The NYPD would continue to feed information to the feds, but it was a one-sided deal.

The discovery of Ralph Torres's tortured body in the feds' backyard had Owen Reed's boys "jumping like bunnies," Henry cracked. What's more, he said, the feds believed Bennie and Ralph killed Jaime Santiago and tried to kill Esmeralda because they had a grudge against Edgar Watelу.

"That's all off the record," he admonished.

"Of course," I replied.

I acted appropriately dumbfounded, as if this were all new information. It jibed with what Arthur Melendez had told me earlier.

"What about Esmeralda?" I asked. "How does she fit in?"

Henry sighed and took a slow, wide turn around a corner. "Nearly eliminated as a suspect, still sought as a material witness or possible accomplice. She turned up in the emergency room of Metropolitan Hospital the same night your girlfriend and the Santiago kid died. Claimed she was given bad cocaine by an unknown male Hispanic. What's interesting is that her blood and urine tests showed traces of scopolamine in her system, too, but nothing compared to the dose your friend got. Scopolamine is tricky; it seems to work better with depressants—if you're trying to knock someone out."

Henry continued: "Esmeralda checked herself out of the hospital in the company of another male Hispanic, light-skinned, pockmarked face, tattoo on left hand, age twenty-five or thereabouts. Bye-bye Esmeralda."

I made no reply. We rolled through the night in silence. What intrigued me now was Edgar Wately's role. We cruised west, toward the Hudson River, through the Chelsea warehouse district. Henry found a desolate block, pulled into the curb, and cut his lights. At that point, my mouth was very dry but the cold sweats had me shivering. Henry noticed and pulled a pint bottle of Courvoisier from the glove compartment, smiled, and handed it to me. He plucked a thermos full of decaffeinated coffee from a gym bag on the seat and produced two paper hot-cups. We laced the coffee with plenty of cognac and took a good swallow.

"The feds are playing games with us," Henry said.

"Maybe they're covering something up," I ventured. I was tightrope walking.

Henry rested his cup on the dashboard and gave me a long, searching look.

"Let me ask you something, Mr. Darenow. Be straight. What do you know about the three men who were shot on Avenue A?"

My heart sank. I grasped the cup with both hands and blew on it.

"I know what you told me," I lied.

"Did you ever meet those guys? Have anything to do with them?"

I was about to ask him why he wanted to know, but that was too defensive.

"I knew the one guy," I said. "The guy who lived there. A musician. He hung out in some of the places where Denise used to go. Village places. I think he sold a little weed from time to time."

"Maybe a little coke from time to time?"

"I wouldn't be surprised," I said.

"When was the last time you saw him?"

"Jesus!" I gasped. The coffee rolled in the cup, but I hadn't moved. "The last time . . . ages ago. I've been out on Long Island a month and it must be . . . months before that. I stopped seeing Denise six months ago."

Phew . . . distance yourself, my boy.

"Did these guys, or this guy, have a grudge against you or your girlfriend? Did she know they were dealing drugs?"

"Grudge, no. No . . . why?" The fucking coffee cup was trying to jump from my hand.

"Where were you the night those men were murdered?"

The sixty-four-dollar question! A strange calm settled over me. My hands stopped trembling, but the sweats, and my heart rate, increased. I stared straight ahead.

"What night was that?" I replied. I needed a sip of cognac, but I couldn't move.

"Tuesday," he said. "Actually Wednesday morning, according to the ME's report."

"Yeh," I said thoughtfully, looking him in the eye. "I was shit-faced drunk. I had just found out about Denise. I took it pretty hard. I wound up sleeping on somebody's couch. It didn't do me any good."

It was the big lie, the Mafia alibi. I was perfectly composed as I delivered the line.

"Would you know anyone who'd want to kill Bennie and Ralph Torres, or Manolo Pearson, the man you knew?"

"Certainly not," I said. I glanced away quickly, too quickly to read his eyes. If I thought I was off the hook, I was wrong.

"*You* would have no reason to do so?" he said.

"Kill?" My voice cracked. It almost sounded convincing. I looked at him, my brow in a knot. A truck rumbled past and the digital clock on Henry's dashboard ticked off the seconds while I searched for a better reply.

"If you knew they killed Denise?" he asked. Henry's voice was soft and conciliatory, but he had more up his sleeve. This was cat-and-mouse interrogation. I caressed the cup and tried to draw its warmth into my chilled bones.

"If I knew they killed her and I had the chance to kill them, would I do it?" I stared at the clock. 2:47. There was another knot forming in my throat, but I felt a lot better asking the question rather than answering it. I hoped my voice wouldn't crack again. "I don't know," I said, my voice fading.

"OK," Henry said. "I'm not saying you shot those guys. That's not the point. I'm trying to tell you as a friend that someone called 911 two days ago and suggested you might know something about how Bennie and Ralph Torres and the other man got hit." He gave me another searching look. "That's between you and me."

911? I had called 911 to report the murders, but that wasn't what he meant.

"Someone called 911 and gave my name?"

"A female Hispanic."

I didn't say what I was thinking. Aurora Carrera!

"Maybe it was one of the drag queens I interviewed," I replied uncertainly. I couldn't admit I suspected Aurora was the caller. Not yet, anyway. And what about my own call to 911?

Voice prints. Would they have voice prints?

"There was another call," Henry solemnly informed me. "Detective Gonzalez heard both tapes. Someone else called 911 and requested an ambulance at that address the night it happened. The bodies weren't even cold. A hit man does that if he needs publicity."

"Needs publicity?" I blurted it out while I tried to steady my hand. The coffee was getting frisky again. I thought about that inspector who called from police headquarters. *Hi, Mr. Darenow, recognize your voice?* Is that why they want me to drop by?

"A hit man gets paid when the contractor is satisfied the guys are dead," Henry said. "Having a picture of three corpses on the front page saves him the trouble of bringing back ears or fingers."

Sounds good to me. I nearly smiled. If they don't make voice prints, my phone call to 911 may have been a good idea. Blame it on a hit man.

I looked Henry in the eye and wished I could tell him the truth.

"Someone must know you're interested in this case and they're making trouble for you, Mr. Darenow," Henry added with some concern. "That's why I say: be careful. Other people are gonna ask you questions like I did, but maybe a little bit less open-minded. Just tell 'em what you told me. Shit! No one's gonna believe you ever walked out of a three-way shoot-out and lived to tell the tale anyway."

"Right . . ." I croaked again.

I was shivering. Henry started the engine to power the heater. This was far from over and getting worse.

"I had a call from an Inspector Rossetti at police headquarters," I announced.

"Oh, Rossetti," he said lightly. "I'm not surprised."

According to Henry, Inspector Dante Gabriel Rossetti ran a tight little unit within the department's Bureau of Special Services, the intelligence-gathering division. Rossetti's job was to keep track, as best he could, of all covert operations, and covert operators, doing business in the Big Apple. There were legions of them. I thought of Avery Wately, Edgar's father, and what Melendez had mentioned about the Torres boys' links to the CIA.

"Rossetti's in charge of the spook squad." Henry laughed. "The feds go out of their way to protect their agents' identities—too far, I think—to keep us in the dark. Then they worry about accidents. Let's say an agent is armed, or he's undercover around drugs, and the New York cops happen upon the scene. It's either blow your cover or risk getting blown away. That's why the feds don't trust anybody—including each other."

Henry paused and snorted in frustration.

"It's their own fault. They use contract agents—murderers, con men, riffraff that work both sides of the fence. Rossetti's unit, if they're tipped in time, tries to direct traffic so the wrong guys don't get hurt."

Henry stared thoughtfully.

"Look, Darenow, I'm a cop and I'm black. I go to church and I try to uphold the law to the best of my ability, but sometimes I wonder if I'm on the right side. You hear all kinds of things in the ghetto, and you hear all kinds of things on this job, and after a while you don't know who's right and who's wrong."

I said nothing in reply. He was groping for an answer so I let him think.

"There's a rumor in the ghetto that won't go away," he sighed before looking me in the eye. "It started right after the black riots in the 1960s, about the time that drugs started pouring into Harlem. It was heroin then; it's crack now. The rumor was that the CIA was using drugs to dampen the fires of a revolution."

"A new twist on 'opiate of the masses,' " I said.

"Opiates are opiates." Henry grinned bitterly. "If you want to pacify a lot of angry, uneducated black bucks, making sure they have plenty of heroin and crack is a lot easier than getting them into Sunday school and getting them working. Hell, they might become registered voters."

Henry was giving me plenty to think about, but he hadn't answered my question.

"Where did Rossetti get my name, and what does he want from me?" I asked warily.

"He wants to identify the undercover agent working near the Torres boys, but the feds aren't cooperating." Henry shrugged.

"Uh-huh." I nodded thoughtfully. "More CIA stuff. And you guys—New York's finest—are being pulled off the case."

Henry cradled the coffee cup in his lap and slid the car into gear. He resumed cruising. He was heading toward my house.

"Listen, Mr. Darenow, we get a break, we open that case, bring it to court—if we ever get a break. But we're gonna lose time while the feds horse around with all these Cubans. They're burying bodies and leaving false trails. Time is against us. My hunch is that Inspector Rossetti wants to match the people Miss Overton was hanging out with against his own private list of names."

"Do you think any of those men from Avenue A could have been undercover agents?"

"Anything's possible," Henry said. "They're known bad guys, unless . . ." his voice trailed off.

"Unless what?"

"Unless their arrest records were manufactured like their passports. It's in the realm of the possible."

"Their passports?" I had to play it very smooth here.

"The Torres men carried Panamanian passports under different names," he said. "We're still in the dark about that. The feds are acting very hush-hush. Make a note of it but forget I told you."

"Christ, this is turning into a big deal," I said, trying my best to remain nonchalant and matter-of-fact about the whole thing.

"If you can find that transsexual your girlfriend was taking pictures of—before she disappears, if she hasn't already—we might come up with something. You willing to try?"

I wanted nothing else at that moment except to sit down with a lawyer and tell the cops everything I knew.

"But don't take any chances," he said. "Call Rossetti tonight. And let me know if you have to go anywhere dangerous, OK? I'd go with you as a friend."

"That's awful nice," I said, "but I'm never going to get close enough to anything to be in danger." Who was I kidding?

He stopped in front of my apartment building, said goodnight, and I traced a wobbly path to the front door.

I went upstairs, took off my coat, and dialed Inspector Rossetti's number.

A woman answered, not at all sleepy. There was a television on in the background.

I gave her my name and said I was returning Inspector Rossetti's call.

"Gabe," she said as she passed the phone, "it's for you."

Inspector Rossetti came on the line. He was cheerful enough, brief, and to the point. He asked to see me, at police headquarters in a Deputy Commissioner McGovern's office, at 2:30 tomorrow afternoon. *This* afternoon.

"What's the scoop?" I asked blithely.

"No scoop," he replied just as blithely. "*Deep* background, not for the papers. We want to bring you up to date on what we know about Miss Overton's death and a few other things."

I couldn't measure his sincerity. He must have noticed.

"Is there a problem?" he asked offhandedly.

"No," I said. "No problem. I'll be there."

No problem? According to Melendez, someone—Aurora—had phoned 911 and merely *suggested* yours truly might know something about the murders. According to Henry, she didn't say I was *physically* there. It still wasn't a good sign.

I ran back over what Melendez had said. Wately was Esmeralda's lover; Bennie and Ralph worked for Wately; Bennie and Ralph killed Jaime and Denise—and tried to kill Esmeralda. Henry had told me as much. Come on, Darenow. What's two plus two?

It was as clear as the nose on my face. Edgar Wately had ordered all three of them killed. Jaime and Esmeralda were dispensable. Denise knew Edgar was Jaime's and Esmeralda's sugar daddy, Edgar found out Denise knew his dirty little secret and told Bennie and Ralph it was time to clean house.

A bell tolled slowly, mournfully, like the first buoy in a strange, foggy harbor.

I weighed my options: I couldn't tell the cops what I knew without implicating myself in a triple homicide, leaving the scene, hampering an investigation, suborning a witness, and consorting with known gangsters. But I was due at police headquarters in less than twelve hours.

It was after three in the morning. Maybe the Big Guy had already presented his deal to Edgar. I looked at my notes and I dialed the number Wately had left earlier. Might as well keep shaking his tree, and why wait till morning?

The number I dialed, I learned, belonged to the Albemarle Club, an all-male preserve where the quietly rich go to scratch each other's backs and talk about money behind closed doors. Its membership rolls were full of Wall Street sharks playing I Spy. It was a retreat from the world, from all the dicey, unpredictable, nasty things that intrude on an insecure man's sense of order, a place where he can be reassured by like-minded men that if you hold fast to the party line, circle the wagons, and hang tough, those terrible *others* can be beaten back.

The phone rang a half dozen times before a politely sleepy male voice answered. I asked for Mr. Wately and told him who was calling. There was a long wait before he connected me.

"Helluva time to call, Darenow. What's wrong?" The edge in Wately's world-weary banker's voice was back.

I apologized for calling so late.

"What do you want?" Wately asked gruffly.

"Couple of things," I said. "Have you ever heard of a man named Hector Melendez?"

Long, pregnant pause.

"Aren't you supposed to be talking to my sister tomorrow night?" he asked warily.

"I've been invited for cocktails and told to bring my notebook, if that's what you mean," I replied. "In the meantime, I thought you might be able to clarify some things about Hector Melendez."

"What on earth for?" he asked.

"There's been some developments," I said lightly. I filled him in on the deaths of the Torres brothers and the fact that Denise's camera had been found in Manolo Pearson's apartment.

Another long pause.

"I don't get the connection," he said in a dull voice. "What are you trying to say?"

"There's talk on the street that the Torres brothers worked for Mr. Melendez."

Another pause. He was giving it a lot of thought. His voice dropped to a whisper, as if the question had knocked the wind out of him.

"That's wild," he said.

"Do you think it's possible?" I asked.

"I'm not at liberty to discuss any of this," he said in a louder, hurried tone. "Hasn't my sister told you anything?"

"No one's telling me a goddamned thing," I replied. "Except the police and a couple of drag queens." I was all innocence.

"What do you know about a drag queen named Esmeralda Sanchez?" I added. It slid into the conversation so well.

Wately drew an audible breath. Shit! I thought, I shouldn't be doing this over the phone. I'm moving too fast. He's gonna catch wise, or panic.

"She was Jaime's . . ." He struggled to complete the sentence. "She was . . . *this is preposterous*," he squealed. *"What is going on?"*

He was panicking.

"You tell me," I said. "Let's meet and talk."

"Look, Mr. Darenow," he replied with exasperation. "You're all over the map. My God, Hector Melendez has nothing to do with this. This is a very complicated matter you've walked into. We're talking about . . . matters of national security. Hasn't my sister explained any of this to you?"

"Your sister wants me to talk to some friends of hers," I said. "Who are they?"

"The State Department," he quickly replied. "They'll explain everything. This is a family tragedy. My father . . ." He sounded as if he was crying.

"Your father worked for the CIA," I informed him. "Were the Torres brothers working for the CIA?"

"This is *so* complicated," he gasped.

"Why didn't you tell me you knew Esmeralda Sanchez?" I asked. "I'm told you knew her quite well."

"Oh, God, please, sir. I don't know where you're getting your information. Come to our house tomorrow night. Everything will be cleared up." His voice was returning to normal, but very slowly.

"I want to talk to you," I said, "not your sister."

"You'll have to talk to the authorities," he said with finality.

"I'll be at your apartment tomorrow night," I said. "I expect a full accounting then."

"Your friend . . ." he started, and then his voice brimmed with emotion. "You lost your friend. You deserve an explanation."

I told him I'd see him tomorrow night and hung up. I was so far out on a limb I couldn't pursue him any further without jeopardizing myself.

I found the pack of Camels and lit another one up.

I still couldn't get a fix on Edgar Wately. If Esmeralda was really his lover, that would tend to support the blackmail theory. But then why kill her?

I had to speak to Esmeralda, even if it meant suborning a witness. I called Dixie. She picked up on the second ring, as if it was the middle of the afternoon. She said hello like Dinah Shore in a chicken commercial. Everything was hunky-dory on her end except Esmeralda needed more coke and no one had any. Dixie wanted to know if I had some.

The words rustled in my mind like Dracula's cape. I thought about the coke in Manolo's apartment. Don't get so defensive, I thought, Esmeralda's the junkie.

Dixie apologized for asking and turned to the subject of Edgar Wately. I told her I had called him, as instructed.

"Max," Dixie trilled, "Esmeralda has all the dirt on Wately."

I felt dirty myself but I had to talk to Esmeralda. "I'm doing this for Denise," I said for no reason at all.

I told Dixie I'd be right over, after I changed my clothes. If I was going to Dixie's to grill Esmeralda, I didn't want to look like one of the guys who had just kidnapped her. I went into the closet and changed my clothes from the ones I had been wearing at the Waldorf, adding a wool cap to cover my forehead. I was no dope. I knew about disguises. Let them try to catch me now.

I was about to shut the light when an incoming thought made hash of my brain, a sobering thought that twisted angrily as it moved to the fore of other thoughts now receding.

Maybe this whole thing is a bungled CIA caper, unraveling before my eyes.

20

Dixie owned a 2,000-square-foot loft on the Bowery, around the corner from Little Italy, a long, narrow, rectangular space a half-block long, with a kitchen, bath, shower, sauna, and bidet at one end, and Dixie's "parlor" at the other. In between were "the boudoir, library, and nightclub," as Dixie called them.

The decor, except for the kitchen and spa, was part New Orleans and part Hollywood musical. The library consisted of shelves of books and records, stereo gear, a video player, and a twenty-four-inch color monitor. The books were on costume and stage design, makeup, fashion, and beauty. The records were mostly show tunes.

The nightclub portion consisted of three ice cream tables and six matching chairs set at the edge of a pink linoleum dance floor that faced a tiny semicircular stage, complete with curtain and spotlights. There was, I swear to God, a mirrored ball over the dance floor, which was six feet square. ("I use it for backers' auditions," Dixie said. "Sometimes I invite people over to see a new act. It's like court theater. Only you never know who's courting who.")

A queen-sized bed, covered in lavender and lace, was the focal point of the boudoir. The bed was flanked with nightstands and lamps, none of which matched, except the colors, which were predominately lavender and white. Dixie's collection of custom-tailored Barbie dolls sat, stretched, and strutted their stuff on a shelf above the bed. The shelf was edged in ruffled pink and white ribbon. "The Barbies are worth a small fortune," Dixie said. I wasn't sure if the pun was intended.

The walls on either side of the bed were hung with Dixie's show gowns, her own creations as well as designer copies she ran up on her sewing machine. They came in all colors of the rainbow. "Diana Vreeland wants me to leave them to the Costume Institute," Dixie crowed. "I told her I wasn't planning to die." I counted thirty-two frocks and stopped counting.

A powder-blue tulle net was draped on each side of the bed, joined and tufted at the ceiling, framing the Barbies and softening the effect of the gold-flecked, mirrored headboard trimmed in more lavender and gilt. "I thought of a mirrored ceiling, but I was worried it might fall," Dixie hooted. "Besides, I'm always on top so I'd only see myself when I was sleeping."

Four vanity tables of varying shapes and sizes, covered with jars and tubes of makeup, lotions, and potions, were lined against the wall separating boudoir from library. Across the aisle were two sawhorses holding up a table on which rested a dozen wigs, half of them mounted on the heads of old painted plaster millinery mannequins, the rest on white Styrofoam forms.

It was a strange tableau; the painted heads all stared at different points in space while the Styrofoam heads were blank and directionless, as if waiting for a face to be assigned to them. It reminded me of a De Chirico painting.

Painted flats, used as backdrops for Dixie's extravaganzas, were stacked here and there, filling up the available wall space. A pair of painted Doric columns, used for Dixie's Samson and Delilah spoof, framed the entrance to the parlor.

We sat in the parlor, on white wicker furniture upholstered in zebra stripes, under a pink ceiling fan that swept the smoke from Esmeralda's cigarettes into lazy spirals that drifted like frail clouds.

Number One had taken up residence in an easy chair, which he had pulled into a dark corner. He didn't say very much for a long time; he just listened quietly until Esmeralda got a little excited.

Esmeralda was stretched out on the couch in a white terry cloth lounging suit and gold high-heeled boots. Her hair was blond again. It was her own hair, piled atop her head and fastened with a gold clip and lots of bobby pins. The dye job had been done on a wig.

Her features weren't softened by the blond tresses. Esmeralda had a strong face, no matter how you framed it; it was a mask, void of character—except for her eyes.

Number Two sat in the library, his attention wandering from the telephone to the door to the wrestling matches on television, and sometimes to the action, or lack thereof, in the parlor. He kept falling asleep.

Dixie played hostess, changing into a flowing white peignoir and matching gown, with white tufted high-heeled slippers to match. At various times she made coffee, sandwiches, fudge brownies, mixed drinks, and light of the situation—all at the right moment. When she wasn't doing that she was sitting on the edge of a wicker rocker, her legs crossed, a tufted slipper dangling precariously from her painted tootsies.

It took several hours to pry a story out of her. Number One helped. So did Dixie. So did the pizza delivery boy, who brought a thick Sicilian pie with sausages and a side order of three grams of cocaine at around 7 A.M. The pizza was for Numbers One, Two, and me. The cocaine was for Esmeralda. Dixie finished the brownies.

Dixie had warned me, upon my arrival, that Esmeralda was unaware of exactly how much we knew about her boyfriend, Edgar. But Esmeralda didn't seem to care. She considered herself a celebrity of sorts, and took it for granted that we recognized him as a big enchilada. Number Two made it clear he wasn't impressed with pedigree, didn't like baby-sitting for Esmeralda and advised me to proceed with the grilling. I sat opposite her and began by asking how she had met Denise.

She said Denise had approached her one night in the Toucan Too and asked her to pose. "I am like a product of modern technology," Esmeralda added in a rehearsed voice. "A beautiful example of woman, so naturally she wanted to photograph me." Esmeralda said she wasn't interested, "not even for money," until Denise agreed to include a wedding portrait "like the ones from Bachrach."

She flashed a diamond engagement ring as big as the Ritz and said Edgar Wately had given it to her. She referred to him as her husband.

"Where did you meet Bennie and Ralph Torres?"

"They were like servants," she shrugged.

"They were killers," I said. "They were big-time drug dealers, too, until some people got tired of them. Now they're dead. You could wind up the same way."

It didn't faze her. She slipped off her booties, stretched her legs out on the chaise, and flexed her toes, revealing a ornate silver ankle bracelet worn over her hose. She cocked her foot and gazed at it wistfully. It was a custom-made job, seven disks of hammered silver, with words engraved on the disks.

"A present from my husband," she said. "It's Mexican." She stretched her leg to give me a better look. "What does it say?" I asked. I was trying to put her at ease. I wanted her to relax and spill her guts before someone else did.

"For Esme—he call me Esme, tha's his pet name for me—with love and something else, I forget. And the date of the year. It's nice." She twisted her ankle around so I could see it better. She liked it because it was shiny and expensive.

I had to get up to take a closer look.

The inscription said "For Esme, With Love And Squalor" and was dated three years ago.

Poor Edgar Wately. Maybe he did love her. Or maybe he was just having a little fun, a cruel, private joke. The inscription was taken from the title of a J. D. Salinger story about a soldier who meets a war orphan, a scared, scarred, teenage girl and leaves a farewell note signed "For Esme, With Love And Squalor."

"Why do you think Bennie Torres tried to kill you?" I asked.

"They was jealous of me and Jaime 'cause we was beautiful and they was ugly," she said dismissively. She dodged the subject and inquired about the coke, which hadn't arrived yet.

"Did Ethel Wately know you were living with her brother?" I continued.

Esmeralda raised an eyebrow and smiled; her eyes narrowed and her tongue poked at the inside of her cheek. "Of course," she said mockingly, amazed at my naïveté. "She would be my sister-in-law."

"So you've met Mrs. Wately?" I asked incredulously.

"She called on me," Esmeralda replied easily. "It is the custom."

"What did you two talk about?" This was rich.

Esmeralda's smile turned into a wide-open, silly grin.

"She wanted to see my pussy," she laughed dryly.

"When was this?" It was jaw-to-the-floor time.

"Fuck you," she snapped. "Where's the coke? You're getting too personal. Find my husband and bring him here."

We were getting no place until the cocaine arrived. That loosened Esmeralda's tongue.

She was born in Puerto Rico. Her father had been a merchant seaman who came and went in one night. She was christened Jesus LeMer, LeMer being her father's name. She later adopted her mother's name,

Sanchez, as a surname. Her mother, whom Esmeralda implied had been a prostitute, turned "her" over to an older, single woman who raised her as a girl and named her Esmeralda. By the time Esmeralda was fifteen, she was on the stroll, working the hotel lobbies and the parking lots. That's where she claimed to have met Edgar Wately for the first time.

"He took me to a nightclub and kept telling me how beautiful I looked," she said dreamily.

"I knew how to dress," she bragged, "so I could go anywhere."

When she turned eighteen, she moved into Old San Juan. She was taking hormone and silicone injections by then, adding curves to an already girlish figure. She became the Toast of La Perla. One night, in a hotel bar on the Condado, Esmeralda picked up an Albanian merchant seaman. The man broke Esmeralda's jaw upon discovering "she" was a "he." Esmeralda had been warned about men of his ilk and so carried an antidote—a six-inch steel letter opener filed to a fine point that she plunged through his back, into his heart. Esmeralda had a woman's charm and a surgeon's eye. Her plea of self-defense earned her an acquittal and the further admiration of the people of La Perla.

The talk shifted back to Edgar Wately.

"He was perfect," Esmeralda said wistfully. "He was handsome, good manners, plenty of money, but there were all these problems."

Esmeralda thought those problems could be connected to his bank. In any case, she said her troubles really began about six months ago when Wately began avoiding her. Wately had bought her a house in Tampa, she said, and an apartment in New York for Jaime. But suddenly, Wately had told them both they would have to move to Puerto Rico, or maybe Costa Rica, for reasons that weren't clear to her. She balked at the idea. It would only delay the wedding. Wately compromised by letting her stay at a house he owned in Puerto Rico in a place called Las Conchas. He forbade her to call him at home or at the office, and only communicated with her through the Torres brothers, who served as her warders. These developments obviously upset her; her mood turned uglier as the dream faded.

"I was a prisoner," she complained. "Bennie and Ralph only let me go out at night for walks on the beach. I was going crazy until Jaime came to visit me. Then they left to go to Tampa to see my husband on some business so Jaime and me slipped out and came to New York."

"When was that?" I asked.

"About two months ago," she said. "My husband was so mad. But he came to see me and he promised we'd go away after everything was over."

"Until what was over?"

"I dunno," she said. "Some important business he had to do."

"Did it involve the Torres brothers?"

She shrugged her shoulders and looked blank.

"What did the Torres brothers do for your husband, Edgar?" I asked her.

"They ran errands," she frowned. "My husband called them his 'problem solvers.' "

"Maybe they were one of his problems," I suggested. "And maybe you were one of his problems, too."

"Maybe," she sighed.

It was like that for the next hour. She either didn't know or she held back. The gravity of the situation didn't register.

We started to discuss the night Esmeralda met Denise in Rocco's joint, The Crib, when she began to beg for more cocaine. Number One was holding the stash. He threw the three bags on the table and shook his head in disgust as she dived for it.

"You gotta take some, too," Esmeralda said to me. "Then we be equal."

"I've had enough," I said. "And don't take too much yourself. There's a lot of things I have to know before I can help you."

"Who's gonna help me?" she said. "Him?"—she jerked her head towards Number One—"Or you?"

"Maybe both of us," I said quickly. "Your husband, Mr. Wately, is in trouble. Perhaps he's the one who wants you killed."

Esmeralda looked at the drug and at me. There was a sneer in her voice. She ignored my comment.

"Come into my life, baby," she said with all the wrong feeling. "Then we'll talk."

I took a matchbook cover and scooped up enough white powder to make her happy.

"Who gave Denise the drugs?" I asked.

"Bennie," she said. "Their fucking aunt was jealous of me."

"Rosa?" I said.

"Yi!" she said, dipping into the drugs for a second hit, "that one!"

"Did Jaime ever talk about his father?" I said. "About inheriting money?"

"Oh, sure," she said. "He had lots of money. This is good cocaine."

"Was Bennie Torres, or Ralph Torres, trying to blackmail Edgar?" I asked.

She couldn't grasp the question.

"We were like man and wife," she said indignantly. "We lived together."

The memory caused her to pause and reflect. Her eyes grew colder. "His sister told me I wouldn't ever be accepted as a woman by his friends. She said I should find another husband."

"Maybe she hired Bennie to kill you and Jaime," I suggested. It was just a probe. Nothing seemed impossible with these people.

"Never," she said with finality.

"Why not?" I said.

"Why?" she demanded. "I told you Bennie gave us the drugs. He gave me some and he gave everybody some. He always had drugs."

"Did *your husband* know that?" I asked.

"I don't know," she said. A faraway look crept into her eyes.

"I want to call him. I want him to come and get me," she said, getting up and pacing around the chaise, stopping in front of Number One's chair. Number One grinned up lazily at her.

"Get him for me, baby," she said to Number One. "Bring him to me. You'll make a lot of money."

She faced him with her legs spread apart and her hands on her hips. She cut an imposing figure. The jumpsuit fit her like a glove. When she stretched into one of her Cosmo girl poses, all the silicone curves fell into alignment. The Toast of La Perla! I could imagine her strutting her stuff when the fleet sailed into Old San Juan.

She thrust her pelvis in Number One's direction and shook the silicone bazooms at him with the skill of a burlesque queen.

Number One exhaled but made no comment. His grin faded behind the cigarette smoke. I liked him. I hoped he never did anything to make me change my mind.

"Edgar hopes you'll disappear. Can't you see that?" I said.

She didn't like that at all. Her dream was sacrosanct. She turned on her heel and came toward me with her left arm trailing stiff behind her. She was winding up a roundhouse slap to my face. I started to get up and out of the way when Number One bolted off the chair, grabbed Esmeralda's arm, and spun her around so she faced him. He wasn't much taller than she was, but he leveraged her down without effort.

She didn't resist. Her body went limp and she sagged toward him.

"I'll treat you better than a woman," she whispered.

"Sit the fuck down," he snapped.

Esmeralda brushed herself off, pouted, and sat down. She wanted to be Edgar Wately's wife but she only knew how to act like a whore.

"Did Bennie give Denise a Tuinal?" I asked gently.

"I dunno," Esmeralda shrugged. "Maybe Jaime gave her one of his. Bennie only gave us drugs to see if they were good quality." She shoveled into the coke with her pinkie nail and sucked about a quarter gram up her nose. "They must have made a lot of money," she sighed.

She didn't seem to care they had tried to kill her. She admired them for making money.

"They tried to kill you," I said, as evenly as I could muster.

"I don't know," she said. "*Somebody* wants to kill me. That's what my husband think."

"*Edgar told you someone wanted to kill you?*" I said. We were finally making progress. She crinkled her nose and sniffed the air. She was thinking about the question, but it was racing away in her mind. She dipped her pinkie into the coke again and took two ladylike snorts.

"That's what he tell me," she said, licking her fingertips.

"And you have no idea who these people are?" I said. "That's hard to believe."

"He knows lots of people," she replied. "Some of them are very jealous."

Her offhand manner had a rousing effect on Number One. He crossed into the light, scowling.

"Can it!" he said. "Call your boyfriend up right now. Tell him to get his ass down here or we're throwing you to the wolves. You got his number? There's the phone. Dial it!"

Esmeralda looked at the coke. She wanted to suck up the rest of a gram before she dialed.

"You got anything to drink?" she asked Dixie. She remained totally oblivious to Number One.

Dixie went to get her another drink. Esmeralda looked cooly at Number One. "What should I tell my husband?" she said nonchalantly.

"I told you," Number One said impatiently. "We're gonna turn you over to the cops and they're gonna hang a murder rap on you unless your boyfriend sits down and deals with us. You want to spend your life in a woman's prison now that your dick's cut off? You fucking stupid or something?"

His logic was sound but I didn't like his approach. It was abundantly clear the mob wanted to lean on Wately for their own gain. I wanted no part of that.

I took him aside and tried to explain that I was still trying to act like an honest reporter, albeit one who was going to extraordinary lengths to get a story.

"I can't let her tell Wately that," I said. "It's going to make me look bad. I'll talk to Wately myself, at the proper time."

"So what are we gonna do with this fuckin' thing? She ain't telling you nothin' so far." The expression on my face told him I didn't have the answer. He leaned over and tugged my lapel.

"She'll talk," he whispered. "I'll do a razor job on her snatch."

"Let's take a break," I said. "Let's calm down."

"Does anyone want coffee?" Dixie boomed. She came bounding in with Esmeralda's rum, scanning the room like a nervous hostess who knows the party has taken a bad turn. "Not you, honey," she said to Esmeralda. "You're wired already."

It didn't register as a joke with Esmeralda. She sat down on the chaise and looked tired. She drew her legs up and stroked her arms. Her world was in tatters and she was just beginning to realize it.

"Why would Bennie kill Jamie," I asked, "unless someone hired him to do it?"

"I dunno," she said.

Number One snatched the coke off the table. Esmeralda lunged for it but Number One straight-armed her back into the chaise.

"Daddy's gonna give you some candy when you start talking," he said. "Tell me, never mind him"—he jerked a thumb in my direction—"tell *me* what kind of trouble your husband is in."

"My husband lend Bennie and Ralph money and they wouldn't pay him back."

"Did Edgar back them in the Toucan Too?" I asked.

"They needed some place to sell retail, you know? What you think, they gonna stand on the street corner and sell quarter grams?" She couldn't imagine I was so stupid. "Everything bad happened when they went retail."

"Like what?" Number One demanded.

"Guys from Miami came up and killed *all* the people who was working for Bennie and Ralph," she said without any emotion. "So I guess Bennie and Ralph got mad."

"What do you mean? Threatening Wately?" I asked.

"Yeh," she said, "like that." She was losing interest. Her eyes wandered over to the bags of coke Number One was holding like a quarterback about to throw a pass.

"Give her another hit," I said. He handed me one of the envelopes. I dumped some coke on the table and jammed the rest in my pocket.

"Call my husband and tell him I'm all right," she whined. "I have to talk to him!" She stared at the coke and started to cry. The tears were real; the sobs shook her breast implants.

"Tell us who your husband is afraid of," I said. "And then everything will be all right and you can go away."

"They'll kill me!" she shrieked. She was bawling now, a keening wail that brought Number Two into the parlor with a worried look on his face.

I felt sorry for her. I didn't feel sorry for Edgar Wately.

"Ask her again," Number One said.

"The police are going to think your husband tried to kill you unless you tell us what you know," I said.

She searched my eyes but she didn't answer. She was plenty scared of someone, and I believed she had some idea of who that someone was.

"The girl needs her beauty sleep," Dixie winked. "You want to take a nap on my bed, honey?"

Esmeralda nodded and rubbed her runny nose on her sleeve. Her cheeks were streaked with black mascara. She was a mess; she didn't care what she looked like. She just wanted daddy to come and get her. Dixie gave her a tissue. Esmeralda curled up on Dixie's bed. Dixie laid a quilt over her and rubbed her back. She gave her a Darvon and told her to get some sleep. But Esmeralda said she couldn't sleep until I called Edgar and interceded on her behalf.

"That's what Dixie said you would do," she sobbed. "But you're not doing it!" She wanted to be forceful but she was burned out.

I told her I'd speak to Wately. I didn't know how I'd handle it but I gave her my promise. She was either an innocent screwball or she was cleverly witholding information, protecting someone or stalling for time until Edgar came to the rescue. The Darvon pulled her eyelids down like the last curtain of a bad act.

Number One came over and took note of the sleeping Esmeralda. He looked at me and said: "Go."

"What are you going to do with her?"

"If we can't get nothin' out of her soon we're goin' to have to lean heavy on the boyfriend," he replied casually. "It depends on what he says when you tell him we're baby-sittin' his little chickadee. He's worried about his image. He oughta be worried, hanging around with this trash. Look, either the cops will chew her up or someone else will get her, right? So we're her best bet."

"You're not going to harm her," I said.

"Naw, naw," Number One said. "She's worth more alive than dead. Just make sure you see this Wately guy tomorrow."

"Yeh," I nodded.

I was a liar. I had to see a deputy police commissioner tomorrow. And suddenly I didn't want to see Wately again, ever. I wanted to go home to a nice warm bed, get a good night's sleep, and wake up to discover that none of this had ever happened.

Dixie walked me to the elevator. I was having reservations about everything. I felt as if I had accomplished nothing at all.

"Do you think Denise would approve of what I'm doing?" I asked her.

"I don't think she'd care, Max. You're doing this for yourself and I don't think you realize that. You might get some satisfaction out of putting the people who murdered her away, but it won't bring Denise back.

"Max," Dixie continued, "Denise thought you were a great lover." Dixie sighed and crossed her arms stoically. "But she wasn't about to give up her career because you thought marriage and children could solve your personal problems."

"I could have been anything she wanted," I cried.

The elevator lurched into place and yawned.

21

PATRICK SARSFIELD MCGOVERN was all the sign said. It was engraved on a heavy brass plaque outside the office nearest to the commissioner's own. It was a relic carried over from the old, baroque police headquarters on Centre Street, which had been converted into expensive condos, and it was a reminder of First Deputy Commissioner P. S. McGovern's clout.

McGovern was known as "The Cardinal," or "His Eminence," for several reasons. For one thing, he bore an uncanny resemblance to John Houston, who had played a Prince of the Church in *The Cardinal*. For another thing, McGovern was the commissioner's confessor, his *éminence grise*. He was a confirmed bachelor, a devout Catholic, and a Knight of Malta—an honor conferred by the church mainly on certified movers, shakers, and the particularly generous. McGovern knew the city; he knew where certain bodies were buried, and in whose closets skeletons rattled. His integrity was cast in granite, and his talent for diplomacy and behind-the-scenes maneuvering were highly regarded. As the commissioner's hatchet man and ex-officio secretary of state, McGovern wielded great power, inside and outside the ranks. He was a deal maker, a power broker, and, most important, the soul of discretion. He had to be: he liaisoned with everyone of importance, from the mayor to the mob.

McGovern's secretary, Maude Callaghan, was a reserved, tightly corseted spinster in her fifties who had a hard time concealing her devotion to her boss, who was pushing sixty himself, and whom she had served faithfully six, sometimes seven, days a week for fifteen years. She held him in awe. So did everyone else.

Maude was on duty when I arrived. She had no trouble figuring out who I was, and she took my coat before knocking on the inner sanctum and announcing my presence in tones appropriate to an abbess.

McGovern's office was full of personal touches, a far cry from the spartan decor that prevailed elsewhere in the gleaming new headquarters building. He had a Chinese carpet on the floor. He had a carved oak desk, a phony marble mantelpiece with phony logs in it and two leather couches facing across a cocktail table fashioned out of a sewer cover that sat atop a brass pedestal. He also had a pair of telescopes. One was a brass antique, the other I recognized as a $4,000 job that could make the moon look like a closeup of a rivet on the Brooklyn Bridge, which it also picked up very well.

We were joined by Chief Inspector Dante Gabriel Rossetti, a soft-spoken, mild-mannered burgher who lived on a quiet street in Queens three blocks from the house where he was born. He was a man without pretensions, a man who weighed his words very carefully, a man whose demeanor belied his stature as head of the department's "spook squad."

Rossetti liaisoned with the heads of security from all the city's foreign consulates and missions. In the city that played host to the United Nations, that task was formidable.

Spies were Rossetti's meat; the study of the world's intelligence services was his hobby. His exploits were legend among veteran cop watchers. They say his boys once found a shipment of plutonium, the kind you use to make atom bombs. It was turned over to the Atomic Energy Commission without fanfare. How the NYPD found it remains a mystery. It was rumored that Rossetti's men had saved several heads of state from national dishonor, averted the assassinations of several ranking diplomats, saved more than one sheik from disgrace, and helped avert the assassination of an Israeli premier.

Rossetti and I were offered seats on the leather couches that flanked the sewer cover. The Cardinal, after the formality of introductions, took a seat behind his desk. He was a big man, with massive shoulders and a head to match. His sparse gray hair was combed flat and lay smooth against his skull, like a carefully plowed field. He moved in a dignified stoop.

On top of the sewer cover, which was "protected" with a glass top, were ashtrays, a vase with no flowers, a pitcher of water, and plastic cups. There was also a battery-operated cassette player that wasn't turned on. The atmosphere last night at Dixie's had been better.

His Eminence got right to the heart of the matter with a demonstration of dry humor and no-nonsense candor.

"We have a problem, Mr. Darenow," he said, resting his steel-blue eyes on me. "All of us."

If he meant to instill fear, he was off to a good start.

"I'll be glad to help," I said, rearranging the lump in my throat.

"I appreciate your enthusiasm," he deadpanned. "Let's see if it lasts. Gabe, why don't you start?"

Rossetti turned the recorder on. He wasn't recording. He wanted to play something for me and it wasn't the "Moonlight Sonata."

"These are transcriptions of calls into 911 made by two different individuals," Rossetti said matter-of-factly. "Let me know if either one of the callers sound familiar."

I knotted my brow to divert attention from the nervous smile that was asserting itself.

The first voice was mine, announcing that three men had been shot in an apartment at 76 Avenue A and were probably dead. It was mercifully brief, but I was dumbstruck nonetheless. Was this a joke?

"Recognize the voice?" Rossetti asked.

I concentrated real hard. My Spanish accent and the roar of the subway masked my voice. I hoped they hadn't run the tape through a voice analyzer. I kept concentrating, as if I was really trying. I held my breath and squinted my eyes, as if that was going to prove something.

"Play it again," I said. Rossetti played it again. Christ, why had I called the cops?

"I don't recognize it." I said.

He played the second tape. It was Aurora Carrera's turn. She was mercifully brief, but angry.

"Ask the reporter from the *New York Graphic* who killed Bennie and Ralph Torres," Aurora said. "Ask him what he knows." Click. That was it.

I looked appropriately puzzled. The nervous smile flared. *How much do they know?*

"Well, somebody thinks I know something," I said. "Or ought to know something." My sweats weren't visible yet. Nothing on the brow.

"You recognize the voice?" The Cardinal asked. His chin was cradled in his hands. His elbows rested on the desk, forming a big M that accentuated his stare.

"I don't know," I said, hoping my mind would think of something more brilliant to say before I blew myself away in a gale of nervous laughter.

"I honestly can't say; there's something familiar about the voice. I can't pinpoint it," I mused. Why the hell don't they just snap the cuffs on me? I thought. Or open the sewer cover and let me float out to sea.

"Did you know Bennie and Ralph Torres?" The Cardinal asked.

Here we go, Darenow.

"Never had the pleasure," I said. "But I did know the kid whose apartment it was."

The Cardinal looked at Rossetti without changing his pose.

"Manolo Pearson," Rossetti said. "A Cuban refugee."

"Right," I said. "I knew him because Denise Overton, the girl who died of the drug overdose, introduced him to me. He was a punk musician who thought I might want to write about him and his band. He was rumored to be a drug dealer."

"Pearson had the girl's camera in his apartment, chief," Rossetti said. McGovern didn't move.

"Do you think he killed her?" I asked Rossetti. "Is that what you're saying?"

"Maybe," Rossetti frowned. "We don't know. Did your girlfriend take drugs? Or buy drugs from Pearson?"

"She didn't take drugs. This guy was just another face, a character study. That's the only reason she knew him." I didn't mention the fact Denise knew *I* had bought drugs from him. But I wasn't doing this for Denise anymore. I was saving my own ass. Dixie was right.

The Cardinal leaned back and crossed his hands on the desk. Big hands. "Do you know why anyone, especially the woman whose voice you heard, would have a reason to suggest you would know something about these murders, Mr. Darenow?"

No dry humor this time. He even sounded like John Houston.

"Not a clue," I said. I tried looking hard at him; my heart skipped a beat.

We all exchanged glances. The Cardinal leaned forward.

"Do you know a man named Hector Melendez, Mr. Darenow?" The Cardinal asked.

Holy shit! Here go the lies.

"I've heard of him," I said. "I'd love to know how he figures into this."

More glances all around. McGovern lazily stroked his chin. Rossetti leaned forward expectantly. I decided to wait before opening my mouth again.

"What do you know about him?" Rossetti asked.

"He's supposed to be worth a couple of hundred million," I said. "And he's supposed to carry a lot of weight in Florida. He's a Cuban exile and he's on the board of directors of a bank owned by the Wately family. Mrs. Wately's ward, Jaime, was killed along with my girlfriend."

The Cardinal leaned forward for emphasis. "Is this how you came across Melendez's name?" he asked. "Digging around in Wately's affairs?"

"In fact, no," I said. "A transvestite prostitute implied that he was behind the Torres brothers. They owned a joint called the Toucan Too. I later asked Wately if he knew Melendez." The lies were piling up. How was I going to remember all this?

The Cardinal looked bemused. "Really?" he said. "When was that?"

Rossetti was all ears.

"Last night on the phone. I found out Melendez came from Tampa so I figured Wately might know him."

"What did Wately say?" Rossetti asked.

"He told me Melendez was on the board of the bank. He was sort of in a hurry but he indicated that he wouldn't mind talking to me about it."

Rossetti glanced quickly at The Cardinal before replying. "Do you intend to pursue it with him?" Rossetti asked.

"Yeh," I said.

If I don't wind up in jail myself, I thought.

"And that's all you know about Melendez?" The Cardinal asked.

"That's all so far," I said.

Jesus! Do they know I met his son? The thought drew a nervous smile to my lips. Watch it, Darenow. Don't get cute with these guys. Swallow that smile. Only guilty people smile at moments like this.

"Am I on the right track?" I asked. Rossetti looked at The Cardinal, who looked at Rossetti, who looked at me.

"You might be," The Cardinal said.

More glances were exchanged but nothing was said. His Eminence nodded to Rossetti. It was a cue. I gave Rossetti my undivided attention.

"Hector Melendez visited New York in 1957," Rossetti announced in a conversational tone. "He stayed at the Astor Hotel under an assumed name. He was in the city for about forty-eight hours, during which time Albert Ducatti, boss of all Mafia bosses, was shot dead while getting a manicure. Ducatti was killed because he didn't want to bring heroin into New York."

"But no proof?" I asked.

"No proof. Melendez wasn't even picked up at the time. His name only came up years later. We made some discreet inquiries then, but Mr. Melendez had a perfect alibi. At the time of the hit, Mr. Melendez was a guest at a breakfast meeting with a Cuban diplomat. Three embassy employees attested to his presence there. None of this is for publication, of course. It's all hearsay. I just want you to know who you might be dealing with."

"Where did Hector go after that?"

"Back to Havana," Rossetti answered.

"Three years later he fled the Castro regime and emigrated to Miami Beach," he continued, "where he joined the liberation army. You've heard of the Bay of Pigs?"

"Oh, yes," I answered dutifully, somewhat insulted by his implication.

"Hector was in the first wave to hit the beach," Rossetti said. "He lost some blood and was captured. He escaped from a Cuban hospital and turned up in Key West a month later. Very interesting man."

"He started out as a hit man?"

"Hearsay," The Cardinal interjected.

"That's all you have on him?" I asked.

"He thinks he's the Donald Trump of Florida," Rossetti said. "Which is not to cast any aspersions on Mr. Trump, only to say that Melendez knows how to get things done. Otherwise, he's clean as a whistle. You said it yourself. Upright citizen, patriot, businessman. That's why I say: this is off the record.

"Incidentally," Rossetti added, "your editor, Walt Hurley, speaks highly of you." He paused. "So do some other people."

What the hell was that supposed to mean? Does he know I've been wining and dining with Charlie, The Big Guy? I nodded as if I understood. The more I knew, the less I wanted to. On the other hand, I was surprised to hear a word or two of commendation. Was it a friendly sign, or was it designed to lower my guard?

"What do you know about Edgar Wately's relationship to the deceased youth, Santiago?" The Cardinal asked before I had time to answer my own questions.

"That's an interesting question," I replied awkwardly.

Interesting, I thought, but not as interesting as Hector Melendez's connection to Wately. I was dying to ask Rossetti about Melendez's CIA connections, but I was afraid of compromising Detective Henry. Cops are mind readers and mine was being read by two of the best.

"Have any answers?" The Cardinal asked, nonchalant as a circling shark.

"The servants, at least the elevator operator," I began slowly, "told me Wately didn't bother much with the boy, but maybe that was just for show. The Watelys lead a very private life." I was treading water, trying not to disturb my surface calm.

"What about the rest of the servants?" Rossetti asked.

"I spoke to the housekeeper and Mrs. Wately's secretary," I said.

"You spoke to the secretary?" Rossetti said, flicking a glance at His Eminence.

"Yeh." Slow down, curve coming.

"What did she tell you?" The Cardinal wanted to know.

"I introduced myself as a reporter and told her Denise Overton knew Jaime Santiago and some of the crowd he hung around with. I told the same thing to Wately, Mr. *and* Mrs."

"What did *they* have to say?" The Cardinal replied.

"Not much," I said. "Edgar Wately said he thought a drag queen, probably a prostitute, poisoned them."

The Cardinal managed a very thin smile and glanced at Rossetti.

"Do you know any of the drag queens who posed for Miss Overton?" The Cardinal asked. "The one they call Esmeralda?"

Another heart-stopper. I directed my reply to Rossetti. He seemed far more friendly than McGovern.

"I'm trying to find her," I lied. "I'm pretty sure that's who Denise was meeting the night she died."

His Eminence addressed Rossetti.

"What do we know about Esmeralda?" he asked.

"Someone answering her description was seen frequently in the company of the Santiago kid at his West Side apartment in the past couple months," Rossetti replied. "No record, at least under the name we have. She gave an address in Tampa when she checked into the hospital the night the others died. She claims an unknown gave her bad drugs. We have the lab tests. Right now, she's among the missing. Oh, yeh. She's had a sex-change operation."

The Cardinal frowned, nodded his head slowly, and looked at me.

"You see we have a mystery on our hands, Mr. Darenow. Anything you can contribute will be appreciated." He paused for effect. He was squeezing me for reasons all his own. I suddenly had the crazy idea that he knew everything I knew and wasn't letting on. I gave him a wide-eyed, innocent look. What the hell is he up to?

"We want you to know the detectives are doing their best, Mr. Darenow," McGovern continued. "And to assure you that the department will continue to pursue leads wherever they find them."

Was he reminding me that I'm still on the hook for the Avenue A murders? I turned it over in my mind and decided to play it another way.

"I take that to mean the case is still active," I said, not too eagerly.

His Eminence looked at Rossetti and then at me.

"It's active as far as the deaths that occurred in our jurisdiction are concerned," The Cardinal said.

His Eminence stretched, stood up, and went to the window to adjust the shade. The morning sun had just moved over the building and McGovern was bringing more light to bear.

The Cardinal asked Rossetti and me if we wanted a cup of coffee. I said thanks very much. The meeting was far from over. McGovern buzzed Maude and ordered three cups, then turned his back on us and gazed down at the East River. Silence prevailed until Maude entered with a tray full of paper cups containing fresh-brewed coffee, real cream, cookies, and cocktail napkins.

We munched while The Cardinal sipped his coffee and leaned against the windowsill. He repeated his invitation to have me contribute whatever "leads, ideas, theories, and rumors" I might pick up that related to the homicides of Denise and the others.

"Poisoners are complex people," he said at one point. He might be an *éminence grise*, but he was still a cop.

"They say women poison more than men," I offered.

"That's usually the case," His Eminence said drolly. "That's why we'd like to know who the woman was who called 911."

I let out a long sigh of resignation. I couldn't hold it in. It was better than a smile or a nervous laugh. If His Eminence noticed it, he wasn't letting on. I screwed my forehead into a knot as if an idea had suddenly occurred to me.

"Let me listen to the tape again," I said. I was going way out on a limb.

The Cardinal motioned with his hand and Rossetti played Aurora's voice again, skipping mine, thank you.

I listened carefully, nodding my head in thought. Don't think too much, Darenow, go with the flow.

"She sounds a little distraught," I said. "And she sounds like Aurora Carrera, Mrs. Watelyʼs secretary." I had a hard time delivering that calmly, but I did. I decided I was far enough out on the branch. I started climbing back in.

Rossetti smiled and looked at The Cardinal. The Cardinal remained impassive. What the hell was up?

"When did you last talk to Ms. Carrera?" The Cardinal asked smoothly.

"Uh . . . yesterday." I thought again and corrected myself. "No, the day before."

The Cardinal looked hard at Rossetti. Rossetti ran his tongue over his lips and looked deep in thought. He looked at His Eminence but His Eminence had no comment.

"*I'd* like to know more about Aurora Carrera," I said, boldly taking the initiative.

"Aurora Carrera is Bennie and Ralph Torres's cousin," Rossetti said. "Rosa Torquenos, Mrs. Wately's maid, is their aunt."

I nodded thoughtfully. I couldn't let on that I knew of the relationship from my meeting with Hector Melendez's son.

Rossetti started to speak. I cut him off; I shouldn't have.

"Mrs. Wately has invited me to a cocktail party tonight," I chirped. "She says she's going to introduce me to people who know something about all this. What do you make of that?"

Rossetti looked momentarily stunned and shot a glance at The Cardinal. The Cardinal looked at me and squinted. It was as close to being incredulous as he'd ever get.

"Have you accepted the invitation?" The Cardinal asked.

"Yes," I said. "Why not?"

I thought I saw a smile flicker across The Cardinal's face. "I hope you'll let us know what goes on," he said. "We weren't invited."

"I wish you'd let *me* know what's going on," I replied.

"More coffee?" The Cardinal asked.

I told him no. I had plenty left in the cup. I hoped it had some metaphorical significance.

"Gabe," he said, "tell Mr. Darenow why you're here." He crossed over to the brass telescope and ran his hand idly over it.

I took a swallow of coffee and waited.

Rossetti had the floor. He sat back and talked about things I knew nothing about, until that moment.

"Mr. Darenow, the federal authorities—a task force comprised of various agencies and directed from Washington—are very interested in the murders of Bennie and Ralph Torres, and in the deaths of your girlfriend and the Santiago boy."

Rossetti scrutinized me before he continued. He was feeling me out, trying to get an emotional fix on me as he took me into his confidence. I nodded attentively.

"Why they're interested, we're not sure," he said. "According to the people in charge of the task force, it has something to do with 'national security.' That covers a multitude of sins, but it usually means an agent of our government—" he paused to pick the right words— "is involved in an operation that somehow . . . touches upon our own investigation."

"Is this person known to us?" I asked. "I mean, could it have been one of the Torres brothers?"

Rossetti smiled and looked at The Cardinal. The Cardinal was moving around his telescopes, but he returned Rossetti's smile.

"Unlikely," Rossetti said. "From what we know so far."

"Let me ask you something," he continued. "How well did your girlfriend know Esmeralda Sanchez and the Santiago boy?"

"I think Denise may have met Esmeralda once before the night she died. So that was probably their second meeting. I'm not sure if she knew the Santiago boy before that night, either."

"What is your impression of Edgar Wately?" The Cardinal asked.

He was leaning over his scope, the expensive one, blowing dust off the armature. Rossetti looked idly at the corner of the ceiling, lost in thought. McGovern's question took me by surprise. What could I say: the Mafia thinks he's queer?

"I haven't formed one yet," I said. "He's pretty smooth."

Rossetti's gaze drifted down from the ceiling, over to The Cardinal, then over to me.

"We'd like to know more about him," The Cardinal said.

"The Torres brothers are our chief suspects," Rossetti picked up. "For several other murders as well as your girlfriend's. There's information from the street confirming they were dealing drugs and hitting people who got in their way. They're tied—remotely, but still tied—to rubouts in the Bronx and Queens. But these guys weren't poisoners. They shot people. They threw people off roofs. The question is, why did they suddenly change their modus operandi and use drugs to kill the Santiago kid and your girlfriend?"

"Would Aurora want to kill the Santiago kid?" I asked.

"And call 911 and say you knew something about it?" Rossetti said. "Why would she do that? It's a theory, but . . ."

My mind was going in another direction. I was thinking about something Manolo said before he died. He said the Torres boys had fucked up trying to kill Esmeralda. He implied *she* was the target, which added weight to the theory that Edgar may have wanted her killed.

But I couldn't tell the cops that. Not yet, anyway. I let out a sigh of frustration.

The Cardinal frowned and looked glumly serious. "I'm going to ask you to help us," he said. "I want you to work with Inspector Rossetti on this."

"Sure," I replied. "Sure, what can I do?"

"We'd like to know who these people are that his sister is inviting you to meet," The Cardinal said.

I took another sip of coffee. It was cold but I was stalling for time. McGovern had a lot of balls in play. Whose side was he on? I knew that protecting the department's reputation was foremost in his mind, but why was he taking me into his confidence regarding Wately?

And the mob? What about them? Did McGovern know that the Italians were jockeying for position? Did he know they were protecting me? I decided to toss him a lob.

"What's all this talk about a mob war?" I asked.

"What mob war?" McGovern said sharply.

"I've heard talk that the Mafia might have been behind the rubouts of some of those Latin drug dealers who've been turning up dead around the city," I said. "Anything to it?"

Rossetti remained silent.

"May I ask where you got this information?" The Cardinal asked.

"A federal source," I lied.

"If that's what the feds believe, good luck to them," The Cardinal said testily. "We're satisfied, at this point, that Bennie and Ralph Torres were the shooters in at least eight of the homicides you're talking about. We base that conclusion on the fact that the guns found in Manolo Pearson's apartment were the same guns used in those homicides. We have ballistic tests to back it up. We also have information—from the street, nothing to build a case on, yet—that the victims in those homicides were criminals from Florida who had done business with the Torres brothers at one time or another. I know nothing of a mob angle. Do you?"

I shook my head.

"Just checking something out," I said.

"You know something, Mr. Darenow?" The Cardinal said. "I'm glad you're checking things out. We have lots of laws on the books, and an awful lot of people breaking them every minute. Law enforcement in this town is a hit-and-miss proposition. When you get up around Park Avenue, where the Watelys live, it's sometimes impossible to separate the good guys from the bad guys. We can't enforce every law every time it's broken. What we try to do is keep the peace."

Rossetti nodded somberly. The Cardinal scowled. I had a feeling the meeting was over.

"Once again, this has *all* been off the record," The Cardinal said. "If anybody asks you—anybody—just tell them that."

"Of course," I said. "What about the feds, though? What if they ask?"

The Cardinal smiled.

"Tell the feds," he said, very slowly and deliberately, "that if they have any more questions about what we discussed, to speak to me. Got that?"

"Got it," I said, trying to convey complete obedience.

The Cardinal came around and shook my hand. Rossetti shook my hand and gave me a piece of paper with two phone numbers on it.

"You can reach me there night or day," he said. "Call whenever you think you have something to say. Even if you don't think it's relevant."

"We'll decide what's relevant," McGovern added pointedly.

The meeting was over. Maude handed me my coat and smiled warmly, as if she shared my sense of relief. Rossetti walked me to the elevator.

"What do you think of His Eminence?" he asked.

"He seems like a straight shooter," I said truthfully.

"He is," Rossetti said. "And if you play straight with him, he'll stand up for you, long after the inning is over."

"That's good to know." I nodded sincerely.

I liked Rossetti. I hoped he liked me. I wanted desperately to trust in him, to confide in him if necessary. Now wasn't the time, but I hoped he was reading it in my eyes.

"Aside from what we've discussed, I wouldn't advise you to make any more moves on your own from this point forward," he added. There was more than a hint of warning in his tone.

Rossetti's warning stayed with me on the elevator ride down, but by the time I reached the lobby I had artfully convinced myself that it had to be applied with some precision. People like Wately and Melendez were above the law. It was going to take more than The Cardinal and the New York City Police Department to bring them in. I had to let my hunches run out, unhampered by the police, at least until I talked to Wately. I'd survived The Cardinal's interrogation and that gave me a certain confidence. I left McGovern's office feeling better than when I went in.

22

The good blue suit was coming in handy these days. I nixed my yellow Hermes power tie, it was out of style; the call was for cocktails at seven at one of Manhattan's better addresses. I opted for Sulka accessories—muted white-on-white shirt, a midnight blue silk tie with vertical pink stripes, and a well-worn pair of black tasseled loafers from Lloyd & Haig, brushed to a high sheen—the Euro look. I wore my cashmere overcoat, leaving the trenchcoat behind. If the Watelys were going to try and buy me, I wanted to look expensive.

I rolled into the Watelys' apartment about 7:10 P.M., checked my coat with a rent-a-maid, and came face to face with Ms. Aurora Carrera, who gulped in surprise and blushed as I introduced myself, a formality that had not taken place during my prior visit. It wasn't the reaction I expected from someone who might be able to place me at the scene of a triple homicide. Was she, *or was she not*, the person Pepe was talking to on the phone before the lead started to fly at Manolo's? She was certainly the person who called 911 to suggest yours truly knew *something*, but her reaction did not suggest she thought I had blown Bennie Torres away. Maybe she wasn't the person Pepe had been haranguing after all. Then why did she call 911?

She certainly wasn't bad-looking. Blushing softened her Indian cheekbones, making her less of a threat but still attractively brazen. She wore a green wool dress, peplumed at the waist and padded at the shoulders, a purple scarf, black earrings, and low-heeled patent leather pumps with big satin bows, just the look for her tough, compact body. Her hair was brushed to one side and fastened with a gold clip. She fit right in to the drawing room atmosphere.

"I'll tell Mrs. Wately you're here," she said defensively. "Please go into the living room." I did so, and promptly drew an approving smile from a blonde who was standing near the serve line in the tennis-court-sized parlor. She was in a group comprised of two couples in their thirties who were ordering drinks from another rent-a-maid. Mrs. Torquenos was conspicuous by her absence. She would have been out of place anyway, intimidating the guests like a waiter from the Stage Deli. The ladies were taking white wine and sherry; the men were having scotch on the rocks. Scotch sounded good to me; I wanted to fit right in.

I eased into the conversation with a drink order and drew another smile from the blonde. I introduced myself.

"Oh," the blonde said approvingly, "you're Mrs. Wately's friend."

"I hope so," I replied. I certainly wasn't going to say no. The blonde introduced me to the others. The men were investment bankers; the women were wives. They were all from Houston.

The blonde, whose name I forgot, proudly announced, with what I thought was a Midwest twang, that her husband, Bart, had been "advising the Watelys" for some time; this was their first social call. Bart and his buddy kept their chins tucked firmly into their necks and said little.

The blonde asked me if I covered the stock market. Ethel had apparently told her I was a journalist, and little else. Nothing about my proclivity for trouble-making, for instance. I couldn't decide if that was a good sign or not. I told the blonde I kept an eye on the market, but merely to protect my own meager interests. I said I was currently on general assignment and asked her how she liked living in Houston. The talk had turned to the oil economy and sagging real estate values in the Lone Star State when Aurora returned to see if we had ordered drinks. The maid appeared with the drinks at the same time; Aurora got flustered. She was trying very hard to be the perfect surrogate hostess and got tongue-tied instead. Everyone laughed.

The doorbell rang and Aurora wriggled off with a body language dirty look intended for me. Two more couples arrived, older, in their forties, deposited their coats, shook off the cold, and joined us. They knew the crowd from Houston. Hello, hello, hello, hello. Jim and his wife, Nancy, Ed and his wife, Gloria. Brown curls for Gloria and a blond flip for

Nancy. I pegged the men for bankers and wasn't far off. They were partners at one of the big-eight accounting firms. We exchanged perfunctory handshakes. The new wives nodded politely and sized me up. If I left them alone, they'd find out soon enough that I was Ethel's new friend. It was no trouble excusing myself and slipping away. They were all engrossed in renewing old acquaintances and they weren't my crowd.

I wandered off to examine the paintings on the wall which I hadn't seen up close on the previous visit. The Hockney and the Rivers were hung in gilt frames, which made them a little less incongruous against the slubbed silk wall covering. At first I couldn't figure out whether Ethel or Edgar was the collector. The Rivers was a collage, of course, with a chorus line of dancing girls drawn across the bottom in old master's style. Atop that were a couple of tongue depressors set into a rosette made from red-hued paper currency. The currency was drawn on the Bank of the Confederate States.

The Hockney showed a Hollywood sunset from the deck of a house in the foothills: flat planes, green and gray into mauve and a strip of muddy blue for the ocean, the sunset a smear of bloody scarlet. A leisurely dressed man stared, in three-quarter profile, into the sunset. He was standing behind a chaise, from which a pair of high-heel-clad legs stretched into the foreground. Otherwise, the occupant's body was not visible. The man in the picture was Edgar Wately, no mistake. The cut of the high heels—they call them mules, I think—did not suggest they came from Ethel's wardrobe.

Esmeralda? Of course. Why not. How subtle. How does Ethel stand it? She's jeopardizing herself to protect Edgar, who is rubbing her face in his dirt by hanging that in the shadow of their parents' portraits. The bastard. He stole the family bank, peddled drugs to cover his losses, and was somehow responsible for Denise's death. No wonder I saw murder in Ethel's eyes. She loathed her brother and was too proud to vent it. Wately will get his, I fumed to myself, Ethel just needs a man she can trust.

The fuming tired me. I sat down on a sofa, of which there were three. There were more wing chairs than I had previously noticed and a trio of easy chairs covered in yellow silk, grouped around a mahogany coffee table covered in more beige marble.

It was all very nice, but where was Ethel? And why did everyone—the mob, the police brass—think it was so vital *I* speak to the Watelys?

The cocktail party may be a ploy to buy me off, but maybe it was also a cry for help from Ethel. I was pondering all that when I caught Ms.

Carrera's eye again. She blushed and—*mirabile dictu!*—smiled a strained smile. I decided to take advantage of the friendly overture. I beckoned her over with my index finger. She swallowed hard, thrust her cheekbones into the air, and came over wrapped in an air of mild exasperation.

"I told her you were here," she began apologetically. "It's just that she's so busy. All these phone calls."

I would have loved to know more about the phone calls but I shifted gears and expressed innocent surprise that Mrs. Watley was having a cocktail party so soon after Jaime's funeral.

Aurora wasn't surprised at all.

"Oh, no, that's Mrs. Watley," she said, shaking her head. "Life must go on. It's more than just a cocktail party, anyway."

"Oh?" I said.

"People from Washington, all over, old friends, very close friends of hers, are here."

"Is *Edgar* going to be here?"

"I don't know," she said, glancing expectantly toward the entrance to the room. "Maybe not."

Aurora was hiding things and it showed.

"Where are you from?" I asked.

"I was born in Puerto Rico," she said. "But now I live here."

"Is that how you know the Watelys," I asked, "from New York?"

"Uh, yes," she said hesitantly. "Mrs. Watley hired me . . . I . . . needed a job."

I was going to ask if her Aunt Rosa had helped, but I put that aside for a minute. I flashed back to Manolo's apartment again, me watching Pepe on the telephone. Me snorting coke and playing detective. But if Aurora was on the other end of the line, why was she now backing off, acting defensive? Wasn't she still curious? What was her story? She avoided my eyes, looking around to watch a group of new arrivals. She wanted to flee and didn't know how. I grilled her.

"How long have you been working here?"

"A year," she said distractedly.

"Must be interesting."

"Yes," she replied with a start. "Here comes Mrs. Watley now. I'm sorry we can't talk." She looked at me warily, paused to pick up a dirty glass on a nearby table, changed her mind, looked at me again, and put it down. *Agita*. By that time, Ethel had swept magnificently into the marble foyer to greet the new arrivals, including a distinguished looking man in his fifties who looked familiar.

Ethel wore a black-and-gold checked dress, cut extremely low and squared at the neck. It accentuated her bosom, which heaved gently under the gold and ebony necklace around her throat. Her hair was brushed back, high off her forehead, swept off her face, and anchored by a pair of golden earrings also set with ebony stones. The pale violet-blue eyes glowed against her lightly bronzed cheeks. She had gold bracelets set with more black stones that must have weighed a ton, but her hands still moved like little birds. She wore a pair of black lizard pumps, with very straight, very high heels, and sheer stockings. Her hemline stopped well above the knee, showing off a pair of slender, tanned, muscular legs that a much younger woman could easily envy.

She was perfection, and every man in the room wanted her. So did I. I had a crazy notion I'd get her. She was a rare bird, an exquisite trophy few men would pass on. Let me tell you something about men, and why I wanted her so terribly. It mattered little at that moment that she might be covering up Denise's murder. I'd square that with my conscience after the fact, after I put her brother Edgar behind bars for the murders of Denise and Jaime Santiago. In the meantime, she was fair game, fairest of the fair. She wanted to walk and talk and turn me on? Fine, let her pay the price. I'd never see her kind again. She was a once-in-a-lifetime conquest.

Of course I was being a fool, but who knew?

Two of the men among the new arrivals settled into a quiet conversation with the two accountants. Their wives compared notes on life in Manhattan, loud enough so I could hear. Names were dropped, but they were places and things; objects, not people: shopping at Trump Tower, a soiree at the Museum of Modern Art, a trip to Sotheby's to see the Duchess of Windsor's panther bracelets, gallery hopping on Madison Avenue—locales that provided a parameter of value in their erstwhile society.

I bided my time—sitting on the silk couch, sipping scotch, and watching Ethel move. I only had eyes for her and I wanted her to know it. Every gesture Ethel made was an artful one, a smile, a look, even the way she tilted her head or moved her shoulder had meaning. Ethel needed a man. It was in her eyes, in every move she made. I'd sit on Ethel's couch until hell froze over to get my chance.

I thought for a moment she was about to come over and say hello, but she was offering her cheek to the tall, distinguished man in a gray suit and red tie who not only kissed the offered cheek, but grabbed her around the shoulders and pulled her closer. Ethel laughed, stepped into his embrace, and put her hands on his neck, stroking his cheeks before she stepped back and surveyed him. She took his hands in hers, then turned like a top and introduced him loudly as "one of the brightest men in the State Department" to the others.

It was neatly done. Ethel was bright as a button and fast as silk.

On closer inspection, the State Department's bright star looked to be in his late fifties or early sixties. He had dark gray hair, worn fashionably long, and his clothes looked custom made, right down to his shoes. Ethel kept him by her side while she gave orders to Aurora and the maid and told them to make sure everyone got a drink, and fast. And then Ethel shifted her stance and let her gorgeous eyes meet mine. I smiled.

She smiled back and pointed me out to the man from State, who looked in my direction while Ethel whispered something in his ear. Aurora had brought his drink first, and he took a swallow before turning his attention back to Ethel, who was now talking to a young, good-looking man on her left. She released her grip on the man from State, excused herself, took the younger man's arm, and waltzed him in my direction.

"Hello, Mr. Darenow! We're not ignoring you. I don't believe you've ever met Owen Reed, except over the phone. Our mothers grew up together in Philadelphia. Owen told me you had called him so I thought, why not invite you both here. I think you two will get along just fine. Owen, Max Darenow of the *New York Graphic*, in the flesh." Ethel beamed.

I grinned stupidly; Ethel was stupefying me, but I got up and shook Owen's hand. Ethel wasn't through.

"I'm afraid Owen isn't aware of your reputation, Mr. Darenow. He much prefers Washington to New York. But I've assured him you're a thorough professional." She smiled mischievously, pursed her lips, and addressed Owen Reed, the man who headed LEGAL, the federal task force.

"Max has a unique approach to reporting," she explained. "You either love his stuff or hate it. He takes sides and scolds people who don't match up to his ideals. I'm becoming one of his fans. He's at least interesting and isn't afraid to state an opinion." God, she was some piece of work.

My grin broadened; I tried to look humble, but the lust flared up and she recognized it. Her eyes danced and bowed gracefully.

"An idealist! Not many of us left," Owen Reed cut in, nearly smiling.

He was far more animated than he had been on the telephone, but he still came across as a stiff.

"I told you you'd have a lot in common," Ethel said.

"Well," I said to Mr. Reed, "what news do you bring?"

"There you go," Ethel remarked. "Just like a reporter!"

Reed asked if it was all right to sit down, sat without waiting for my response, took a swallow of scotch, and asked if I minded if he smoked. I said no, as long as I could have one too. We lit up and watched Ethel waltzing the guy from State around.

"Quite a woman," he said. There wasn't much emotion in his voice, but I knew he meant it.

I agreed.

He proceeded to tell me what brought him to New York and, more specifically, what brought him to Ethel Wately's apartment and why he wanted to talk to me.

Reed was an assistant attorney general in the Justice Department's division of intragovernmental affairs. He was forty years old, married, three children, graduate of Yale and Harvard's School of International Law. He was the administration's man in charge of the federal task force that had set up shop in New York.

"We just wrapped up a six-month investigation in Florida," he began, "mostly into money-laundering operations. We have indictments coming down next week." My Tampa source, Terry Compton, was right on top of things.

"Is the Wately bank involved?" I asked. I thought I'd get that out of the way first. If this was Ethel's production, it was smooth as silk and as soft as the inside of one of those old dollars. If it was a setup, I wanted to force their hand. My heart wouldn't stand the suspense, anyway. I was torn between the wonder of it all, the big mahoffs currying favor with the ink-stained wretch in the nice blue suit, and the way the story—or whatever they were cooking up—was being railroaded my way. The Wately bank remark had a nice effect.

Reed grinned. I felt better. I liked it when people smiled, even when they lied.

"Yes and no," he said. "That's what I'd like talk to you about. Some funds were laundered through the Wately bank, completely without Edgar Wately's knowledge," Reed said flatly. "We know who's responsible and as soon as the indictment is confirmed we'll apprehend that individual."

"Is that all?" I said.

I thought I was throwing him a curve, but he ignored it.

"No," he said glumly. "Edgar's a banker with a soft heart and big ambitions. He loaned a lot of money in the past ten years to companies in Mexico and Latin America as well as investing in oil and gas leases that aren't paying off fast enough. Some of the loans are in default. The Watelys can handle it, but it comes at a bad time. No one wants a run on the bank. The Comptroller of the Currency is straightening things out, but it's going to take time. There's also evidence of fraud involving collateral for some of the Latin American loans. Unfortunately, the people who engineered that swindle are dead."

"Two brothers named Torres?" I interjected. I was acting smart, and I shouldn't have bothered. If he was looking for scapegoats, he didn't need my coaching.

He looked at me, for an instant, in what would have passed for astonishment in a more animated individual, but he took it in stride, filed it away, and went on. He was a cool customer.

"You got it. They set Edgar up real nice. There's more, which is where you fit in."

He and I both took a hearty gulp of scotch.

"The Cuban revolution is in trouble," Reed began. "Castro needs dollars. We think a lot of the money that's missing wound up in Havana, by way of offshore banks and money transfers in Panama and Mexico City. Edgar Wately, or rather, the bank, was hustled by people we suspect were acting in the interests of Castro's finance ministry."

I listened; some of it I already knew, the rest was "in the realm of the possible." What he said was interesting, but I wasn't buying it just yet.

"And you think the Torres brothers pulled this off all by themselves?" I said in disbelief.

I shouldn't have phrased it like that, nor raised an eyebrow, but I did. I raised both of them.

"We think someone made them an offer they couldn't refuse," he said carefully. "The same person, or persons, provided them with false documentation for the loans. The paperwork is impenetrable. Lots of phony companies owned by other phony companies."

"What was the Torres brothers' motive for killing the Santiago boy?" I asked.

He smiled ever so slightly. He was letting that one slide over the plate, too.

"Ethel said you were on top of things. I'm glad we're having the opportunity to talk before any of this winds up on your front page."

"What are you trying to say?" I asked. "Are you asking me to hold the story?"

"Until the indictments are handed over, yes," Reed said confidently. "Give us a week. We don't want people taking sudden vacations. There's also a national security angle I'd prefer you discuss—" he paused for emphasis—"with the gentleman Mrs. Wately is talking to."

We looked in Mrs. Wately's direction. The gentleman from State had his arm around her waist. Ethel leaned on him and looked very comfortable.

"She seems to like him," I said.

"They're old friends," Reed said. "Stu Metcalf is old enough to be her father. He doesn't look it, but he is."

"What does he do?"

"Undersecretary of state for political affairs. Handles Latin America and the Caribbean Basin. Staff advisor to the National Security Council. Too bad he wasn't on watch when the flotilla from Mariel set sail."

"Why is that?" I wasn't trying to be funny, but the question drew a big grin from Owen Reed.

"He wouldn't have let half of them in!" he huffed delightedly. "Stu knows his way around Latin America. And Washington. He has the President's ear."

I was wondering whether to take that as a warning when the object of this praise turned his attention to us. Or possibly had his attention turned by Ethel Wately, who had since linked her arm around Stu Metcalf's waist and was leading him in our direction. Ethel waltzed in, got right to the point, and waltzed off again. A prima ballerina.

"Stu, you know Owen. Now I want you to meet Max Darenow, the columnist I told you about."

I stood and shook Stu Metcalf's hand while Ethel headed in the direction of the kitchen. My eyes were on her.

"Pleasure to meet you, Mr. Darenow. Ethel speaks very highly of you."

"That's terrific," I said, acknowledging him.

Metcalf was an imposing presence. He looked you hard in the eye when he addressed you and showed lots of potential for being overbearing.

"Has Owen filled you in on what's going on?" he asked.

"More or less," I said. "He indicated you could fill in some of the blanks."

"Ethel thinks you should be briefed and I agree with her," Metcalf said. "I'm talking to you as a friend of the family, not as a journalist. Can you make that distinction?"

His eyes waited for my reply.

"I think so," I said. Friend of the family, indeed.

"Ethel told me about your fiancée, Max. I want to express my deepest sympathy. One reason Ethel wants you to hear the whole story is because it involved someone close to you, possibly as close as Jaime was to Ethel."

"Is this about Denise?" I asked.

"As much as we know so far," Metcalf said. He ran his hand idly through his hair and scanned the room. "You know, on second thought, maybe we ought to talk this over in the library."

His suggestion carried the weight of a command.

"Owen, will you join us? I'll need your input if Max has questions about your end of the operation."

The Watelys' library was a bit different than Dixie's. This was an old-fashioned, oak-lined room with floor-to-ceiling books, a cathedral ceiling, and two ladders to help you get around the stacks. There were plenty of reading lamps with soft lights, comfortable chairs, an antique partner's desk in the middle of the room, a warm, cozy glow from the fireplace, and stained glass windows depicting a hunting scene. Two polo mallets and a helmet were crossed above the fireplace. About a half-dozen manila file folders were stacked in a row on one side of the partner's desk. The ashtray was full. It looked as if someone had been working there recently.

A Telex machine in a corner of the room looked as if it hadn't been used in a while, but a small red light burned on the compact telephone facsimile transmitter that sat on an carved oak writing table under the stained glass windows.

Stu Metcalf and I sat on a green tufted-leather couch. Reed sat in an armchair covered in what appeared to be antelope hide. A maid came in and said Mrs. Wately wanted to know if there was anything we wanted. Drinks, pencil, paper? The orchestration was phenomenal.

Metcalf waved away the remark about pencil and paper by stating flatly that no one would be taking any notes for the time being.

Metcalf ordered single malt scotch on the rocks with a splash of water. Reed and I settled for what the house was pouring. I had plenty of time to be nonplussed while everyone settled down.

I may never be one of the boys, I thought. This was the big leagues, all right, but it wasn't exactly my crowd. There was plenty of talent in the room, plenty of clout too. We could probably solve all the world's problems right here, among ourselves. But that's not what this crowd did; they didn't solve problems, they disposed of them. Sometimes they created them and *then* disposed of them.

Metcalf began by asking some questions about my background: where had I gone to college, how long had I been a reporter, things like that. I should have brought résumés.

"I know you served in Vietnam," Metcalf said warmly. Of course, I thought, isn't that a requirement for entry into the club?

But there was more to it than that. He was letting me know he'd checked me out. He had pulled my service record. I had nothing to hide. What else did he know?

"Two years, four months, and three days," I said slowly.

"I imagine Owen told you about some of the problems at the bank." It was a statement, not a question.

I nodded in agreement. I wasn't ready to swing on his pitches. The drinks arrived. Metcalf wet his whistle before continuing.

"The Torres brothers were trying to shake Edgar Wately down, Max. They were trying to blackmail him. Blackmail is a terribly bad business—especially when it's not true. Unfortunately, the lie would be sufficient to cause great harm to the Wately family."

"What were the grounds for blackmail?" I asked.

"I'd prefer to let Ethel talk to you about that, Max. It's ugly, it's false, and it could cause irrevocable harm to the man's reputation.

"Blackmail," he said, "is sufficient grounds, I think, among gentlemen, to be left alone, like a snake under a rock. But that's not the only reason I'm asking for your cooperation in presenting this story to the public." Reed affirmed that with a nod. Metcalf punched the next sentence home with several quick stabs of his hand.

"We believe the Torres brothers may have been working for Fidel Castro's secret service. The credit for that discovery goes to Edgar Wately alone. At least one of the Torres brothers' businesses was used to launder money for a firm we *know* is linked to the Cuban Communist Party."

I leaned forward, took a drink, and tried to digest his theory. It had a lot going for it but it raised a few questions. I had one ready.

"Why did the Torres brothers want to kill Jaime Santiago?" I asked.

Metcalf didn't bat an eyelash. He delivered his lines with the snap of a soap opera regular.

"They wanted to put pressure on Edgar Wately," Metcalf went on. "They wanted to hurt him indirectly, hit a loved one. They may have suspected he knew they were dealing with Fidel's people."

He punctuated that with a glance around the room. A grandfather clock chimed the quarter hour with a discreetly modulated tinkle.

"How did Watelv find that out?"

"In the course of reviewing those outstanding loans Owen told you about—not, incidentally, made by Edgar himself, but rather by his chief loan officer."

Metcalf glanced at Owen Reed and frowned.

"I'm sorry, Owen, maybe I shouldn't have said that," he said.

"This individual is facing indictment, Mr. Darenow," Reed said. "We wouldn't want him to be tipped off until we're ready to pounce."

I turned to Metcalf.

"You're saying the Torres brothers poisoned the boy as part of a blackmail scheme against Edgar Wately?"

I wanted to believe it, but now that it was being presented on a silver platter I was having trouble accepting it. There was something else. It was all too simple, and murder is never that simple.

"That's what it looks like," Metcalf said. He made no eye contact this time.

"Where's Rosa Torquenos, Mrs. Wately's maid?" I said. "She's supposed to be their aunt. Did the Watelys know that?"

Metcalf sighed, nodded gravely, and stared into his glass of single malt.

"That's why the Watelys trusted them, Max. That woman had been with Ethel for a long time. Of course, Rosa didn't know what the hell was going on. She didn't have a clue. If she did—" he shook his head sadly— "this might never have happened."

"What about Aurora Carrera, the secretary?"

Metcalf looked puzzled for a second.

"I don't think there's a problem with her," he said, reverting to a stare.

"What are you asking me to do?" I said. "Sit on part of the story? If so, which part?"

Reed started to say something but words failed him. He set his wooden smile into place and tried starting again. Metcalf cut him off.

"I think, Owen, it might be appropriate if you gave Max first crack at the indictments coming down on the bank officer," he said with an appropriately hard stare.

"It's a deal," Reed said amiably.

I got the hard stare next.

"So far as the blackmail, Max, and the cloak-and-dagger stuff, let's put that on the back burner. Our counterintelligence guys are zeroing in on some of Castro's operation in Florida and elsewhere." He paused and trimmed the hard stare into a searching gaze. He was taking me into his confidence again.

"Someday there might be a helluva tale to be told about that, Max. My deal with you is that that story is yours—when and if it can be told."

Was I supposed to thank somebody for this?

"What about Wately's bad loans?" I countered.

"The Comptroller of the Currency," Metcalf said smoothly. "They're handling it. I can tell you that the bank will come out smelling like a rose. It's a heavy loss, but Ethel and Edgar have put their own resources on the line and the stockholders are in total accord with the program.

"If Ethel permits," he said, "I'm sure her accountants will walk you through it. In fact, a good, solid business-page story would go a long way toward clearing the air. I think she'd agree."

Metcalf studied his wrist as if he wanted to check the time but changed his mind. He was finished with me. I wasn't finished with him.

"How does Hector Melendez figure into this?" I said.

Metcalf's stare blazed into high voltage, then dimmed in a scowl.

"Hector Melendez is holding the board of directors together and being a perfect gentleman," Metcalf said. "He's been a tremendous help in preserving the bank's integrity. The Torres brothers tried to smear him, too."

My mouth formed a perfectly silent O. Metcalf was indeed Mr. Fixit, the man in charge of client states and investor relations. He was covering everybody's ass—his own, Edgar's, Ethel's, and now Señor Melendez's. Hemingway was wrong when he disputed Fitzgerald's claim that the rich are different from you and I; Hemingway thought the difference was strictly money. It wasn't money; it was connections, the sort the hoi polloi would never have.

"Gentleman, may I intrude?"

The voice was Ethel Wately's.

Metcalf got on his feet and greeted her. She took his hand and clasped it in hers.

"Did you give Max the sordid details?" she asked. She didn't flinch or show any emotion. "I really don't care anymore," she added. "It's been a nightmare." She hunched her shoulders, shivered, and turned to face the fireplace. Metcalf put a protective arm around her shoulder. She shook some more and sniffled, as if she were holding back tears.

It was an awkward moment, but Ethel regained her composure and turned around. She bravely announced that Mr. Metcalf would be late for the opera if he didn't leave soon. She rubbed the corners of her eyes with her fingers, as if wiping the tears away. I didn't see any, but the light was dim.

"I left the sordid details out," Metcalf said testily. "You'll have to decide how to deal with that yourself, Ethel." He'd said enough; his watch was over; his duty done, begrudgingly, I thought.

Ethel sat down beside me and took my hand in hers.

"I think I'll confide in Mr. Darenow and trust his understanding," Ethel said.

I squeezed her hand.

"Do you want to save this for another time?" I asked.

"No," she shuddered. "I'd rather you got it from me than put my brother through it. It's cruel."

"Ethel, we *should* be going," Metcalf said. "Don't bother seeing me out. I'll be in touch. Owen, can I drop you somewhere?"

The dog-and-pony show was over. The high-wire action was beginning.

Metcalf shook hands and gave me one of his State Department calling cards. Reed did the same. Wham, blam.

"I'm leaving you in Ethel's very capable hands," Metcalf said in parting. "I'm afraid our wives are dragging us to the second act of *Tannhäuser*." He gave me an atta-boy wink, no smile.

Ethel waited until they left the room before leveling me with a pair of warm, searching eyes.

"Can you stay for a while?" she asked. "I'd like to talk."

"Sure," I said.

We sat down on the couch; she rested her head on the back of it and stared at the ceiling, then into the fireplace. She was enjoying the comforts of home.

"Stu Metcalf has been a pillar of strength," she said.

I couldn't disagree; I hardly knew the man. But why she was taking me into her confidence, treating me like one of her old friends? Her eyes reflected the flames. She stretched her legs toward its warmth, a cat's move. If she expected me to respond, this wasn't the time; I felt like a moonstruck calf. Two scotches go a long way when you're staring into the eyes of a beautiful woman. Ethel, as usual, covered the silence.

"I'm scared," she said, looking into the flames.

I shifted ever so slightly, moving about an inch closer to her. She was three feet away.

"Of what?" I asked.

"The world." She sighed. "It's different. Men are different. They no longer keep their word."

"We have the same complaint about women," I said. "What really frightens you?"

She showed the Giaconda smile and said: "I don't expect you to wait by the fire for me. Come meet some of the other guests."

She linked her arm with mine and steered me to the door. She uncoupled as we passed into the hall and ran into a pudgy blonde and her husband.

The blonde was about thirty; her hair was bleached and she was slightly tipsy. She was pulling herself away from her husband, who looked about twenty years older than she, and she was throwing daggers with her eyes; a fun blonde with a mean streak. When she spotted Ethel she beamed delightedly.

Ethel ignored her and moved briskly and deliberately down the hall into the living room, where the accountants and their wives were still chatting. It seemed as if none of them had moved.

Ethel introduced me to a couple I'd met briefly before, one of the big-eight accountants and his wife, then excused herself to work the room.

I decided to play the perfect guest and do exactly what was expected of me.

"Stu Metcalf says the restructuring of the Watelys' bank would make an interesting story for the business page," I said for openers. The accountant's eyes brightened and then narrowed warily.

"What's the angle?" he replied evenly.

"From what I hear, it's being handled very smoothly; the stockholders like the plan; there might be a lesson in it for some other banks," I said just as evenly. He knew what I meant; stories about billion-dollar bank bailouts were a dime a dozen. I was adding a positive twist to a tired tale.

"We're simply cooperating with the banking authorities," he said woodenly.

"Talk to Ethel about it," I said, looking toward Ethel.

I'd pursued the business page story far enough to suit me, so I drifted back to the library, where I'd left my drink.

The pudgy bleached blonde and her older husband were in the library by themselves. He was wresting a glass from her hand and she was resisting. I apologized for the intrusion and looked for my glass but the maid must have taken it away.

"Hi," chirped the blonde. She was all fun again. The husband dropped his hand glumly; she quickly took a sip of her drink.

"You're the reporter, aren't you?" the wife asked. She had a Georgia drawl; her name could have been Peaches.

I admitted I was a reporter and introduced myself.

Her husband smiled grimly and introduced himself and his wife. I won't disclose their names. I asked him if he was with one of the big-eight accounting firms. He wasn't; he was a bureaucrat in the Florida state banking commission; he wasn't on the list of people I was supposed to be chatting up.

"What's the story with the Watelys' bank?" I asked pleasantly. "I hope everything turns out all right."

"Oh, it undoubtably will," he said. He had a Florida drawl.

I asked him why he was so optimistic and he launched into a ten-minute lecture on government regulations, market forces, and the ins and outs of laundering drug money. Getting a bureaucrat to talk to a reporter is easy; their political bosses never pay much attention to them, despite the fact the bureaucrats are usually the only ones who know what's going on.

I asked him to be more specific.

"The Wately bank has lots of Latin loans, some of them backed by paper corporations used to launder drug money," he explained drily. "It's up to the courts to determine if the bank is entitled to that money in order to recoup the loan, despite the fact the money was gained illegally. We act as agents of the court in tracing the money."

"I see," I said, and I did. I saw Edgar Wately having his cake and eating it, too. *Edgar*, possibly with the help of the CIA, set the Torres brothers up, made them the patsies, and now Edgar stood to recoup his "losses" with the help of the court. Beautiful!

"Well, here you are!"

It was Ethel, right on cue.

I turned to greet her, but not before Peaches drawled, to no one in particular: "My husband says the easiest way to rob a bank is to own one."

I grinned and tossed her a wink; she *was* fun, and mean; I don't think Ethel caught it; if she did, she let it drift.

"Everyone's leaving. Thank God," Ethel said, heaving a sigh of mock relief. She looked as radiant as ever, framed in the doorway.

"Thank you for coming," she said, addressing Peaches' husband. She stepped inside the room, just enough to clear his path to the door, a clear signal that he was also expected to leave.

"Well, *thank* you," Peaches replied sarcastically.

Ethel nodded politely in the woman's direction, then stepped forward, took her husband's hand, thanked him again, and waltzed him nimbly out the door. Peaches and I followed in their wake.

Ethel summoned the maid and ordered her to bring their coats. No request was made to retrieve mine.

"Will you stay for a minute, Mr. Darenow?" Ethel added nonchalantly. "I know we have to talk."

I wandered around the hall, inspecting the moldings and the marble, while Ethel gave the bureaucrat's hand one more squeeze before she closed the door, nearly catching Peaches' heel in the motion.

"We're alone," Ethel said, snapping the lock for emphasis. "Let's go into the library."

23

Ethel asked me to throw another log on the fire while she called the maid and ordered a bucket of ice, glasses, and seltzer. I completed the assignment before the maid returned and sat on the couch. Ethel perched on the arm of the same couch, a position that caused her already short skirt to slide farther up her leg, exposing wonderfully compact thighs encased in nylons that shimmered in the light. She was in glorious shape.

The maid returned with a tray laden with a couple of grand's worth of crystal glassware and placed it atop a bar that slid neatly out from one of the bookcases when she pushed a lever. It was a wet bar, fitted out in copper and brass, and the crystal—ice bucket, matching glasses, and soda siphon—was massive, diamond-cut, and old. Ethel thanked the maid and told her she wouldn't need her anymore.

"Where's Aurora?" Ethel asked before the maid left.

"She paying the bartender," said the maid, who looked and sounded vaguely Polynesian, maybe Filipino.

"I want to see her before she goes," Ethel said.

The servant nodded and left.

"Can I get you something?" Ethel asked. She went over to the bar and began dropping ice cubes into a glass.

"Very weak scotch and soda," I replied. She made it and then held the glass out toward me. Go get it, Darenow, she's not a waitress.

I got up and accepted the drink and stood alongside her while she made another for herself.

She poured a rather stiff shot of vodka into a small silver cocktail shaker, added ice and a splash of white crème de menthe, then handed it all to me.

"Stingers," I said.

"Shake it for me," she smiled.

I put my glass down, capped the shaker, and shook it. It was small enough to shake with one hand.

"Fifteen shakes gives it froth," she said. "Do you like stingers?"

"Brandy stingers," I said, trying not to lose count.

"Join me," she said.

I said I would. She threw my scotch away, allowed me to pour her drink into a glass, then she took the shaker, tossed the old ice away, rinsed the shaker quickly in the sink, and produced a bottle of cognac that came in its own Baccarat crystal decanter. I had seen something like it in a *très chic* French restaurant where it went for seventy-five bucks a shot. A shot. When you ordered a bottle for the table, they let you keep it—provided you drank it all there. The state liquor authority prohibited it otherwise. You had to leave with an empty bottle. Money is just so silly when you have too much of it.

"That's awfully good stuff," I said. "It's a shame to spoil it with crème de menthe."

"Trust me," she said. "Crème de menthe—" she pronounced it *en français*— "is good for the digestion."

She poured for about twelve seconds, a triple shot for a wide-necked jug, and uttered a crystalline laugh. She splashed some crème de menthe on top and handed me the works. I hoped Denise couldn't see me entering the gilded cage.

"Shake," Ethel said.

I shook it fifteen times. I wanted some froth, too.

She waited until I poured my drink and offered a toast.

"Chin-chin," she said.

"Good health," I said. I went to touch her glass with mine but she pulled it away. Was she afraid the glass would break? Or was she hedging her bets?

"Salud." I shrugged, thinking of Number One. I wondered how he and Esme were getting along. I watched Ethel take a swallow of her vodka stinger and listened while she reminisced about the wondrous sliding wet bar.

"My parents had been living here since before the war and my father had all these important contacts in the government and they'd have these meetings that were so hush-hush you couldn't have servants present because you couldn't trust them. We had all these Germans and Hungarians from Yorkville working here and Daddy's friends wouldn't tolerate it. I mean, they were dividing Europe into banking consortiums and the last thing they needed were communists listening in."

"So he installed a wet bar so everyone could make their own drinks?" I asked.

"You got it," she drawled, crossing back to her perch on the arm of the couch and straddling it so her skirt hiked higher this time. I followed amiably and took up my old position by her side. She was staring into the fireplace again. I was staring at her legs.

"Those were the days." She sighed languorously. She smiled the Gioconda smile and let it wash over me, then told me what those days were like.

Ethel's memories tumbled out freely. She grew up somewhere between Park Avenue, El Morocco, and the Stork, the opera in winter and the April in Paris Ball, private schools for the kids, and then Tampa—land of sun and oranges, polo and the beach, rocking asleep to the sound of waves from Mexico caressing the teak hull of a 125-foot Evans motor yacht. Her father's business interests had earned him a seat on the war production board and then carried over to a spot on the international banking commission that divided the spoils. Avery Wately preferred Manhattan to Washington, since "some of his interests were always on Wall Street." After the war, when these interests and her mother's abhorrence of New York winters took the family south, to Tampa, the Watelys' Park Avenue apartment was only used in the spring and fall.

Life was different in Tampa. It was a purely southern town, far more xenophobic than Palm Beach and too staid to ever get confused with Miami. Ethel called it Pasadena East.

"Daddy did a lot of business south of the border and his bank was tied to Chase, and Nelson Rockefeller sort of ran the Caribbean for Chase so Nelson was always here when we came to New York." She threw her head back and laughed the tinkling laugh. "I used to sit on his knee! In those days people knew how to drink and I'd help Daddy make cocktails. I knew how to make sidecars and Cuba libres and martinis and manhattans."

She smiled wistfully but the smile faded and turned down as her eyes roamed the room. If she was acting, I was a perfect foil.

"Chin-chin," she said again, this time touching her glass to mine ever so lightly.

She lifted herself off the arm of the couch and moved around the room, stalking like a cat, pointing out this and that, a book, a painting, a Tiffany lamp, an embroidered, framed map of Cuba she said was given to her father by a Bay of Pigs widow.

"What's his connection to the Bay of Pigs?" I asked innocently.

"He was the paymaster," she said, "or rather the bank was. It's no secret and it was all legal. Not like today, where they have to launder the money."

"I see," I said, somewhat abashedly. There was no surprise, no evasion in her response. It didn't sound like someone covering up a bungled CIA operation.

She stopped and gave me one of Metcalf's cold, hard stares. I felt strangely confident, now that we were alone. She still looked gorgeous and my eyes let her know it. Her manner somehow reminded me of Denise. Both women could be soft and hard at the same time.

"What *do* you see, Mr. Darenow?"

"I thought we were on a first name basis?" I said.

"Yes," she said in a voice that was too loud and carried the wrong inflection—for she wasn't addressing me. She was addressing Aurora Carrera, who was standing in the doorway.

"You wanted to see me?" Aurora asked.

"Is everything finished and are you going out?"

Aurora looked blank and bit her lower lip. Her eyes flickered over to me and back to Ethel.

"I think I will," Aurora said after a moment. "I know it's going to be busy tomorrow so I'll try not to be late."

"Where are you going?" Ethel treated her servants like children.

"He's giving me a ride downtown to this place where I'm going to meet my girlfriend," she said compliantly.

"Who's *he?*" Ethel inquired. "The barman?"

"Yes," Aurora said demurely. Her eyes shone in a poker face.

"Lock the doors and the elevator," Ethel said. "I'll be alone. When you come back, go directly upstairs. I'll be asleep."

Aurora bit her top lip now and flicked another eye at me before replying.

"OK," she nodded.

"Good night," I said, but she was already gone.

"Now we are alone," Ethel said.

"She's locking the elevator?" I asked.

"You'll be trapped here with me," she grinned.

I smiled, looked pleased, and said nothing. The fool on the brink.

"This apartment is a triplex with its own elevator," she said. "When I'm alone the last servant locks the elevator so I have some degree of privacy. I walked into the kitchen one night in the altogether when I was about sixteen and there was this stranger sitting there eating a sandwich. I shrieked like a banshee and he threw himself against the wall. He was more frightened than I. Daddy came bursting in with his gun and the poor man fainted."

"Who was he?"

"Oh, some brother or cousin or God-knows-what of one of the servants, who came down for a midnight snack. So the rule now is, take your midnight snack upstairs before the elevator is locked."

"Your father always carried a gun?"

"Oh, not really," she said pleasantly. "He always had them around because he loved guns. He used to go hunting with the Seminole Indians at Okeechobee and he kept some guns at home for protection."

"What was he afraid of?" I asked.

"My father was afraid of nothing except women," she said without hesitation. "Would you care for another drink? I'm having one."

I shouldn't have bothered to ask. Avery Wately had lived through two world wars, a depression, and the bomb, most likely with a deep fear of anything that might imperil his fortune, particularly the red menace. His world ended in the fifties but he didn't believe it until Joe Kennedy's son moved into the Oval Office. Avery Wately hobnobbed with gangsters and let the CIA use his bank. His wife's money kept the family solvent while he swaggered through history. Of course he was afraid.

Ethel tossed her head, sighed dramatically, and swallowed what was left of her stinger. "Is that 'yes' on another drink?" She sprang off her perch and headed for the wet bar.

"I'm fine, thanks," I said. I began to think that I had better make my play before Ethel got sloshed. One or two stingers went a long way with most people. If you weren't ready to fade after a couple, you were on the road to ruin. I wasn't sure I wanted to be around when Ethel crashed.

"Can we talk about your brother?" I asked.

"I suppose we must," she said. She finished pouring the crème de menthe and paused. "But only if you shake it again."

I left the couch and went through the motions. Fifteen shakes. I poured the mixture into her glass.

"Come on," she said. "Bring your drink. I'll show you the house while we talk." My pulse beat quarter-time.

We walked into the foyer. Along the way, Ethel talked about some of the small paintings that lined the hall. They were muted, pastel-laden abstracts that, from a distance, resembled Manets, but had been painted by the same man who painted her parents' portraits.

"My father bought these in the fifties," she said, "before he commissioned the portraits. He loved abstract expressionism, but he thought Pollack and the others too violent. This man was perfect for his taste—the violence was all underneath. You have to get close to see it."

I've forgotten the artist's name, but she was right. Under the pastels, which were applied like washes or watercolors, was a bloody canvas of dark colors frantically threaded with torturous white lines. I told her I preferred Manet's vision, where the violence came from nature and the artist restored the calm.

"My father's world was ruled by violence," she replied, "but he had a terribly gentle side. It really only flourished in the year he died. All the men those days thought might made right." She looked thoughtfully at one of the paintings.

"I suppose nothing's changed, has it?" she said. "We taught man how to destroy himself and now we're paying the price."

She forced a brave smile and her eyes searched mine. Anything I might have said would have sounded dumb. I wanted to hold her in my arms at that moment. We walked into the foyer in silence and she paused again under the chandelier.

"This marble is very rare," she said, "particularly the borders, which come from the same quarry as the marble in The Breakers—you know, the Vanderbilts' place in Newport? You don't see that purple grain very much, do you?"

I had to admit I hadn't. The last time I saw it was during a tour of The Breakers which cost me five dollars. I was in Newport for the America's Cup, having persuaded Hurley that we needed a different angle. I came up with stories and pictures on the girls who followed the races and profiles on the people who "crewed," which seemed to involve more girls. Hurley finally made me interview Ted Turner. We wound up talking about the girls, too.

"We live in different worlds, Ethel," I said. "I appreciate the tour but I've really come here to try and get to the bottom of something."

She waved me off and then pulled me back with the old Giaconda smile. She wanted to be held by a man, but she wanted him to make the first move. I felt like a four-year-old preparing for his first plunge into the surf.

"I know," she said sweetly. "Come upstairs. I'd like to show you something."

We went upstairs, to her mother's bedroom, a vast chamber full of floral prints, cream-colored furniture, and soft memories, all of which had faded with age. Ethel told me to make myself comfortable but it wasn't easy. I felt like an intruder. I was standing in someone's past.

I sat down in a flounced and ruffled chair while she rummaged in a bureau drawer. She pulled out two photo albums, lay them on the bed, sat down, and patted the bedcover next to her. She meant for me to come and sit beside her.

I hesitated because there was something odd about Ethel's behavior. This new friendly, open, and confiding manner was in stark contrast to the correct behavior she was so adept at. But I was giddy with anticipation. I suppose that is how it feels when you get inside the tiger's lair and the tiger rolls over so you can scratch its tummy *once*—before it takes your arm off.

She opened her parents' wedding album to the first page, which featured a formal full-length portrait of her mother in her wedding gown. Ethel's mother, Sissy, the real Mrs. Wately, had more than just a Giaconda smile. The madness in her eyes was buried in the portrait by the guy who dabbled in abstract expressionism, probably on purpose. He painted it into the portrait so you never got tired of searching for it. The camera made the madness plain, and very unattractive. You didn't want to look at the photographs too long because of it.

"I know what you're thinking," she said. "She looks like my brother. It's the eyes. I have her skin and the shape of her face, but that's all. The rest of me is my father, particularly his eyes. My brother is very much like my mother."

She turned the page, pointing out various bigwigs who had been at her parents' wedding.

"Do you know who that is?" she asked, pointing a perfectly manicured finger at a serious looking young woman standing in a group of young men in tuxedos and military uniforms.

"She looks familiar," I said.

"That's Fay Bayne," Ethel said. "She's still a dear friend of ours."

Fay Bayne controlled one of the free world's media empires—radio, TV, and newspapers in half a dozen countries, mostly in the U.S.

"I want you to meet Fay," Ethel said. "But I want you to send me some samples of your work first. I know you're good, but it's better if she sees it with her own eyes."

So that was the pitch. Now I really had to know why Ethel wanted to buy me—before I put myself on the block.

"How do you know I'm looking for a job?" I asked.

Ethel shut the album and looked at me with a mixture of condescension and understanding.

"Max, let's talk about my brother for a moment."

"Let's," I said.

"He's weak, Max. He's like mother. Neither of them were tough enough to face up to the world. They're dreamers at best, fools otherwise."

Something told me to take her hand, touch her, but something else was holding me back. What if she's snowing me? I thought. Playing me for the amorous sap. She hasn't once asked about Denise. Is she jealous? Or simply not concerned?

"What do you know about Esmeralda Sanchez, or Esmeralda LaMer?" I asked as gently as I could.

Ethel closed her eyes and nodded her head gravely. Her eyelids took a deep bow.

"She was with Jaime the night he died," she answered evenly. "She was apparently a friend of Jaime's who the police suspect may have had something to do with his death. She is a sex-change. Did you know that?"

She was being very cool.

"What was her relation to Edgar?"

She turned away and kept nodding her head. She put the wedding album aside, turned, and faced me. She was going to push the blackmail angle.

"Edgar tried to help her. She was a drug addict, like Jaime. The two men who killed Jaime were her boyfriends at one time. They didn't like homosexuals and so they probably just—" her hand fluttered in the air—"killed them. They owed the bank a ton of money. We think now it was their way of giving Edgar a warning to lay off. He was trying to foreclose. They were my housekeeper's nephews, you know."

I nodded my head. Ethel had all the answers and she delivered them in a firm, even voice. I wanted to believe her; it would make everything a lot easier.

"Where *is* Mrs. Torquenos?" I asked.

"Probably in Colombia by now, back in the jungle," Ethel said. "Just packed up and left."

"And Ms. Carrera? Isn't she related to them, also?"

"She's not a Torres," she said. "She's related by marriage, but I don't know how. They're all like that. You know," her hand fluttered again, "they have these huge families and different fathers. It's so difficult to follow them. Everyone loved Jaime, though. It was a total shock. It's amazing what men will stoop to when money is involved, isn't it?"

Damn it! I thought. Why do I find this drivel so charming?

She got up and paced around the room, picking things up and putting them down and talking about the concept of an aristocracy and how there wasn't any in this country anymore and what a pity.

"Darenow," she said. "What kind of a name is that?"

"Anglo-Irish," I said. "The Norman invasion. Originally French, according to family lore. Someone dug up a coat of arms that spells it 'D'Arnou.' We're satisfied with our origins."

"My mother's family, the Simpsons, were strictly Anglo-Saxons. They made a fortune in England, refining sugar from the West Indies," she said brightly. "Hence our love of the Caribbean."

"They probably fought my ancestors." I grinned. She liked that. She liked a good fight. Nothing else had changed, either. The Simpsons were still plying a rum triangle, only now the commodity was cocaine and heroin.

"We desperately need a revival of European blood in this country," she added fiercely. "We've completely tipped the scales. We may as well turn the bloody country over to the Spanish and be done with it."

"You invited them in," I said without emotion. I thought of the Eurodollars fueling Manhattan real estate, the polo revival, and a host of American industries devalued in the fast food shuffle. Why couldn't she tap that lode? Why play the Latin card and gripe about it? My comment provoked another outburst.

"They're cheats and swindlers," she replied in a very uncharacteristic, high-pitched whine. "Edgar let Mrs. Torquenos co-sign the Torres's mortgages, for God's sake." She stuttered over the words, but she got them out forcefully all the same. She was more than a little distraught. I was intrigued by the fact she had decided to answer at all. Maybe the third stinger had something to do with it. Maybe I touched a sore point. Maybe now that she knew I had a coat of arms she was letting her hair down. Maybe she was just crazy—like a fox.

"It seemed harmless at the time. Edgar never bothered to check their bank references. He thought it was all in the family. They were supposed to be working for the government. I mean, that was the point of all this."

"My brother felt he had to care for these people," she said, "because Jaime was one of them. I'm glad those men are dead, but I'm sorry Jaime had to be their victim. Jaime's mother was Rosa's friend and Edgar felt an obligation to the family." Something had upset her. She put her hand to her throat and gasped.

"It was," she said softly, deliberately, "the most tragic result of father's many indiscretions. I can't blame Edgar for trying to help, can you?" She was acknowledging that Jaime was her half-brother and begging my sympathy, but her delivery was contrived and old-fashioned, like an operetta performance. It gave me the willies to see someone covering up like that.

"Could the Torres brothers or Rosa have benefited from Jaime's death?" I asked.

She threw herself up off the bed and stood facing me. It was a quick move that took me by surprise. She pointed her finger and shook her jewelry at me.

"That's it!" she exclaimed, her eyes wide in anger. "They thought Rosa would be the beneficiary if Jaime died. *That* was their motive!" She made two fists, locked her arms to her side, and trembled. "I wish they were alive," she said. "I'd like to see them hang."

She stood there looking shocked and stunned, stunning in a fiercely determined, purely feminine way. It was a feral quality certain women cultivated—if they had it to begin with. Ethel had it but it didn't look cultivated. It seemed like raw emotion. She was made for the stage.

Her eyes grew wide again and then snapped shut. Her whole body shook.

I stood up and grasped her by the shoulders.

"It's all right," I said. "It's all right. Maybe we're starting to understand some things, both of us."

"I hate those men," she said. "I hate them."

The blood had drained from her face. She opened her eyes and looked at me in desperation. She clasped her elbows with her hands and started to draw into herself.

"Please be my friend," she said, dropping her arms. "Hold me."

I released my hands from her shoulder and was about to pull her closer but it was unnecessary. She folded into my chest and as I put my arms around her she put her arms around my neck.

Her eyes brimmed with desperation.

I remember thinking that was how Denise might have looked when she knew she was dying. Maybe that's what made me put my mouth to Ethel's.

I kissed her. Her lips were pink, perfectly soft, and pliant; her cheeks were hot and moist. Her body was a magnet that drew every atom of my flesh into its field. I started kissing her with my mouth closed and then we had passed that stage. She let me devour her, and then she did the same to me.

She ran her hands through my hair while we kissed. I ran my hands down her back. I released her and held her face in my hands. She shivered and moaned, and let me stare deep into her eyes, as deep as I could dive. It was plenty far, but I had no idea just how deep she was taking me.

We stayed like that for I don't know how long. We kissed several more times while she ran her fingers idly down my spine. When we separated, it was because she made the first move to part. She wanted to talk some more. She stepped around me and toyed with a paperweight on her mother's dresser.

"My brother was in love with that exotic creature, Esmeralda," she said, staring into the mirror. "And in the worst way: he was fascinated with her. But he never told me the Torres brothers had threatened him. He had all these Latin loans. He was frantic with worry. I tried to get him to see a psychiatrist, but it was to no avail." Her eyes grew large and crazy, like her mother's.

Was she really upset, or was this an elaborate backdrop for her brother's defense? Damn it, I thought, why does she keep talking? She's just prompting more questions. Ah-ha, Darenow. Isn't that what you came for? Ask her one. She wants to talk.

"All right," I said resignedly, "let's go back to Rosa. *Could* Rosa have benefited by Jaime's death?" I was trying to eliminate suspects.

"Of course not," she said dismissively.

"Who gets his share?"

She came closer and put her hands on my shoulders.

"Let's go to my room," she said. "I'd prefer it."

"Wait a minute," I said. "Who gets his share?"

"My brother," she said wearily. She slipped out from my arms and sat back down on her mother's bed. She looked at me and shook her head slowly as she spoke.

"You're thinking—ah, there's the motive! I know. It's far from the truth, though. My brother loved both those poor creatures. You see, he had begun to think he was a homosexual, too. Like his half-brother and that pitiful friend of his, what's its name? Esmeralda? She was a prostitute, you know. My brother always went after the wrong women, even when they weren't real women. They just walked all over him and, you know, he never really liked it?"

I made no reply. I went over, picked up my brandy stinger, and downed it. I suddenly had no stomach for what I was about to do but I was going ahead with it anyway.

She led the way down the hall, turning left into a room that was sleek and dark and full of the smell of her perfume. The furniture was Chinese, lacquered red and black. A cut-glass vanity table shimmered in the stark light from the hall. The bed was covered with a silk throw in an elaborate Oriental design. She turned on a lamp next to the bed, stepped out of her shoes, and stood with her back toward me. She wasn't so big anymore.

"Unzip me," she said.

Her body was soft and hard, perfectly tanned and tuned to racing standards. She was either a very good actress or a woman who hadn't been laid in a long time and loved it all—the celibate interludes as well as sex itself.

"Don't think I'm a whore," she said after we were both undressed and in bed. "I've only had six men in my life, God's truth. You, Darenow, are the sixth."

"Why are we doing this now?" I asked.

"We're both very smart people," she said. "I like smart people."

I wondered who the rest of her partners were and turned out the light.

She was everything a man could ask for—in the boudoir. She must have been a terror in the boardroom.

Tell the truth, Darenow.

The truth is, she *was* wonderful. But something about the passion she displayed rang false. We weren't in bed and lost in lust for more than an hour when the phone rang. She clicked right into a business mode and that was the end of our affair.

It was her brother. He was at "the club." I knew which club.

Why wasn't he at the party? I wanted to speak to him, but it didn't seem like the time. In any event, Edgar must have been sorry he interrupted us for Ethel was giving him hell. She took the phone to the other end of the room and dropped her voice, but she wasn't mincing words. Edgar was getting a tongue-lashing.

She finally slammed the receiver down and put the phone away, but her mood had changed considerably.

"What's going on?" I asked in all innocence.

"Edgar's at his club, giving a deposition to George Cartwright from Stu's staff so we can straighten this damn business out, and he's just falling apart, poor thing. He doesn't know when charity stops and prudence begins. He's a goddamned weakling."

She went into her closet and pulled on a silk robe. She took a gold pill box out of a bureau drawer, took a small white pill, and popped it into her mouth. She swilled it down with the remnants of her stinger and announced that the evening was over. I went limp. I half-expected her to leave a hundred-dollar bill on the dresser, neatly folded under my drink.

"I must rest," she said. "Edgar needs me. He's going to be there for a while and I might have to talk to him again. I hate to chase you out.

"This will be the last time it'll happen," she said, pulling the robe tight around her body and adjusting her cleavage until it hung just right to tweak my interest again.

"You understand, don't you?"

I nodded, but I didn't like getting tossed.

"I want to talk to your brother," I said. "I'd like you to be there."

"Why don't we do that?" she replied. "Perhaps in a few days when everything settles down."

"I'd like that," I said, weakly. I was suffering from *coitus interruptus.*

"You'll like him," she said. "Really you will. He's a darling, a throwback. A gentleman."

I dressed and she wasted no time seeing me to the door and getting my coat.

"It's better you leave tonight, anyway," she said. "Edgar will come home eventually and I'd rather he not know we've become intimate."

"Better for the servants, too," I said woodenly. Why did I care?

"Oh, don't worry about Aurora," she said mischievously. "She likes you."

She kissed me lightly on the cheek and sent me off into the night.

There was a new man on the elevator. He said nothing on the way down. The doormen were changing shifts. The old Irishman scrutinized me while the new man held the door and asked if I wanted a cab.

I told him no. I walked a block and made up my mind where I was going.

I was going to the Albemarle Club to catch Edgar Watery in a lie.

24

The Albemarle Club was on East Forty-eighth Street, near Madison. I'd been there once before, to interview the governor on a plan to house the homeless with private sector money. But the tax write-offs were so blatantly huge even the Republican legislature wouldn't approve it. The rich felt safe in the Albemarle Club; you had the feeling everyone there was armed to the teeth, even the little old men nodding asleep in Queen Anne chairs.

There was a gray Buick parked at the curb with State Department plates. Two men were dozing in the front seat. I made a mental note of the plate number and went up the steps to a big door of oak and brass and glass. I was dressed for the occasion.

A doorman was standing on the landing at the top of the stairs, next to a raised desk. I assumed a deferential air and walked upstairs to meet him.

"Hello," I said. "I'm supposed to meet Edgar Wately here. I believe he's upstairs."

"Mr. Wately, right! Upstairs one flight, first door to the left. Shall I tell them you're going up?"

"Don't bother," I said. "I'm just picking something up."

"Good," he said. I think he'd been nibbling at the members' port.

So far, so good. I went up stairs carpeted in royal blue pile, with a

Greek border running up both sides. The staircase curved around in the federal style and carried me in good taste to a second floor rotunda, lined with marble busts of dead men.

I heard a man's voice and then I heard Wately's voice coming through the first door on the left, across the hall from a door marked LAVATORY. I checked the lavatory. It was empty; I didn't have to worry about someone waltzing out, zippering his fly and finding me with my ear pressed to the opposite door. Then I realized I hadn't quite figured out what I was going to say to Wately when I waltzed in on him. I started getting cold feet.

The voices grew louder as I approached the door. I had no trouble making out the conversation. Wately was catching hell from the man named Cartwright whom Ethel had mentioned.

"You've caused a lot of trouble and you can't handle it, Eddie, so stop trying. Bite the bullet and quit while you're ahead. We have a fall guy at the bank. Ethel is your savior. But you're going to have to give up a few things. Grow up. Take it like a man."

Cartwright had a prep school voice, spiked with age and polite contempt.

I couldn't make out Wately's reply, until his voice rose into a chastened whine.

"I don't want her hurt!" Wately fumed. His performance must have been driving Cartwright up the wall.

"That's the deal, Eddie," Cartwright said soothingly. "Ethel won't stand for it otherwise. You *need* Ethel. And she needs you, for God's sake. Why are you insisting on the impossible? And, listen, your little friend won't be hurt if she fades away as instructed. Who knows? If you like her that much you could join her in five or ten years. Retire to Domingo—if that's the way you want to go. But, Jesus, Eddie, everyone would be a lot happier if you found a real woman."

I heard voices and someone coming up the stairs. I ducked into the bathroom.

I waited until the hall was quiet and went back to my listening post. Wately sounded as if he were repeating instructions, and not very enthusiastically.

"I need assurances," I heard him say.

"Don't worry, Eddie," Cartwright said. Prep school guys are big on nicknames. "Everything will be taken care of. Get rid of your girlfriend and go home and get some sleep."

* * *

The tone of his voice indicated the meeting was over. I scurried downstairs without waiting for Wately's reply.

"I'm supposed to wait outside," I told the doorman as I passed him at a slower pace. "Can you beat that?"

"You can wait in there," he offered, pointing to a wood-paneled reception room.

"Naw. Too stuffy. He'll be down soon."

I hit the sidewalk and turned up my collar against the chill. The State Department car was still there but now the two men in the front seat were awake. They saw me and gave me the once-over. I got nervous and turned around for lack of anything better to do. I decided to go back inside. I had to speak to Wately, if only because I had promised Charlie and The Cardinal.

I was heading up the stairs, smiling at the doorman, when Wately came into view. Another man, older and more distinguished looking, accompanied him. Wately was donning his topcoat and didn't see me. The other man wore only a suit.

I made myself inconspicuous by bending down to tie my shoe. I was wearing tasseled loafers so I had to change that to an imaginary pebble, forcing me to take one shoe off, examine it, and shake it vigorously while the two men passed by. I played that until they were out the door and then said good night to the doorman, who had grown suspicious and was waiting for me to leave.

I shuffled along, taking my time, limping now from an imaginary blister. Wately was saying good-bye at the curb, his back toward me. Cartwright's chauffeur was holding the door for him. I stepped lightly down the steps, nodding deferentially in Cartwright's direction for the benefit of the bodyguard in the front seat. I turned left and headed for the corner at a leisurely pace. I heard a car door slam, then another. I hoped Wately was right behind me. I was counting on him to be heading back to the Waldorf.

The light changed and I crossed the street, not looking back until I reached the other side. When I did, I saw Wately crossing. I read the interest rates on time deposits in a bank window to pass the time until he caught up, then I turned around and smiled at him.

He didn't recognize me at first; there was a big question mark in his eyes before he caught on.

"My God! Are you following me?" he said indignantly.

"Not really," I said. "I wanted to talk to you but they wouldn't let me in. Then I thought you probably didn't want to be seen talking to a reporter so I gave everyone time to leave gracefully. Are you going to the Waldorf?"

The last sentence hit him like greased lightning.

"Who the hell *are* you?" he said indignantly.

"Who's Cartwright?" I asked.

"A family friend," he said evenly. He looked over his shoulder. "Let's keep walking. Then I have to go."

He studied me as we walked and he talked. There was puzzlement in his eyes. He couldn't figure me out.

"Cartwright's with the State Department," he said. "Did you see my sister tonight?"

"I did. We had a nice chat. I met Stu Metcalf. And Owen Reed and a couple of big-time accountants."

"Well," he said, pulling up the collar of his coat against the wind, "you know as much as I do."

"Esmeralda is no longer at the Waldorf," I said. "I'm told she's staying with friends."

He stopped in his tracks, turned, and stared at me.

"Who are you?" he said. "Some spook from Langley? Journalism your cover? Stu Metcalf will grind you and whoever you're working for into dust."

Maybe there was something to be said for the conspiracy theory and the Castro operatives and all the rest of it. Wately was so paranoid he thought I was one of them.

"I want you to tell me what Hector Melendez has to do with this," I said. "You tell me what you know and I'll tell you a few things. I'm not a spy and I'm not working for anybody except myself, not even my newspaper. A friend of mine died and I want to get to the bottom of it. Is that something you can understand?"

The wind bit my ears and blew down my collar. Wately paused in the glare of an electric sign and searched my eyes.

"Melendez is their responsibility," he said. I figured "they" meant the State Department.

"We're talking serious politics, Mr. Darenow. This is not for publication. Most of what I know is classified. You may have to sit on it for a while. But don't worry. There's plenty more you can write about."

"Why didn't you tell me Esmeralda was your lover?" I said. "She's a material witness, possibly a suspect. You can't go on with this charade, *Eddie*. They're going to put you in jail."

He hunched his shoulders and sulked before he replied.

"Is this for your smut sheet?" he said. "Is that it? So you can disgrace me? Disgrace my family? For a lousy headline?"

"Not true," I replied. "If Esmeralda's guilty, there's no need to mention your name. She'll have an opportunity to tell the police her side of the story. The word is that she knows who killed Denise and Jaime."

"Have you talked to her?" Suddenly his tone was tender and concerned.

"I'm planning to. She's scared, Eddie. She says you're abandoning her."

"Who told you . . . I was her friend?" he asked.

"Your sister," I said.

"*She* told you Esmeralda was at the Waldorf?" That concerned him.

"I found that out myself," I said. "I've been talking to a lot of drag queens. A lot of people, in fact."

"What did Stu Metcalf tell you?" We walked on.

"Metcalf said he 'believed' the Torres brothers were working for Castro. He says they were blackmailing you. I don't like Metcalf's story. I have it on pretty good authority that Esmeralda was the prime target and the others were a mistake."

He stopped again. If any of what I'd told him was a surprise, he wasn't letting on, but something formed in his eyes: it was either fear, a lie, or both.

"Of course it was blackmail," he said. "They thought I was fooling around with Jaime and Esmeralda, but I was only trying to help them. That was my only crime."

"What was your only crime?"

"They thought I was homosexual," he said, walking on again. "That's what was wrong. They wanted to hurt us, embarrass me.

"There weren't any grounds for blackmail, but they tried it anyway. Isn't that what Stu Metcalf said?"

I ignored the question.

"What kind of work were the Torres brothers doing for you?"

He twisted his head against the wind and looked at me with suspicion.

"They had accounts at the bank. They had outstanding loans. What the hell did Stu tell you?"

His eyes veered from right to left, as if he was expecting boogeymen to appear. I damn near laughed with delight at his perplexity.

"They were drug dealers, Wately. You bankrolled them. You're holding out. You lied to me from the start. Who killed my girlfriend has more to do with you personally than it does with Metcalf's clandestine operations."

It was still just a hunch but I didn't tell him that.

He quickened his pace and shouted into the wind.

"You're a madman, Darenow. No one's buying your story. I have no ties to the Torres brothers, except for the fact they were related to my sister's housekeeper and they owed the bank some money. There's no way . . ."

"It goes deeper than that," I said, trotting to keep up. "You're not protecting your housekeeper. You're protecting yourself or somebody else."

He slowed down and turned on me.

"Who?" he snapped. "If you're so goddamned smart: who?"

He resumed his pace. I kept up.

"It's freezing," he said. "Come to the Waldorf. Maybe we *should* talk. Your information is wrong. It's dangerous. I know."

He wagged his head in wonder and crossed against the light. Something I said shook his resolve. Something else shook mine.

I suddenly remembered the greaser we had left in Esmeralda's room.

"Esmeralda is not at the hotel," I said. "I was told she had a disagreement with her bodyguard, a man hired by you. He didn't want her to leave. There was a rumpus. It could be embarrassing if you make an inquiry. They might start asking you about the trash she left behind."

He turned on his heel and stared at me. His eyes were glazed with doubt and fear.

"You're preposterous," he stammered. "Who are you? Who's feeding you this information? Are you trying to shake me down? What did my sister tell you?"

"Let's go somewhere for a drink," I said. "Somewhere warm." It seemed ironic to talk about warmth with Wately; I felt as though I'd never feel real warmth again.

"Yes," he said. "I want to find Esmeralda. I'll take my chances, thank you. I have nothing to be afraid of. I've done nothing wrong. If you want the truth, come along."

He stepped off confidently, heading for the hotel.

25

We walked the remaining three blocks to the Waldorf in record time. The wind had shifted from north to northeast and was blowing furiously down the Park Avenue canyon, howling off the impervious facades of the skyscrapers and scattering swirls of dirt and debris in frustration. I preferred the breezes that swept Montauk clean with sea salt and warm kisses, courtesy of the Gulf Stream's northern meanderings. Go there now, I told myself. Wish this sorry asshole good luck and leave. You're too old, or too young, and it's too cold.

The wind precluded conversation, but every time we had to wait on a corner for a light to change, Wately would turn, look at me querulously, and smile. Once he smiled, shook his head, and again muttered, "Who the hell are you?" He acted a little tipsy.

We reached the Waldorf and Wately breezed right past Harry's Bar for Peacock Alley. We were going to have a tête-à-tête with soft lights and music. Nice and quiet in Peacock Alley. The only thing stirring was a dozen well-heeled customers who spoke in three different languages. They lazily stirred drinks to the strains of "Begin the Beguine." A statuesque brunette in a crimson velvet gown and a page boy haircut was tickling the same ivories Cole Porter tickled when he lived in the Waldorf Towers. Those were the days Ethel remembered so fondly.

Wately crumpled a five-dollar bill into the captain's hand and got us a nice quiet table in the corner. He ordered a double scotch on the rocks and a side of water and then asked if I wanted anything. He had lost his manners but recovered his nerve. I ordered a beer.

Wately took a long, satisfied look around the room, drummed his fingers lightly on the edge of the table, and started telling me the story of Cole Porter's piano. I cut him off.

"I know the story," I snapped. "We're here to talk about you, Esmeralda, and the Torres brothers."

"I'm not saying a goddamn word to you," he said waspishly. "I'm not authorized to tell you anything! Do you know who you're fooling around with, man? What did Stu Metcalf tell you?"

He frowned a rich boy's frown. He was insulted. How dare I question him?

"Esmeralda's been running around town telling people you're going to marry her," I said offhandedly.

"Oh, don't be a fool." He laughed nervously. "That's absurd."

His face twitched in four places. I scared him; he was lying and it showed.

I tweaked him again, and added some prep school sadism. I had gone to prep school, too.

"I have people in Florida checking into your affairs, Eddie. Your bank is in trouble. You were using the Torres brothers to bail it out, and now they're dead. Metcalf is covering for you because the CIA owes your father a favor."

He drew back, puffed up and got haughty.

"My father was a shit, Darenow. He robbed my mother's estate, he robbed my inheritance. He stole from us! And I worked and I slaved and I recovered the inheritance he almost lost. Now I'm losing it again. Don't you see?"

"History repeating itself," I said. "You're exchanging one set of gangsters for another."

I leaned a little too far across the table and made the candle waver. The flame threw shadows across Wately's face. He shifted his eyes and changed the subject.

"Esmeralda's in a lot of trouble," he said, taking a deep breath.

"*You're* in trouble," I replied. "Why did the Torres brothers want to kill Esmeralda and Jaime? To deprive Jaime of his inheritance? Because you needed money?" It was a long shot and he knew it.

"It was blackmail," he said arrogantly. He looked away, ran his fingers up and down his tie, then eyed me suspiciously. "What did my sister tell you?"

"Your sister is trying to cover up for your crimes. Come clean with me and I won't drag the family name through the tabloids if I can help it."

Wately didn't need my charity. He leaned back and gave me a malicious smile.

"Talk to Ethel," he said sarcastically. "She has all the answers."

The pianist was introducing Porter's "Love for Sale" with a few brief remarks. Wately politely applauded the opening bars. He was going to enjoy himself despite anything I had to say. He was very much like his sister. They had the knack of changing their emotions in the flick of an eye.

The waiter arrived with our drinks. Wately threw half of his down and ordered another before the waiter departed.

"You're kidding yourself," I said angrily. "You can't brush murder off so lightly. You lived with Esmeralda in a place called Harbor Heights. I have proof of that. And I can prove the Torres brothers were working for you."

He winced, shook his head, looked annoyed and then distracted. I had to be careful of what I told him.

"You know," he said, shifting into a wistful voice, "I wanted to be a writer once. I tried writing a novel when I was sixteen. If I knew then what I know now I would have had a bestseller. I remember the title— 'Mask of Hypocrisy.' "

He sighed, crossed his legs, and sat back. He must have had a wonderful childhood.

He finished his scotch and looked around for the waiter. I didn't want anything this man had to offer except a small truth. I leaned across the table and beckoned to him.

"I'm going to probe so deep into your life and affairs, Wately, that even you're going to be surprised. I'm going after your bank, *and* you. I'm going to hound you until you tell me why the Torres brothers did what they did. Do you understand me?"

Something registered in his eyes, but I didn't know if it was fear or the lie. He licked his lips and reached for his glass. I grabbed his arm.

"Do you understand me? I can wreck you."

"Threats will get you everywhere, won't they?" He smiled.

"Let me tell you something," he said, putting the glass down slowly. All he had left was ice. He had wanted to throw it. "Do you know how important fathers are? They shape your life."

He was going to try and charm me with confidences. A candid chat after lights out.

"Yeh," I replied. "My father told me to keep my nose clean and stay out of trouble. You have a problem, Eddie, and it's not going away. You fucked around with the Torres brothers and they wound up killing my girlfriend. Someone's going to pay for that."

Wately pulled the stirrer from his drink and sucked on it.

"What exactly did Stu Metcalf tell you?" he asked politely.

"Esmeralda's mad at you, Eddie," I said. "She cut her dick off for you and then your thugs tried to kill her. She's a woman scorned; there's nothing worse."

The waiter arrived with his second drink. The pianist had shifted tempo on the chorus and Wately waved his finger, trying to catch up to the beat. He was feeling his scotch.

"Didn't Stu Metcalf tell you this whole thing is classified?" he replied.

"Why classified? Because the Torres brothers were selling drugs and you and the CIA were bankrolling them?"

"For God's sake!" he scoffed indignantly. "Banks don't ask where the money comes from, Darenow. If the Torres brothers sold drugs and deposited the proceeds in my bank, that's no crime," he said.

"Laundering drug money's a crime, mister. The Torres brothers were acting on someone else's orders. That someone put a contract out on Esmeralda and Jaime. I want to know why, and I want to know who."

"The story will be told to a grand jury in Tampa," he said dreamily.

"And what happens when Esmeralda goes before the grand jury?" I asked. "What happens when that comes out in the wash?"

Wately looked idly in my direction. His eyes glazed over and he went from spoiled kid to dazed middle age. He stared at his drink before picking it up and swallowing half of it again in one gulp. He shook his head slowly from side to side.

"I don't know where Esmeralda is," he said in a thin, weak voice. He turned his head abruptly away. Was he holding back tears?

"What were the terms of the blackmail?" I inquired gently.

Wately slumped back in his chair so abjectly that his legs had to crab to follow his body when he turned to answer me. He acted as if he had taken a blow to the chin and was trying to find his corner. The waiter came by, eyed our table warily, and scampered off with a blind eye when Wately signaled for a third refill.

"Where is Esmeralda? Where is she?" He drawled the words painfully, but he was addressing no one in particular.

"I think she's with friends," I lied. "Other than that, I don't know. Shall I give her a message if she tries to contact me?"

"I don't expect you to understand." he said. "We were all very close. Jaime, Esme, we had something rare . . ."

Rare, all right. Too rare for words.

"If she contacts me I'll give her a message," I said. "The cops want to talk to her before she . . . wanders again."

He stared dully across the room, frowned, and put his hands together as if he were praying.

"They wanted to hurt me, Darenow. The Torres brothers and all the rest. They don't like me because I'm gay."

"Who are 'they'?"

"Everybody," he said. His eyes welled with tears and he didn't hide them.

"Jaime was my brother, conceived in rape. My father was probably drunk, but that's no excuse. My father was very handsome. We tried to make Jaime part of the family. It didn't work. Later, much later," he continued, "my sister allowed Stu Metcalf to use our bank as a front for a CIA operation. The cash was for the contras, the freedom fighters. Some of it, I admit, went to cover my father's losses. That has been paid back."

Several questions formed in my mind.

"I'm thinking of Melendez," I said. "I've been told on the highest authority that Hector Melendez is a very bad guy."

"My God," Wately said, his eyes lighting up. "Hector Melendez wants to be governor of Florida."

"Try this," I said. "Is it possible Melendez is still working for, or with, the CIA, planning new invasions, new espionage operations? Is that a possibility?" I was playing devil's advocate.

Wately pouted and shook his head.

"No way, José," he droned disdainfully. I couldn't tell if he was drunk or just being arrogant. I took another tack.

"Why did Melendez break with Santo Trafficante?" I asked. I was beating the bushes again.

Wately liked the question. He narrowed his gaze and a thin smile stretched across his face.

"Santo Trafficante controlled the Tampa docks," he replied casually. "He was in charge of heroin imports from Mexico. Melendez knew that and wanted no part of it. He was smart."

"Someone was financing a drug racket through your bank," I said sternly. "If it wasn't you, who was it?"

"You may be aware of things I don't even know, Darenow. You're sharp. My sister thinks you're terrific, you know? The truth is that Metcalf was running an operation through the bank. He'll deny it, of course, and there's no way to prove it. The operation is being dismantled as we speak."

"*Could* Melendez have been involved?"

"No way," he said. "Hector's too smart for the CIA. He'd been burned by them before." He sniffed and dabbed at his eyes.

"Hector Melendez is not the problem," he said, shaking his head in irritation. "It's rather obvious. Stu is at war with Cuba."

"Who declared war?" I said, not believing my ears. "I thought Congress declares wars in this country."

Wately gave me his "dear boy, don't be silly" look.

"Stu Metcalf reports to the White House, Darenow. You can't go any higher than that." It made perfect sense to Wately.

I wanted no part of this. It wasn't my war! It wasn't Denise's war, either, but she died in it.

What would she want me to do?

Blow these bastards right out of the water.

I pushed my beer away. I'd hardly touched it. Wately was going to get good and sloshed, and that was that. I stood up and threw my coat over my arm.

"Call me when you're sober and ready to tell the truth," I said.

He turned his head and gave me a pathetic cockeyed look.

"Tell Esmeralda I love her," he said. "Find her for me. I'll tell you anything you want when I know she's safe."

"Tell me now," I replied.

"No," he said stubbornly. "Have another drink with me."

I took a five-dollar bill from my pocket and dropped it on the table.

"That's for the waiter," I said.

26

I left Eddie Watley crying in his scotch. I knew he was going to check Esmeralda's room. I didn't want to be around if he discovered the greaser bodyguard that Number One slapped silly. I wondered how he'd react to that. Let him swing. I hadn't seen the last of him, but enough was enough.

I walked down Park Avenue to Grand Central, and stopped for a beer at that wonderful café overlooking the concourse. I was the last customer. The porter swept under my feet as I sat and watched two couples laughing gaily as they ran to catch the last train to Larchmont. When the gates shut behind them the only thing left to watch were the homeless, maybe a dozen of them, men and women, drifting aimlessly under the map of the sky put into place for the enjoyment and edification of the public.

I took my beer over to a pay phone and called my apartment to see if I had any messages. No one had called. I should have been grateful for that, but I wasn't. I had a job and a roof over my head, but no one to tell my troubles to. Don't be a sap, Darenow. Do you think Ethel Watley is home waxing sweet for her roving reporter? Dream on. You get one toss with a dame like that. The rest you pay for, one way or another. I still couldn't make up my mind about Ethel. It was so stupid.

I called the city desk and asked them if there were any messages for me. There were none, but a package from Tampa, Florida, had arrived.

It was Terry Compton's packet of clips. Hurley got on the phone and wanted to know what the hell I'd been doing.

"The publisher wants to know what kind of story you're writing," he said. "I had to tell him I didn't know. Why the hell is he getting involved? What the hell kind of a story *are* you writing?"

Metcalf must have alerted him.

"I want you in the office tomorrow," he said. "And so does the publisher!"

He slammed the phone down.

Good, Darenow. Soon you'll be out of a job. No job, no future. And you'll have two mobs and the CIA on your back besides.

I walked out to Forty Deuce and hailed a cab. I asked him to go downtown and to drive slowly because I hadn't made up my mind about where I was going. I didn't particularly want to see Esmeralda again, but I knew it might be the last time I'd have the opportunity. From what Cartwright implied during the session at the Albemarle Club, she was to be taken to a safe haven, all expenses paid.

Why? As a simple favor to Wately, her pitiful swain? I don't think so. Esmeralda knows something. Cartwright wasn't trying to save Esmeralda, he was disposing of her. She was no threat. She was a dumb kid with dreams. Cartwright was housecleaning for the Watelys. The trash went out in the morning. He's part of Mr. Fixit's operation.

And who's taking the rap for the money-laundering? Metcalf, Cartwright, and Wately know who the patsy is, but he won't be unveiled until Monday when he testifies before a Tampa grand jury. I'd better alert Terry Compton to that one.

I had spent a year in Washington, working for the Associated Press, and I developed a strong dislike for the clubby atmosphere, the backbiting and favor currying that went on. Everybody, for the most part, tried to play it both ways. Wately was sixteen when he discovered his father's world was an orb of hypocrisy, but he opted to go for it anyway. Fuck him and the horse he rides on.

And fuck Stu Metcalf and his troopers, too. He wasn't even a politician. And he wasn't an aristocrat, either. I could understand politicians, even sympathize with the hard choices the good ones had to make in order to survive and try to do some good elsewhere. That type was in short supply. These days, it was every man for himself and the public be damned. The pols governed by taking soundings of how deep the debt could pile before the eagle started to scream. You don't want the socialists taking over, after all. That's consensus politics. There was no attempt at intelligent guidance—only intelligence operations. Imagine letting The People decide foreign policy! It isn't in the Constitution. Neither is an imperial presidency. The answer, as usual, was hung in the middle of the Senate cloakroom, like a coat someone had left behind eons ago and no one ever moved it because they thought the owner might return someday.

No, Metcalf wasn't sending in an entire flying squad so Esmeralda Sanchez could be retired from the game. There had to be a lot more to it than that.

We were flying through the intersection of Park and Twenty-third Street when I decided where I was going. I was happy with the way things turned out the last time I changed my mind about seeing Esmeralda. I'd try it again. But first I'd retire to the comfort and security of my apartment for a strategy session. I directed the cabbie there and told him to stop along the way so I could buy a pack of cigarettes and some more coffee. I had a lot more work to do before I could sleep.

I was dialing Terry Compton's phone number before I took my coat off.

Compton was wide awake and eager to talk.

"Your Wately banking scandal is taking off," he said. "They found Oscar Herrera, his loan manager, hanging from a tree in a cemetery on the south side of town shortly before eleven P.M. So far no suicide note. The word is that he was to be indicted in connection with a money-laundering scheme, but that's all we know. I'm leaving early to catch some sleep because I want to be down at the bank and police station in the morning." *Oscar Herrera.*

I grabbed a pad and pencil and took notes. Herrera was the guy whose name was on the lease of the Toucan Too.

"This is good," I said. "This is good. I'm going to go through the clips you sent and then I want you to follow up some leads I'll provide. I'll have a better idea of things in the morning." I didn't tell what I knew about Herrera.

"Here's what I was thinking," he said. "Edgar Wately is in New York. I thought you might run him down for a quote on this."

"I ran him down last night," I said. "This guy Herrera's death opens new vistas, but it's also shut some doors. Somebody is getting rid of a lot of witnesses and that means one thing."

"A cover-up?"

"You got it."

"Well, I'm digging in," he said. "I'll keep you posted. How was your interview with Edgar? I'm surprised he wanted to talk to you."

"Keep it under your hat for a while," I said, not really caring whether or not he did. "Wately was apparently having an affair with a transsexual who was also a friend of his late little brother's. He, and some State Department guys I also met last night at his apartment, they all claim Wately was being blackmailed for that reason by the two men I—" I stumbled over the words— "that were killed here in New York."

"Holy smoke!" was all Compton said.

We signed off, promising to call each other as soon as we had moved on to the next development.

I hung up and, I don't know why, started humming a Strauss waltz. I wandered into the bathroom and peeked warily into the mirror. I looked like a man who had just gotten laid but still wasn't satisfied.

I went to the kitchen, put up some coffee, slipped out of my shoes, pulled out my little black book—actually Bennie Torres's little black book, but mine now—and sat down to work.

Compton's parcel had arrived already. I cleaned off the top of my desk, opened the parcel, pulled out a Tampa street map and telephone directory, and spilled the bundle of newspaper clips on my desk.

27

Time flies when you're having fun, but the crick in my neck told me it was time for a break. The air in my bedroom had grown thick with cigarette smoke so I opened a window and let the night roll in, bringing with it echoes of the big tuning fork, the great urban hum. The breeze felt good.

Unfolded, the Tampa street map covered most of the bed. The news clips Compton sent were arranged in a semicircle around the map. Different colored grease pencils and highlighters spiked the crown. The diadem was the Tampa telephone directory. It formed a nice, orderly pattern. I sucked on a Camel and eased the taste with a swallow of stale coffee while I contemplated the fruits of my labor.

A scatter of black dots on the map represented the approximate street addresses of most, if not all, of the Latinos blown away in New York. They had all lived in a Tampa suburb on the edge of a scrub pine wilderness where the CIA had been training mercenaries since the early 1960s. A rash of red dots represented branch offices of the Wately bank and other "family holdings," including a water company, two citrus warehouses, and a few mini malls. A lot of red dots were clustered in the suburb where the New York victims had lived. The bank alone had three branches within a few miles of each other. Blue dots represented some of the things Melendez owned, like the cement plant, a trucking company, and a downtown office tower that headquartered his shipping line.

I figured that out thanks to Terry Compton's reportorial diligence. Compton had pulled enough clips from the files of local newspapers to give me an overview on all the things we'd discussed thus far, not just police blotter items about the Torres brothers and their thugs, but business-page stories on the Wately and Melendez holdings, and background on the CIA's use of Florida's pine barrens as a training ground for covert operations throughout Latin America.

Those clips, the Tampa map, and Bennie's address book revealed yet another connection between Wately, the Torres crew, and the CIA.

I found out about the subdivision from a story in the real estate section which mentioned that Wately's bank had underwritten the construction and development costs. No mention was made of the fact that it bordered on land used by the CIA, or that the land had been the site of a depleted phosphate mine once owned by the Wately family and leased to the Department of the Navy in 1961. That information came from a slim file slugged CIA—MISC. As usual when reading a newspaper, the real story is found by reading between the lines. That's always been taken for granted in places like Russia and Poland, but it's a recent development in the United States, where the inclusion of juicy tidbits and irony once helped weave a good news story. Now they leave the best parts out and call it objectivity. I really had to find another way of making a living.

The name of the subdivision where the CIA barracked its peon army and their dependents was Liberty Village, a wonderfully ironic touch the real estate editor missed, or purposely omitted because it might hurt sales, especially sales of the full-page ads heralding the no-money-down terms that made owning a home in Liberty Village so easy. The ads made no mention of the fact that the head of the house had to put his ass on the line occasionally to fight a rich man's war in the jungles of Central America. How innovative of the CIA, I thought. Someone in Langley discovered that Latin armies traditionally brought women, sometimes whole families, into the field, and decided to offer free housing as an inducement to serve. George Washington and the rest of *our* Founding Fathers would have been appalled.

That wasn't all I discovered. Just for the hell of it, I checked to see if there was a listing for Torquenos in the Tampa directory. There was one for Iris Torquenos, at an address in the same subdivision. I went and found a corresponding number in Bennie's address book, under T, with the name Iris next to it.

I was feeling good about my discoveries, good enough to emit a satisfied yawn and check the clock. It was nearly five in the morning. Another night gone, me still up, and much to do tomorrow. I had promised to call Rocco and Inspector Rossetti after my meeting with the Watelys. I couldn't sleep until I figured out what I was going to tell them. My tangled relationships with the police, the Mafia, the CIA in the person of Stu Metcalf, the feds in the person of Owen Reed, the Watelys, the Melendezes, *père* and *fils*, all needed untangling, at least in my own mind.

It was a common pitfall. The reporter finds that he's become part of the weave, and it's difficult to extract himself in order to see the picture with a keen, objective eye. I needed a stimulant so I took a quick, brutally cold shower while the water for coffee boiled, then settled down with a cigarette and a yellow legal pad. I stared at the cigarette for a long time before I lit up. I hated to think I needed it to think, so I lit up, took a drag, and snuffed it out again before proceeding.

I worked for a long time, taking notes and trying to separate the strands of the story. Finally, when I could scarcely hold my eyes open, I gathered up my notes, exchanged my coffee cup for a bottle of beer, and called Dixie. It was nearly six A.M. but I didn't care. Dixie thrived on chaos.

Number One answered the phone.

Not good. *I hadn't expected him to answer the phone*. I figured he'd be sleeping or watching TV wrestling.

I lapsed into a Tallulah Bankhead voice that scared the pants off me. "Dahling," I sighed, "let me speak to Dixie."

Number One said nothing. He'd had enough of drag queens for one night. The next thing I heard was Dixie's voice.

"Say nothing," I said. "It's me. I can't talk right now. Do exactly as I say. Get a tape recorder. Hook it up to your bathroom or kitchen extension, and let Esmeralda dial the number I'm about to give you. Do you understand what I'm saying?"

I was counting on Wately's going back to the Albemarle Club.

"Yes," Dixie said. "And then what? Who does she call?"

"She calls Wately and you tape the call. Don't let her know you're taping it. Do you have a tape recorder?"

"Yes, but—"

"You were right, Dixie, but for the wrong reasons. Esmeralda's dead meat, but it's not the cops she's afraid of. Wately might have been blackmailed by the Torres brothers on account of her, but I don't think they're the only ones who want to see her disappear."

"What should I tell the boys?" she whispered. I knew that was coming.

"I'll talk to Rocco myself. Tell Number One I'm a drag queen, a friend of yours, calling with a message from the grapevine for Esmeralda. The message is to call Wately. Tell her Wately wants to help her escape. I want to tape the call—for my own reasons. Charlie Big Guy can have the tape, for all I care. I just want Wately on the record. I'm sure Charlie will approve."

There was a pause. It was a lot for her to swallow.

"I think so," she said. "Why can't you come here?"

"I'm a reporter and my career can't take a blackmail rap, or a charge of suborning a material witness in a murder investigation."

"Where are you now?"

"Home," I said, "and you're the only one who knows it. Capice?"

If she wasn't on my side I'd know soon.

"Got it, darling," she said. "Thanks for the tip."

Now I had to straighten things out with Rocco and Charlie. A little diplomacy would go a long way. It wouldn't hurt to mention my fling with Ethel, come to think of it. It would boost my machismo as I wriggled off the hook. Rocco was probably still at The Crib, counting the night's take. The crowd there tended to linger well past the four A.M. closing time ordained by the state liquor authority. Rocco picked up on the first ring.

"Hello," I said. "It's me. I have a message for Charlie."

I filled Rocco in as best I could on what went down at the Watelys'. I told him about meeting Stu Metcalf and Owen Reed and the big-time accountants and I told him about drinking stingers around the fireplace with Ethel.

"The upshot is this, Rocco: we're dealing with extremely well-connected people. They have the CIA on their side, and they've concocted a neat scenario that takes Mr. Wately off the hook. Some poor sap named Oscar Herrera, the loan officer at Wately's bank, was being set up to take the fall for the money-laundering, and he's been found swinging from a tree in a Tampa cemetery."

"Dead men cannot testify or defend themselves," Rocco said without hesitation.

"You're right, Rocco. That's why no one misses the Torres brothers. I don't want to be next on their list. Do you?"

"They won't mess with you," Rocco said. "Charlie won't stand for it."

"Rocco, this is the CIA. They don't play fair. The only thing they want from me is sealed lips, and they have other ways of ensuring that."

"So what are you saying?" he asked glumly.

"I'm saying that I have to keep my distance from Esmeralda, and from Charlie. I appreciate his help, but I have my own axe to grind with Wately."

"Charlie's not gonna like that, Max. He went the distance for you. He's backing up your alibi."

I was expecting that. The Mafia doesn't like to see its pigeons leave the coop without permission. It was time to stir the Italian's machismo.

"I probably shouldn't tell you this, Rocco, but I thought Charlie might want to know that I nailed Edgar Wately's sister last night. She was delicious."

"You boffed the sister? You gotta be kidding. Charlie hears she's gorgeous! Melendez's son gives her a ten. You really boffed her? You got in her pants after a few stingers?" Rocco was impressed. "Jee-sus! Them rich broads are just like anybody else, huh?" But I wasn't getting off that easy. It made him think.

"See," he said, "Charlie thought they were gonna try and buy you off, but they knew you didn't care about the money, so she spread her legs for you. Wake up, baby! Charlie won't steer you wrong. Melendez knows these people and he's on our side."

"Melendez is on Melendez's side, Rocco. He's holding a gold card from the CIA. Charlie can't match his clout, I'm sorry. Metcalf, the guy from the State Department, says Melendez is bailing out Wately's bank. That's his payoff. He doesn't care who murdered Denise."

"Who are they blaming for Denise's murder?" Rocco asked. "Who gave her the knockout drops? What does the government say about that?"

"All Bennie and Ralph Torres's fault," I said. "The motive was supposed to be blackmail. That's what the feds claim. Wately denies they worked for him, of course. We'll see about that. In the meantime, I overheard one of the government guys telling Wately to get rid of Esmeralda."

"He said '*get rid of*' her?" Rocco asked.

I told him how Dixie was going to try and tape a call between Esmeralda and Wately. I told him Charlie could keep the tape, but I wanted to listen to it first.

Rocco thought about it for a minute and agreed to my terms.

"It sounds all right," he said. "I'll tell Charlie. Where can he reach you?"

I told Rocco I was going to the office to do a little research. I felt better not letting him know I was staying home for some reason, partially because I wanted only Dixie to know. I didn't trust anybody anymore.

"OK," Rocco said. "I'll tell him to call the office."

"Fine." I sighed. I didn't care if the newspaper knew I was dealing information with the mob. So what?

"How about Esmeralda?" Rocco said. "You get anything out of her?"

"She thinks Wately wants to marry her," I said. "She's a fruitcake and so is he."

"See!" Rocco chortled delightedly, "The Big Guy knew he was queer!"

I left Rocco laughing.

So much for the Mafia, at least for the time being. The cops were next on my list. Rossetti and The Cardinal expected a full report and Rossetti had told me to call day or night.

But I owed the first call to Henry, the man who first tipped me to the spy angle and coached me through my ordeal in The Cardinal's office. That was good manners. If Henry hadn't warned me it was coming, I would have spilled my guts on The Cardinal's sewer cover when Rossetti played the tape of Aurora's call to 911. I wanted to return the favor. I'd rather have a man in the trenches carrying my spear than a man in the tower. That was *my* pecking order.

Henry was either coming on or going off a shift so I called his place of work. He wasn't in.

I sat on the couch to take a break and promptly fell asleep. It was nearly seven A.M. and a new day was under way.

Lieutenant Henry called at 7:40. No rest for the weary.

I told him about my audience with The Cardinal and Inspector Rossetti. Henry had spoken to Rossetti since then and seemed quite up to date on our meeting. He was more interested in how my meeting with Owen Reed and the State Department brass went.

I filled him in on as many details as I could, leaving out the time in Ethel Wately's bedroom. I told him about tracking Edgar down at the Albemarle Club. He listened attentively and seemed pleased with my report.

Henry had been pretty busy himself. He had gone to Harlem early last evening to interview a sixty-three-year-old black man who had been the Watelys' butler for many years. Prior to that, and to my visit to the

Watelys, Detective Gonzalez, the man assigned to the murders on Avenue A, had gone to the Wately residence and interviewed Aurora Carrera. No wonder Aurora had seemed nervous during the cocktail party.

We compared notes and came up with a not-so-startling conclusion: there were big holes in the stories being peddled by the Watelys and Aurora. Holes too big to cover up.

"No one's telling us the whole truth," Henry huffed.

I asked him if he had heard about Oscar Herrera's alleged suicide. He hadn't. "The feds aren't telling us shit," he complained.

"They found Herrera's body at eleven o'clock last night. He was supposed to be indicted Monday, according to Metcalf and Reed."

"Look, pal," he said, "what we have to do is tie the Watelys or Rosa to Bennie and Ralph. Then we have to establish probable cause for the murders of Santiago and your friend. Then we prove the brothers weren't acting on their own. Right now the district attorney is satisfied with the feds' explanation. The buck stops with Bennie and Ralph and case closed."

"I don't think they acted alone," I said.

"I don't either," he said, "and I'm not the only cop on the force who doesn't. These people are making an all-out effort to snow you, Darenow. You gotta be careful."

I could only agree. I had been offered everything short of a blowjob. The truth was, Ethel had hinted that might be forthcoming, too. So how come I knew I was being snookered and was still denying it?

"There's a lot of things the Watelys didn't tell us, or are just telling us now," Henry said. "Like the fact that Bennie and Ralph were related to Rosa. Why didn't Mrs. Wately tell us that right away? Other things don't jibe. We found men's clothes at the kid's apartment, which we think belonged to Mr. Wately, right? This is the same guy who never told us the kid had his own pad. I let it slide, figuring these rich people don't know what their left hand is doing, but then when we found the clothes . . ."

"They're strange people," I said. "What did the butler have to say?"

"It's a long story, as usual." He yawned. "Any chance of meeting tonight, before I go back to work?"

"I've been up all night, too," I said.

"Come to my place around eight o'clock," Henry said. "I'm baby-sitting. That's if you don't mind three kids."

I told him I wouldn't mind at all and we arranged to meet. I started to get up and strip for bed but I knew that once I hit the hay I'd be out like a light. I decided to call Rossetti and get it over with. If the CIA was going to be on my case, I'd like Rossetti and The Cardinal in my corner.

Rossetti's wife answered the phone in a sleepy voice. I gave her my name. She yawned in reply and passed the phone to her husband. He didn't sound too wide awake, either. I offered to call back at a more convenient time.

"There's a place on Carmine Street," he said. "Tre Pesci, a coffee shop. You like espresso? Good desserts?"

"Absolutely," I said.

"All right, Tre Pesci, between Sixth and Seventh Avenues, on the north side of the street, and, let's say, four?"

"Four is perfect," I said.

"See you there," he said.

I set the alarm for 2:30, figuring that would give me plenty of time to get organized before my meeting with Rossetti. I sat down on the bed, kicked off my slippers, lay back, and wondered what would have happened if Denise and I had gotten back together before she died.

Would she be alive today? I was too tired to think about it. I closed my eyes for a second, wished she was lying next to me so I could rub her back once more, and fell asleep, still wearing the pants to the good blue suit.

28

The phone rang at quarter past one in the afternoon. The light was streaming through open blinds. The pants to the good blue suit needed pressing.

It was The Big Guy. He drove right to the point.

"Everyone is looking for the drag queen," he intoned gravely.

"A lot of people want her, Charlie," I said easily.

"Yeh, well, she's hot," Charlie growled. "So here's what we're gonna do." There was a new timbre in his voice. He wasn't laconic, he wasn't cool.

"You're still my friend, right?" he said. "Everybody treating you OK?"

"Yeh," I said. Keep your trap shut, Darenow, you simpering, lying dog. This is no way to win a Pulitzer, but it's OK.

"OK. I want you to have some information from a source in Florida. He's seen the address book. He's a private dick. He's gonna give you the lowdown on Wately." He paused for effect. "You take it from there, scoop."

"I have to see the information first," I said. "See where it leads."

He thought about it.

"That's good," he said. "You do that. I can tell you you won't have any trouble proving anything after this guy talks to you. Meanwhile, everybody's sitting tight, waiting for your next edition. So go to it, scoop."

Scoop growled. Oh, be a nice dog, Darenow, roll over and let the man play with you.

"I'll let you know," I said. "How do I know this guy's legitimate? The guy from Florida?"

"He's legit. He's Frank Reilly! Frankie the Cop. He's totally loyal. He's in court all the time testifying. He's tops in the private eye racket. He's been in Florida for fifteen years. Shit!

"Listen," he continued, a little more timbrously, I thought, "just do your job and don't worry about anything. You're backed up. Clear?"

"Clear," I said. "But I also have to back up the story."

"Talk to Frankie," he said. "He'll call you in half an hour, or less."

I tried going back to sleep.

I tried, but it was no good. No sleep for Darenow. Smell the coffee. I got out of bed and put some on and thought a shower might help. It often does, at least while you're in it. I was tired and mad at myself. I wasn't Charlie's personal scribe. Oh, tell them all to fuck off, D'Arnou. Isn't that Ethel's pet name for *her* house scribe? Norman French, right? I was serving too many masters, or mistresses.

I jolted myself awake with a hard, cold spray and thought about the state I was in. The stinging chill of the water was nothing compared to the heat that was coming down.

I toweled off, had two sips of coffee, and jumped successively into skivvies, Levi's, a corduroy shirt, socks, good tennis shoes, and an old tweed jacket. I was going fence walking. I didn't want to look too good if I fell and got arrested, but I wanted a comfortable pair of shoes on my feet. I didn't wear a belt, either; they take it away from you before they put you in a cell.

I went back to the desk and wished it was four o'clock so I could call Terry Compton. Never mind Compton, I thought, go out and call Dixie. Use a pay phone. Find out if Esmeralda reached Wately. The more ammunition you have, the better off you'll be when the shooting starts—or it's time for plea bargaining.

Wait again. Frankie the Cop is supposed to call. What if they tap that call? And what if they've already tapped the call with The Big Guy? Any dunce could see I was lying when I said I didn't know where Esmeralda was. Or could they? Stop it, Darenow, you'll fret yourself to death. Call

Dixie on your way to the Village. Organize your notes. Get your ducks lined up.

Coffee wasn't going to be enough. I made myself a fried egg sandwich and sat down at the desk to eat it when the phone rang.

It was Frank Reilly, AKA Frankie the Cop, hard-boiled Florida sleuth.

"Mr. Darenow?" he said. He sounded like an aging tenor.

"Yes," I said.

"I'm Frank Reilly. I have some information for you if you're ready to take it down."

"I'm ready," I said, pushing the egg sandwich aside and picking up a nice fast pen.

"This is from round-the-clock surveillance while the subject was in Tampa, as well as background checks on the subject and other individuals. There's a lot of details involved, places, times, that you might wish to pinpoint, so I'm sending you the surveillance logs certified mail. OK?"

The guy's voice was worn smooth as my old corduroys and sounded just as tough. There was some comfort in dealing with a pro, even if it was double-dealing.

"We picked up the subject 12/19 at his residence in the Palm Towers, a downtown condo near his bank's main office. He drove a Buick station wagon to the Fort Leigh Racetrack, where he unloaded four gym bags, big ones, heavy load, at a feed room near Barn Twelve. We had two men on him, so we know that the bags were picked up while he went over to watch the morning workout. The bags were taken into the clubhouse by a groom. Subject spent an hour chatting with some people at the rail and then went into the clubhouse, to a members-only area where we couldn't go. He came out ten minutes later with a big leather satchel, like accountants carry, took it back to his car, and drove to a seaplane base in Tampa Bay.

"Am I going too fast?" he asked.

"No," I said, scribbling notes furiously. "Go ahead."

"You get the picture?" he asked.

"He was laundering money?"

"Exchanging small bills—God knows what denominations were in the gym bags—for big bills—maybe hundreds, five hundreds. Who knows? How many five-hundred-dollar bills could you fit in one of those accountant satchels?"

"I wouldn't know," I said.

"Figure a few hundred thousand dollars."

"And then he got into a seaplane. Where'd he go?"

"Either Miami or beyond," Frankie said. "He headed inland and south. My guess is he dropped the satchel off in Miami or Bimini for transfer to the Caymans, where it is now drawing interest."

"I see," I said. "Can we find out where the plane was going?"

"I'm working on it," he said.

"What else do you have?"

"Subject returns to Tampa the following day. We pick him up at his sister's house. He keeps a condo downtown but stays at the mansion sometimes—2304 Shore Road, big mansion, two gatekeepers, patrolled grounds. We leave him at the driveway at eleven A.M. Four other cars arrive shortly thereafter. I have a make on all the registrations, which is included in the report, if you can wait. Otherwise I can give it to you now."

I took the names and addresses of the owners of the four cars and told him I could wait for the rest. Hector Melendez headed the motorcade. The others were lawyers and accountants.

"OK," Frank continued, "those people departed two hours later. Wately drives downtown to his bank, departs there five P.M., walks two blocks to condo, departs there an hour later. Cab to home of Mr. John Masters, his sister's attorney of record. He and sister depart Masters' house eleven P.M. in a chauffered Buick and return to mansion, where Wately spends the night.

"He leaves at six the next morning heading for Tampa International Airport, flight number 267 to Washington. That's the last time we've seen him."

"What about his sister?"

"Our instructions were to cover him and him alone."

So Wately stopped in Washington on his way to New York. And he's still laundering money. And carrying the bags himself! This is lovely, I thought. What do I do with it?

"What about those names and phone numbers you were given?" I said. "Have you been able to do anything with them?" I was referring to Bennie's address book.

"You got mostly criminals in that crowd, but you got businesses that are interesting and you got some law enforcement people and customs people, too."

"Law enforcement? Customs?"

"DEA people and some FBI. Home phones and work numbers, both.

Customs people, it's mostly the customs office they got. We're still checking those numbers, sir, it takes time."

Frankie the Cop was a diamond in the rough and nothing if not thorough.

The businesses he thought were interesting included marinas, boatyards, and yacht clubs up and down the Gulf Coast, as well as flower importers and wholesale florists there and in New York.

"Florists?"

"Sure, do you know how many flowers arrive in Florida from Colombia every day, not to mention coffee beans? How do you think so much cocaine gets through? You can't check every box, every sack of coffee. It's pretty obvious these guys were importing something. I'm just telling you what the investigation shows so far. You draw your own conclusions."

Reilly had run a check on all the Florida residents who had been blown away in New York. They all drew steady paychecks from businesses owned by or connected to the Torres brothers. Most of them had arrest records. That I knew. Most lived near each other. That I also knew. According to other known criminals in and around Tampa, all of the New York victims were believed to be part of the Torres brothers' organization. It wasn't something to offer a grand jury, it was something to go after.

What I hadn't noticed until then was that three of the New York victims—the married couple from Kew Gardens and one of the men shot in Queens—had shared the same surname, the woman through marriage. The surname was Herrera.

"Oscar Herrera was Wately's loan officer," I piped.

"I was going to say," said Frankie the Cop. "Oscar Herrera is dead. They're calling it suicide. He was supposed to be indicted tomorrow for laundering money. Two of the deceased New York men were his brothers. Oscar Herrera was a big deal around these parts."

"They found his body swinging from a tree in a graveyard," I said.

"Bennie and Ralph must have spent a lot of time with Mr. Herrera," Frankie said cheerily. "You won't have a problem drawing connections there. Wately's bank holds mortgages on all their homes."

Frankie had also run credit checks on Edgar and Ethel Wately.

"Love to hear something on that," I crooned.

"Mr. Wately has four banks listed on his credit sheet, Mainline Trust, Manhattan Trust, Gulf Bank of Houston, and the Chase in New York. Assets slightly over twelve million dollars, *not* counting stocks and bonds.

The twelve mil is real estate and cash deposits. Not bad, huh? He sounds liquid, right? But listen to this.

"We checked his sister's credit sheet, too. It's identical. They seem to share everything. The credit reports read like carbon copies. I thought it might interest you."

Frank Reilly was low-key.

"Bennie and Ralph would have been great to tail," he said. "From the looks of things, they got around and met a lot of interesting people. I'd love to have been watching them through a telephoto lens."

And had a sense of humor.

I gave him some more things to check out and we arranged to speak again the next day.

I stared at the notes I had jotted down during our conversation, then tucked them into my jacket pocket. I got up and put an overcoat on over the jacket and went out to call Dixie and meet Inspector Gabriel Dante Rossetti.

The sun was out and the wind had died down to a few hearty gusts. I found an outdoor phone booth on a sunny corner and called Dixie's. She answered on the first ring and whispered hello.

"What's the story?" I said.

"They're all sleeping. He wants her to leave tonight on a flight to Puerto Rico; she's supposed to pick up a passport there and fly to Costa Rica. It's all on tape. He cried; she cried."

"Is she going?"

"Uh-unh," Dixie said. "He wanted to send over money and a passport, but Esmeralda doesn't even know the address here. 'One' got on the phone because she started getting hysterical, yelling 'Get me out of here.' Number One told Wately he wanted to meet him and talk."

"And?"

"Wately got pissed. He demanded that Esmeralda get back on the line but 'One' wouldn't do it. She got hysterical again and Wately hung up."

"But the tape? He tells her she's got to leave?"

"Oh, yeh. I was in the sauna. I made a mouthpiece for the phone from a piece of sponge, turned the volume up, and laid the receiver right over the built-in mike. Soundproof room, perfect reception. She doesn't even know I taped it. Wait till you hear it."

I asked Dixie if her phone was secure.

"Max," she replied, "Charlie thinks of everything."

Dixie was too much.

Wately was taking the bait. Relax, Darenow. You're holding good cards. Don't lay those cards down yet.

Inspector Gabriel Dante Rossetti was a bookworm. He liked to browse the used and rare book stores, of which there were still a few left in the Village. Tre Pesci, he explained, was the centerpiece of his serendipitous journies. He either fueled up there before he started his browsing, took a breather at midpoint, or ended up there.

"It all depends on where I park my car." He smiled. He moved a shopping bag full of books off a chair and invited me to sit. He had finished a piece of chocolate cake and was ordering his second cappuccino when I arrived. He asked me to join him. Everything looked delicious but I passed on the desserts. The waiter was disappointed.

"Make mine a special." Gabe winked to the waiter. It meant they'd add a shot or two of anisette.

"Two specials," I said. "Make mine extra special, it's cold out there."

Gabe patted his book bag affectionately and told me he had something in there for me.

"It's required reading for what you're getting into."

We sipped steaming cups of cappuccino while Gabe talked.

"Oscar Herrera's suicide is not a good omen," Rossetti began. "The guy was loaded with sedatives when he died. It's a question whether he could have climbed on the box and put the noose around his neck at all. They still haven't found a note. The feds weren't happy when we called Florida for a report. Your friend Owen Reed called one of our guys and complained. He's right, of course, it's completely out of our jurisdiction. We told him we were concerned for the lives of Mr. and Mrs. Wately and possibly their servants. He said they were all under federal protection. Reed apparently got a little snotty with one of our detectives. He asked why we haven't found Esmeralda yet."

"Look," I said, bending the facts to fit, "I don't know what this is worth, but I've been sending out feelers and I've gotten some more feedback from the street, just drag queens with rumors, but it looks as if Esmeralda is still in town and trying to get out. Wately, in fact, as much as admitted that to me."

Slow down, Darenow.

"You spoke to him?"

"I cornered him last night after I left his sister's apartment, after I'd met Reed and Metcalf, the guy from the State Department. I overheard another State guy tell Wately he had to get rid of Esmeralda. The same guy told him not to worry because they had 'a fall guy' at the bank. Those were his exact words—'a fall guy.' About the time he said it, the 'fall guy' was dropping on a rope in Tampa."

Rossetti broke into a wide grin. He was a great audience.

"The guy from the State Department is named Cartwright," I continued. "I tailed Wately to the Albemarle Club. Much to my surprise they let me in. I went upstairs and heard Wately's voice so I stopped and listened. That's when Cartwright told him in no uncertain terms to get rid of Esmeralda."

Rossetti looked at me with a mixture of bemusement and benign curiosity. He liked me, I thought, and I liked him. He was from the old school, the son of immigrants who cherished the American dream, and knew it must be earned, not ripped off.

"Esmeralda knows something," he mused half to himself. He waved his pipe idly in the air. "I'd hate to see her skip."

I nodded earnestly. I couldn't tell him I knew he was right. On the other hand, I had to move fast before Cartwright's cleanup crew disposed of her or she accepted Wately's ticket to ride. Maybe it was one and the same. Fly her to Costa Rica and throw her out over the rain forest.

"This Cartwright, did you meet him?" Rossetti asked.

"No," I said. "I'd heard enough so I beat it. I picked Wately up when he was leaving and we went and had a drink."

I left out the fact Esmeralda had been staying at the Waldorf and I helped her check out.

I changed the subject and recounted my conversations with Edgar and Ethel Wately, Owen Reed, and Stu Metcalf.

"Wately told me point blank that Metcalf was running a covert operation through his bank," I said, knowing that would catch Rossetti's interest immediately. "Wately swore me to secrecy. After talking to Metcalf, I believe him. If so, they might be responsible for the murders of Denise Overton and Jaime Santiago. Let's call it criminal negligence."

"*If*," he said, giving me a lawman's hard stare, "*if* it ever became necessary, would you be able to testify to the conversations you overheard, or your conversations with the Watelys?" He smiled, but it was a very questioning smile.

Be careful, Darenow.

"I don't know," I said. "What do you have in mind?"

"Nothing at this point," he said. "We need more than hearsay. I'm still trying to determine who the bad guys are."

"So am I," I said.

We both went back to sipping our cappuccino. Rossetti asked me how long I'd been a reporter and I asked him how long he'd been a cop. He told me he had nearly twenty-five years on the force, and three years as a military policeman in Korea. I told him I'd been in Vietnam and had been assigned to an intelligence unit. He liked that and asked me what exactly I had done in that job. I told him I had been an unsuspecting part of Operation Phoenix, a CIA concoction aimed at eliminating suspected Viet Cong agents who were doubling as legitimate village leaders. The Army's job, my job, was to collect names. More gung ho boys, Green Berets and Cuban hit men from the CIA, did the dirty work. I told Rossetti frankly I didn't like the assignment and had gotten transferred. He mulled that over for a long time.

"You ever hear of the De Leon Society?" Rossetti asked.

"Nope."

"I'm not surprised. It's a secret fraternity, a brotherhood of Cuban exiles who like to think they're picking up where Ponce de León left off. You know who he was?"

"The Spaniard who went looking for the fountain of youth."

"He discovered Florida in the seventeenth century," Rossetti said sarcastically. "The boys in the De Leon Society discovered Florida when Castro kicked them out of Cuba. The new conquistadores."

"Sounds like Hector Melendez and his boys."

"Hector Melendez liaisons with everybody in South Florida, including the feds. No one makes a move without Hector knowing about it."

"He's untouchable, I'm sure," I said. I didn't want to press Rossetti, I merely wanted to create a favorable climate to loosen his lips.

He sat back and lit a pipe. I knew if I reeled out more information I'd get him talking again.

"If I had some proof linking Melendez to the Torres brothers, I'd feel a lot better," I said. "I have a source in Florida who's looking into it for me."

Rossetti expelled a cloud of smoke.

"The Torres brothers were ass-kissers," he said dismissively. "Lowlifes trying to break into the big time. Melendez wouldn't give them a tumble. They're not even Cuban-born; they grew up in Tampa."

He tapped the pipe stem on his teeth and gave me a long, thoughtful look.

"I think Edgar Wately's the weak link in the chain," he said. "I'd like to sit him down with a couple of really sharp homicide detectives, but before we do that we have to pick up his girlfriend, Esmeralda, and lean on her."

"What about the servants?" I asked. "Rosa's gone, and maybe the feds had something to do with that, too. But Aurora's still there. She seems to know what's going on."

"We're on her like glue," he said. "OK? We're doing everything possible."

"Hey, I'm not complaining," I said. "You guys are great."

"Look," he said, rummaging around in his book bag, "I picked up a few books you ought to read."

He pulled two hardcover books out and put them on the table. One was the story of the CIA in the Bay of Pigs called *The Fish Is Red*. Among the real-life characters were several who had figured prominently in the Watergate scandal.

The other book was an autobiography of Wild Bill Donovan, the Wall Street power broker and World War One hero who founded America's first formal espionage agency, the OSS, forerunner of the CIA.

He stacked the two books neatly and pushed them across the table.

"If you see any familiar names in there, let me know." He smiled.

"You run across these guys in your work?" I said.

"I spent six months in Florida, part vacation, part work," he said, laying his pipe down. "What I saw disgusted me. It's not America; it's a separate country; it's a staging area for operations throughout Latin America. It's a nest of spies, counterspies, naive politicians, mercenaries, scam artists, and con men posing as patriots.

"The CIA presence there, friend, exceeds any other single station outside of its headquarters in Virginia. They created the problem and now they're paying the price. They took in every secret police chief and torture artist, death squad leader, and neo-Nazi politician and threw a lot of money at them in the name of fighting communism. They're armed criminals out to make a quick buck while they look for another country to rape."

Rossetti shook his head and studied me carefully. He'd been listening to the lies the cloak-and-dagger boys dished out for a long time. He was sick and tired of it, and glad to have someone to complain to. I was all ears and let him know I supported his view.

"The CIA lost control of this mob years ago," he said bitterly. "The people they supported soured on them, until it dawned on them: why not start an oligarchy in Florida, using the CIA's seed money—that's my taxes, friend, and yours—like Monopoly dollars. Build some condos, finance little wars, finance a couple of drug deals. These are people, my friend, who are not acting in the interests of the Constitution of the United States."

He pushed his chair back, sighed, and called for the check.

"Read these books, Mr. Darenow. I think you should know the kind of people you might be bumping into as you pursue your story."

"I'm gonna stay," I said. "I can start my reading assignment right here."

"Fine," he said. "Enjoy yourself. Just remember: don't rattle any cages prematurely and don't count on guys like Metcalf to be your buddy. There's more ass-kissers and assassins out there who'd love to do him a favor—without his even asking. You understand? *Without his even asking.* Boom! Problem disposed of. These guys are wild."

"Thanks," I said.

"The first cup was on the NYPD," he said.

"Thanks again," I said.

I picked up *The Fish Is Red* and put the book down an hour later. I was enthralled.

You haven't seen anything, yet, Darenow. These guys play for keeps. Facts just bounce off them. They don't respect truth. They make it up as they go along.

I paid the bill, bundled up against the cold and the gathering darkness, and tucked the books under my arm.

I crossed Carmine Street and stepped into St. Anthony's Church. I sat in a pew in the back and watched the votive candles flicker crazily on the altar. Two old Italian ladies, all in black, of course, knelt elsewhere in the church, unconnected to each other except through their devotion.

I opened the other book, *The Last Hero*, Wild Bill Donovan's story, and thumbed through it. It was a reviewer's copy and there was a publicity release folded into its pages. It contained an excerpt from an interview with the author, Anthony Cave Brown.

"The intelligence service is not just a bunch of spies rushing around the world finding out other people's secrets," he was quoted as saying. "Nor is it a system for blowing up bridges and power stations. That's elementary stuff. Its true purpose in Russia, America, Britain and France is as a praetorian organization which exists to protect the established power."

I read it again and then once more. Then I watched the candles flicker.

I watched the candles flicker for a long time and thought about all the poor, tired old ladies—mothers and grandmothers—lighting candles in churches like this throughout Latin America. What were they devoted to? Offering their sons and husbands as a constant reenactment of the crucifixion?

I went up and lit a candle for Denise. Then I lit another one. I didn't ask for anything. I just stuffed two bucks into the hole and knelt there for a minute and hoped everything would work out for everybody.

And what happens if you get cut down in a hail of bullets when you step outside, Darenow? Do the good guys ever win? I kicked that around in my mind while I walked up Bleecker Street. Why sure, Darenow. Where's your faith? There's always someone out there more interested in truth than money.

Isn't there?

29

Lieutenant Henry wasn't expecting me until eight o'clock so I stopped and ate dinner in an Indian restaurant further along Bleecker Street. I read throughout the meal. Christ, I thought: here it is, all spelled out, and I can't do a goddamned thing about it except cluck my tongue like the rest of my fellow citizens and treat it as entertainment. Except the people in the books were real. And so are Stu Metcalf and Hector Melendez and Oscar Herrera and the Torres brothers and the Watelys.

And so *was* Denise. But it wasn't her war!

I bundled up again, clasping the books in front of my chest to ward off the chill, and wondered if the books could stop a slug.

I walked to Broadway, headed to Canal, and cut through the streets between Chinatown, the criminal courts, and the Tombs. Visiting hours at the Tombs were just over and the tired, poor relatives of the incarcerated—those who got caught and couldn't swing bail—poured into the street behind the jail, their musical Latin chatter bouncing off the brickwork and fading away into the traffic's roar and the night sky.

I quickened my pace. The temperature seemed to drop a few degrees every half block. My ears were numb by the time I stepped into the elevator at Lieutenant Henry's apartment building.

I stepped off the elevator at Henry's floor, found his apartment, and rang the bell. I heard men's voices behind the door. It sounded as if Henry was bidding adieu to some visitors. Cops.

The door swung open. Henry appeared, said something about "perfect timing," and moved aside to let one of the men out. I recognized him immediately. He was the same mean cop I had met at Denise's place when we were going over the photos of the drag queens. He nodded curtly and stepped into the hall to button his coat. A second man, short, dark, and stocky, brushed past Lieutenant Henry, then paused deferentially, as if he was going to let me pass, but that wasn't his intention. He stopped, about three feet away, and scrutinized me from head to toe. He "made me," as the saying goes, then smiled faintly and stepped into the hall.

"Don't let these guys scare you," Henry said cheerily. "They're off duty. Come on in."

Henry shut the door and explained that the second man, the one who gave me the twice-over, was Detective Gonzalez, who had been investigating the deaths on Avenue A.

"We call him Pancho," Henry said. "He interviewed Rosa Torquenos and Aurora Carrera after he found they were related to Bennie and Ralph. When he went back there yesterday he found out Rosa had taken a powder. The Watelys weren't at home, so he leaned on Miss Carrera. Pancho don't like it when his own people lie to him. Pancho acted on his own, of course. As you can see, we're not letting the feds tie our hands completely."

Henry's remarks and the scotch and soda he poured for me put me at ease.

"Gonzalez is convinced they're lying," Henry said, meaning Aurora, Edgar, *and* Ethel. "He asked Aurora to write out a statement and she froze. She speaks English but she can't write it. She's no secretary, that's for sure."

"And listen to this." Henry smiled. "The elevator operator said Bennie and Ralph came to see Rosa a few days before the Santiago kid was found dead. Aurora claims she doesn't know why they were in town."

"Has anyone asked Aurora why Bennie and Ralph would kill Jaime?" I inquired. "She might shed some light on the blackmail angle."

"Gonzalez asked her," Henry said. "He caught her in a lie. He had already found out from the elevator man that she and Mrs. Watley were on the premises during the Torres brothers' last visit. He pressed her and she started to cry. She swore she didn't know why they murdered

Jaime, but she implied that they might have had a motive for trying to kill Esmeralda."

"So it *was* Esmeralda they were after," I said. "They have been lying from the start."

"Mrs. Wately didn't lie," Henry said. "She just didn't tell us what she knew about Esmeralda and her brother. I don't blame her. It was a lot to accept for a woman of her caliber."

"But she lied," I protested. "She lied to me. She didn't tell me any of this. She never told me the Torres boys came to visit."

"Aurora says Mrs. Wately was fed up with Edgar's relationship with Esmeralda," Henry said. "Aurora said it got to the point where Rosa told her either Esmeralda had to go or they were all out of a job. Rosa smelled trouble."

"Jesus," I muttered, only half believing what I was about to say, "maybe Ethel Wately is the one who wanted Esmeralda disposed of."

Ethel?

My heart skipped a beat.

Henry nodded somberly.

"Something's wrong here," I said.

Henry laughed dryly. "If we had more information we could trip Aurora up," he ventured, "find a hole in her story or something, but we don't, and since there's a freeze on the case from the feds, we can't go down to Tampa and start digging around. Aurora's worried, but money buys a lot of silence."

"And Rosa, a material witness, if not a suspect, walks away. Just like that."

Henry saw the frustration in my eyes.

"Immigration and Naturalization is hot on Rosa's trail, but do you know how many cases immigration handles per man?" he said. "Forget it, Darenow. Rosa's gone.

"Esmeralda was a real embarrassment to Mrs. Wately," Henry added firmly. "Rosa could have passed word to her nephews that Mrs. Wately wanted Esmeralda gone. To them it would be just be doing someone a favor."

We were back to what Rossetti had said earlier, about people like Stu Metcalf just saying the word and boom! there would be people waiting to carry out his orders.

Maybe Metcalf's attitude rubbed off on Ethel. I could imagine Ethel getting into a snit over Edgar's relations with Esme and Jaime, and Rosa asking, out of turn, what was wrong. And then Ethel snarls something nasty under her breath about Esmeralda, and Rosa gets worried.

Would Rosa then have padded calmly back into the kitchen to put the deadly plan in motion? Is she the one who told Bennie and Ralph that their lives would be better if Esmeralda, and Jaime, weren't around anymore? And then Bennie, who knew how to shoot and little else, did Bennie dispose of them accordingly? But why use poison?

"I think Rosa knows why Bennie killed your girl and the kid," Henry summed up. "It's in the realm of the possible, but I have a hunch Rosa didn't give the order. There was someone else."

We sat and sipped our drinks quietly for a moment. Both our thoughts were leading in the same direction, but . . .

"So where do we go from here?" I asked. "Even if Ethel Wately gave them the idea, the only witnesses are Bennie, maybe Ralph, and Rosa, and they're either dead or gone."

Henry got up and closed the bedroom door. There was a small commotion in the living room. The kids were having a pillow fight during a commercial break.

"We're going to lean on Aurora," Henry continued, "Not hard, just enough to remind her she's in deep. Violence is always a possibility to these people. Aurora said she suspected Bennie and Ralph were bad guys, but blood's thicker than water, I guess. After all, she and Rosa owed their jobs to those boys."

Henry got up to freshen up our drinks. I told him I'd pass. I was thumbing through one of the books Rossetti gave me when he returned.

"You're in good hands with Rossetti," Henry said. "Did he tell you about the time he met the Russians?"

"No," I said.

"Great story. Rossetti gets called to the Russian mission when one of their big guys is in town and they're worried because the Ukrainians want to hit one of their leaders. So they want to show Rossetti pictures of the guys they suspect, right? So Rossetti goes over there and all these Russians are sitting around in this room in wigs and phony mustaches. They're all disguised because they're KGB agents and they don't want to blow their cover. So Rossetti keeps them there, studying them and asking questions, trying to be real serious, and the Russians are sitting there and the wigs are sliding and the mustaches are falling off. It must have been a riot."

We laughed, though neither one of us thought it was funny.

"Look, Mr. Darenow," Henry continued seriously. "If a crime's been committed we'd still like to know who did it, even if we can't build a case," he said thoughtfully. "Even if you can't make the arrest stand up in court, you get the satisfaction of knowing who done it. And they know you know. Sometimes knowing the truth is all the job means."

It rallied me.

I left Lieutenant Henry's and caught a cab back to my apartment. I got out on the corner, stopped in the deli, and bought a loaf of bread, a couple of cans of soup, a couple of cans of sardines, a six-pack of beer, and walked home. I saw two couples, a block apart, scurrying home with bundles of firewood. The girls both reminded me of Denise.

It was nearly ten. I wanted to get a good night's sleep. Denise was being buried tomorrow and I wanted to be fairly alert when I met my publisher in the morning.

I popped the top on a can of beer, bowed to the answering machine, and rolled my messages out. Terry Compton. Rocco. Mary Collins. Ethel Wately.

I called Compton. Tampa's U.S. attorney confirmed that Herrera was due for a grand jury appearance in connection with a money-laundering probe. An unnamed supervisor at the bank said Herrera had been "despondent" lately and was acting strange.

Nice work, I thought. If I ever have a disposal problem, I'll call Stu Metcalf. I asked Compton to hang on for minute while I snapped the top lock on the door and made sure the bedroom shades were drawn down. I wasn't being paranoid; I was being careful.

I spent some time on the phone with Compton, outlining the things I wanted him to do. I had to put more pressure on Wately and his cronies. If I couldn't trap them, I'd stampede them and see where they ran. I suggested to Compton that he tip other reporters, preferably in the state capitol bureau, about some of the things I'd picked up from Rossetti and Reilly.

"You're really in a hurry to bring this guy down, aren't you?" Compton said. "You don't care who breaks the story."

"The more the merrier," I said.

Let there be chaos.

Rocco was my next call. He wanted to know "what kind of a story" I'd gotten from Frankie Reilly. He was feeling me out for The Big Guy. I told Rocco I thought Frankie the Cop was terrific. Charlie wanted to know how soon I'd run a story.

"We can't baby-sit Esmeralda forever," Rocco said.

"I know," I said.

The Mafia was getting tired of Esmeralda.

I called Ethel Wately. I felt blue. The phone rang twice and she picked it up herself.

"Where have you been, Max? I'm worried about you."

"I'm a working stiff," I said. "I work for a daily paper."

"I tried your office," she said. "You weren't there. You didn't tell me you were in contact with Esmeralda," she said sweetly.

"I'm not in contact with her," I said drolly. "I merely told your brother I'd heard she was trying to reach him." I was unusually calm.

"He told me," she said icily. "Oh, Max. Edgar is such a fool. Why must you do this to me? Let the police find her. If you know where she is, tell Owen Reed. Tell *me*, for God's sake, and I'll call Owen immediately."

I'll bet you will, I thought. I told I'd call her if I heard anything.

"Max, why did you go the Albemarle Club? Edgar is devastated that you intruded like that. Frankly," she scolded, "so am I. I thought we were friends. Maybe loyalty is no longer in fashion, though. I should have expected it. There's a difference in our ages, and I guess some other things, too."

"That's not it," I said.

You're crumbling, Darenow, you're crumbling. Don't let her snow you! She's in this up to her neck.

"When are you bringing your clips over?" she said timorously. "I'm serious about helping you. Your career is stale. Am I going to see you again?"

"Yes," I hedged. "I have to meet my publisher first and go over some things. I guess Metcalf or someone spoke to him."

"I'm not surprised," she said. "This is serious business, Max. It doesn't lend itself to cheap stories in the tabloids. You're better than that."

"It'll work out," I said.

"Max, come see me tonight. Edgar went back to Tampa and Aurora's out. I'm alone and I'm scared. I know it's an imposition . . ."

She let it dangle. She was clutching at straws now. Edgar must be climbing the walls. I wouldn't be surprised if Stu Metcalf were having second thoughts about getting involved in this mess himself. Ethel had a lot to worry about.

"I have to meet my publisher at nine-thirty in the morning and I have to prepare for the meeting. Otherwise I'd . . ."

I let it dangle. This was hard work. I wanted to like her but she wasn't so likable anymore.

"Oh, what's to prepare?" she snapped. "If you're desperate for a story, I'll speak to Stu Metcalf. He'll get you something to keep your publisher happy. Is that all it is?"

"More or less," I sighed. "Look. I'm not happy about this. I'd rather get to know you in different circumstances. But not tonight."

"Have it your way," she said icily. She paused.

"Is there another woman?" she asked meekly.

"No," I said.

"Good," she said. "I'm acting terribly silly."

She was falling back on the old cocktail party charm. I felt sorry for her.

"Lock the doors and make yourself a stinger," I said. "Make two of them and drink mine, too."

"You make one down there," she cooed. "We'll toast each other in separate beds."

"It's a deal," I said. I was relieved. My brain resumed its long climb back to reason. It had fallen below my belt.

I called Mary Collins. She wanted to tell me that Denise was being buried tomorrow morning at eleven in Greenlawn Cemetery in Brooklyn. There was going to be a brief service at the funeral home at nine-thirty. She was disappointed that I hadn't dropped by yet.

"Just be there tomorrow, Max," Mary commanded. "Denise would have wanted you there."

That rubbed the callus off my heart. I suddenly felt as I had that morning in Montauk when Dixie had called to tell me Denise was dead, and it felt as if the earth had given way under my feet. I hadn't had time for mourning. The same angry tears began to swell but I dammed them, as I had been damming them ever since.

I told her I was in hot water with my publisher and couldn't be at the funeral home, but I'd definitely be at the cemetery.

"You know," Mary added thoughtfully, "sometimes we resent the loss of a loved one."

Just like a woman, I thought. Always handy with advice.

"Give me a break, Mary," I snapped. "I've been trying to find out who killed her."

"I don't think Denise would care," she said. "I think she'd want you to get her work published. That would mean something."

"See you at the grave," I said.

I got up and drifted idly about the apartment, picking up glasses of stale beer and the remains of sandwiches left uneaten. The place smelled of old memories and disuse. It wasn't a home, it was just somewhere to flop, somewhere to hang my clothes until I found another woman and settled down. I'd been saying that for how many years? I brought the dirty dishes into the kitchen, scraped the food from the plates, and left the rest in the sink. Maybe Dixie would drop by and wash them, if I asked her.

I stopped and scooped up a couple of dust balls, dropped them in the wastepaper basket, and moved a sweater from one chair to another, closer to the closet where it belonged. I picked up the pack of Camels I had foolishly brought home, extracted a couple in case I had a nicotine fit, and then crumpled the rest of the pack and pitched it into the trash. Bad for the lungs. It was time to clean up my act and move on.

30

The meeting with the publisher was a piece of cake.

I woke up at eight and went into the living room, where I stared for a long minute at the map of Florida I had since taped to the wall. I took a quick shower, shaved, and went into the kitchen in my robe and slippers. I popped a piece of bread into the toaster, cut up an onion and sautéed it in olive oil and garlic, beat a couple of eggs into submission, poured them over the onion, and scrambled them until it smelled good enough to eat. I turned the radio on for a second and turned it off again. I was going to a funeral.

I wore a charcoal gray suit, a blue shirt, and a red wool challis tie. I put on my black tasseled loafers and my cashmere overcoat and went out the door, wondering again when I'd be back. I wasn't in a great mood.

I got to the paper around 9:20 and spent ten minutes in Hurley's office, giving him a very broad outline of where things stood, half the time grinning like a nervous fool and the rest acting like I knew exactly what I was doing. I said nothing about Rocco, Dixie, or The Big Guy, but I mentioned Esmeralda for the first time and said that we had an obligation to explain her involvement as a witness to the murders, despite the clamor it might cause. In return, I wouldn't insist on mentioning the espionage angle or the blackmail motive. If anything, we'd call it a vendetta.

Hurley agreed, as I knew he would. That decided, we walked together up the back stairs to the publisher's office.

"I'll do the arguing," he said. "Just tell him what you told me and then I'll take over."

That was fine with me. The publisher was an amiable but moody man who came from the business side of newspaper publishing. He started out as an order taker in the classified department of the old *Daily Mirror*. Half a dozen newspapers had folded under him as he worked his way to the top. His stock in trade was knowing how to talk to the labor unions. His moods shifted with the price of the holding company's stock and the presence in town of the owner, who fancied himself a full-fledged media baron and acted accordingly. The publisher also had a grand view of the East River, the Brooklyn Bridge, and the seaport. I told my story, briefly and well, I thought, and sat back and enjoyed the view while Hurley worked out the details with the boss.

It was agreed I'd write a story aimed at helping the police find Esmeralda, without mentioning the fact she was tied to Edgar Wately. We wouldn't pursue the story unless Esmeralda was arrested and tried.

The boss admitted he had spoken to Stu Metcalf and Owen Reed. Reed wanted to set up another meeting to brief me on the grand jury investigation in Florida. The publisher told me to follow up and make an appointment with him, pronto. Otherwise, the boss thought I was doing a fair job. He was just worried that the owner, *his* boss, who hobnobbed with people like Metcalf, would pull the rug from under both of us. Metcalf had him scared. He drummed nervously on the edge of his desk while he spoke and constantly shifted his attention from Hurley to me and back again.

"I want you to keep Mr. Hurley here informed of *everything* you're doing," he emphasized. "I don't want us to get blamed for the death of some undercover agent. The goddamn television news people would have a field day with that story. We're going to stay out of it. Understand?"

I nodded my vigorous assent.

It was 10:10 A.M. when Hurley and I descended to the newsroom after our brief visit to Olympus.

"I need a car and driver, Walt. Denise is being buried at eleven in Greenlawn. I have to be there. And then I have to come back and write a story."

Hurley said it would be no problem.

Having a car gave me a couple of extra minutes to make some phone calls. I couldn't stop to think so I kept working. It was time to cast my nets a little wider.

I had realized something: there was no doubt Metcalf et al. could quash the real story, but could they put the lid on rumors? You can bury news, but you can't bury gossip.

I called our Washington bureau and put a bee in the bonnet of the assistant bureau chief, a twenty-eight-year-old graduate of Ole Miss with a designer wardrobe, several thousand dollars' worth of cosmetic surgery on nose and chin, and a fierce ambition to be an anchorperson in a major market. She had more contacts than the distributor cap on a V-12 Jaguar and ran her mouth without a muffler. She was a straight pipe to Foggy Bottom's rumor mill.

I innocently requested that she dig up biographies on Stu Metcalf and Owen Reed, just in case I needed to profile them in connection with a story that may, *or may not*, be developing in New York. She took the bait and began pumping me mercilessly for more information.

I told her that indictments *might* be forthcoming in a money-laundering scheme and I just wanted to be on top of it. I dropped the name of Wately's bank and the fact that polo star Avery Wately had been paymaster for the Bay of Pigs. I explained that Stu Metcalf was an old friend of Ethel Wately's, and a real fine gentleman to boot. I described Ethel as one of the most "glamorously fascinating" women I'd ever met. Finally, I told her the real story was on permanent hold due to the sensitive nature of the investigation. I merely wanted the biographies in case it ever broke.

She ate it up.

"Max," she crooned, "I dated a guy who covers the capital for a chain of Florida newspapers. I wonder if he knows anything?"

"Gee," I said. "Why don't you ask him?"

I knew damn well she would, and I knew the story would be circulating within the D.C. beltway within the hour.

You can't bury a rumor, Metcalf, no matter how deep the hole.

We rolled up to the gate of Greenlawn Cemetery at 11:02 and the attendant directed us up a road that wound through a landscape of imposing tombstones and mausoleums where the burghers of a once sylvan Brooklyn now rested after milking the land for all it was worth, incorporating it into the City of New York, and moving themselves to Park Avenue so they wouldn't have to look at the slums that bloomed in their wake. Funny how they came home to be buried.

The road curved up and around a stand of rhododendron that went on forever and must have been dazzling in bloom. I saw the crowd as we turned the corner.

There were forty or fifty people milling around a snow-covered knoll ringed with young oak trees. There were men, women, and two lofty transvestites, one of them wearing a dark fur coat, high heels, and a black hat with a veil, the other in a stylish parka, designer jeans, aerobic booties, and oversized sunglasses. There were far more women than men, and the crowd was thick with Manhattan's downtown scenemakers. Familiar faces, faces I knew from the streets and bars of SoHo and TriBeca. I waved glumly to a few I knew quite well but was too ashamed to talk to, since I knew they were privy to all the sorry details of my failed romance. What could I say: "Hi, it's me, I've cleaned up my act and I'm looking for another girl. Got any suggestions?" I saw several of Denise's neighbors, including the two elderly sisters who lived across the hall and a man who ran the local Laundromat.

I saw Mary Collins talking to the man who owned the gallery where Denise's photographs had been on display, and I headed toward them. That's when I spotted the mean-faced cop I first met at Denise's apartment and later at Lieutenant Henry's. He was working the crowd, looking to see if any of the mourners stood suspiciously alone. I knew he was itching to see what was under the veil on the fur-clad drag queen. He saw me but didn't acknowledge me. I reached the top of the hill, gave Mary a hug, shook hands with the gallery owner, looked around at the number of people who cared enough to come and say good-bye, bit my lip, and fought back the tears. Those people were her life; I'd been a part of it too, but I was ashamed of the fact that my part fell short of having made her life any better.

Mary said we were waiting for an Episcopal deacon who happened to be a woman, and who, she had been informed, was running late. The gallery owner told me what a brilliant photographer Denise had been, and what a wonderful career she would have had, if she had lived. He pointed out a couple of mourners who were editors at one of the publishing houses interested in Denise's work. He suggested I introduce myself, since Denise had told him I might collaborate on the text. I told him it wasn't the right time. He shook his head in disappointment and asked why I hadn't brought a photographer with me. Push me, pull me. I ignored him and went over to talk to the two elderly sisters and the guy from the Laundromat.

"You must feel terrible," said one of the sisters. She was the one who had kept telling us we ought to get married. She didn't mention it there at the grave, but I knew she was thinking of it and the unspoken memory of my time with Denise brought tears to all our eyes again.

I chatted with a few more of Denise's friends until the deaconess arrived. Mary Collins, who seemed to have taken charge of things, took my arm and walked me to the edge of the grave, where we stood for a simple service from the Book of Common Prayer. The deaconess must have known Denise; she paid tribute to Denise's creative spirit and her love of people.

"Denise had a woman's love of humanity that characterized her life and work," the deaconess eulogized. "She had a special knack for showing the spiritual hunger in her subject's eyes. Her soul was full of love. Love was the lens through which she viewed the world. She taught us to love the bizarre for the spiritual hunger it reflected. Denise's own spirituality was profound enough to support that view."

That was that. No drums, no rifle salutes over the grave, no lone bugler blowing taps. A few scattered sobs, lots of red-rimmed eyes that could be the result of too many late nights, some sniffles that could be blamed on the damp cold that clung to the earth where we stood. I wished there could have been more, and suddenly there was.

Someone, Mary said it was some girl who had been collecting Denise's work for several years, cried out loudly: "I know Denise would embrace us if she was here today and we were in the ground instead. Why can't we embrace each other before we leave, and show her her love was not taken for granted."

That was it for me. I crumbled and began sobbing and couldn't stop or catch my breath. Mary put her arms around me and then someone else came up and wrapped us both in a hug and when I opened my eyes I saw everyone hugging each other.

Mary and someone else, I have no idea whether it was a man or a woman, held me and walked me down the hill. Mary asked if I needed a ride, and when I told her no, she asked if I wanted someone to ride back with me. I told her I'd be all right. I should have asked some of the others if they needed a lift into Manhattan, but I didn't.

I climbed into the back seat, slumped down, closed my eyes, and realized I'd never get a good night's sleep until I evened the score with the lousy bastards who killed her.

I went back to the office and pounded out a story on Esmeralda: eight tight paragraphs saying she was seen in the company of Denise and Jaime Santiago right before they were killed. Lieutenant Henry told me to describe her as "a mystery witness" rather than a suspect, which I did. Unbeknownst to me, a police sketch artist had supplied the paper with a rendering of Esmeralda's face, based on police descriptions gathered from drag queens, neighbors at Jaime's West Side apartment, and the emergency room staff at the hospital where Esmeralda had her stomach pumped.

Danny Tung showed it to me. It was fairly accurate, although it made Esmeralda's nose too little and her eyes too big. The makeup must have thrown them off. I had no comment. After all, for the record I hadn't ever seen her.

I turned the story in and called Owen Reed to set up an appointment. I had the distinct feeling Reed himself only knew half the story, but was trying to be a good soldier. His future—at least the kind he foresaw for himself—depended on his being a good dog. We made an appointment for lunch Wednesday.

At Hurley's request, I drafted a memo outlining my approach to the series we were now calling "The War on Drugs," rather than "the drug wars." The publisher thought it was a more "positive, dramatic" approach. On a whim, I threw in the suggestion that I ought to spend at least a week in Florida talking to law enforcement officials, customs agents, and immigration people. What the hell, go for it.

I was getting ready to leave the office when Number One called. My first instinct was to put him on hold and walk away. The publisher's meeting and Denise's funeral had drained my already depleted reserve of spunk. I was supposed to be distancing myself from Esmeralda and the mob, but no, I had to be there when the phone rang.

The mob wanted to take one more shot at contacting Wately before they turned Esmeralda loose. Number One had instructed her to call Wately again, but he wasn't at home. They had reached Ethel instead.

"Did you tape the call?"

"Dixie taped the call."

"What did the sister say?"

"She told Esmeralda to go to the police and turn herself in. She said she'd get her a lawyer and post bail if necessary. She told her not to worry, she wouldn't get blamed for your girlfriend. She said everyone knew the Torres boys did it."

"What did Esmeralda say?"

"She said she'd think about it, she wanted to talk it over with Wately," Number One replied. "The sister started asking questions so I made her hang up." He was getting impatient. He didn't enjoy baby-sitting the silicone princess. Or maybe he enjoyed it, and that scared him. According to Dixie, Number One had a taste for showgirls.

"Here's what we're gonna do," Number One said. "Esmeralda will make a deal with Wately so she can leave, and you'll witness the deal, guarantee it."

This had to stop.

"No way," I said. "She's a hot potato."

"Dixie promised her you'd help. That's how we got involved in this crap in the first place. Over you. You don't have to say anything. You just pick up a package from Wately and bring it here, then we let Esmeralda stroll."

Ransom money and I'm the bag man.

"My boss is calling me," I lied. "I have to go. I'm in a lot of hot water as it is. I'll call you back. I'll talk to Charlie."

"I talked to Charlie! Charlie's giving Wately one last opportunity to come to the table." He ground the words out. He was on a slow boil.

"Let her go," I said. "The cops have plenty of evidence on Wately. Esmeralda's of no value to anybody."

Number One growled.

"Charlie wants to hear Wately's side; he'll decide if she goes or what. I'm not working for charity," he added, his voice rising to a full bark.

I knew what that meant. Numbers One and Two worked on a contingency basis. Part of Esmeralda's ransom was going to pay their salaries. No ransom, no paycheck. All that strong-arm work for nothing. Stealing Cadillacs was far more pleasant.

I told Number One I'd work it out with Charlie. He didn't like it, but he had no other choice. I was glad the conversation wasn't face to face.

"Just find out a time and place where this fruitcake can call her boyfriend," Number One said reluctantly. "We'll handle the rest."

I had to end this whole game, and soon. I was too far over on the wrong side of the law. It was time for a man-to-man chat with the cops.

I called Gabe Rossetti at police headquarters. A cop with a poetic air, a monsignorial presence, and a distinguished Italian name was exactly what I needed. I felt good when Gabe invited me to come over right away. In fact, there was a note of pleasant surprise when he heard my voice.

I walked the ten blocks from my office to headquarters, stopping along the way to buy fifty dollars' worth of vitamins. I needed long walks, and vitamin therapy, too. A couple of mail-room clerks were chucking dirty snowballs from the last snowfall at a pair of keypunch operators on Pearl Street, and the girls were pitching them back. It was as close to nature as most of them would ever get. The bicycle messengers cursed the snow and threw dirty looks at the taxi drivers.

Rossetti was all smiles when I showed up at his office.

"Let's go to down the fourth floor," he said. "Lieutenant Henry is down there with a friend of yours."

Uh-oh.

"I was beginning to think I hadn't any friends," I said, playing for a laugh. It came out sounding hollow.

Rossetti smiled mischievously and started walking to the elevator. I said nothing. He pressed the down button, turned, and said, sans smile: "Detective Gonzalez and Lieutenant Henry picked up Aurora Carrera this morning. She was about to board a flight to Miami. She's about to leave our custody with the permission of a federal magistrate, but she told us a few things before the feds claimed her. She'll remain in New York until the grand jury convenes. We were able to do that much."

Great, I thought. The cops aren't going to let the feds steal their thunder.

"We thought you might want to talk to her before we let her go," he added.

Uh-oh.

"Why . . . should I talk to her?" As if I didn't know.

"She claims you were in the apartment on Avenue A right before the bodies of Bennie Torres and two others were found," he deadpanned.

The elevator arrived before I could reply, not that I could have. We stepped inside, joining a couple of police cadets. The two cadets stopped talking. The elevator was bursting with silence.

"Were you there?" Rossetti asked. He sounded nonchalant, but we both knew it was a serious question.

I wasn't ready for this, but the question deserved an answer and I was tired of running.

"I was there," I replied. "Before they got shot." I said nothing more until we reached our floor, then I stepped out, sighed glibly, and started reeling out half-truths as we walked down the hall.

"I had information that Denise had been seen in Manolo's company the night before she died," I began, as convincingly as possible. "I went over there to ask some questions, but I got no answers, so I bought some coke to cover my ass and beat it." I was taking the Mafia's advice: cover a big crime with a smaller one. "The atmosphere was very strained, to put it mildly. I had the impression I wasn't welcome."

My heartbeat was louder than our footfalls. Rossetti stopped at a door marked MAJOR CRIMES, MANHATTAN CENTRAL.

"Why in hell didn't you tell us this before, Darenow?" There was more disappointment than disapproval in his voice. I think he believed my story.

I took a deep breath, nearly swooned, and lied again.

"I'd just come back to work," I said feebly. "I was supposed to be drying out and I wound up doing coke and getting drunk that night. I'd just found out about Denise. When I heard about the murders the next day I got scared. Can you blame me?" I held my breath until he replied.

"I can see your problem," Rossetti said. "It might have been better, though, if you had said something right away. You said the atmosphere was tense. Did you think there was going to be trouble? Did you see any guns?"

"Manolo was there with another guy, called Pepe. Pepe wanted me to stay but I told them I had someone waiting for me outside in a car."

"Did you?"

"No," I said.

"Good thinking," he said. "What time did you leave and where did you go after that?"

Alibi time. We were still standing in the hall. People sauntered along without a care in the world, happy in their work. My knees were starting to shake.

"It was after midnight. I found a gypsy cab on First Avenue and went to a friend's house, a friend of Denise's, and drank too much cognac. I slept there for a while and she insisted on having someone drive me home. She called a car service."

I hoped it came out all right. I threw the gypsy cab into it because I knew they couldn't trace it and it kept me off the streets in case I'd been spotted.

"What was Manolo's reaction when you started asking questions about your girlfriend?" Rossetti inquired.

"He said he *might* have run into her Friday night. He couldn't remember. That's when things got uptight."

Rossetti fixed me with a gray, inscrutable cop's stare. He eyed me like that for a very long time before he spoke again.

"You're lucky they didn't kill *you*, Darenow. You left just in time, before the shooting started."

"I think you're right," I said.

He shook his head in wonderment and we went inside the office; it was quiet, a lot of empty desks, including one with Lieutenant Henry's nameplate but no Lieutenant Henry. Henry was in the interrogation room, a twelve-foot-square cube of nothing much except a table, three chairs, a one-way mirror with a shade on both sides, two entrances, and a peephole for the video camera. It sat in the middle of floor like a bunker. The shade inside was pulled down.

Rossetti paused about ten feet from the room and asked me to wait; then he went inside, closing the door behind him. *Denise,* I thought, *I need you now to watch over me*. Rossetti was in there for about five minutes before he beckoned me in. Lieutenant Henry was seated at the table with a notebook and pen in front of him. An odor of lilac perfume hung in the room; Aurora's scent; I remembered it from the cocktail party. I wondered where she had gone but I didn't really care. Rossetti asked if I had any objections to making an official statement, no cameras.

Henry asked me to repeat what I had just told Inspector Rossetti minutes before. Rossetti stood behind me and listened. I said as little as possible, emphasizing things that might take me off the hook.

"I knew something was wrong," I said. "I'd been there once before to score coke, and the atmosphere had been very different. Manolo was very uptight this time. You could sense it."

"Was there any indication that they were expecting other visitors?" Henry asked.

"The one guy, Pepe, told me to hang around because there was going to be a party. That's when I lied about having someone waiting for me in a car. It wasn't party time."

The big lies came when they asked me what I did after I left Manolo's. I really think Denise was standing over me because I suddenly got very clever.

"I went over to see a friend of Denise's who happens to be a lesbian," I sighed ruefully. "She's pretty hip; I thought she might know something. Her name is Carol Lundgren. She lives in a loft on the Bowery and likes to drink. We knocked off a bottle of cognac. I passed out, then I woke up because I got sick and wanted to go home. I couldn't even walk, but I wanted to be sick in my own apartment. Carol called a car service and took me home. She wound up sleeping on my couch."

Henry glanced at Rossetti and closed his notebook.

Carol Lundgren. I couldn't believe the ease with which the name rolled off my tongue. Maybe it was someone from my past. Or maybe it was a name Denise conjured for me.

In any case, they bought the story, which kept Dixie and the Italians, temporarily, out of the picture. I think we all shared a sense of relief. If worse came to worse, I'd say I was too embarrassed to admit in whose loft I really had been.

I turned and asked Rossetti where Aurora was. He said they'd released her into federal custody a short time ago. What's more, Rossetti confessed that he'd had no intentions of having me confront her. It was a ruse to see how I'd react. My reaction satisfied them.

They had used a similar ruse to extract new information from Aurora.

"Aurora says Bennie and Ralph rushed to the Watelys' apartment the very next day, set up camp in the kitchen, and made lots of telephone calls while Rosa ran back and forth carrying messages to Mrs. Wately, who stayed in the library the whole time. Aurora claims no knowledge of what transpired among them."

The scenario fit right in with what Henry and I had been thinking about the day before. I felt like a man going over the falls in a barrel while the crowd cheered. Ethel grew less and less attractive to me.

"I'd like to hear Ethel Wately's version of what went on that night," I said.

"So would we," Rossetti said tersely. "Henry called her; she's not in. The problem is, we had to let Aurora go. The feds caught wind of what we did fifteen minutes after we collared her. We all got scolded. It's a losing battle."

"No, it's not," I said.

Lieutenant Henry went back to his desk and began typing up his notes. Rossetti escorted me out to the elevator.

"I may as well tell you something else," Rossetti said as we stepped into the hall. "I have information that both Hector Melendez and your friend Stu Metcalf wanted to permanently remove Bennie and Ralph from Edgar Wately's sphere of influence."

"How did you find that out?" I asked politely.

"You have your sources, I have mine," he replied. "What's important is that it weakens the blackmail motive; it also weakens the theory that Bennie and Ralph were double agents. If Metcalf was really telling the truth, he'd have spared them, if only to lead him to bigger game. If the feds were telling the truth, they'd want Bennie and Ralph alive so they could prosecute them."

It made sense, but it made me dizzy. I slumped against the wall for support.

"So Melendez is involved," I said.

"Hector Melendez and Metcalf had entirely different motives for wanting Bennie and Ralph out of their hair," Rossetti answered patiently. "Hector wants Wately's bank, without strings, free of vermin. He doesn't want a CIA front; he wants to make money."

"And Metcalf?" I asked.

"He was cleaning Edgar's house for reasons of his own," Rossetti said. "I have it on good authority that neither Bennie or Ralph worked for Castro. Castro's boys knew them too well; they knew they were CIA thugs and wouldn't get near them. If that's so—and I trust my source—Metcalf's a liar."

I pulled on my coat and we continued down the hall.

"I'd like you to pass something on to Ethel Wately," Rossetti said. "Tell her you've heard that the NYPD is very keen on having both her and her brother testify before a grand jury, if and when a jury is called. Mention it in passing, as if it was just some tidbit you picked up in a squad room. Don't attribute to anyone in particular."

I nodded my assent, but I wondered what made him think I was going to be talking to Ethel again?

It wasn't the only thing that was going to make me wonder.

As we reached the elevator, Rossetti, with a side glance, asked if I knew "a female impersonator called Dixie Cup."

My mouth flew open in amazement before I managed a reply. The curve balls were still sliding in.

"Uh, yeh," I stammered. "She was a good friend of Denise's." I shut my mouth and prayed for the elevator to come.

"He, or she, might have a line on this Esmeralda," Rossetti added while we waited. There was no indication in his tone that he suspected any connection between Dixie and me. "See if you can get us a phone number or something. There's no Dixie Cup in the residential phone book."

"I'll ask around," I said.

Rossetti frowned, shook his head and looked at me with eyes that revealed nothing but weariness.

"It's a crazy salad, ain't it?" he said. "Spooks, Wall Street guys, drag queens. Makes you wonder."

I nodded and stared intently at the elevator button. I wanted to roll my eyes and shake all over like a crazy person but I just concentrated on that button. Denise must have interceded. The button blinked red and the doors sighed open.

"Call me if you hear anything," Rossetti said in parting.

"*Absolutely*," I said, waiting until the door closed before I treated myself to a deep breath and a silent nod to Denise, who was up there, somewhere, watching over me.

I walked for another ten blocks, then hopped a bus going up Sixth Avenue.

The telephone answering machine winked its electric eye at me when I arrived at the apartment. I ignored it, went to the kitchen, poured myself a beer, and swallowed a handful of vitamins. I found one of the cigarettes I'd stashed, sat down, and smoked it. I had to make a move, a strong move. I had to bring this to a head. I couldn't take it anymore. The next trap to spring might have my foot in it.

It was going to be another long day. I had started it thinking I was going to get everything off my chest, make a clean breast of things, but no. No, I had to lie. Who the fuck was Carol Lundgren? And why did Rossetti go out of his way to ask me if I knew Dixie, saving the question for last? So they could trap me in the lie later on?

These guys are cops. They don't trust me any more than they trust Ethel or her brother.

I went to the kitchen and pried open a can of sardines. I was looking forward to a nice quiet dinner at home, maybe a little classical music, when the phone rang again.

I picked it up, of course. I'm a glutton for punishment.

It was The Big Guy.

"Frankie Reilly is sending you a picture of Wately and the drag queen Esmeralda," he said. "I think it would look good in your paper."

I swung on the ball.

"Color or black and white?"

"What difference does it make?" Charlie said testily. "It shows him up. Frankie got it from a neighbor of theirs, a guy who lived next door to them in Tampa when Wately was shacking with her. You gonna use it or what?"

"We don't run color," I said. "It'll be all muddy. You won't see anything."

Charlie snarled and cleared his throat. It sounded like it was coming up from his gut.

"If it's black and white you print it, OK?" It wasn't really a question.

"It's a smear," I said. "The publisher won't stand for it. It won't mean anything. Get me a picture of Wately with Bennie and Ralph Torres and I'll print that—guaranteed."

Not bad, Darenow. Give yourself two bases.

Charlie wasn't giving up yet.

"Esmeralda wants to talk to you," he said. "Call her up. Find out what she wants and do it. You owe me that much."

Man on second, two outs, you're up again. Now what?

"Can't do it, Charlie. It's asking too much. I'm out of it. I have my own problems."

"With the feds, right? They're leaning on you, right?"

"Right," I said.

"OK," he said. "I'll be in touch."

He hung up.

The inning wasn't over. Charlie was just calling time out. Maybe he was going to put in a new pitcher. My own lineup didn't look too good. I had used most of the nine lives my team had.

The sardines weren't bad, but I had lost my appetite. I took a couple of bites of sandwich and swallowed more vitamins, minerals, and a couple of odorless garlic tablets. Didn't Mel Brooks say garlic was responsible for the thousand-year-old man's longevity? When the angel of death comes in the middle of the night, you take a deep breath and say: "Who's there?" Your breath knocks the angel over.

But not if it's odorless garlic.

Oh, well, I told myself, while I'm sitting here grinding my teeth, the rumor mill is grinding away, making things difficult for Wately and Metcalf and their cold warriors.

It was no comfort.

31

Tuesday was a very bad day. Denise was giving me a tongue-lashing from on high.

It started raining around midnight; rain turning to sleet that slapped against my bedroom windows in a frantic tattoo. I'd been pacing the floor, trying again to fathom Denise's obsessive interest in the sexual conundrums of the Latin underclass. It opened old wounds, bringing to mind the argument we'd had about devoting a book to a bunch of goddamned drag queens. She'd be alive today if she had only listened to me, not in trouble, not dead, I kept telling myself. Denise was wholesome. Her favorite singer was Patsy Cline, for crying out loud.

I pulled out Patsy Cline's greatest hits. I put it on, sat up in bed with a couple of beers, and read the liner copy. The songs were eerily appropriate.

"Heartaches," "Faded Love," "I Fall To Pieces," "Walking After Midnight," "Imagine That."

Innocent songs from an innocent time, in Patsy's ethereal down-home soprano. These were the songs people were humming while the CIA was plotting to assassinate President Diem. And most people didn't know where the Mekong Delta was.

"Walking After Midnight" came on.

Forget it! There was no way I could listen to that one all the way through. I jumped up, flipped the record over, and buried my face in the pillow.

I drifted off to sleep somewhere in the middle of side B, listening to the rain and Patsy Cline singing "Who Can I Count On (If I Can't Count On You)."

Denise was coming in loud and clear.

I got up around noon because the telephone answering machine was laboring away, spinning and clicking, beating a path to my dreams.

I got out of bed, made coffee and played back the messages.

Frank Reilly had called and left a number in Tampa where he could be reached.

Rocco had called. He sounded anxious. "Where the hell are you?" he asked. How the hell should I know?

Hurley called, asking if I planned to file a story for any of today's editions. No, I was taking the day off.

Mary Collins called, asking when the police were going to take the seals off Denise's apartment so she could start organizing things.

Edgar Wately had called. He had some things to tell me.

Terry Compton had called.

Two callers had hung up without leaving a message.

I put on clean socks and skivvies and climbed back into the clothes I wore the day before. The rain had stopped but the sky outside was dark and moody.

I called Frank Reilly. He wasn't in.

I called Lieutenant Henry and asked him when we could get into Denise's apartment. He said the seal wouldn't come off until the grand jury met, but if there was something I needed he'd gladly accompany me over there. He also said he'd found Dixie Cupps's phone number in Denise's address book and left a message on her answering machine.

Uh-oh. My time was running out.

I called Mary Collins and left a message on her machine, repeating what Henry told me about the seal.

I called Terry Compton. The scandal was spreading according to plan. Two Florida state legislators were interested in pursuing leads concerning the role of Wately's bank in a possibly illegal covert operation.

That cheered me and scared me at the same time. My campaign to turn on the heat was working, but it was going to be a toss-up to see who felt it first—me or the Watelys.

I made myself a bowl of soup, burned my mouth slurping it, drank more coffee, and sat at my desk making notes to myself, trying to reconstruct my conversations with Edgar and Ethel, or anyone else who could answer my questions.

I kept coming back to Pepe's last telephone call from Manolo's apartment and wishing I had been more proficient in Spanish. I wished I had one more snort of Manolo's cocaine to bring my memory back. Forget it, Darenow. But wait! I had the package I took from Esmeralda. Was there anything left in it?

I went into the closet and got the pants I'd worn that night. The package was there, crumpled into a loose ball. I held the pants pocket over a newspaper so I wouldn't loose anything as I removed the contents. Some of the coke had fallen out of the wrapper and was now mixed with pocket lint and spare change. I wasn't that desperate.

But I opened the crumpled packet to see if anything clung to the wrapper.

Two, maybe three lines.

Before I had a chance to think twice about snorting them I took the three lines into the bathroom and flushed them down the drain. I rinsed the paper, discarded it, and went back to my seat at the desk. I tried concentrating again on what Pepe had said but my mind whirred and spun and all I could do was make more notes to myself, drawing lines from one name to another. Wately to Melendez to Metcalf to Bennie to Rosa to Ethel. Big circle around Aurora's name. More lines, from Metcalf to Ethel and from Ethel to Bennie, from Ethel to Rosa.

I gave up after a while. I began pacing from the kitchen to the bedroom and back again, pulling records from the stacks and then not playing them. I needed a brisk walk.

Then it hit me. I knew what I had to do. I *had* to talk to Ethel. I had to put her into a room with Esmeralda and her brother, lock the door, and tell them they weren't coming out until I was satisfied with their stories.

But how would I arrange it? I dressed for the weather and was looking for my keys when the phone rang. I monitored the call before picking up the receiver. It was Frank Reilly.

He'd been out to the Harbor Heights development, the subdivision east of Tampa comprised of ranch houses on two-acre lots where Wately maintained his expensive honeymoon cottage.

Wately was seen there frequently by neighbors, mostly families with children whose curiosity was aroused by the scantily clad, buxom blonde who lived there and tooled around in a BMW convertible with an androgynous young Latin male who wore makeup and painted his nails.

The photograph of Esmeralda and Edgar Wately, the one Charlie had courtesy of Reilly, had been obtained from the teenage daughter of a neighbor who said Esmeralda had given it to her to prove that Wately was, indeed, her lover. According to Reilly, the picture, a Polaroid snapshot, showed Esmeralda hugging Wately from behind, her hands around his crotch. Wately had a big smile on his face.

I didn't think Hurley would use it if it was a sharply etched black and white glossy.

But that wasn't all. Reilly had delved deeper into the Torres brothers' affairs, calling on underworld contacts who owed him a favor.

Bennie and Ralph had been running drugs for two years, using a variety of means to slip them past the Coast Guard and customs. According to Reilly, the success of their modus operandi depended on their role as government informers.

When the brothers had a big shipment of cocaine coming in—by air or sea—they'd finance a less costly shipment, marijuana, usually, and tip the authorities off to it. The authorities would concentrate on that shipment and while they were busy making the small bust, the big haul would slip by.

It was neat and cruel and it made a good story, but it was all hearsay. They'd laugh it out of court.

"What you have to do," Reilly explained, "is find the people they burned and double-crossed and get them to talk. If they're still alive."

I told him I'd think about it.

"You have to understand the employment situation down here," Reilly said. "Drugs provide jobs for people with no skills and big ambitions. It's a perfect environment. Especially if Bennie and Ralph promise to pay for lawyers and take care of your family while you're doing time in the joint."

Reilly asked me how I wanted to proceed from this point.

I told him I didn't know. I told him I wasn't sure how much longer I was going to need his help.

He said his instructions were to keep digging until he received further orders. He made it obvious that the orders weren't coming from me.

I let him go. I told him to make a copy of the Polaroid and send it to me. I told him to keep the original in his files.

I hung up and decided to call Gabe Rossetti and tell him, without naming my source, what Reilly had just told me.

Rossetti was in his office. I told him I had evidence linking Esme and Edgar. He wanted to talk about it, but not over the phone.

"Meet me in the same place as Sunday in half an hour," he said. He didn't mention the name of the place and neither did I.

My brisk walk was a laughable slog through three-inch mush that was turning to ice underneath. A steady wind and drizzling rain didn't make navigation any easier. I tried jumping over a foot-deep lake that had pooled on the corner of Seventh Avenue and Twelfth Street and missed. My left loafer shipped a lot of water.

I pulled my hood tight around my face and tried hiding behind the umbrella without its turning inside out in the wind. I cowered behind it until I was inside the doorway of Tre Pesci.

The windows of the place were fogged and it was nearly empty except for two backgammon players who looked like Sacco and Vanzetti and a pair of lovesick college kids who held hands and stared into each other's eyes.

The waiter recognized me from the other day. I ordered a double espresso, heavy on the "special." He nodded and came back with a full-sized china mug that was mostly anisette.

Rossetti was fifteen minutes late, but he showed.

He was pissed off because he'd had to park in a no-parking zone and he knew the meter maids were going to ticket him regardless of the Police Department emblem on the visor of his own car, which was registered in his wife's name. He'd beat the fine, but it was going to involve needless paperwork.

He ordered cappuccino and dessert and skipped the anisette. He filled his pipe and frowned.

"The remains of the other occupants of the apartment on Avenue A were found three hours ago," he announced dryly, "stuffed in a couple of fifty-gallon oil drums in a shed behind a Union City auto body shop, owned by the late Torres brothers."

So much for the missing Kooks and whatever light they might have shed on Denise's death. Ralph Torres must have killed them before he got whacked himself. *Damnit!* Didn't the Mafia understand that Ralph Torres might have been pressured into testifying against Metcalf or whoever his boss was? Of course not, I thought, answering my own question. Ralph slandered the Italians, and that demanded instant punishment. So much for Mafia justice.

I couldn't tell Rossetti what I was thinking so I merely sighed and shook my head. He smiled benignly but it was no comfort.

"Let's hear what you have to say," he said. He had a twinkle in his eye, as if he had *plenty* more to tell me.

I described the photograph showing Esmeralda grabbing Wately's crotch. I told him about the training camps, and the subdivisions where the families of the mercenaries were billeted. I told him about how the Wately bank held mortgages on the homes of the Torres boys and their friends. I wished I could have told him about Esme's ankle bracelet and the engagement ring.

"I dropped by the Cuban mission to the UN," he said. "There's a guy over there who owes me and I thought I'd ask him if he knew anything about Bennie and Ralph or Edgar Wately. It was a very instructive meeting."

Rossetti was relaxing and letting his hair down. He told me how the lives of several members of the Cuban mission had been lengthened considerably by the intervention of his unit, which had picked up a tip concerning an assassination plot engineered by unnamed anti-Castro "activists."

The contact, Rossetti said, was very much aware of Bennie and Ralph Torres's activities. Bennie and Ralph had been trying to establish their own contacts in the Cuban mission over the last three months. The deal was simple: they would trade hard Yankee dollars for hard drugs and Colombian emeralds to be be smuggled in diplomatic pouches. In addition, for every safe shipment, the brothers would provide the names of people here and in Cuba who were working for the CIA.

The Cubans didn't go for it, according to Rossetti's source. The reason was simple: " 'The Torres brothers weren't even trusted by their fellow patriots,' " he said, quoting his source verbatim.

"Of course," Rossetti added, "my man insisted that his communist colleagues wouldn't think of dispoiling the integrity of the revolutionary cause by trafficking in drugs." He smiled and puffed heatedly on his pipe.

"You believe him?" I asked.

"Of course not." He laughed. "Our own narcs traced payment for a major shipment of cocaine last year to a bank account in Mexico City maintained by an Angolan export firm. There wasn't an Angolan connected to the company that had the account. They were all Cuban "graduate students" supposedly studying economics in Mexico. 'Economics of the Global Drug Economy' should have been the title of the course."

"Did you bring up Metcalf's name, or Edgar Wately's, or Hector Melendez's?"

"Didn't have to. All the commies know Melendez. They call him the prime minister of the government-in-exile. Melendez thinks he'll be invited back to reopen the casinos and the cathouses when Castro dies. And Bennie Torres offered Wately's bank as a reference when they first approached the Cubans. Naturally Wately's name rang a bell in certain quarters of the mission. But the Torres brothers' reputation for double-dealing is what really scared them off."

"Is Wately the agent Metcalf is protecting?" I wondered. "Not so much for the blackmail angle, but because Wately was actively participating in Metcalf's operation, just as his father did before him?"

"Here's what I'm told," Rossetti said. "Bennie and Ralph were loose cannons. They played Wately for a sucker and when Melendez caught wind of what was going on he ordered Metcalf to clean house. Wately is an embarrassment to everybody.

"There's no doubt in my mind that out-of-town shooters were brought in to blow Bennie and Ralph away," he added. "The CIA lost two guys trying. We know that now. Chances are a more experienced man was sent in to finish the job at Manolo Pearson's house. The guy was a pro. He staged it to look like a shoot-out and made a nice getaway."

I suppressed a smile of relief by pursing my lips and wondering aloud whether Metcalf or Melendez hadn't been behind that cleanup, too. I should have been an actor.

Rossetti shrugged. "Why not?"

Hooray! I thought, I'm off the hook. At least for the time being. To be comfortably off the hook, Rossetti should have winked and smiled as he delivered the line.

Rossetti beckoned for the waiter and ordered another round of cappuccino before continuing. He was in an expansive mood. Things were falling into place and he liked it.

"Bennie and Ralph were trying to set up some of Castro's boys in a drug-smuggling deal, very likely at the request of someone like Metcalf," he said. "But they were also dealing for themselves, either on the sly or with the feds looking the other way. Don't forget, they needed a cover. But half the time they were genuine cutthroats and the other half they were patriots working for the CIA."

He paused and dropped some sugar into his cappuccino. He laughed to himself.

"Shit," I said angrily. "How the hell can we prove it?"

"Look," he said. "You're going to have to decide, as a reporter, whether you're only interested in why your girlfriend died, or whether it's worth your while to blow the whistle on the CIA's dirty tricks."

Rossetti blew the steam away from his cup. He didn't mean to, but he was blowing the wind out of my sails, too.

"It's a tough call," he said, reading the doubt in my eyes. "I can't see Metcalf plotting to eliminate the Santiago kid *or* your friend Denise. Where's the motive? Those guys aren't thrill killers. On the other hand, there's a grain of truth in Metcalf's blackmail theory. Bennie and Ralph would have betrayed their own mother if the price was right. The obvious target was Esmeralda—she's expendable. But why kill Jaime and your girlfriend? The question remains: who were Bennie and Ralph working for?"

"Try this," I said. "If Metcalf was cleaning house to protect Wately, why not include Esmeralda in the trash? Maybe Ethel Wately was the one who tipped the scales and convinced Metcalf it was in everyone's interests to get rid of Esmeralda."

"Good luck," he said. "It still means you're going have to expose the entire operation. These guys are so far removed from what they do they may as well be on another planet. You'll never pin it on Metcalf, and I doubt you'll pin it on Mrs. Wately. It'll wind up looking like a cheap smear."

He sucked on his pipe but it had gone out.

He was right. The case was at a dead end. We sat in silence awhile until my thoughts turned to what Lieutenant Henry had said, how people in Harlem thought the CIA regularly sent drugs into the ghettos to ensure domestic tranquility. Rossetti put his pipe aside and polished off his cheesecake. He was being very candid, and since various other theories were being propounded, I decided to ask him what he thought of that one. I repeated what Henry had told me, without mentioning Henry's name.

My query drew a dark look from Rossetti. He said nothing at first; he was giving it thought. A lot of thought.

"You hear a lot of things," he said.

"Yeh," I pressed him, "and after what I'm seeing and hearing now, I'm about ready to believe it."

Rossetti relighted his pipe. He was still thinking. The conversation wasn't over.

"Remember Santo Trafficante?" he said.

I smiled. Santo Trafficante might be dead, but he still cast a long shadow.

"Sure," I said. "He was chummy with Edgar Wately's father, according to Tampa gossip. And Edgar's father was very chummy with the CIA."

Rossetti nodded, wreathed himself in pipe smoke, and continued.

"Trafficante was supposed to have ordered the hit on Albert Ducatti in 1957, with Hector Melendez as shooter," Rossetti said evenly. "But according to my sources, Melendez wasn't told why Ducatti had to be killed, and when he found out it was over drugs he and Santo parted company. Hector might be a killer, but he drew the line on drugs. Sex and gambling were his rackets."

"The story gets better," Rossetti added somberly. "Years later, a Green Beret colonel was on a mission in Thailand, looking for MIAs and POWs. He approached the leader of the Shang Army, a Chinese warlord, whose outfit protected the poppy crop up there in the Golden Triangle."

Rossetti narrowed his eyes and pointed his pipe in my direction.

"The colonel then went on a lecture tour and told anybody who'd listen that the warlord swore to him that the *CIA* was his best customer."

Rossetti paused for effect.

"Yes, indeed," Rossetti said. "The warlord was very accommodating. He said there were no MIAs in the area, nor were there any deserters or prisoners of war. But he used the occasion to extend an offer to destroy most of his opium crop in return for entering a new relationship with the Americans.

"*A new relationship*," Rossetti emphasized, "means that a relationship already existed."

"But how does Trafficante figure into this?" I asked.

"The warlord gave the colonel the name of a high-ranking CIA official who, he claimed, had approached him and arranged for the regular transfer of heroin to this country. This guy was deputy director of the CIA. Once the initial deal had been made, the CIA man stepped aside and told the warlord that guess who, Santo Trafficante, would henceforth take charge of stateside distribution."

"Everyone from the White House to the CIA denied the allegations, of course," Rossetti continued. "The CIA dismissed it as an example of disinformation, a wild rumor started by the communists. But the warlord wasn't a commie. He loved Americans. He wanted to set up a trade mission and hire Peace Corps workers to teach his people how to grow vegetables for export."

"I believe it," I said.

"I've met a lot of fine people working in intelligence," Rossetti said, almost apologetically, "but I've met just as many crackpots. The crackpots are convinced that armed revolution is possible here, inspired by black radicals who are either Marxists or Muslims."

"So the CIA keeps the ghettos supplied with drugs to defuse the threat," I ventured.

"How could you prove that?" I wondered aloud. "What a story that would make."

"Good luck," Rossetti said and loudly tapped the ashes out of his pipe.

32

There wasn't much to say after that. Our parting was awkward again. Rossetti asked if I'd been able to get a line on "Dixie Cup." I told him I hadn't even tried yet and promised to keep in touch. He went off to retrieve his car, muttering about "the brownies," the meter men and maids who delighted in ticketing policemen's cars.

I walked two blocks through a paste of dirty snow and litter, side-stepping vagrants poking through garbage cans overflowing with junk food wrappers and dodging a half-dozen panhandlers. I made my way to Sixth Avenue, renamed the Avenue of the Americas to honor our Latin neighbors, and chanced upon a dreadlocked Jamaican who caught my eye.

"Smoke?" he asked expectantly.

Why not. My whole world had gone to pot.

I bought a twenty-dollar bag and walked to the nearest liquor store, bought a bottle of Remy, and caught a cab back to my apartment to wait for the end of the world.

I ignored the messages on the answering machine, smoked the grass, listened to some Lou Reed and more Patsy Cline. I love Lou's "Original Wrapper." I moved around in nearly total darkness, drank cognac, and ate sardines from the can. I slopped sardine juice and cognac all over my notes and didn't care. I drank until I didn't care about anything. The pot made me feel lousy. There were all kinds of thoughts tossing around in my mind—Denise, Ethel, my own role in all this. And now I was regressing, hiding from what I knew I had to do.

The answering machine whirred and clicked but I wasn't taking any calls. I checked them off, though, on a piece of paper as they came in, one by one. Rocco. Terry Compton. Edgar Watelv. Two hang-ups. Edgar Watelv again. Another hang-up and then Rocco again. Rocco was sounding very pissed off.

Edgar Watelv's voice grew more plaintive each time. "Please call. It's important." Very mannerly, very low-key. Very psychotic.

At one point I picked up the phone and started to dial the Watelys' apartment, but I changed my mind. I was too drunk.

I fell asleep until I heard somebody knocking on my door around one A.M. It was Rocco. He whispered my name a few times and kept knocking. I didn't answer. I sat and listened to my heart beat. He knocked softly, so as not to arouse the neighbors, I guess, and then he went away.

I was way up in the clouds, like a bird, and then a storm came up and I was in a helicopter and the helicopter started to fall through the sky but I didn't care. I knew it was a dream and I laughed at how funny it was because I wanted the helicopter to take me to wherever Denise was hiding. She wasn't dead in the dream. She was just playing hide-and-seek.

I woke up at six in the morning with a bad taste in my mouth and the beginning of a hangover. I got undressed, flushed the rest of the grass down the toilet, took two aspirins, and went back to bed. I pulled the covers over my head and somehow managed to fall asleep again.

By ten the answering machine was making such a racket that I had no choice but to get up and face the world. I turned the volume up. Rocco was calling. He didn't sound angry anymore; he sounded worried.

I figured I may as well get it over with. I could run, I could sleep, I could get fucked up and say I no longer cared about anything, but I knew I might as well keep going.

I picked up the phone and said hello.

"Babe," Rocco sighed in relief. "We were worried about you. I got some bad news."

I didn't care.

"Let's have it," I said.

Big, brave Darenow. You set all the balls in play and then you say fuck it. That's how people die, dummy.

"I don't think we're gonna be able to store your pigeon anymore," he said. "She's a problem. She's too much trouble to feed. Capice? So you got to talk to Wately soon, OK, pal? Otherwise, we're leaving her with Dixie."

"I have nothing to say, Rocco. I'm tired and I'm hung over. I buried Denise yesterday and I really don't give a shit what happens. What else can I say?"

"Yeh," he said. "I can dig it. We're square, right? Nobody knows nothing about anything, right?"

"Right," I said.

I brushed my teeth, took a cold shower, drank a cup of stale coffee, and put on the charcoal gray suit and red tie I wore the day before. I didn't care. I had to meet Owen Reed in half an hour.

I wore my black tasseled loafers again because they were the only shoes I had that were dry. I put my damp parka on over the suit and brought the umbrella.

I hadn't bothered to look out the window. I had assumed it was still raining. By the time I got downstairs I realized I wouldn't need it. The sun was shining but the wind was blowing. The streets were a sheet of ice, despite the sunshine. I stepped back into the lobby of my building and jammed the umbrella behind a radiator. The radiator didn't work but I didn't care if it did. I just wanted to divest myself of all excess baggage.

Lunch with Owen Reed went a little worse than I had expected. If Stu Metcalf was master of the hounds, Reed was his whipper-in; he had to make sure the pack didn't stray. So naturally, Reed was late. It was either a power play to remind me who was top dog, or Metcalf was giving him one last briefing.

I arrived on time. The restaurant was The Bull and Bear, near the World Trade Center. It was full of smoke, noise, and Wall Street gamblers selling the country's future short.

I presented myself to the captain, gave him Reed's name, and followed him through the place to a table way in the back where another man was sitting.

The man was one of Reed's assistants. I won't embarrass him by naming him. He was just following orders. He was a bit on edge, a bit too chirpy. I was still coasting on harmful substances from last night's drugfest. The pot had damped my fears and given me a sore throat, but the cognac had enabled me to sleep it off. I was weary, but mellow enough not to care. I had to sit through half an hour of this joker's song and dance about how "the grand jury" was "a real good bunch of people from all walks of life," and how the New York cops "know more about what's going on than anybody else in town, bar none."

I asked him what grand jury he was referring to. I knew plans for a grand jury had been brewing, but the fact that jurors had already been selected was news to me. He said Reed was convening one in New York to deal with the wave of drug-related murders. These boys could move fast if they wanted to.

Flattery came next. He praised my "attitude and ability to see through the bullshit" and told me "what a treat" it was to be working with me. His wife was one of my biggest fans, he said, and so was his fifteen-year-old son, who, he noted, "wants to go into politics someday too, like his father." For a moment he looked as though he felt important.

I refrained from asking him why he didn't include himself among my fans. I just sucked on a Campari and soda and kept my peace—for the time being.

The closest I came to being provocative was to ask him to describe his relationship to Owen Reed in the federal pecking order, and to inquire about who they planned to summon before the grand jury.

"My God," the man replied to the first question, "Reed's my boss." It carried a note of finality that would have been cruel to pursue.

He dodged the question about the grand jury rather well. He tucked his chin in before he spoke. He was just a face in the crowd, a spear carrier, a lackey. He wore a suit and a tie and his hair was parted neatly and he looked like everybody else in the room.

"We don't usually give names out," he said cautiously, "and I'm sure Owen wouldn't make an exception in this case, considering the national security angle." Brief pause, clearing of throat. "You can ask him, of course."

Reed finally arrived, the epitome of Potomac charm, larger than life. You could almost hear ruffles and flourishes in the background. He was another Metcalf-in-training. Money meant nothing and power was just a heavy burden. They were in the game because they enjoyed belonging to the fraternity that taught the praetorian guard dirty tricks.

And I'd been invited to ride with the pack. Me, a deliberate bolter.

Reed's charm faded as soon as he took his seat. His smiling entrance was for the luncheon crowd—lawyers, judges, senior bureaucrats, bankers, and brokers who considered the restaurant their preserve. Reed scowled at me and sat down. He didn't acknowledge the other man's presence at all.

"Let's order," he said.

He smoothed his hair and locked me with an earnest gaze.

He was warming up to something, or cooling down. Maybe he had just lost a game of squash.

He ordered vodka on the rocks and suggested we order food right away. He ordered sliced steak, I ordered chicken, and the other man ordered something unpronounceable. Reed lit a cigarette and laid the pack on the table. He thought for a moment and addressed the other man by his first name. Let's call him Tom.

"Tom," he said, "what I'm going to say to Mr. Darenow is off the record—for the time being. But I'd like you to listen in, informally, of course, with a prosecutorial ear. All right? I'm merely after an opinion."

"That's my job," the faceless one said gravely.

My alarm bell trilled, but didn't go off. If poor Tom was going to carry the ball in this scrimmage, it meant Reed was distancing himself. All the same, it implied a threat.

"I'd like to ask *you* a few questions," Reed said next, flexing his jaw at me. "*If* you're gentleman enough to know what off the record means. No one's sure about your ethics, your motives, or your sense of moral obligation."

I reddened, my pulse quickened, and I sank into the plush velour. See what you get, Darenow, for going out on limbs with the wrong monkeys? No respect. Maybe Reed thinks you're part of Charlie's blackmail racket.

"How many people have you talked to since Stu and I briefed you at Ethel Wately's place the other night?"

"My publisher and the senior editor I report to," I lied. "Do you mind if I take one of your cigarettes?"

"Help yourself." He shoved the pack contemptuously in my direction.

"Let me tell you how many people are in on this officially, Darenow. The director of the CIA, me, *you*—" he stabbed his finger at me— "Stu Metcalf, and a handful of deep-cover people, some of whom are already dead.

"Someone's talking, and I sure as hell know it wasn't the director, this man—" he stabbed his finger at Tom— "Stu, or myself." He jerked his thumb into the knot of his tie.

Reed was plenty sore, but something told me he wasn't only mad at me. He was mad at the world, especially Metcalf, for having screwed things up and then leaving him in charge of the cleanup crew. Besides, he was wrong in assuming we were the only people aware of Metcalf's operation. According to Inspector Rossetti, the Cubans at the UN Mission had gotten wind of it through Bennie and Ralph Torres. I could blame the leaks on them, but I wouldn't. I'd have to betray Rossetti's trust, and I'd never do that.

I hid behind the cigarette I was lighting and let him go on.

"How come every newspaper in Washington wants to know what's going on at Wately's bank?" he said. His eyes bounced from me to Tom. "We also have three young snots from the house committee on intelligence—three hotshot liberals, incidentally—asking us if the CIA is running an operation through Wately's bank."

He fixed me with the hard stare, the one Metcalf taught him, then put it on the other man. My networking was more successful than I had expected. Our Washington bureau must have acted fast, and who knows what tremors were being felt in Tampa as we spoke.

Tom nodded dutifully.

"I don't have to tell you the law, Tom, I'm sure you're aware of the national security sections in the federal code. If we find out who is talking to the press, we're going to prosecute them. Metcalf's furious. He wants to make a test case out of this."

He turned his wrath on me.

"The rotten thing, the despicable thing, is that the rumor—call it slander, a case could be made for it—started in his newspaper's Washington bureau."

He was talking about me.

"Maybe Oscar Herrera made a couple of phone calls before he put the noose around his neck," I said.

He flinched and reared up again.

"He's a victim of the leak," he said, his upper lip quivering. "We know he was the laundry man. That's why we indicated him. We were leaning on him so he'd lead us to the goddamned Cubans."

"Which ones?" I said, "Metcalf's or Castro's?"

That was the last straw for Owen Reed. He brought the whip down hard. He curled his lip. A real Saxon was Mr. Reed. No Norman French in his family tree.

"Listen, mister," he seethed, "your ass is grass. You won't be able to get a job selling papers on a corner, never mind writing for them. Your career is finished—finished, understand?—if Metcalf finds out you're the source of the leak."

If they find out I'm the source.

I took a long swallow, finishing my drink. I put it down and signaled a passing waiter.

Reed turned his attention to Tom, whose eyes were now swimming in wonder.

"He's talking about a guy who may have been strung up by one of Castro's mob," Reed said.

So that was how Metcalf planned to explain away the disposal of Oscar Herrera. Blame it on the commies, as usual.

Tom looked baffled. I wanted to laugh. The waiter came over. I told him I needed a glass of red wine.

Reed grabbed angrily for the pack of cigarettes, fumbled for a minute with the opening, then ripped the whole top off and made a big deal out of lighting up. He blew a lot of smoke into the air.

He was setting up for his next act. Metcalf would have been proud of his performance, except for ripping the pack of cigarettes apart and taking too deep a drag. That was overkill. He was going to play good cop next. The shift was nearly flawless. Pat the doggie, then whip the doggie, then pat him again.

"Because the information concerning the operation is patently false, Metcalf will be satisfied if we cut our losses right here," he said.

He gave me the hard stare. That's how it's done. You lie without blinking and the other dog is supposed to slink away.

I bit my tongue and saved my speech for later. I wasn't going to embarrass him with the fact that Edgar and Ethel had both told me Metcalf was "running an operation." Quote, unquote. Metcalf had even admitted it himself. He didn't say the goddamned Cuban agents dropped into his lap. The story changed every time I heard it. I let him go on. Sooner or later he was going to trip over his own dogs. I merely had to stay on my feet until it happened.

"If we can have your word, Darenow, that nothing more gets said about this, Stu is willing to let it slide—and that's only because Ethel Wately is still behind you one hundred percent."

"Who's appearing before the grand jury?" I queried.

"You want to be called?" Reed huffed. "Sign him up, Tom."

"I'll consider it," I answered, drawing on the cigarette I'd bummed from Reed, "depending on who else appears."

That's it, Darenow. Gentle pressure accompanied by bold move.

"Stu Metcalf intends to make a full and complete statement before the panel—*in person*," Reed said, as if that made all the difference.

"What about Edgar and Ethel Wately? Aurora Carrera? What about Cartwright?" I asked. I have no idea why his name came to mind. He was the man Wately was talking to at the Albemarle Club. It just rolled off my wicked tongue.

"Cartwright!"

The name shot off Reed's tongue, too, but it came out strangled in a comical falsetto. No one dared laugh, of course. He knew exactly who I meant.

"What the hell does Cartwright have to do with this?" he blustered.

"My question, exactly," I said.

"Listen, pal," he said. He waved the cigarette at me like a pointer, or a knife. "You better have a chat with Stu Metcalf. In fact, you better see Ethel first and let her know what you're doing."

"Why Ethel?"

It was a legitimate question.

"She's your only friend, buddy," Reed said.

The food arrived. I had lost my appetite. I felt the same way I felt when Edgar Wately was buying drinks for me. I didn't want to be at the same table with this man, either. Reed was lying through his teeth. Maybe for different reasons than Edgar, but he was lying.

If I was wrong, I was going to be in deeper shit than I thought.

"Food's good," Tom said, chewing happily.

Reed's appetite had failed him, too. He sliced a couple of tender morsels from his steak and chewed automatically, but he left most of it on his plate. He picked thoughtfully at his baked potato but skipped it, opting instead for a couple of forkfuls of green salad.

He signaled for the waiter and told him he was finished. The waiter looked at his plate in mock horror.

"Is something wrong, sir?"

I wanted to crack a smile but I didn't.

"Everything's fine," Reed said brusquely. "Bring me some coffee."

Tom was only halfway through what looked like swordfish steak covered in a horrible green sauce. I pushed my plate aside. I wanted to mimic Reed's act. I don't know why. It seemed right. Two hungry dogs circling each other was a more interesting match than one hungry dog circling a well-fed, lazy one.

I reached for his cigarettes again.

"Do you mind?" I asked.

"Go ahead," he said. "I'll have one, too."

He had damped his anger somewhere between the steak and the salad.

Maybe I was back to doing the right thing.

I didn't care.

When Reed's coffee arrived, I ordered one, too. Tom was just getting into his julienned carrots. He looked at Reed apologetically every now and then, as if he expected Reed to take his food away at any moment. A dog's life.

Reed was warming up for the next round. He played with his coffee for a while. Stirred it. Dumped half a pack of sugar into it. Put the sugar down. Stirred some more. A little milk, a little more sugar, and he was ready.

"I can understand how upset you must be," Reed said soothingly. It was supposed to represent sincerity. "Let's see what the grand jury says before we get at each other's throats," he added. His tone was wary but cordial.

"Tom's here to assist in any way he can. He's presenting the case. He'll consider any leads you might have. I'm sure Stu will back me up on that. Stu has nothing to hide."

"Why did Rosa take a powder?" I said. "No one stopped her. Aurora might have skipped too if the cops hadn't pulled her in for more questions."

Reed nodded thoughtfully. His eyes were glazed with a limpid calm.

"I doubt Aurora will testify against her aunt." Reed shrugged. "But we'll try. We could threaten to deport her. I don't know. Tom? What do you hear from your side?"

Tom cleared his throat.

"We're just gearing up," he said shakily. "Uh, the city cops . . . uh, we're gonna run down what they've gotten out of her and go over it. But sure, we'll call her."

He cleared his throat again. He wanted to say something that would please Reed.

"A detective told me this morning that they found Bennie Torres's prints on Miss Overton's camera," Tom said brightly, "*and* on a roll of exposed film found in the back of Ralph Torres's car."

He looked to Reed for approval.

Reed looked at me.

"You see, Darenow," Reed said. "We've still not satisfied that this isn't just a servant problem. Latins can be very vindictive people. We know Rosa had her money mixed up with the nephews. You know that, don't you, Tom?"

"Yeh," Tom said. "I heard something . . ."

"So we're pursuing that angle," Reed said.

"What does Ethel have to say about that?" I asked Tom. "She and Rosa were supposed to have had a long talk one night while Bennie and Ralph were in the kitchen. Shortly before the murders of Jaime and Denise."

Tom looked at me like I had just shoved a piece of bad cheese under his nose.

I glanced at Reed to see his reaction.

"Neither one of us has questioned Ethel Wately, Mr. Darenow," Reed cut in sharply. "But I'm sure she will be questioned."

Tom looked like he'd like to question Ethel himself, but he held his tongue.

"Let's get the check," Reed said. He picked up his cigarettes, put them into one pocket, and took his wallet from another. He pulled out a platinum American Express card and laid it on the table.

"Say, Tom, would you mind if Darenow and I have a word together alone?"

"Not at all," Tom said pleasantly. "I'll get the coats."

"I don't have one," Reed said. "The car's outside."

"Sure thing," Tom said. "Max, a pleasure, really. Let's hope everything works out. I'm sure it will."

Reed nodded curtly in his direction and Tom dogged off to get his coat.

"Look, Darenow," Reed said, "Ethel Wately is one fabulous woman. She did her best to try and give that kid an education, but it didn't work out. I think we both know her brother is another problem. He doesn't know whether he's straight *or* gay. At least the kid was an out-and-out case. I believe Ethel deserves every break we can give her, and I hope you feel the same way."

I started to say something but he waved me off.

"Let me finish," he said. "Ethel thinks you're OK, Darenow. She likes you. She can pull a lot of strings and she's a brilliant woman. I know you both lost someone you loved and cared for. But Ethel isn't letting it get to her. Stu Metcalf doesn't go for hysterics. You're letting it get to you."

He reached across the table and laid a fraternal pat on my arm.

"Your girlfriend's death isn't connected in any way, by any wild stretch of the imagination, to anything Stu might, or might not, have had his hand in," he said. "Take my word on that, buddy. Believe me, I'm trying to save you from a whole mess of problems."

"I'd like to peek at the grand jury minutes when it's over," I said. "I think that would clear up some of my problems."

Reed smiled condescendingly.

"Tell you what, scout," he said, making a gun out of his thumb and forefinger and pointing it at me, "you got a deal. But it's between you and me. You want to look, just look. You come around when it's over and I'll have a copy for you to read. For your eyes only. No story."

I walked him out to the coatroom, where Tom was waiting. Reed apologized for not being able to take him around the corner to his office. He had to "shoot uptown."

The *Graphic* was only six blocks from the restaurant, so I walked there, stopping to browse in a storefront travel agency that advertised "sun tours." I checked economy fares to Tampa, Miami, and Colombia, just in case.

Normal conversation stopped as I strolled into the newsroom. I tried covering the silence with long, purposeful strides. Darenow, star reporter, full of piss and vinegar on his way to show the feds a thing or two. Or were they thinking I'd gone off the deep end again? Danny Tung flagged me down on the way to the mailboxes before I could decide.

"Max! I got something for you," he yelled. He pulled me down so he could whisper in my ear.

"Some guy called twice, wouldn't give his name, says you should call Frankie or Rocco as soon as you get in," he said.

I knew who that had to be. My buddy, Charlie, The Big Guy.

Danny was hoping I'd shed light on the mysterious caller, but I remained inscrutable.

"Anything else?" I asked.

He handed me a dozen phone messages.

All the people I hadn't called back the day before.

Rocco. Dixie. Rocco again. Frank—no last name—my friend in Tampa. Rocco again. Frank again. Ethel Watley twice and Edgar Watley three times, the last message from him marked "Urgent!!!"

There was no mail worth reading: invitations to taste a new salami at the Carnegie Deli, with models from a famous agency doing the slicing and serving, and two tickets to a lecture at Town Hall featuring an Indian swami who had a new plan for world harmony.

Everyone in the newsroom wanted to know what I was up to. One jealous asshole said he was surprised to see me because he'd heard I'd been fired. The price of fame.

"Not fired," I said. "Shot."

His jaw dropped. He said: "Really?"

I grinned and walked away.

I decided to call Dixie first. I used an extension way in the back of the room that offered more privacy. The phone sat atop a scarred wooden desk, the bottom remnant of an old rolltop, rumored to have once belonged to Bat Masterson, a turn-of-the-century gunslinger who retired to New York and became a sportswriter.

I got Dixie's answering machine, but she picked up when she heard my voice.

"Hi, babe," she said. "Everything OK?"

"Yeh," I said. "How about you?" It was almost a relief to hear her voice.

"Esmeralda's still here," she said. "Her 'husband' wants her to take a vacation, but she wants to talk to you first. When can you get over here? I'd like to get on with my life. I have a showcase this weekend."

Dixie was very breezy.

"Are you alone?" I asked.

"Just us girls," she said. "The baby-sitters are gone. Can you come over, Max? Please?"

Numbers One and Two had undoubtedly tired of waiting for the big payoff and had probably asked to be relieved. Maybe Charlie was finally giving up the ghost. Otherwise, why leave Dixie in charge? Now was the time to make my move—before Wately, or worse, Metcalf's, exterminators caught up with Esmeralda.

"I'm coming over now, Dixie, but I have to warn you. When I'm through with Esmeralda, she has to make a statement to the cops before Wately takes her under his wing. Is that clear?"

"Honey, I've already spoken to my lawyer," Dixie drawled. "I'm to say that I *just* found out Esme might be involved in something. I knew *nothing* until I read your story in the paper, so *naturally* I called you right away."

"Fine," I said.

Well, here we go.

"Max, there's one thing: I want you to promise you'll *not* throw Esmeralda to the wolves. I know you don't like her, but *I* believe her story. She's been used, Max. She's a victim."

Esmeralda was nothing to me.

Dixie was.

"I promise," I said.

I couldn't say no. She had saved my life.

I told her I'd see her in an hour.

I leaned back in my chair and put my feet on Bat Masterson's old desk. Or was it Hart Crane's? It's probably a myth, anyway, I thought, perpetuated by someone in personnel to prop up the J-school grads' hunger for nostalgia and tradition—the days when reporters were fearless, editors and the public cheered them on, circulation soared, and the accountants kept quiet and counted the money. You want news to *sell*, tell the fucking truth.

I called Rocco.

Rocco said Charlie wanted to see me sometime soon. Had I spoken to Frank Reilly recently? Could I drop by The Crib on my way home?

I figured Charlie wanted to renew our marriage vows. I told Rocco I'd drop by before I went to Dixie's.

But first I'd call Frank Reilly.

Frankie the Cop was still plugging away, tapping into Tampa's criminal underground for all he was worth, which Rocco told me later was $2,000 a day, *plus expenses*.

He had some interesting new theories developed from "impeccable sources," as he called them. It backed up everything Rossetti had told me and more.

To wit:

Bennie and Ralph were "ferrets," CIA contract agents charged with making contact with Cuban communists in this country who wanted to deal drugs or buy information. The CIA fronted them "minimal" amounts of money to buy drugs which, ostensibly, were then to be destroyed and any profits turned over to Nicaraguan counterinsurgents, the contras. This was considered the best way to make contact and handle a hot potato.

That was only a part-time job, of course. Frank repeated more of what I'd heard from Gabe Rossetti: no one trusted Bennie and Ralph. Any "Cuban communist" they ferreted out was most likely another bullshit artist, like Bennie and Ralph. And the drugs were never destroyed.

The profits, according to Frank Reilly, were to be pumped back into Wately's bank, in order to forestall a takeover attempt engineered by Wately's sister and certain members of the bank's board of directors, led by—you guessed it—Hector Melendez.

Frank, always the decorous professional, saved the juiciest gossip until last.

"I went out to the neighborhood where the Santiago kid and the drag queen were brought up," he began. "Not where Watelv was shacking up with them, but where they lived after they were born."

"Esmeralda was raised in Puerto Rico," I corrected him.

"According to my source, Esmeralda was born in Tampa, Mr. Darenow. It shouldn't be hard to prove that. I'll pull her birth certificate—or his."

"Are you sure?"

"Okay Darenow, ready for this? According to a neighbor, a Mrs. Esther Garcia, Esmeralda and Jaime Santiago had the same father. Mrs. Garcia says the old guy came around regularly for about six months after they were born. I'm goin' out there tomorrow with a picture of old Watelv. I'll let you know what she says."

"Esmeralda is Avery Watelv's kid?"

"Right-o. The Garcia woman claims Esmeralda and Jaime are *twins*," he said gleefully. "She's willing to testify to that effect. Says she wants to see them get their just due, collect their inheritance. I didn't have the heart to tell her that one kid was dead and the other changed its sex."

Holy Mother of God. Edgar Watelv was in love with his own half-brother.

"Will this woman testify?" I croaked.

"If the remaining kid doesn't get a square deal. Mrs. Garcia says she heard how Rosa's nephews got knocked off and that started her thinking about the kids."

I shifted over to autopilot and called the Watelys' apartment. It was too much to swallow.

The new Filipino housekeeper answered the phone. I asked to speak to Mr. or Mrs.—it made no difference to me. I'd squeeze either one.

Edgar was out. Ethel was in.

Not quite perfect, but it would have to do.

"Max!" Ethel exclaimed when she got on the line. "What's going on? The bank is flooded with calls. What have you done?"

"Nothing," I said.

"Nothing! Max! No one else knows anything about this!"

I couldn't decide if she was angry or just bewildered. Neither could she.

"We have to talk soon," I said.

"You bet we do," she said emphatically. "Edgar's on the verge of a breakdown. Oh, Max, I hope it's not you who's been spreading these horrid rumors in Washington and Tampa. Do you think I've been *lying* to you? Didn't Stu Metcalf tell you *everything?*

"Please," she said huskily, "please don't hurt me. Please, Max. *Please.* Don't do this to me. Edgar is my brother. He's flesh and blood. He's the only thing I have."

I tried tuning her out. Her brother wasn't my problem. I tried to read between the sobs.

"Let me ask you something," I said calmly. "Did Jaime Santiago have a twin brother?"

Long silent pause. I could hear the wires humming. Her voice dropped an octave or two before she spoke.

"I don't know what you're talking about," she said hoarsely.

"Can I see you around five o'clock?" I asked.

"Here?" she sniffed.

"Yes."

"I'll be waiting for you," she said. "Don't disappoint me."

"I won't disappoint you," I said, and hung up.

I didn't bother asking her where her brother was. If he was in New York, I'm sure he was sitting around a table with his lawyers and accountants. If he was in Tampa he was probably shredding paper.

I lay the phone down as if it was an atomic weapon and let out a long sigh. Edgar *must* have known Esmeralda and Jaime were twins.

Now I had to find out if Ethel knew as well.

I was shaking my head in wonder when I heard Danny Tung clear his throat. He was standing behind me and I hadn't noticed. I swung my legs off Bat Masterson's desk, or was it Hart Crane's? I jumped up and damn near knocked Danny over with a phony twenty-four-carat grin. How long had he been standing there?

"You want coffee, Max? A bite to eat? I'm sending out. The company's paying for it."

"Gotta run, Danny."

"Is everything OK, Max? You look awful." The grin hadn't fooled Danny. He was a good kid. Another immigrant's son who believed in the American Dream and knew it all came from hard work. And faith.

I was already out the door. I thanked Danny, hung the trenchcoat over my shoulders, Euro-style, pulled my collar up, and waved to the jerk who thought I'd been fired. I was putting on a brave front for the youngsters in the newsroom.

I had a funny feeling Denise wasn't going to like what I was going to do. Even if I was right.

But I was more concerned with how Ethel was going to react. Especially if I was wrong.

I headed over to meet Rocco. I had to know where I stood with Charlie's family. Obviously, blackmailing Wately wasn't a dead idea even though Charlie was letting Esmeralda go. Frank Reilly wasn't collecting two thousand bucks a day because someone forgot to tell him to quit. Frank was still getting instructions from Charlie, which meant Charlie was still interested in leaning on Wately. Well, I wasn't going to help him in any way.

I hoped Rocco would understand and plead my case. I wondered whether my alibi was still in place.

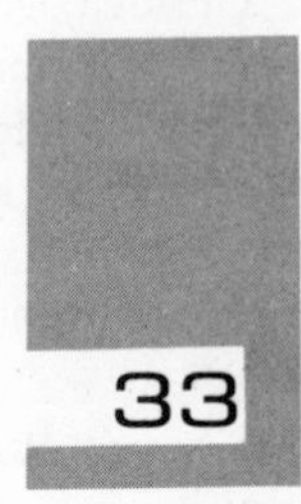

Rocco and Charlie, The Big Guy himself, were sitting at a booth in a far corner of The Crib. I didn't see them when I came in. The place was as dark and murky at four in the afternoon as it was at four in the morning. A couple of leather queens were shooting pool. Didn't these people work? One of the lumberjack clones led me to the booth where Rocco and Charlie were waiting. It was like naptime at nursery school except the jukebox was going full tilt, blasting out a tune called "It's Raining Men."

We all shook hands. The Big Guy initiated it, which I thought was a good sign. It's when they kiss you you have to worry.

Charlie wanted to know if Frank Reilly had given me the dirt on Esmeralda being Jaime's twin.

I told him I had been so informed.

"So go take a picture of Mrs. Garcia and put it on your front page," Charlie said. He waved a finger in front of him; he was conjuring a headline: NEIGHBOR SAYS SUSPECT IN MURDER IS WEALTHY HEIRESS. "And under that you say, "Did Sex-Change Twin Murder Its Brother?"

Motives were still a dime a dozen.

"No good, Charlie," I said. "The publisher wouldn't print it unless it comes out in court or she's formally charged."

"The cunt got to you, right?" Charlie said.

Rocco, who had been quietly sucking on a match, seconded the notion with a grunt. They were referring to Ethel. It didn't matter. I let it drift.

"No," I said. "But the idea of Esmeralda's killing her brother is interesting. It's another avenue to explore. However, I'm leaving it to the cops."

"The fucking information is gonna check out, believe me," Charlie said. "Frankie Reilly will find a baptismal certificate, if he can't get a birth record."

"The fact Esmeralda was Jaime's twin, if true, doesn't prove she killed him," I answered. "In fact, Jaime was probably her only real friend. So what's her motive?"

But Charlie wasn't interested in motives. He just liked making mischief.

"We're putting up for you," he demanded. "Now you gotta put up for us. What are you, crazy? You owe me, pally."

Now what. Maybe I should ask Stu Metcalf to straighten Charlie out. Ha.

"Reilly is terrific," I said. "But I've made up my mind that the Torres brothers killed Jaime and Denise. I just don't know why."

"Forget the Torres brothers," Charlie said, waving his hands. "We can help this Esmeralda get her share of the fortune. We can do a blood test. That will prove who the father is. See what I mean?"

He was losing patience, but he was losing steam, too. He was taking one last shot before Esmeralda walked, but his heart wasn't in it. If he couldn't get to Wately, he'd cut a deal with Esmeralda. Hey, she might be an heiress.

"The father's dead," I said. "You can't draw blood from a corpse, even a blue-blooded one."

"Listen to me," he hissed. "What do think I'm wasting my time for? Frank Reilly don't come cheap. Use it!"

"You want to help Esmeralda, be my guest," I said. "If you're really concerned, hire a public relations firm. I'm after Edgar and his pals in the State Department."

"Fuck them!" Charlie said. "Forget about his pals! You can't hurt them. Leave them alone."

"Why?" I probed. "Did Melendez tell you to lay off? Or did Metcalf offer you a deal, too?"

Big bad Darenow shoots his mouth off. Charlie looked stunned, but he turned it around and made light of it.

"Nobody tells me to lay off," Charlie sneered. "Fucking blue nose, that's what they used to call you guys. Not a brown nose. A blue nose."

"From being around that Wately dame." Rocco nodded approvingly. "I knew you were gone when you told me you boffed her. Fucking blue bloods give you a blue nose."

"Look, Charlie," I said. "It'll all come out in the wash. I know Wately's been lying and his sister hasn't been telling the truth either. I'm seeing them tonight."

"What's the difference who killed them?" he scoffed. "The fucking truth ain't bringing them back. The only way to get satisfaction is to break Wately's balls. Make him pay through the nose."

"Not my style, Charlie."

"Fucking blue nose." Then Charlie smiled.

"What about the broad at your paper who writes the gossip columns? What's her name, Woozie? Maybe she'd do a line if you asked her."

He waved his hand again idly. He was composing a suitable line for the gossip columns.

" 'What well-known society figure has sex-change son suing for damages?' Something like that?"

No wonder the Mafia had managed to hold onto its power for so long. They never ran out of ways to squeeze a buck from sin.

"Call her up, Charlie. She might even answer the phone herself. She might even use the item. I can't stop you from doing it." I was getting tired of Charlie's constant prodding.

Charlie looked affectionately at Rocco.

"This is my daughter's 'rock,' " Charlie said. "My daughter needs a rock because she's pretty tough herself." Rocco was Charlie's son-in-law.

Rocco beamed. No wonder he always had Charlie's ear.

"What do you think of this Darenow guy?" Charlie asked his favorite son-in-law.

"Forget the whole thing," Rocco replied. "You're fucking with the fucking CIA and everybody. Max says he's gonna squeeze Wately's balls, so that's enough. The money is dirty, anyway, and I don't trust Wately's friends. There's a lot more spics with guns than there are Italians. You wanted a truce, you got it. Enjoy it."

It was Charlie's turn to beam.

Everything was working out.

"Tell ya' what," Charlie said, a big shit-eating grin on his face, "I won't push it if I can get into Ethel's pants."

"It'll be the first thing I ask her when I see her tonight," I said, putting on my best poker face.

Charlie laughed.

Since everyone was in such a good mood, I decided to pop a serious question, one that might have all, or nothing, to do with Denise's murder. Knowing *why* Denise died was as important to me as knowing who dunnit.

So I asked Charlie what he knew about Santo Trafficante, the CIA, and the drug trade.

Charlie stopped laughing.

"That ain't so funny, pally," Charlie scowled.

"Let's hear it, Charlie."

He scowled again. I tried elaborating but it was a lot for Charlie to handle; too many big words, too many big concepts. Deniability in the name of national security was the CIA's code and it bothered Charlie to think about it. The Italian mob operated under a violent code of its own, but the Mafia's saving grace was that they only killed each other, and then only consenting males.

"People don't want to hear that shit," Charlie muttered. From his point of view, the clandestine service simply had hired the wrong gangsters. He lowered his eyes, bowed his head, and the scowl faded to a slight blush. A touchy subject all around.

"But I'm on the right track, Charlie, aren't I?" I smiled. A smile was my umbrella.

"Santo made a bad deal," Charlie replied morosely. "He should of never gotten involved. Those guys came to him."

"That's no excuse, Charlie," I said softly.

"Society makes people greedy, Darenow. For some people, at some time, drugs are the only way to make real money." Charlie smoothed a paper napkin, avoiding my eyes.

"The fact is that people in government knew about Santo's deal with the CIA and said nothing, Charlie. Them's the facts. What those people did was wrong. You can't do that and live here."

Charlie blinked once, soft and slow, before meeting my gaze, a strong man taking a punch.

"Drop it, Darenow," he said simply and without rancor. "That's all over now. I'm in charge."

"I hope you're right," I said wistfully. "Why spoil an otherwise pleasant afternoon? I'll give Ethel your best."

"Do that," Charlie said.

I stood up to leave and paused. I thought about shaking hands but I wasn't sure if it was a good move. I was about to settle for an exchange of friendly glances when Charlie offered his hand.

I shook it and departed.

I walked a block, found a cab, and headed over to Dixie's. I decided not to call the detectives until I had spoken to Esmeralda one more time.

Maybe, I speculated, maybe Esmeralda's parentage is what Rosa laid on Ethel the night they argued.

Sex-change heiress?

Esmeralda would probably blow it all on cocaine and face-lifts.

34

The "heiress" was in the middle of a crying jag when I arrived at Dixie's. She had been drinking rum since Numbers One and Two left and she wasn't a happy drunk. It might have had something to do with the fact that Number One had flushed the rest of her cocaine down the toilet before he checked out.

Esmeralda was losing it. She was a doused, disoriented hen, pacing the floor, clenching her fists, and cursing the Wately name. She didn't know who she was, or what she was, or who she belonged to. She had nothing except the clothes on her back and a leather satchel full of makeup.

She'd gotten her wish to be a woman and this is where it had led.

"You gotta help me, baby, please," was the first thing she said when she saw me.

I had hoped to talk to Dixie first but that wasn't to be. Esmeralda grabbed my lapels and started pawing me, stroking my face, and blubbering gibberish. She wanted me to look at her.

I wanted to look to see if I could discern a resemblance to the Wately family, but I couldn't meet her eyes. Whoever she was, or had been, had been painted over, hidden deep. The real Esmeralda, or Jesus, or whatever name she was given at birth, had been altered and stitched and reshaped into an envious cartoon of a woman. It wasn't the truth and never could be. Esmeralda thought she was alive when she looked into a mirror, but she couldn't see any further than that. She hated who she was and she hated what she'd become. No one wanted her, except dead.

"I called my husband but his sister won't let me talk to him," she gasped. "I don't even know if he's alive anymore. What's wrong? I didn't do nothing to anybody. Why do they want to kill me?"

"You tried calling Wately again?"

She nodded her head. "They gonna kill him, I know," she sobbed. "They gonna kill him and then me."

"Esmeralda," I said slowly, "did Jaime ever tell you you were related to him?"

"He always say I'm his sister. But it isn't true," she said feebly.

"Do you have a birth certificate?"

She shook her head. She didn't know.

"When you left Puerto Rico, why did you go to Tampa?"

"My mother—the one who raise me, not my real mother—had relatives there," she said.

Talking about it made her focus on something far away, something she couldn't figure out.

"And you met Rosa?"

"And Jaime," she said. "He live next door to Rosa. Rosa knew his family."

"When was the first time you met Edgar Wately?"

"No," she said, "no, no, no."

"Where did you meet him first?" I pressed.

"No," she said. "I met him myself. I knew him before."

"Not in San Juan," I said. "That was a lie, wasn't it?"

"No, no, no," she screamed. "Not there. I know what you're thinking. No! That was just a joke."

"What's a joke?"

"He's my husband!" she shrieked.

She came at me with both fists. She wanted to hurt me bad. I grabbed her left arm but I was too late for the right. I should have let her slap me. Instead, she raked her nails across my cheek and nose, drawing blood and missing my eye by a fraction.

I slapped her hard, twice, and pushed her down into a chair. She wailed and shrieked in a voice unlike anything I'd ever heard before. It curdled my blood and it scared the shit out of Dixie, who was running back and forth with a telephone in her hand.

"Don't call anybody," I said.

Dixie looked frightened but smart enough to admit it. Her eyes flashed like high beams, on, off, and on again as she corrected her path and came toward me. She had something private to say. She blew her cheeks in exasperation and sidled alongside me, talking from the side of her mouth.

"Max—someone's trying to kill her. The New York cops may not be able to protect her now. Call them. Anyone near Esmeralda is a walking target. She's frantic with worry."

Esmeralda shrieked again, but it wasn't as blood-curdling. Dixie moved to comfort her. I grabbed Dixie's arm but let go fast. I saw how she had moved when the greaser at the Waldorf grabbed her.

"Dixie, if the New York cops believe Esmeralda's story, they won't turn her over to the feds," I implored. "You're right and I'm right. I'm taking Esmeralda to see Ethel Wately. I want them both in the same room. That's the safest place for Esmeralda right now."

Dixie looked up at me over her low beams. She glanced at Esmeralda. Esmeralda was crying, like a gargoyle grinning in the rain.

"Just don't torture her, Max!" Dixie hissed.

I turned and, in a calm voice, asked Esmeralda if Edgar Wately had ever made love to her. The gargoyle's grin folded into a distracted smile of pleasure. Her smile turned to wonderment and then she shook her head in denial, but she wasn't thinking of my question. She was mulling her own.

I asked her one more time.

"Did Edgar ever make love to you?"

"He is my husband," she shrieked. "He never told me we had the same father."

"How did you find out?"

"Jaime . . ." she screamed. "Jaime tell me."

"Did Edgar know you were . . . his half-brother?"

She responded immediately.

"No." I believed her.

"How did you find out?"

She tossed her head angrily, plucked at her hair, and concentrated on a spot on the floor.

"When I tell everybody Edgar was gonna marry me one of the neighbors said don't do it. She tell Rosa I was Jaime's . . ."

She couldn't finish the sentence. She looked at me and uttered a hollow, voiceless scream. The light in her eyes shifted and dimmed, as if a filter had been drawn over them. They weren't Esmeralda's eyes anymore. They were Jesus Sanchez's eyes and they were Avery Watley's eyes—and they were Ethel Watley's eyes, too.

"Mrs. Garcia? Was the neighbor's name Garcia?"

"Esther Garcia," she sniffed. "You know her?" She looked at me like someone stirring awake. Her voice was an adolescent voice, soft, full of wonder, and still ignorant of the rites of men. She fumbled for a tissue, found one, and blew her nose loudly.

"Get your coat," I said. "I'm taking you to Edgar's apartment."

"They'll kill him too," she said woodenly. "I can't."

"Who are *'they,'* " I asked. "Who wants to kill Edgar?"

"I dunno," she replied, wiping her nose on her sleeve. "He told me a long time ago that some people were jealous of us."

"His sister is there," I said. "No one's going to hurt you."

A new look crept into Esmeralda's eyes. A look I'd seen before. Hard and soft. I shuddered at the comparison.

"No," she said primly. "I don't want Mrs. Watley to see me like this."

"Get your coat," I said evenly. "Let's go."

Esmeralda stood up and smiled wanly through her tears at Dixie.

"Imagine," Esmeralda sniffed.

Dixie draped her coat over her shoulders and put an arm around her.

"I'd like to go with her," Dixie said.

"Let's go," I said.

The three of us went down to the street and hailed a cab.

Dixie let Esmeralda slide in first, then turned to me and whispered: "Don't you think we should have the police meet us there?"

"I'll call them when I get there," I said.

"Let's call them on the way," Dixie said. "I'm scared."

"Don't be scared," I said. "I know what I'm doing."

I was only half right, or half wrong.

I climbed into the front seat and went on autopilot again. It was nearly rush hour but traffic was moderate. The driver said more snow or rain was expected and people were leaving their cars at home.

The driver kept glancing in the mirror, eyeing the two dishes in the back seat. He couldn't make up his mind if they were drag queens or not. The Bowery to Park Avenue flight plan had him intrigued. A fine mist rolled in off the East River as we proceeded up the FDR Drive and he put the windshield wipers on so he could see better.

He was one of the few cabbies left who smoked, or allowed smoking in his cab. I bummed one from him, lit it, and stared out the window, my thoughts veiled in a fine mist of their own. I made a checklist of all the things I wanted to ask Ethel.

What had Rosa told her the night Bennie and Ralph came to visit?

Did Rosa threaten to expose Esmeralda's affair with Edgar?

I weighed the blackmail angle very carefully. Maybe Rosa demanded money from Ethel and Ethel refused. If she refused, that might explain why Bennie slipped the poison to Esmeralda first, to show Ethel he was serious and Jaime could be next.

But that was killing the golden goose.

But what if she paid them off and they took the money and tried to kill Esmeralda anyway, as part of Cartwright's—or Metcalf's—house-cleaning operation?

What about Esme? I couldn't come up with a motive for her to kill Jaime. I believed her story, at least parts of it.

It all came down to just two options, maybe a combination: blackmail and/or a CIA-sanctioned money-laundering scheme that backfired, and killed innocent people, one of whom I had wanted to marry. But it wouldn't have happened without the CIA.

All right, I said to myself. A woman got me into this and another woman is keeping me at it. That other woman is Ethel Wately.

35

It was a couple of minutes after five o'clock when we got off the drive and headed over to Park Avenue. Nobody was saying very much because we were all on different moonbeams. The cab driver, for whom time is money during rush hour, was intent on finding holes in the traffic. There was an occasional murmur from the back seat, but that was all. Esmeralda stared listlessly out the window and Dixie chewed on her lip. As for myself, a strange calm had settled over me, as sometimes happens before a storm breaks, or a gambler plunks down his last chip. I hated to think Esmeralda was mine.

I'll admit I had qualms of my own, right before leaving Dixie's, about stage-managing a production where the curtain speech was missing. I had considered calling Lieutenant Henry and having him meet me at the Watelys' apartment, but the consequences of that, at the time, were wholly unpredictable. I was still trying to cover my own hide; I had promised Dixie I'd protect Esmeralda's, up to a point still undefined; and, there was Ethel, silken skinned and drenched in Chanel. I still had mixed emotions about Ethel; I felt a certain, increasingly slim, obligation to keep it all in the family until I was 100 percent sure who was ultimately responsible for Denise's death. I'd call the cops *after* I spoke to Ethel. That was an internal compromise. I didn't want to come on like gangbusters: enter Darenow with an entourage of bluecoats, a couple of homicide dicks, a drag queen, and a sex-change who may, or may not, be a missing heiress, or heir. Hi, Ethel, we have a surprise for you.

The doorman at the Watelys' apartment wasn't happy to see us. He remembered me and I think he recognized Esmeralda, either from the police sketch that was in today's paper or from a previous visit. He eyed her and Dixie with curious contempt while he buzzed upstairs. I knew he wanted to spoil the party.

"Mr. Darenow—and two others with him," he barked into the intercom. I hoped the maid was on the other end and not Ethel. I admit I wanted to see Ethel's face when she first saw Esmeralda. I had a feeling that would tell me a lot. I planned to use that moment to judge my next move.

The elevator operator was surprised to see us, too. He nearly fell over himself closing the doors. He never asked which floor we were going to. He knew.

Dixie smiled and patted Esmeralda's arm.

I let the ladies out first when we arrived, then stepped forward and rang the bell. The elevator operator didn't close the doors. He stood there, staring.

Aurora Carrera answered the bell. Her expression went from apprehensive calm to shock when she saw Esmeralda. She looked over her shoulder nervously, but the great marble hall was empty.

"Hallo," Esmeralda said dully. Aurora's response was barely audible. They had obviously met before.

"Is Ethel here?" I asked.

Aurora nodded, dumbstruck. She continued to stare at Esmeralda and I thought I saw the faintest smile creep into her eyes. She was another born liar and I don't think her brush with the law had broken the habit. She stepped aside and let the three of us file into the apartment.

"You and I ought to have a talk sometime," I suggested. Aurora looked at me, glanced again at Esmeralda, and back to me.

"You don't need me," she said. She turned and started down the hall to the living room. She walked as if she was carrying a lot of weight on her shoulders.

The three of us trailed along after her.

I saw Ethel as she came out of the library. She saw us at the same time and stopped in her tracks.

Ethel's mouth opened but nothing came out.

Esmeralda broke the silence.

"Hallo," she said lazily.

"What is this?" Ethel said. Her eyes grew dark and angry. Her wrath was on me.

I walked a few feet down the hall and she met me halfway. The reservoir of calm I'd built up in the cab was now being tapped.

"Esmeralda wants to turn herself in," I said quietly. "As a material witness to the murders of Jaime and Denise." I was bluffing, of course; at that point I was still uncertain of what would happen when the sparks began to fly. Her eyes dimmed and flared again. It was the first and only time I saw Ethel show fear.

"I think we should talk before she goes to the police," I added quickly.

One quick breath was all it took for Ethel to regain her composure. She was a paragon of grace under pressure.

"Yes, of course," she replied. "Just you and I?"

"Just you and I," I affirmed.

"Wait a minute," Esmeralda said warily. She had edged down the hall, closer to us. There was a hint of panic in her voice. She had been led to believe I would help arrange her safe passage.

"It's all right," I told her. "You have my word nothing will happen to you."

Esmeralda looked skeptical. I ignored the look and told her to wait in the living room with Dixie. Dixie threw me a skeptical look of her own. I held up my hand and offered them my most sincerely reassuring look. Dixie took Esmeralda's hand and turned her around. She was easily distracted, like a child.

She looked up at the chandelier and smiled. She just needed a little more sedation.

"I'd like a drink," she said.

"Get her a drink," Ethel said curtly.

Aurora showed them the way to the living room and then went into the kitchen to get the drinks. I heard Dixie asking for a Diet Coke.

Ethel and I stood in the hall, in front of the little abstract painting full of innuendo and hidden meanings. All pastel surface and chaos underneath.

"Where did you find her?" Ethel asked.

"At the other one's apartment," I said. "The other one knew Denise." I felt slightly disloyal, referring to Dixie that way, but I wanted to keep my explanation simple. My relationships were tangled enough.

"Of course," Ethel said. "Your friend . . ."

"My late friend."

"Has she told you anything?"

"She says Bennie passed out the drugs—a smorgasbord—a little of this and that to appeal to everyone's taste. He had the Tuinal caps, the ones that killed them, the ones loaded with heroin and scopolamine . . ."

"Did she say why he did it?"

"She says she doesn't know. She says your brother told her some people wanted to kill both of them."

"Your girlfriend and Jaime?" she asked incredulously. She didn't believe it. Maybe she's innocent after all, I thought. That would be good.

"Jaime and Esmeralda," I said.

"Where did she get that idea?" She seemed genuinely puzzled.

She turned away and looked toward the living room. Aurora came back from the kitchen with a tray of drinks and more wary looks for Ethel and me.

"Let's go in the library," Ethel said. "She won't try anything, will she? I mean, she's a little wild. Is the other one . . ."

"She's a personal friend," I said.

If I had expected that to shock her, I was wrong. She nodded silently and went into the library. She went over and pressed the button to the bar.

"So, what else did Esmeralda say?" she asked, but not as nonchalantly as she wanted. She pulled out two glasses and a bottle of sherry and started to pour.

"She said you came and checked her out after her operation. She said you didn't approve of her affair with Edgar."

"Certainly not," she said unequivocally. "Would you?" She was keeping a very stiff upper lip. She filled one glass and was about to fill the other.

"Especially not if she was Jaime's twin," I said, underlining it slightly.

She looked at me in astonishment and continued pouring sherry into the second glass. It filled the glass and ran over the bar.

"How stupid of me!" she said angrily. She set the bottle down hard and used her hand to stem the tide of sherry from going on the floor.

I took my handerchief out and started moving toward her to help her mop up.

"Did you know?" I asked. I already knew the answer.

"Know what?" she asked peevishly. "Oh, don't bother cleaning up. Sit down!"

"That Esmeralda is Jaime's twin?"

It took a lot for me to say it, to goad her while the fear swam in her eyes.

"Oh, hogwash," she said. She handed me a glass of sherry. "That's absurd." She brushed it off; it only made her look worse.

"Is it true?" I said, putting my own glass back down on the bar without drinking.

"She told you that?" Ethel asked sharply.

"A neighbor who knew them from the time they were infants," I replied firmly. "She says she'll testify that she saw your father come to their house on numerous occasions. She wants Esmeralda to get a share of his estate."

I stood tall and got the words out, but I was ready to duck if the crystal started flying.

"Those goddamned parasites and their babies!" she snarled. Her jaw was clenched so tight the words came out slurred. She took a rather large swallow of sherry and then spat it violently back into the glass.

"Goddamn sediment!" she said.

She nearly tripped as she threw the sherry, glass and all, in the direction of the fireplace. The sherry flew all over the couch and rug and the glass bounced off the fireplace screen and broke on the hearth.

I flinched, but I stood my ground. Let her clean up the mess herself. I knew it was coming.

"Is it true?" I repeated. I emphasized each word so she couldn't ignore me.

Ethel's agile poise wasn't so easily disturbed.

"Oh, who knows?" she replied, as if it was some small matter. "Let her prove it. They all want a goddamn free lunch, don't they?"

She was revving up for a change of subject, maybe another attack on Latins in general. I cut her off before she started.

"You said you didn't want me to lie to you," I began. "But you're not telling me the truth. If you're protecting your brother, I can understand. I can even understand if you're protecting Metcalf and his operation. But I don't want to be lied to, by you of all people."

She still had a hold on me. Why? I remember standing there, holding my arms out for a reason I couldn't fathom. Was I asking her to come to me? Was I imploring her to come clean? It didn't matter. She shrank in horror at the gesture.

"Why don't you just leave us alone?" she hissed. "Why must you pry, and pry, and pry?" I was expecting another outburst, but she was merely shifting gears again.

"Oh, Max, darling . . ." She stepped toward me and put her arms around my neck. I pulled my hands close to my body and felt it contract and harden with revulsion. A chill swept me from head to toe. I positioned my hands lightly on her hips, at an angle signaling rejection, but I didn't move a muscle after that. I was in the spider woman's embrace. I stared straight ahead at the opposite wall, lost in the embroidered map of Cuba that some soldier's widow had woven for her father.

"Hold me," she whispered. "Be my friend. Listen to what I say. Let her go. She's suffered enough. Do the police know where she is?"

"They're on their way here," I lied, suddenly wishing I had called them. She dug her nails into my sleeve and then released them and glowered at me.

"You goddamn idiot!" She geysered the phrase and stormed out of the room.

I don't know where she was charging off to, but she never got there. She heard the front door chimes and wheeled around again.

"I won't let them in," Ethel said frantically. "This is a private matter. Stu has to take care of this for me. I don't know what to do. Oh, God, I wish I'd never met any of you!"

Aurora was already trotting down the marble hall to answer the door. She must have been in the living room with the girls. Or eavesdropping in the hall.

Ethel stood ramrod straight and snapped her fingers quickly three times. Strong, loud snaps. Ethel had lots of power at her fingertips, and plenty of practice commanding attention.

Aurora stopped, looked quizzically at Ethel, and waited for the next command.

Ethel waved her hands negatively and motioned for her to come down the hall.

"Don't open the door," she whispered. "Take those other people upstairs in the elevator and lock it behind you. I'll tell you what to do after."

Aurora looked at me. Was she expecting me to intercede?

"I doubt if it's the police," I said. "I haven't called them yet."

Ethel looked exasperated and started into the kitchen. I followed her. Another thin smile crept over Aurora's face as we breezed past. It amused her to see Ethel so rattled.

Ethel went to the kitchen intercom and called downstairs to the doorman.

"Who just came up?" she inquired lightly.

"Is this . . ." he started to say.

"Of course," she snapped. "Who came up?"

"Mr. Wately went up a minute ago and the others before him," the doorman replied in a perfectly flat Irish brogue. "The man from the newspaper . . . and the others."

He dropped "the others" into a space of their own with a trill of the "r."

"Thank you," Ethel said, clicking him off.

She turned and went into the hall. Aurora was there, waiting.

"Open the door," she said.

Edgar Wately stepped inside, saw me, and said nervously: "What's going on?"

"Nothing, darling," Ethel replied, shaking her head for emphasis. She told Aurora to get back to the living room.

"And don't let *anyone* leave," she added. "Scream if she bolts." "She" obviously was Esmeralda, but Edgar didn't know it yet.

"What's going on?" Edgar repeated. He looked at me and at his sister. "Who's here? Who's here?" he begged. His nose went up like a dog smelling fire.

"Esmeralda," Aurora trilled wickedly.

Edgar's face fell into permanent despair. The lights had gone out and the cage door had just slammed shut.

He looked meekly at his sister.

"Come into the library," Ethel said firmly. She was in charge again, but Edgar was too dumbfounded even to obey anymore.

"Esmeralda?" he said. "Where?"

He looked toward the living room, but Ethel tugged at his sleeve.

"Go to the library, Edgar," she ordered.

He did as he was told. I followed him. He looked twice at me, but he kept marching.

I knew I could count on Ethel to keep him in line and I knew I could count on Dixie and Aurora to keep Esmeralda entertained.

I'm afraid," Ethel glibly informed her brother, "that Max isn't satisfied with Stu Metcalf's explanation."

Edgar now resembled a dog caught peeing on the rug because its owner had forgotten to put papers down. He still hoped to escape a scolding.

"Well," he said carefully, "it's your problem, isn't it?"

She dismissed his reply with a fluttering hand.

"Max," she said, "why don't you tell my brother what you just told me?"

"Let me ask him something first," I said. "What was he doing at the Tampa racetrack early the other morning? When he dropped off four bags and left with one."

I hadn't told Ethel about it. It was a dirty trick.

"Are you allowing this?" Edgar fumed, looking desperately at his sister.

Ethel blushed to the roots of her coiffure, smiled, and bit her lip. Was she enjoying this? Her brother found the question annoying, but it didn't stop him from going over to the bar, finding a bottle of scotch, and pouring himself a neat double. No water, no ice.

"You're not answering my question," I said.

"I have no intention of answering it," he huffed. He took a drink and let it linger in his mouth.

"Please, darling," Ethel said. "Tell Max you were helping Stu run the Torres brothers. That's all he wants to know. We'll forgive your dalliance with Esmeralda." She was her old self again.

"Hah!" said Edgar, seemingly engrossed in his scotch.

It was a transparent gesture of avoidance. His brain was going a mile a minute to catch up with what was going down. His concentration, if that's what screwed his brow into a knot, was on his sister, not me or the single malt. The trouble with nailing bastards like Wately to the wall was the confident impunity they could wave like the old school tie, even when that's all they had left. Accusations from the hoi polloi were cheap cloth.

"When did you find out Esmeralda was Jaime's twin?" I said. "Before or after Stu Metcalf started cleaning up your act?"

"Ask big sister," he said lightly. But it made him think. He turned and looked at me, contritely. "Everything changed when I found out Esmeralda was part and parcel"—he shifted into a more sarcastic, confident tone before he made his point—"*of the inheritance.*

"So far as Stu is concerned," he said with finality, "he's Ethel's friend, not mine. She's in the driver's seat now, ask her."

He downed the scotch without savoring it and refilled his glass. Edgar was going to get loaded again. He looked at me and sneered.

"It's wonderful how my sister keeps adding to her stable," he added flippantly as he poured another double. "I've known plenty of women and believe me, there's none like her."

"And there never will be," Ethel said, her body stirring into place like a Porsche revving up.

"I'm too smart for them, Max," she said, shifting her frame into a more comfortable pose. She moved imperceptibly, but her moves were studied and exact.

"I've had to compensate and conceal and cover up all my life for men. They'll never learn." She crossed her arms on her chest and glared at little brother.

I heard a parade of high heels coming down the hall and Dixie telling Esmeralda to "be nice or they'll think you're crazy." Edgar heard them, too.

"My sister wants everything her way or not at all," he said. "Isn't that right, Ethel?"

"Edgar, say hello to Esmeralda," she said dismissively.

The high-heeled delegation milled outside the door. Aurora stood guard but Esmeralda slid past her. Her glamour paled as she rushed to Edgar's side. They were more than friends.

"Poor butterfly," Edgar said.

Esmeralda hesitated, smiled, burst into tears, and buried her face in his shoulder.

"Max wants her to testify before a grand jury, Edgar," Ethel said, raising her voice to be heard over Esmeralda's sobs. "He thinks she can fix the blame on the Torres men."

Edgar looked surprised, but only mildly surprised. He smiled sardonically and told Esme not to cry.

"Gladly," he said. "We'll all testify. I'll call the police now." He smiled into Esmeralda's eyes and looked benignly at me.

"She'll be safe in their hands, Darenow?" he asked soberly.

I was about to reply to him, but Ethel cut me off.

"She'll make a statement and then Stu is going to have to move her to a safe house," she said testily. "Where have you been?"

"I've been trying to save my father's bank," he said bitterly.

"Well, it's saved," his sister said curtly. "So say good-bye—for a while, that's all—you'll have plenty of time later to cuddle or whatever you do. Take her into your office, please, and explain to her what's going on."

Be glad she's not talking to you, Darenow. She's a holy terror.

"I don't know *anything!*" Esmeralda cried. "I don't! I swear! Edgar, tell her!"

Edgar glowered at his sister. "Why don't *you* brief her, Ethel? That way she'll get the real story and you won't have to bother Stu or Owen Reed again," he said contemptuously. He looked at me with a strange glint in his eye and then back at Ethel. "Unless you've made some arrangement with the press that I'm not aware of," he added drolly.

Ethel opened her mouth haughtily but nothing came out. Esmeralda looked at Edgar with dumb admiration. She hadn't the faintest idea of what he was talking about, but she saw him as her husband and she was proud of him. Edgar took her hand and started out of the room.

"Wait a minute," I began nervously. "We're not through."

"Let him say good-bye to his little creation," Ethel said sourly.

Edgar paused and looked scornfully at me and his sister.

"My creation?" he asked. "Really? I take the blame then?"

Ethel waved him away and I let her. She told Aurora to get Dixie another drink and go back to the living room. Edgar rubbed the back of Esme's neck and led her out of the room.

Dixie gave me a anxious look before following Aurora down the hall.

"I know you think it's all Stu Metcalf's fault," Ethel said to me when her brother left the room. She employed her cocktail party voice. "You do, don't you?"

I bobbed my head in confirmation.

"He's not to blame, Max." She nodded with some conviction. She was being candidly charming. I had to admire Ethel, and that was my problem. She could get away with murder.

"The Torres brothers were terrible people. They played both sides. So did Rosa. Greedy and ungrateful is what they were," she said, crossing to me and then pausing before she continued, looking straight into my eyes.

"Edgar and Esmeralda, of course, are another story," she stated smoothly. "*I* don't know how to handle it. It won't serve any purpose creating a scandal, will it?"

She didn't bat an eyelash. Nor did I.

"What did Rosa tell you the night that Bennie and Ralph came to visit your house, right before they killed Jaime and Denise?"

Her brow knitted slowly, almost imperceptibly, and then she ran her eyebrows up full mast and ran her tongue over her lips as if she was entering a roomful of people. I'd seen her do it before.

"Who told you that?" she asked deftly. "Aurora?"

"Yes," I lied. Her eyes were drilling into mine with the same mesmerizing gaze I remembered from the night she took me into her bedroom.

"Rosa complained," Ethel smiled thinly. "She threatened me. She said she'd . . ." Her smile turned to a frown. "Oh, I don't know . . . something about exposing Edgar." She dismissed the recollection with an agitated wave of her hand and moved over toward the bar.

"Did she ask you for money?" I asked gently. I wanted her to think I was still on her side.

She picked up the bottle of sherry and very carefully poured herself a drink so the sediment wouldn't contaminate it.

"What do *you* think?" she asked.

"I wasn't there," I replied sagely.

"That started it all," she sighed. "After that I don't know what happened." She had recovered nicely and thought she was in control again.

"What did Rosa say? What were her demands?" I persisted.

Ethel's hands rose like birds in flight. She was waving me off. "No demands . . . I mean . . . they were reasonable. I tried to buy her off."

She swallowed some sherry but it didn't seem to please her. She thrust out her right leg and looked at it. She wanted to see something that pleased her. She had gorgeous legs.

I wasn't giving her an inch.

"When did you find out Esmeralda and Jaime were twins?" I asked.

Her eyes wandered around the room before they came to rest on mine.

"This is getting us nowhere," she said with a halfhearted twinkle. "You do realize that?"

"When did you discover they were twins?" I said deliberately. My lips outlined every word.

"Ages ago," she said with a shake of her head. "But I did *not* know Edgar was involved." She came down hard on her words, too, and then bit her lip and came toward me.

"Oh, Max, I need you now," she said, "I wish they weren't here. I wish . . ."

Run, Darenow, run.

"This is crazy, Ethel," I said. "You and your brother are both crazy. He accuses you of wanting it your way, but *he's* having it both ways. He was doing Metcalf a favor by fronting for the Torres brothers and letting them pose as secret agents, but at the same time, he was using them to raise money to stop you and Melendez from taking over the bank."

"You're right, Max. So right I could cry. Hold me." She balled her hands into fists and pulled them toward her.

Her face looked as soft as silk. She wore no jewelry and very little makeup. It would have been out of place with the "Pieta" look that swelled in her eyes.

Give me a break, I thought.

"Edgar's going to have to face a grand jury," I said. "They'll want to know why Bennie and Ralph had him so neatly tied. And they'll want to know why he was still laundering money at the track after they were dead and gone. Is Metcalf going to cover all that?"

She flushed, but it wasn't the flush of passion. It was embarrassment. It was her scandal, not mine. Let her crowd handle it. *Her crowd.*

"Will you allow Stu Metcalf to hide our secrets?" she stage-whispered. "Will you do that much, please?" She was Lady Macbeth now. She was mad, as in crazy.

"If Esmeralda testifies and doesn't get hurt," I said gently. "If she's entitled to share in your father's estate and she gets her share, I won't stand in your way."

I looked straight at Ethel.

"Have you ever seen your father's will?" I asked.

Ethel looked at me quickly and drew away.

"No," she said. "Why?" It was a little shrill.

"Because I've heard that Jaime was left something. If Esmeralda's his twin, she ought to get something, too. Your brother seems to think so."

She thought about it, but not for long.

"She'll get something," Ethel said.

I thought about what Lieutenant Henry had said: Sometimes it's enough to know who did it, without the satisfaction of a conviction.

"If your brother testifies and tells *me* the truth, I'll let it all fade away."

Darenow! It was my conscience talking: *Your brains are in your prick! You're not finished. It's not over till it's over.*

"I'll make him tell the truth," she said.

I heard footsteps in the hall. The click-clack of Esme's cowgirl boots and Edgar's padding tread. They were coming back from his office.

Edgar entered the room while Esme stood in the doorway, looking pleasantly calm.

He presented Ethel with a sheet of white paper written on in longhand. She took it and read every word.

"You and my brother are on the same wavelength, it seems," she said, handing it over to me when she was done.

It was a waiver, written in legalese, headed as if it was a letter from Ethel and addressed "To Whom It May Concern."

It called for "Ethel Simpson Wately" to promise she wouldn't *"interfere or in any way hinder or prevent Esmeralda Sanchez (née/AKA Jesus LaMer) from exercising claims against the estate of her father, Avery Wately."*

It carried a pledge, to be signed by Ethel, that she would *"provide whatever means necessary, legal and otherwise, to see that said Esmeralda is adequately provided for during any term of litigation, if such a term exists, otherwise to see that Esmeralda receives all due proceeds and benefits stipulated in her natural father's will."*

"I think you're supposed to witness that, Max," Ethel said. "Isn't that the deal?"

I gave Edgar one of Metcalf's hard looks and tried holding it as I addressed Ethel.

"Why don't you two tell me, just me and no one else, exactly what happened and why it all happened," I asked.

Neither one said a word. Edgar motioned for Esme to come into the room, but she wasn't budging. She kept her eye on Ethel. So did I.

Ethel pursed her lips and swept a nonexistent wisp of hair from her flawless brow.

"Just the three of us," I said. "Do you mind?"

I was talking to Edgar but Ethel answered.

"That would be better," she agreed. "That would be wise."

Edgar went to the door and whispered to Esmeralda, who clicked away in the direction of the living room with a lighter tread. She probably didn't want to scuff the floor in case she owned a piece of it.

Edgar stepped back inside and closed the door until only a crack was left open. He stared at his sister.

Domestic strife, like war, isn't good for children and other living things, I thought. Time to lighten the mood.

"Don't everyone talk at once," I said. Ethel chimed right in.

"Edgar may have unwittingly helped Bennie Torres swindle some money from the bank, Max, because Bennie told him certain accounts were part of Stu's operation," Ethel said. "We're not sure how much is involved yet. It's a mess that could make all of us look like complete fools."

Edgar's eyes drifted back and forth between Ethel and me. He was wrestling with a lot of demons.

"Let's hear your side," I said.

"He doesn't have a side," Ethel interjected. "Let him go. You've terrified him. He's been through enough. He is my brother."

"That might be enough for you," I said, "but it's not enough for me. I want him to tell me the truth—for my own benefit, not for the newspaper."

I caught myself before I included a grand jury in that gesture and went over to stand alongside Ethel in expectation of hearing her brother's confession. I had the idea somehow that would cement our relationship—the one that hung in the balance between Ethel and me.

Edgar looked at me blankly.

"I have nothing more to say. Let her sign the waiver."

His eyes dimmed like the taillights of a vehicle you notice just before they fade away into the black of night.

"Sign the waiver," he said to Ethel. "And let him bear witness," he said to me.

Ethel grinned and shook her head. I couldn't tell if it was a yes or a no.

"Sign it," Edgar said.

Ethel asked for a pen. I gave her mine. She balanced it on the flat of her hand for a moment, then put the document on the top of the bar, signed it quickly, and moved her finger to the line where I was to sign, returning my pen. I signed, dated it, and held it out toward Edgar.

"What are you going to tell the cops?" I asked him.

"That I was doing a favor for my government and that I was a fool to trust anybody." He smiled benignly.

I still wasn't sure I believed him.

"Why did Bennie and Ralph kill Jaime?" I asked. I was speaking to Edgar, but my eyes darted in Ethel's direction. It was a question I'd asked her before.

Edgar refused to answer and I didn't press him. He dejectedly shook his head, folded the piece of paper in half, and went silently into the living room. He was downed, a beaten man; I had no intention of kicking him. Let the cops handle him.

Ethel looked worried, excused herself abruptly, and went after him. She caught him in the hall, no doubt in front of the little abstract painting, the one with the pastel veneer and the violent undertones. I heard them talking but I could only hear Edgar's reassuring voice.

I sat on the back of the couch and thought about allowing myself a swallow of sherry but decided against it. I felt serene and secure in my surroundings. I still admired the way Ethel Wately handled herself, but I was thinking of Denise. Dixie was right; Mary Collins was right: Denise wouldn't want any part of this horseshit. Ethel came back and stood outside the door, her arms crossed on her chest, her eyes trained on the end of the hall.

I stayed put and waited, too. It seemed like a long time before Edgar returned, his step a bit softer down the hall. Ethel said something about Stu Metcalf as Edgar walked on by; he was heading back to his office.

Ethel grabbed his sleeve. He slapped her away.

I moved from the couch toward the door. Ethel ignored me and followed her brother. I stepped into the hall and watched her. She disappeared into her brother's office and closed the door. I walked slowly down the hall and stopped when the door flew open.

Ethel steamed out.

"Call the police," she said. "Edgar's acting stupid."

We started into the library and I stepped aside, expecting her to point me to a phone, when I heard the shot. It rang up and down the hall before it faded away. A single pistol shot.

Ethel froze. She didn't flinch or show any sign of emotion.

I flinched. I'd heard enough guns going off to last me several lifetimes by now. I wished the cops were here, but it was way too late for that.

"Don't go," Ethel said. "He's bluffing."

I had no intentions of moving.

I heard Esmeralda's voice as she came charging down the hall, trailed by Dixie and Aurora.

"Dixie!" I shouted. "Come in here!"

Dixie stopped and looked confused. Esmeralda lunged past Ethel and headed for the office.

"Stop her!" Ethel yelled.

"Esmeralda!" I shouted her name, but she had already gone into Wately's office.

Dixie and I didn't budge until we heard the scream, a keening wail that reverberated through the house before decaying into a hysterical sob. That's when I ventured down the hall, with Dixie at my elbow. I kept going despite myself. We heard Esmeralda moaning and quickened our pace.

I shoved Dixie behind me, dropped into a crouch, and peeked cautiously around the corner from a low angle. You get to be a combat veteran by peeking around corners from low angles, not by sticking your neck out.

Esmeralda was standing in back of her former husband and brother, gently stroking his hair. Edgar was seated in his desk chair, his arms hanging limply at his side, his jaw tilted up to the ceiling. He looked bewildered and very dead. A blue .32 caliber revolver had fallen from his hand to the floor. Esmeralda's hands were covered with the blood, which ran from Edgar's ears, his eyes, and his mouth.

I took his wrist and felt for his pulse. There was none. I picked up the desk phone, dialed 911, and told the police operator a man had been shot and to send someone over right away. I gave her the victim's name and address and told her to notify Deputy Commissioner McGovern's office as well. I gave her my name and the number on the dial plate. She asked if the victim was seriously injured.

"He's dead," I replied.

"A car is responding," she said. I thanked her and hung up.

In the middle of the desk was a note, in Wately's hand, headed "Dear Sister." I wondered if he meant Esme or Ethel? I told Esmeralda not to touch anything and tried to pry her away from his side, but she wouldn't have it. She had wailed only the one time; now she just cried soft tears that ran down her new face. It was a pale, washed-out face, but it was a real face, not a mask. Esme's facade had been blown and no amount of makeup would ever restore it. She didn't resemble the Watelys anymore, any more than she did the Esmeralda I had known. She looked like a woman, but one I hadn't met before. I had the strange feeling that she looked like Jesus LaMer's mother, Avery Wately's last mistress.

Dixie and Aurora tiptoed into the room. Dixie went straight to Esmeralda and held her while she wept. I told them not to touch anything.

I pulled out my notepad and made a quick shorthand copy of the suicide note while Aurora stood, icy calm and stone-faced, her eyes on me. I took enough time to be fairly accurate.

Ethel was standing in the door to the library, her hands calmly folded in front of her. She shook her head slowly from side to side.

"He's dead, isn't he?" she said.

"He's dead."

"Are you satisfied?" she asked evenly.

I had no answer for her.

"He left a note," I said.

She hesitated and then her eyes scanned the hall. A lot of things clicked behind those eyes. She finally set her shoulders, stepped off smartly, walked into the office, picked up the note, glanced at it, turned, and left the room. She hardly glanced at her brother's body.

She walked down the hall, crossed the marble foyer, and started up the stairs to the second floor. I went after her.

"I'd rather you stayed down here," I said, just loud enough so she'd hear me.

She kept going.

She turned around when she reached the first landing, facing me with "all the calm dignity of blameless womanhood." She very politely asked me to let her know when the police arrived.

I didn't want to follow her upstairs, but I didn't want her blowing her brains out either. I wasn't sure there were no more guns in the house.

I started up to the landing, but she threw up her palm in an imperious gesture, the suicide note rattling in her other hand. She came down two steps to meet me and looked over my shoulder. Aurora was standing at the foot of the stairs, waiting for the next command. Ethel fixed her eyes on me.

"I hope this satisfies your thirst for vengeance," she said in a voice that rang like a cello. Her tone was mellow, almost congratulatory. She thrust her chin out and delivered the next line in a whisper.

"Now leave me alone or I'll have Aurora tell the grand jury who Bennie

Torres was entertaining in one of his drug dens minutes before he died. I have no intentions of taking my life. I have to notify the State Department."

She turned and went upstairs.

I let her go. She marched.

I no longer had any doubts about which "bitch" Pepe Cruz was trying to coax to the telephone that night at Manolo's. Ethel. She, and only she, knew the whole story. She knew I was there; so did Aurora and Rosa. Ethel had played me for a fool from the start, realizing I could never lay down the winning card because *she* was the winning card, the key to the truth—and she'd never reveal it.

There was no way to prove Ethel's involvement. The cops understood that. If I admitted I was there when Manolo, Pepe, and Bennie died, it still wouldn't prove anything; it wouldn't prove Ethel's guilt.

Forget it, chump. You were a sucker for intelligent eyes, firm thighs, and a well-turned ankle.

Ethel and I were in perpetual check.

37

"Mrs. Watelv!"

Aurora cried out and ran past me up the stairs to join her mistress. I let her go, too. It would have been nice to know how both of them felt about my role in the Torres brothers' tragic demise, but Big Bold Darenow didn't think of grabbing her in time. It had occurred to me; I just didn't care. What would I have done, grabbed Ethel's wrist and threatened her life if she said anything? Who knows exactly what she knew? If either of them wanted to hurt me, I'd have been sitting in the Tombs by now. I'd had other threats thrown at me in the past week and I was still managing to tread water. The two of them went into Ethel's bedroom. The door slammed and I heard the lock snap. That ended the chess game. My thoughts turned to the suicide note.

I drifted back to Edgar's office and sat on a couch alongside Dixie and Esmeralda. Dixie was rocking Esmeralda in her arms. Esme babbled and moaned: "She's gonna hate me for this. She blame me. She gonna kill me next. You'll see. You'll see. She hated me. She hated me."

"Nobody's going to hurt you," Dixie said. "You're gonna stay with me. We'll take care of you. Don't worry."

We? I never bothered to ask Dixie what she meant by that. I went over my shorthand notes and tried to make something out of them. I came up with this:

Dear Sister,

I hope this atones for Daddy's sins. I regret the inconvenience but I'm sure you'll handle it perfectly. Thank Metcalf and Reed for their help.

This might satisfy Jaime's mother. Watch out, Wonder Woman, or you're next. Slay no more . . . ?

Daddy couldn't have asked for a better Son than you, Peaches. I was doomed when I saw our little brother in skirts. Pity the natives can't stand paradise. Don't marry—draws flies.

I never hurt a fly. I'm not that kind of man. Good night. If hell exists, we'll meet again. Don't touch Esme! SHE'S CURSED!!!

There was no signature.

My translation was close enough to what he had written. I hoped I'd never have to use it, but I wasn't taking any chances. I didn't like reading other people's mail, but men don't usually lie when they know they're going to die. What did Shakespeare say: "Murder has no tongue, but it doth speak loud?" I ripped the notes from the pad, folded them, and slipped them behind my pocket handkerchief. I put the pad into an inside pocket and moved around the room.

"Where's the waiver?" I asked Esme. "The piece of paper Edgar gave you?"

Dixie had it, tucked in her bodice. She patted her chest and gave me a no-nonsense look. I should have known.

"Slay no more. . . . Don't touch Esme!" That was rich. That was wild. Anyone who could have shed some light on what had happened to Denise was dropping like flies. Except Ethel and Aurora. And they'd never talk, except to lie.

I went over to the desk and was about to dial police headquarters again when the phone rang. I thought it might be the cops so I answered it. I expected Ethel to pick up an extension somewhere but, as it turned out, there was no extension. It was Wately's private line, listed, I later found out, in the bank's name. A man came on the line. He was all cop from the first question.

"Mr. Darenow?"

"Yes."

"Lieutenant Curtis, Police Operations. Are you at the same address you gave the emergency operator?"

I repeated the address of Wately's apartment.

"All right, sir. A patrol car is on its way. Did you request an ambulance?"

"The man's dead," I said.

"Are you a doctor, sir?"

"I'm a reporter," I said. "I happened to be here on another matter when the man shot himself. He was alone when it happened. I heard the shot."

"You asked for Chief McGovern. You know the chief?"

"Only too well," I said. "He's going to want to know I'm here. Also Inspector Gabe Rossetti. Tell them I'm here with Esmeralda Sanchez and Mrs. Ethel Wately, whose brother just committed suicide. You got all that?"

"Esmeralda Sanchez and Ethel Wately. And your name again, sir?"

"Darenow," I said. "I work for the *Graphic*. Can you possibly connect me with Lieutenant Clarence Henry in Major Crimes?"

"Let me put you through to Chief McGovern's office first. I'll ring Rossetti in the meantime and give him your message. You're not going anywhere, are you?"

"No," I said.

"What's the victim's name?"

I almost asked which one.

"Edgar Wately."

"Hang on. I'll connect you with the chief."

Maude answered The Cardinal's phone. He had left for the day. I told her briefly what had happened and asked her to tell her boss to either call or meet me at the Wately apartment. "Poor thing," she tsked. I'm sure she meant Wately, not me.

I was about to hang up and try Lieutenant Henry when Lieutenant Curtis snapped back on the line.

"Hang on, sir, I'm going to put you through to Lieutenant Henry now. We've alerted Rossetti's squad. Just want you to know."

I was talking to Henry when the doorbell rang. I told him to hang on while I answered it. He told me to hang up, he was on his way over.

Two bluecoats and a sergeant were the first to respond. The elevator operator stood gaping in the doorway until one of the blues told him to get his ass back downstairs.

"We're expecting more company," the uniformed man said.

I told the sergeant where the body was and suggested that he might also want to have someone pay a call on Mrs. Wately.

"Where is *she?*" the sergeant asked.

"First closed door on the left, upstairs," I said. "I believe it's locked. She probably wants you to knock first."

The sergeant gave me a dirty look and sent one of the uniformed men up.

"I think there are more guns on the premises," I said.

The uniformed man stopped on the fourth step.

"Really?" the sergeant said. "Is that so?" The two of them exchanged glances.

"Might the sister have a gun?" the sergeant asked.

"Very slight chance," I said.

"Really?" he said.

"She might be a little upset. I'm just telling you."

"Is she psycho?" the sergeant said.

"I don't think so," I said, "but the whole family is a little strange."

I'd rather be safe than sorry. I was having second thoughts about Ethel.

The two cops pulled their guns. The sergeant went to the first landing and covered his partner while he knocked at the upstairs door.

I remembered the room well. It was the room where Darenow had lost his virginity—yet again. The bluecoat who knocked was very relaxed. He held his gun at his side.

"Police," he said.

The sergeant trained his gun on the door. Ethel opened it and stepped into the hall, the perfect hostess. The sergeant quietly slipped his gun into his holster and cleared his throat.

"Hello, gentlemen," Ethel said. "This is my secretary, Miss Carrera." Her tone was appropriately grave.

Aurora stepped into the hall. I joined the sergeant on the landing.

"Where's the body, downstairs?" he said under his breath.

I nodded.

"Can you come downstairs, ma'm?" the sergeant requested.

Ethel took a deep breath, wet her lips, and held out her arm to Aurora. Aurora took her elbow and guided her downstairs. Either Ethel had applied some makeup or she hadn't cried yet. She stared straight ahead, avoiding my eyes. She looked into the sergeant's eyes when she reached the landing, and her lower lip started to quiver. The tears came at exactly the right moment. Two more blues were stepping off the elevator with a paramedic and an ambulance doctor, a skinny white kid who looked about thirteen except he was going bald. I thought he was going to swoon when he saw Ethel. So did the cop on the door.

"Easy, doc," he cracked.

I love it the way cops move through the carnage as if they were watching reruns.

Brava, Ethel, brava. Another perfect entrance.

The house started to fill up with bluecoats, who were soon joined by a pair of detectives from the precinct, including a woman detective who looked like she was the doctor's younger sister. I said nothing about the suicide note. I was back on autopilot, keeping my own counsel. After all, I told myself, I'm not a cop.

At, I believe, Ethel's specific request, Edgar's office room was cleared of all except the police, the "immediate family," and the body.

Dixie and I drifted into the library, where two bluecoats were admiring the decor. I walked over and picked up my sherry. My mouth was very dry.

"That yours?" one of the cops asked.

I nodded in the affirmative and took a swallow.

"You live here?" he asked.

"Just visiting," I said. "We both were."

I used the past tense because I had a hunch visiting hours were over and I had worn out my welcome.

"What's your name?" the cop asked. He was bucking for detective.

I showed him my press shield. He took it from my hand and passed it to the other cop, who muttered something unintelligible and handed it back.

"Who lives here?" the first cop asked.

"Mrs. Wately."

"Was that the husband?" He jerked his head toward the library.

"The brother."

"Didn't they have an overdose here the other day?"

"That's right."

"It broke him up, huh?" the cop said.

"Caved him right in," I said.

There was plenty of traffic in the hall for the next couple of hours. The medics left and an inspector of patrol arrived. He had lots of brass stars on his shoulders and plenty of braid on his hat. He conferred with the sergeant, then with Ethel and the sergeant, then with a couple of blues. He took a look at the body and left, eyeing me but not saying anything.

Lieutenant Henry arrived with Detective Gonzalez, but it was a long time before they got to me. Henry conferred with the sergeant and then with the sergeant and Ethel, and then he took Esmeralda into the kitchen and shut the door. Gonzalez went in with them.

Gonzalez, whom I'd met briefly at Lieutenant Henry's apartment, came out and took statements from Dixie and myself. Henry finished with Esmeralda and sent her into the living room with the woman detective. I saw Ethel and the sergeant huddling in the hall. I wondered where Metcalf was. And Owen Reed.

Neither of them showed, except for a surrogate presence. Reed sent the little dork who had lunched with us at The Bull and Bear. He arrived with a couple of FBI agents in tow. They talked to Henry and the sergeant in the kitchen. Metcalf sent a State Department "duty officer," who arrived with another man. They also went into the kitchen.

The party was in the kitchen and I was in the library.

When Gabe Rossetti arrived alone, he spotted me and came over to say hello. He walked me to the end of the library, to the alcove near the embroidered map of Cuba.

"Did you see the suicide note?" he asked.

I couldn't decide whether it was a cop question or a question question. If it was a cop question, it meant Ethel had either destroyed the note or hidden it. If I said I hadn't seen it and they had the note, everything else I had said would be cast into doubt. If the note bothered Ethel half as much as it was bothering me, she might have destroyed it. On the other hand, Aurora saw me taking notes on it and Esmeralda might also have read it through her tears. If she could read.

I rolled the dice and answered in the affirmative. I thought I knew what he was getting at.

"The line about 'slay no more'?" I asked.

"What do you make of it?" Rossetti asked. "Aside from the fact he was crazy."

"I don't know," I said.

"No ideas, huh?"

"Oh," I said, "I have some ideas."

We both nodded thoughtfully. There are times when that's all men can do.

"There's no reason to hold you up here," he said. "You gonna be home later on?"

"I might have to go back to the office," I said. "Write an obituary."

"Owen Reed is coming up from Washington tomorrow afternoon with this Metcalf guy," Rossetti said, "for a powwow with The Cardinal and myself. Reed's blaming the Torres brothers for most of the murders. He plans to have Metcalf go before the grand jury and swear they were double agents. McGovern doesn't believe a word of it. I'd like you to be there, too, but I'd like to talk to you before that. Can you do it?"

"Sure," I said without enthusiasm. I wasn't at all happy at the thought of seeing Metcalf or Reed. The police department was going to take on the State Department, with me as the soccer ball. Stuck in the middle again. Oh, well, I thought, the burden of responsibility. Isn't that what journalism is all about?

"Call my office before you leave the paper," he said. "They'll know how to reach me. I'll meet you someplace, OK?"

I told him I was looking forward to it, which was a lie. I asked him what they planned to do with Esmeralda.

"Lieutenant Henry wants to book her on suspicion of murder," he said.

"What!"

"Relax," he said, "we need an excuse to bring her downtown now, tonight, just to get her out of here. The charge won't stick, but it gives us a chance to quiz her. The Wately dame will spring her tonight anyway unless I'm wrong. We're waiting for her lawyers to arrive."

"What about Dixie Cupps?"

I was concerned about Dixie's getting into trouble for harboring Esmeralda. I was prepared, at that moment, to take the rap for Dixie and for Charlie, The Big Guy. What the hell, I thought, it would make a good story: STAR REPORTER, FEARING COVER-UP, KIDNAPS WITNESS. I needn't have worried. The law shines in a different light when you're walking after midnight.

"What about her?" Rossetti deadpanned. "She used to run with a mob guy called Tony Piccolo. She was his alibi the night Artie Katzenmeyer was shot. Remember Artie?"

I knew what he was getting at. Artie Katzenmeyer was known as "the porn king." He owned a chain of hard-core peep shows in Times Square and produced most of the films himself. Labor came cheap on Forty Deuce so Artie recruited an army of drifters and decided to handle his own protection. One of the Italian dons didn't like that arrangement. Tradition dies hard, if it dies at all. *Dixie was in the alibi business.* And Rossetti knew it. How wonderfully convincing, to cover a crime with a mere indiscretion. Takes the mind off the real problem. Rossetti was deliberately looking the other way.

"Don't worry about Mrs. Cupps," Rossetti quipped. "She can handle herself." He said good-bye and told me I could leave anytime.

I went around the apartment looking for Dixie and Ethel. It was only proper to say good-bye to the hostess, or, in this case, hostesses. If Ethel wanted to pin me to the scene of a homicide, let her. I'd deal with that when I had to. Innocence is a great strength. I found Dixie first. She was in the kitchen, making tea for Esmeralda and coffee for the cops. Dixie was in her glory. She told me she was going downtown with Esmeralda in case she needed a friend other than Mrs. Wately and her lawyers. Dixie said she planned to let Esmeralda stay at her house until other arrangements were made.

I had told her I just wanted to thank her for everything and was about to leave when she asked me to follow her into the butler's pantry to get some sugar. She wanted to see me alone.

"Esmeralda thinks we're on her side, Max. She won't implicate you, so don't worry about it. She's had it. She thinks Ethel tried to kill her."

"Is that so?" I said sardonically. I was far past the point of being nonplussed.

"Esmeralda and Aurora had a little chat," Dixie continued, finding the sugar and rattling the canister to see if there was anything in it. "The air was rather heavy. Something about Bennie and Ralph being wrapped around the blonde's finger."

I didn't have to ask who the blonde was. Dixie was referring to Ethel. It wasn't something to hang a case on, but it was something.

"Is Esmeralda going to tell that to the cops?" I said.

Dixie put the sugar down and flashed her most vivid camp pose, all raised shoulders and fluttering lashes. She looked me straight in the eye.

"Of course, darling. Why wouldn't she?"

I went to find Ethel and ran into Aurora in the hall. Aurora was bringing Edgar's gold watch upstairs. It had belonged to their father. Ethel was retrieving the heirlooms.

"What do you have to tell me?" I asked. It was a parting shot in the dark.

"Nothing," she said.

"Nothing?"

I didn't believe that and I told her so.

"What were you and Esmeralda talking about?" I persisted. "She's blaming your—" I couldn't find the word— "mistress . . ."

"We were talking about nothing," Aurora snapped. "I feel sorry for her."

"Who?" I asked.

She smiled nervously. "I wanted to thank you for being nice . . . to Esmeralda."

"What about Mrs. Wately?"

"Mrs. Wately is waiting for me," she said, turning away.

Give it up, I thought. You don't need any of these people. You have a story, at least an obituary. Go home and write it.

I told her to give Mrs. Wately my regards and to tell her I was sorry. Aurora nodded sympathetically and went upstairs.

I got my coat and went home.

38

It was ten o'clock when I got home and called the city desk to tell them Edgar Wately had committed suicide. I didn't tell them how I knew. I just told them I was putting together a story for tomorrow's paper. I said I still wasn't feeling well and that I'd write it at home and phone it in to a rewrite man when I was finished.

I sketched out the sorry details of Edgar's life and death, leaving out most of what really counted. I said, "The police believe he was despondent over the recent deaths of his chief loan officer and his sister's ward, who had died of a suspicious overdose." Edgar's story didn't seem so important anymore; Ethel's did.

Hurley thought the obit was *too* brief, so I told him I'd gladly sketch in the Wately family history, starting with Avery Wately's stint as paymaster for the Bay of Pigs and his dead son's ties to Bennie and Ralph Torres. Hurley backed off and said he would run it by the publisher and if the publisher wanted to go the distance he'd say so. I had a hunch my brief obit was going to be judged sufficient to the task of keeping our readers titillated and the boys in the executive suite sweet.

I called Gabe Rossetti's office. He called back a minute later and agreed to meet me at my place in ten minutes.

I made myself a cup of coffee and never drank it. I downed a bottle of beer instead and turned the radio on. I listened to an all-night jazz program, lots of sad be-bop doodling and brush strokes on the snare drums. It fit my mood.

Rossetti arrived on time and accepted my offer of a beer. He stayed just long enough to remind me of what a fool I had been for believing Ethel Wately sincerely wanted my friendship.

Rossetti said Esmeralda told him and Lieutenant Henry that she thought Ethel Wately had paid Bennie to kill her *and* her twin brother. She did not admit giving any drugs to Denise. She blamed Jaime for that. Esmeralda said Ethel wanted her and Jaime killed because she was ashamed of them, wanted to deprive them of their inheritance and punish her brother Edgar at the same time.

Rossetti asked me what I thought about it.

I told him Esmeralda had mentioned something similar to Dixie and suggested Aurora might be able to substantiate Esme's claim by linking Ethel to Bennie and Ralph.

"Aurora's the key," I said wearily. "She was there the night Bennie and Ralph came to visit."

I was spinning my wheels but I couldn't admit it. Rossetti knew Aurora was there. What he didn't know, and what I couldn't tell him, was that Rosa, Aurora, or possibly Ethel herself had been on the phone with Pepe, Bennie, and Ralph's sidekick, minutes before Manolo shot him in my presence. Telephone records might bear that out, but it would serve no purpose. I was the sole surviving witness.

"Aurora won't crack," Rossetti answered. "She *claims* she has no idea what was discussed between Rosa and Ethel, or if Ethel ever met with Bennie at all that night."

"But Aurora probably carried the message," I said weakly, knowing I could say more.

"It's up to the grand jury," Rossetti shrugged morosely. There was nothing more he could say, either.

I was full of mixed emotions and scrambled images. I saw Ethel coming down the stairs after her brother had been shot and I saw her laughing on her mother's bed as she went over the family photo albums. I saw her with her head on a lace pillow. And I saw her lean over on the grand staircase and tell me she strongly suspected that I knew who shot Bennie to death.

Rossetti must have read the discouragement in my eyes. He frowned sympathetically and then grinned.

"Think we could ever build a case to show Ethel Wately is capable of murder?" he speculated. "Paint her as a woman who'd poison her siblings?"

I wasn't sure if he was serious, so I answered with a silly grin of my own. It was the theory I'd been leaning toward. Lieutenant Henry had warmed to it earlier, and now it was getting a rise from Rossetti. If they knew what I knew, there wouldn't be any hesitation on their part.

"I'd like to see the father's will," I mused. "Edgar seemed to think Esmeralda and Jaime were entitled to something. He didn't make it very clear in the suicide note, but he had made a verbal reference that some provision for an inheritance had been made."

"You're suggesting a motive for Ethel?" Rossetti asked.

"I'd like to know if she could have benefited from their deaths," I said. "She claims she *wouldn't* have benefited. She told me so right before Edgar shot himself. But I don't trust her. Lies come too easy for her."

"We're gonna try to get the will opened, at least in front of a judge," he said. "Count on it."

Then he looked at me and smiled gently.

"What are you thinking?" he asked. "That she killed for money?"

"I don't know what to think," I said. "I think knowing what's in the will could help me draw a better conclusion."

"People like that don't kill for money, Mr. Darenow. They kill because they don't like you, or because you annoyed them, or your politics are wrong. They kill to rid themselves of problems they don't have the time or inclination to deal with. They kill because it's efficient."

"What would it take to nail Ethel?" I asked. "Her own brother implied that she knows more than she's letting on." I wasn't exactly volunteering to help nail her, I was just asking.

"Where's the evidence?" he replied. "The suicide note? *'Slay no more?'* The guy was crazy. Who knows what he meant? And when Stuart Metcalf takes the stand, steely-eyed, tall, and distinguished, and portrays the Torres boys as blackmailers, con men, drug dealers, and double agents, the suicide note becomes a footnote in the record. The jury's bound to accept Metcalf's theory that the Torres people killed Jaime in an effort to pressure Wately into handing over more dough. It's believable and convenient. The only people who might have helped us nail Ethel are dead or gone. That's Bennie, Ralph, Rosa, and Edgar."

Nice work, Darenow. You caused the deaths of the first two, scared the other one south—and made it too tough for Edgar to continue living.

"But what about Esmeralda's testimony?"

"Do you think a jury is going to believe her?" Rossetti asked. "It's her word against Ethel's. She has no real proof. The only probable cause is money, and Ethel Wately has plenty of that—always had, always will. And what's the jury gonna think when they find out Esmeralda has a record for prostitution and manslaughter in Puerto Rico? That will come out the minute she takes the stand. And the will, if it's opened, has to show conclusive proof. Otherwise, are they gonna believe Mrs. Wately was jealous of a drag queen? So far as Esmeralda is concerned, where's *her* motive for killing her twin brother? He was the only real friend she ever had.

"My money's on Ethel," he concluded, "but I don't think she'll ever see the inside of a jail."

There was nothing more to say. Rossetti said he'd call me the next morning and let me know what time Owen Reed was coming in for his powwow.

I turned off the radio and lit a cigarette. It was around two in the morning and I was down to the last one in the pack. I smoked it down to the nub, coughed plenty, and lay down on the bed, fully clothed. I watched the smoke drift around the bed lamp and listened to the steam pipes wheeze and cough in response. Smoking was a bad habit. I vowed not to buy another pack, and with one exception, I kept that promise.

I thought about Denise. It was the time of night when she used to call me from her darkroom and ask me what I was doing. I wished she was there now.

I'd go over, of course, my pyjamas under my suit, and wind up cooking us both an omelette while she proudly showed me her latest work. It was the only time she wasn't running around taking pictures, selling them to magazines, or printing them in her darkroom. We'd watch *Star Trek* or a colorized movie while we ate and then we'd usually make love unless we were both too exhausted.

I half expected the phone to ring; but I knew that part of my life was over.

My meeting with Stu Metcalf, Owen Reed, "Cardinal" McGovern, and Rossetti lasted for an hour. It went by like fifteen minutes.

Metcalf renewed his request for keeping the espionage angle out of the papers on the grounds that there was still a possibility of flushing a couple of Castro operatives out of the woodwork.

"It might take months, it might take years," he said wearily.

I told him my publisher made the decision on what we'd print and what we wouldn't about Wately's connections to "the intelligence establishment."

Metcalf gave me one of his hard stares and said he understood perfectly.

Owen Reed announced that he would present the case to the grand jury within a couple of weeks. He bobbed his head up and down like a fawning asshole while Metcalf was talking. There hadn't been enough time, obviously, for Reed to memorize the new script. He tried his best otherwise to act like the tough prosecutor.

"We'll be calling Aurora Carrera, Esmeralda, and, of course, Ethel Wately," he said. "We're calling Ethel last since an accusation has been made against her by Esmeralda."

I put on my "What, Me Worry?" face and tried to look innocent and dumb: Max Darenow, rapidly aging boy reporter. "Are you calling Mr. Cartwright?" I asked. I was referring to the man I overheard at the

Albemarle Club, the aging preppie who talked cynically and easily about fall guys and disposal problems.

Reed looked puzzled and turned to Metcalf. Metcalf charged on cue.

"If you're referring to a man who works for me, certainly not," Metcalf said. "He has nothing to contribute."

"I heard him tell Edgar Wately he had to 'get rid' of Esmeralda," I said.

Metcalf, for an instant, contracted like a stale balloon, but puffed himself up again, flashed the hard stare, and asked me where I'd heard *that*.

I told him about my visit to the Albemarle Club. The best way to preserve my innocence was to keep acting as if I was. Darenow, the happy fool, leads the rest to the brink and skips merrily away at the last minute.

"If you think Cartwright should be called, Mr. Darenow, we'll call him." Metcalf sighed.

If I had really wanted to crack wise I should have asked why he said *we*. After all, he represented the State Department and the grand jury was being summoned by the Justice Department. That hubric display provided the gumption for my next question.

"Are you opening the father's will?" I said. "Avery Wately's will?"

"What for?" Metcalf snapped.

"It might provide a motive," I said.

"Rest assured, we'll open the will," Reed said easily. "A judge will decide its relevance."

Metcalf's eyes blinked a few times. He wanted to glare at Owen Reed but his signals had got crossed. It wasn't an act. I don't believe he knew how Reed planned to handle the issue of the will. Metcalf was from the old school: the public's need to know was limited. Reed's attitude was less imperious, more calculating. Leave it to the judge to decide, as long as the judge was on your side.

"Of course," Metcalf intoned. "The will might shed some light on Esmeralda's motives. Is that what you're trying to say, Mr. Darenow?"

"I'm just throwing questions out," I said. "I have no opinion."

I didn't raise the issue of Ethel's possible motives. As far as these guys were concerned, she had as much on me as I did on her. We were in check. Metcalf might have known it, too.

"That's exactly why we're *not* asking you to testify, Mr. Darenow," Metcalf said slyly. "We're treating you as a journalist and a friend of the court. If you do wish to testify, of course, it can be arranged."

He backed it up with a very thin smirk.

"That's OK," I replied. "But I just want to make sure Esmeralda gets her due."

I thought about something Rossetti had said the night before, about people like Ethel not killing for money. I thought about probate and surrogate court judges who would lie down, roll over, and fetch sticks—anything to make a buck. Probate and surrogate courts were a town pump for lawyer's fees. Carrion feeding on the remains of people who died without the service of a good lawyer to set up and protect their estate. Come everyone, justice is being served, if you're a member of the party.

"She'll get her due," Metcalf seethed before realizing his tone was in bad form. "For God's sake, Edgar admitted that in his suicide note. What more do you want? Ethel's not even asking for a birth certificate."

"Sorry," I said, in what I hoped was a chastened voice.

The grand jury convened in two weeks and took four days to gather testimony and hand up a verdict. The verdict was "no bill," in other words, no charges would be laid against anyone. The jury concluded that Bennie Torres had murdered Jaime Santiago out of a desire for revenge against Edgar Wately, who had been acting at the behest of the United States government in the interests of national security, just as his father had acted before him.

Owen Reed, as promised, let me "peek" at the grand jury minutes in his office.

I didn't take notes; I didn't have to because Gabe Rossetti got a copy for me later.

Metcalf's testimony was censured by the judge, who also ruled the terms of Avery Wately's will to be "irrelevant to the present investigation."

Herewith, an exchange between Owen Reed, fearless prosecutor, and Ethel Wately, friendly witness.

R: What message did Mrs. Torquenos convey to you from her nephews the night they came to visit?

W: She said they wanted more money for the work they were doing for the government.

R: And what did you tell her?

W: I told her I had no idea of what she was talking about.

R: Who did you think they were working for?

W: Look, I knew they were supposed to be working undercover. Mr.

Metcalf explained some of it to me because it involved a bank that I own a portion of. He swore me to secrecy.

R: So they were *not* actually working for your brother, per se?

W: Of course not.

R: And what did Rosa say to that?

W: She went into the kitchen and came out and told me her nephews wanted me to increase her pension. She said they thought I wasn't going to provide enough for her retirement. It was extortion by a different name.

R: How did you resolve it?

W: I wrote Rosa a check for $50,000.

R: Why did you do that?

W: At first I thought they were acting under a great deal of stress, considering the undercover job they were supposed to be performing. I assumed the government wasn't paying them a heck of lot and I thought I could make it up somehow. I later discovered they had also asked my brother for money or they would expose the entire operation.

That last paragraph drove me right up the wall. The galling dose of noblesse oblige Ethel had spooned out to the jury made me furious. The rich stay rich because they can lie so effortlessly. It helped to have Reed stage his questions so skillfully, too. He'd go far.

R: Did Mrs. Torquenos also convey a threat to you if you didn't pay?

W: She said her nephews were very angry with the way they'd been treated and she could no longer control them. She apologized for being the go-between.

R: Did you give her a check that night?

W: I did.

R: Did you have any second thoughts?

W: I tried to stop payment on the check several days later, after my brother told me they had threatened to kill Jaime if we didn't meet their demands.

R: You weren't able to stop the check?

W: Unfortunately, no. She had cashed the check the day before.

R: Was that the last time you saw Mrs. Torquenos?

W: She left my house and employ about two weeks later. I never saw her again.

R: Did she give any reason for her sudden departure?

W: She told me she was ashamed of what her nephews had done and claimed she had turned the money over to them, but she said nothing about leaving.

R: So she just packed and left and you said nothing?

W: She told one of the other servants she was going to run some household errands. But she took several things she considered valuable to her—some jewelry I had given her and at least one change of clothing, probably concealed in the canvas shopping bag she always carried. They weren't the sort of things you take with you to go shopping.

R: Where do you think she went?

W: We assume she took the money and ran. She had cashed the check herself and had apparently lied about turning it over to her nephews.

Nice story, well told. So much for Ethel. At least for the time being.

Cartwright took the stand, too. Reed put on another good show.

R: When you met Mr. Watley at his club, did you say you wanted him to "get rid of" Esmeralda Sanchez?

C: Words to that effect. That person didn't know it, but he, or she, had knowledge of the agents who had been working on our operation. Several of those agents had already met a violent death, most likely at the hands of hostile agents.

R: What did you intend to do with Miss Sanchez?

C: We hoped to move Miss Sanchez to a neutral territory where no threat against her person would exist, and where she would have no opportunity to communicate with hostile agents.

R: Where, exactly?

C: A number of places I'm not at liberty to divulge.

How about the local morgue, Cartwright?

Esmeralda's testimony was the saddest of them all. She knew damn well Ethel had wanted her dead, even when she had bragged to me at Dixie's house about Ethel's visit to her honeymoon cottage. She had grown up with stars in her eyes, like the rest of the world, except she knew in her bones she might stand a chance of reaching them. She was a Wately; if that meant joining a family of murderers, that was the price one paid to belong.

Esmeralda took the stand, broke down, and cried. The court stenographers call crying and other emotional displays "interruptions" or "unintelligible." All the guilt she had stored up about her identity and her parentage and her gender came bursting out in an anguished flood of allegations.

R: What makes you think Mrs. Wately wanted to kill you?

E: She was ashamed of what her father did to my mother.

R: And what was that?
E: I guess he raped her.
R: You '*guess*' he raped her. Did your mother tell you that?
E: I never met my mother . . . (*unintelligible*).
R: Did Mrs. Wately ever threaten you?
E: No, I thought she was my friend.
R: Why did you think that?
E: She always sent money to whoever was taking care of me when I was growing up.
R: Have you ever been arrested?
E: I had to stab a man once.
R: Why?
E: He tried to hurt me.
R: Under what circumstances did he try to hurt you?
E: What?
R: Why did he try to hurt you?
E: He thought I was a woman. I hadn't become a woman yet. (*Interruption.*)
R: Is Mrs. Wately now providing for you?
E: (*Unintelligible*) Fifty thousand dollars a year.
R: Is that voluntary?
E: Yeh, she gonna give it to me for the rest of my life.
R: You get fifty thousand dollars a year from her? In one annual lump sum?
E: Yeh, so I don' have to wait for a check every month. I like that way better. It goes up with inflation, too.

And this:

R: When Bennie Torres gave you the drugs, what did you do?
E: I took some and gave the rest away.
R: To whom?
E: To Jaime (*unintelligible*).
R: Did you give Bennie's drugs to anyone else that night?
E: No.
R: Do you know where Denise Overton, the other victim, got the drugs she ingested?
E: She wanted to take my wedding picture. I heard her say she needed a Tuinal. Bennie didn't give me any of them so it had to be Jaime, because I didn't see Bennie hand her no drugs. Jaime didn't know it was bad drugs, so what could he do?
R: No further questions. You're excused.

40

I knew I hadn't seen or heard the last of Ethel Watley, Esmeralda, and most of the other new friends I'd picked up along the way. There were more surprises in store in the months to come.

Every time I had more than a couple of drinks, which I rarely did anymore, I'd get to brooding, and try to work up a new angle on how to wrestle the truth from the pack of lies I'd been served. I even tried coaxing Aurora Carrera to dinner on one such occasion. I had heard Ethel was back in Florida, and Aurora was staying alone on Park Avenue.

I didn't want to shake the trees too vigorously, not after accepting the Mafia's help in establishing an alibi for myself, helping them kidnap Esmeralda, and then hiding her from the law. Not to mention my failure to inform the cops that the Mafia had undoubtably tortured and killed Ralph Torres and dumped his body in the federal parking lot.

That should have convinced me to mind my own business, but three manhattan cocktails enabled me to throw caution to the winds and give Aurora a call. I know it sounds sexist and conceited, but I thought I might woo her into a position of trust. It came to nothing.

Aurora repeated her assertion that she knew nothing more than what she had already told the cops. And then she informed me, prissily, that it would be in bad taste for her to dine with me because she was an employee of Mrs. Wately's, and Mrs. Wately certainly wouldn't approve.

Aurora's pension fund depended on Mrs. Wately's largesse. Aurora was no dope; she knew which side of the bread the butter was on. But that didn't stop me.

I still had questions. I don't know if I wanted further evidence that Ethel Wately had indirectly caused Denise's death or if I wanted evidence alleviating her of that charge. I made a last-ditch effort to get something out of her over the phone.

I repeated what Dixie had told me about Aurora's telling Esme "the blonde" had wanted Esme and Jaime out of the way.

"I never said that," Aurora replied after a beat.

"I have two witnesses," I bluffed. I only had one and that was Dixie. Esme had been pensioned off herself.

"You know something?" Aurora trilled in response. "*Mr.* Wately had blond hair, too."

That was that.

A month had elapsed before I made a point to take Rocco and Dixie out to dinner one night to a flashy restaurant in SoHo. I had asked Rocco if I should extend the invitation to Charlie, but Rocco said it wouldn't be necessary. The Wately affair was "just another episode" in Charlie's busy life. Dixie and I got rather drunk and cried a few times. We laughed a lot about Denise, wondering what she might have done had she been around to look over our shoulders while I was chasing the story down.

Dixie swore that Denise would have gotten Charlie to pose like a Roman senator, wrapped in a sheet, wearing gold sandals, an olive wreath, and a little makeup, especially around the eyes. I told Dixie I could almost hear Denise telling me she thought Esmeralda's story would make a wonderful book, and I shouldn't waste it on the newspapers.

Dixie took advantage of the occasion, and my newfound mellowness, and made me promise I'd take her out to dinner once a month for a year thereafter, as a reward for saving my life. Rocco said Esmeralda would remain under The Big Guy's protection as long as she behaved herself and remained in Dixie's care. Charlie was doing it "out of the goodness of his heart."

Esmeralda had refused Metcalf's offer to move to Costa Rica at the government's expense. The Big Guy got her a smart lawyer who beat that down at a closed hearing before a federal magistrate. The magistrate, Dixie implied, was also a personal friend of Charlie's. It turned out said magistrate once issued a search warrant on Charlie's residence, which search turned up nothing, of course. Ethel suddenly respected Esme and her new friends.

But Esmeralda's stay with Dixie had turned sour. Esme was spending money like a drunken sailor. She made the rounds of expensive tourist traps, but she also flashed her tits around the seedy drag bars and transvestite haunts, flaunting her new inflation-proof stipend and social status. Dixie got tired of that routine and told Esmeralda she had to start taking her life more seriously.

Esmeralda started going out alone, buying cocaine, and coming in wasted at noon the next day, so Dixie threw her out. Esmeralda moved back to Puerto Rico, where she threw a three-week party for the highway hookers and deadbeats she had grown up with in San Juan. She took an apartment in Old San Juan, got busted for cocaine possession, and got off on a technicality. Ethel had bailed her out.

I ran into both of them a few weeks later in Tampa.

Gabe Rossetti had called me at the office one hot summer's day to tell me that another grand jury was meeting, in Tampa, to deal with the allegations of money-laundering and fraudulent loans at Wately's bank, which now belonged to Hector Melendez and Ethel Wately. The original grand jury probe there had been extended so the authorities could assure the press and rival politicians that a "thorough investigation" had been arduously pursued in the wake of the deaths of Edgar and his chief loan officer.

I immediately put in for a trip to Florida. I convinced Hurley it was worth it to send me down to follow up on our prior coverage. The publisher agreed. Summer air fares were in effect and the Florida peninsula was in the midst of a sweltering heat wave. It didn't look so much like a vacation anymore.

I flew into Tampa International and took a room in Ybor City, Tampa's Old Latin Quarter. I stayed in a hotel overlooking Tampa Bay. The building had been a cigar factory when Cuban tobacco was still being imported and was now part of the gentrification process.

I called Frank Reilly and took him out to dinner. He had tried to find Esmeralda's birth or baptismal certificate but an initial search turned up nothing and Charlie had developed other passions, like staying out of jail. Owen Reed and his task force were looking for new targets. Much to his credit, Frankie felt a professional obligation to me, and asked if he could do me any favors while I was in town.

I told him I wanted to know the terms of Avery Wately's will as it related to Jaime and Ethel and asked if he could arrange for me to take a peek or obtain a copy. I offered to pay for the privilege.

He winked and said he thought something could be worked out. He told me he'd call me when he had something.

I missed seeing Terry Compton. He was smart enough to be in Maine on vacation. I did speak to Miss Vicky Forrestal, the society editor. She declined my invitation to dinner. I think I'd disappointed her. She had been hoping the Watelys' dirty linen would have been aired more thoroughly in the New York tabloids, especially the *Graphic*, so she'd have an excuse to comment on the allegations in her own column.

So I spent my days hanging around the Tampa federal courthouse, making a pest of myself. And that's where I ran into Ethel and Esmeralda.

Esmeralda was staying at the Watelys' family home, a Georgian mansion called Pink Gables on a bluff across the bay. Ethel was taking care of her, had in fact enrolled her in a drug treatment program. They arrived at the courthouse together in a limousine and entered through the garage. They could have walked up the front steps, for all the local papers cared. Darenow was the only newshound who showed any interest.

I was moping around near the elevators on the floor where the grand jury was convened, showing the flag and little else, since the press is barred from the grand jury room and we're not supposed to interview or even know whoever's been called. Ethel stepped from the car, tanned and svelte, looking gorgeous in a nubby blue linen suit, her hair wound into a tight bun. She wore dark glasses, and smiled in my direction. It wasn't a 1,000-watt smile, but it gave the impression she didn't mind running into me. I couldn't believe it; at first I thought she hadn't recognized me, but I was wrong. She acted almost glad to see me. Her old self.

She told me she had expected I'd come down for the grand jury, because she knew I was still curious about the will. She treated the subject lightly, brushing it off with an aside about how she had read it over the judge's shoulders and agreed with him that "it had no bearing on Bennie Torres's case."

It sounded well rehearsed, of course. I didn't tell her my interest in the will was to find a bearing for hanging a motive on her.

I nodded noncommittally and was about to say good-bye when she smiled again, removed her glasses, and flashed her eyes mischievously. She was back to playing the perfect hostess. It was her turf, and she began by asking me how I was enjoying my stay in Tampa. I told her I'd been swimming in the hotel pool and was thinking of taking a harbor cruise some evening before I left.

That's when she squeezed my hand and asked me to join her for dinner at the Tampa Yacht Club. My reaction was immediate. It was easy. I told her thanks, but no.

Still holding my hand, she turned on the high beams and assumed an air of innocent concern. She said she wanted to put "that business" behind her and apologized for having lied to me. We had both acted rashly, she said, in an effort to "protect and preserve" our interests. My interest was to find the people responsible for Denise's death; her interests were to protect herself.

"I know you think I'm to blame for a lot of things," she said quietly. "Perhaps you're right. But I'd like an opportunity to set the record straight before you leave."

She really wanted me to believe her, and she held my hand until I consented to join her for dinner.

Her effusive charm no longer swayed me; I accepted the invitation because I saw it as one more opportunity to try and trip her up; I wanted to see the look in her eyes when I told her that she was considered the guiding force behind Denise's murder, not just by me, but by a couple of smart cops.

My acceptance pleased and animated her again. She made Esmeralda come over to say hello, and then the two of them breezed down the hall in the direction of the grand jury room.

Esmeralda was shy, pale, and withdrawn. Her hair was a mousy shade of brown and she wore it in a simple style. Ethel must have been advising her on what to wear, because the Toast of La Perla was garbed in Lily Pulitzer designs that almost made her look like every other middle-class woman I saw on the streets. She was not invited to dine with us at the Yacht Club that evening. Ethel explained that Esmeralda couldn't even drink anymore. She had to take extra care of herself because the hormones, steroids, and silicones in her body lowered her immune defenses and made her "cancer prone."

Ethel, to be sure I got the right message, had arranged for me to see the grand jury notes from the ongoing Tampa proceedings. Her lawyer contacted me early on the morning of the day I was to meet her for dinner.

There were no surprises.

The jury voted "no bill" in the death of Oscar Herrera, but charged him posthumously with laundering money and conspiring to alter or commit fraud in respect to loan applications. Some dollar figures were thrown around. Backed with false financial statements, the Torres brothers—small-time punks—had been drawing on an $18 million line of credit. The CIA admitted that $3 million of that credit was backed with their money. The rest had been swindled from the bank, or so the story goes. There was insufficient evidence linking Edgar Wately—or his sister—to any wrongdoing. It apparently didn't strike anyone as strange that a man like Wately, an expert at untangling his father's finances, wouldn't have spotted Oscar Herrera's treachery or questioned the amount loaned to two deadbeats like the Torres brothers. All in the family, indeed.

Metcalf's testimony was again censured by the presiding judge. Ethel had turned in another flawless performance. Esmeralda also demonstrated perfect composure on the witness stand. She was seeing a psychiatrist and was taking daily doses of Elavil to steady her nerves. She told the jury she was thinking of opening a beauty parlor or a nail and waxing salon as part of her rehabilitation.

She didn't need rehabilitation. She needed habilitation.

Dinner with Ethel was full of false starts, sad smiles, awkward silence, and much talk about the revitalization of downtown Tampa, in which Ethel, as benefactress, civic and social leader, and financier, was playing a major role.

My plan to try and trip her up suddenly seemed like an exercise in futility. I felt out of place and the surroundings further intimidated me. The heart had fairly gone out of my quest, although I still clung to the belief that if an opportunity presented itself, I might hurl a curve ball. I hoped I'd rally after dinner, right before we said good-bye.

Ethel sipped a glass of wine through dinner but insisted we cap the meal with a glass of Chateau Y'Quem. It was only twenty-five bucks a shot. We had two of them apiece and moved to the veranda on the second round. We stood and watched the lights on the water and the yachts bobbing alongside the pier.

Ethel said she was cold, and accompanied it with a pleading look. She said she didn't want to go back inside just yet, and would I hold her? I stared back at her and shook my head in disbelief.

"I know you think I'm a liar, Max," she said, moving closer. "I had to lie to protect Edgar. It all became such a tangle that I didn't know half of what I was doing. I'm just a woman, Max."

She put her chin on my shoulder and let me feel the richness of her body, wrapped in a black silk. I resisted any sense of pleasure or enjoyment. And I decided to throw a curve.

"*If* Aurora, or Rosa, told you I was there when Bennie Torres got shot, why didn't you go to the police?" I asked, accentuating the qualifier.

After all, I never did know exactly what she knew, but I wasn't going to give her an inch.

"Aurora didn't tell me," Ethel replied, just loud enough that her voice rode gently over the sound of the water. "Some horrible little man who worked for Bennie Torres called me and told me you were there, buying cocaine. He said you knew the whole story, whatever that was supposed to mean," she said pointedly. "He asked me for money, a hundred thousand dollars—to shut your mouth, I believe he said."

I tilted her head up so I could see her eyes. They were all watery innocence. She wasn't lying; she was just twisting the truth.

"There wasn't any reason to pay him, was there?" she added. "I had no reason to shut your mouth. I was completely in the dark, but tired of being shaken down by Bennie and his thugs."

"Why didn't you tell the police this?"

"Oh, I must have," she said, looking away again, over the water. "I don't recall. Maybe they never asked. There was just so much going on all of a sudden."

I wanted to slap her face, and slap it again until she broke down and told me what I wanted to hear. It went something like this: Pepe calls and tells Ethel the price has just gone up on her continuing disposal problem. Pepe's assignment had been to get rid of Manolo, but suddenly there's a nosy reporter in the room, and contracts on reporters run very steep.

My hunch is that Ethel tacitly agreed to Pepe's demands for more money. Pepe was on the phone arguing for some time. And then, I'll bet any money, Ethel called Stu Metcalf to tell him what was going on. She had probably expected Metcalf would send fresh troops to clean up Pepe and the Torres boys, after they'd cleaned up on me. That's why the feds had reacted so quickly to the murders at Manolo's apartment.

Ethel was looking over the boats tied in front of us. I wondered which one was hers, but didn't bother to ask. There was nothing in her eyes except the reflection of dark waters. She turned and looked at me sharply. She was one smooth dame.

"Look, Max, I probably wouldn't have said anything if anyone *had* asked. I figured it was just another lie. I knew you were despondent, too, over your girlfriend. You had your reasons for buying drugs."

I let go of her and took a good long look into the dark water myself. I said nothing.

"You *were* there?" she asked coyly. She smiled when she said it.

"I stopped there for five minutes," I lied. "The drug buy was just a story. I had been told Denise had been seen in the company of the boy who lived there."

"Well," she said casually, "it appears you left just in time."

Long pause while we both stared out to sea.

"Do the police know you were there?" she asked.

"No," I lied. Let's see if she tries to use it.

"Well," she said, "I'll never say a word."

"Just as well," I said as flatly as the lump in my throat allowed. Drop it, Darenow. Denise was right. The glamour of evil is nothing compared to the evil of glamour.

We finished our drinks and went back inside.

She had the nerve to invite me back to Pink Gables. I declined. I said I had too many things to do the next day. We were both liars.

"I'm sorry to hear that," she said. She was relieved. I was relieved she didn't ask twice.

She dropped me off at my hotel, which she thought was quaint. She offered her hand before I got out from the back seat and I shook it. Good-bye, Ethel.

I went up to my room, stood outside on a small deck overlooking an alley, and wished I had a cigarette. It had been months since I'd smoked. The last time was the night Edgar committed suicide. I called the desk and asked the clerk to send up a pack and a bottle of Mexican beer. I wasn't fussy what brand of cigarettes or beer he was sending. I needed something to do with my hands.

I went back on the balcony and in the close, warm night I thought about Ethel. Ethel was a pro, all right; an efficient, accomplished liar. She possessed an extraordinary confidence in her ability to make things go her way. Men were perfect foils. She had all her emotions under control, most of the time, and she spun them like a web. No man, unless he was in a blind rage, could dent her confidence, and Ethel knew just how far she could push it before it happened. Men were an open book to her.

I thought about the night of the shootings at Manolo Pearson's apartment. I thought hard about the phone call.

It was too late to use it against her. She had defused the issue with a simple, innocent admission.

Then I thought of something else. Why did Pepe Cruz, a mere lackey, have the gall to call Ethel? How did he even know her home number? Was Ethel *waiting at the phone* for confirmation that the Torres boys had tracked down the last witness to the murders of Jaime and Denise? Ethel had given Rosa $50,000 to have the job done by her nephews; she expected that job to be well done. But I still didn't know *why* she ordered them killed—whether it was simply because they were a constant embarrassment, or for the money.

Ethel's father's will came to mind. Reilly was on the case. I hoped he had had some luck. But Ethel was so damned good at clouding a man's mind, I wasn't sure I'd ever know the truth.

Had Ethel wanted to kill both twins, or just Esme?

One thing was obvious: Denise's death was pure chance; Jaime, or Esmeralda, had innocently handed her a Tuinal when Denise asked for one. It was a terrible twist of fate. Denise was overworked; she couldn't sleep. What a long sleep she got.

I tossed the cigarette into the alley and threw the pack after it. I was going to start living right again. I waited until the red glow from the butt burned itself out on the dark asphalt and went inside. I had no problems falling asleep.

I slept until the phone trilled at noon. It was Frank Reilly. The best he had been able to do was bribe the county clerk into letting him read the will in the clerk's office. He read it through, took notes, and slipped the clerk another fifty bucks for his interpretation of the legal horseshit that ran more than twelve pages.

"Basically, the elder Mr. Wately left nothing to his daughter, Ethel," Reilly explained. "It says in the will she was amply provided for by money that flowed from her mother's side of the family. It's known around town that Mrs. W. had plenty of her own dough, so that's no surprise.

"The clerk pointed something out, though, that's interesting. Wately left Edgar the bulk of his estate but it stipulates right in the will that if Edgar died, his share—which came to about thirty or forty million mid-1960s dollars—goes to the next surviving male heir. If there's no male heir, Ethel gets it all; she is the executrix of her father's estate. Not a beneficiary, now, an executrix. She's beneficiary by default."

I made him repeat it.

"Esmeralda dropped out of the running when she cut her dick off and legally became a member of the opposite sex. No more male heirs. The will stipulates only the surviving *male* heirs get any dough.

"Get it?" he said. "It seems obvious to me why Ethel is so nice to Esmeralda."

Charlie Big Guy's hunch was right. I was almost sorry I had talked him out of pursuing that angle. Charlie had wanted to help Esme collect what was coming to her, so long as he got a cut. It would have made an interesting case. Is Esmeralda legally a female? Who paid for the operation? I thought I remembered Edgar implying that Ethel had paid for it. Of course, why else drive out to see Esmeralda and ask for a peek to make sure the operation was indeed a success?

I told Frank what Esmeralda had told me about Ethel's coming out to peek at her stitches.

Ethel Wately had given new life to the meaning of the term *castrating bitch*.

41

I returned to Manhattan a different man. Even my new arts and leisure beat started to bore me. My apartment grew smaller every day and the sights, sounds, and smells of summer in the city started making me wish I was elsewhere.

In the fall I applied for a leave of absence, got one, and found a publisher for Denise's photo series on the transvestites of New York. I took a winter rental on a small house in the Hamptons, overlooking a pond with geese who knew they had a free meal every day, courtesy of Max Darenow, animal lover. I sent Dixie out with a tape recorder and $1,000 from the very small advance and gathered enough material to make a book. I had the tapes transcribed and edited and wrote the foreword.

It was hard work, because Denise wasn't there, looking over my shoulder, making suggestions or offering encouragement. Dixie's tapes were swell, but I kept thinking Denise would have been a better judge of what to use. The book needed a woman's touch.

I was halfway through the book when Frankie the Cop Reilly called from Tampa. Esmeralda Sanchez was dead; she had been stabbed once through the heart by an unknown assailant; her body had been found on a public beach in San Juan, where she had returned to live a couple of months ago. She had drifted back into prostitution and cocaine addiction after living briefly on her own in Tampa.

"She couldn't seem to hold on to money," Frank said.

Oh, yes. There was one more thing. Esmeralda had been arrested twice for harassing Ethel Wately before she left Tampa to return to San Juan.

The Toast of La Perla was no match for a woman of Mrs. Wately's caliber.

I thanked Reilly for calling me and told him I hoped I could do him a favor someday.

I stared out the window for a minute and decided to take a walk before the sun went down. It was the week before Thanksgiving, and the thermometer told me that Indian Summer was losing the battle with Old Man Winter so I went into the bedroom and rummaged around until I found my trusty parka, the one I hadn't worn since last winter, and which hadn't been dry cleaned since.

I stuck my hand in one of the pockets, expecting to find a pair of gloves, but it wasn't gloves I found. It was the envelope containing Denise's last letter to me, the letter that came too late. She'd been dead almost a year.

I didn't open the letter. I tucked it away in a scrapbook where I kept some of her photographs, the ones she had taken shortly after we met for the first time, when we were still under the influence of each other's art. I put the parka away, too. I wasn't going to wear it again until it had been cleansed of the smell of death. I put on a sweater instead, and a tweed jacket over that. I felt a chill.

I went into the kitchen, got some old bread I'd been saving for the geese, and walked down to the pond.

The gander saw me coming. He squawked and circled his family, alerting mother goose, who rounded up the little geese and tried to keep them in line while the gander charged, honking loudly, in my direction. It was all a show of bravado, because he knew I was going to feed them, not wring their necks.

I sat on a teak bench that had turned a weathered gray while the geese threw decorum to the wind and happily gobbled my humble gift. A soft southerly breeze rustled the leaves and I suddenly felt unencumbered by the past. I knew if I looked in less traveled places, where there was more light and cleaner air, I'd find the right woman and settle down to life's simpler pleasures.

I still wasn't someone who believed, to the exclusion of all else, that life was beautiful and the world was an idyll, to be pondered and enjoyed, but I was coming around to a view that was brighter than the one I had labored under so long.

Denise was dead; she died horribly, well before her time was due, and nothing could bring her back. Her book would get published. I wondered, though, if that's all Denise would have wanted. Would she *really* not care whether her killers were brought to justice, all of them, Ethel Wately included? Denise's friends, Dixie and Mary Collins, said she would *not* have cared. But Denise was dead, and I'd never know.

I remembered the night I took Rocco and Dixie to dinner in the Village, long after Edgar Wately had committed suicide. Dixie and I had speculated on what Denise would have done if she had been looking over our shoulders while we pursued her murderers with such fierce devotion to the chase.

I remember thinking Denise would have turned on her electric smile, winked, and said: "Max should write it as a book."

This one's for you, Denise. How did Shakespeare say it? *And this gives life to thee.*

About the Author

RICHARD NUSSER is an award-winning reporter whose beat was Manhattan, from waterfront to City Hall, from cops to courthouse. Recipient of the New York City Reporters' Association By-Line Award and the Associated Press Enterprise Award, he is also former international editor of *Billboard* magazine and has written extensively about rock music. His work has appeared in *The Village Voice* and *Reader's Digest*. He is married and lives in Manhattan.